Books should be returned or renewed by the last
date above. Renew by phone **03000 41 31 31** or
online *www.kent.gov.uk/libs*

USA Today and International bestselling author

Lauren Rowe

To Chloe.

You are so brave.
I love you.

Books by Lauren Rowe

The Club Series (to be read in order)

The Club
The Reclamation
The Redemption
The Culmination
The Infatuation
The Revelation
The Consummation

The Morgan Brothers (a series of related standalones):

Hero
Captain
Ball Peen Hammer
Mister Bodyguard
Rock Star (coming 2019)

The Misadventures Series (a series of unrelated standalones):

Misadventures on the Night Shift
Misadventures of a College Girl
Misadventures on the Rebound

Standalone Psychological Thriller/(Very) Dark Comedy

Countdown to Killing Kurtis

Chapter 1
Zander

Have a seat, Mr. Shaw," Reed Rivers' brunette assistant says, indicating a black leather couch in a small reception area. "Mr. Rivers will be with you shortly."

"Thank you." I unbutton my suit jacket, take a seat, and carefully place my résumé on the couch next to me.

"Would you like a glass of water?" the assistant asks.

"Thanks."

I take in the small reception area. I've never been inside a record label before, but this is exactly how I'd pictured one. Modern, minimalistic furnishings. The LA skyline stretching beyond a nearby floor-to-ceiling window. And, of course, what record label would be complete without gold records, album covers, and framed photos of musicians lining the walls?

I scan the photos and spot the face of that white rapper, 2Real—the one who's recently been topping the charts with his smash hit, "Crash." My eyes drift again and stop on the unmistakable green eyes of Aloha Carmichael, the Disney star who grew up in front of the world and, when her TV show ended, reinvented herself as a pop star. My gaze drifts again and lands on the four guys of Red Card Riot. Even if Dax and his band, 22 Goats, weren't poised to jet off to London to open for them on their world tour in a matter of days, I'd recognize that powerhouse band.

My stomach tightens, reminding me how much I want to walk out of here today as the newest member of Red Card Riot's security team. Or, rather, as I like to think of it, *22 Goats'* security team. Getting to watch my honorary baby brother and his band open every night in jam-packed arenas across the world—seeing Dax transform into the global

1

superstar he's always been destined to become—would be a dream come true. Not to mention a welcome distraction from the acute ache that's been ravaging my heart since Daphne blindsided me on Thursday night.

Daphne.

After four days of thinking about it—or, actually, *obsessing* about it—I'm no closer to understanding why she dumped me. I admit I've never particularly wanted to move to New York, but, like I told Daphne on Thursday night, I was willing to do it for *her*. Because I would have done anything for that beautiful girl. For fuck's sake, when Keane—my lifelong best friend, my roommate, my Wifey, my brother from another mother—moved from Seattle to LA three months ago to pursue his Hollywood dreams and the girl of his dreams, I stayed behind for no other reason than to be with Daphne. *I can't follow my Wifey to LA when my future wife is going to art school in Seattle.* That's what I told Keane at the airport three months ago when he pestered me to join him a thousand miles down south. And I didn't even doubt my decision to stay in Seattle with Daphne, despite how excruciating it was to say goodbye to Keane, because I knew I'd found the girl who'd taken Zander Shaw off the market for good.

Well, that and I wasn't going to be a damn fool and give up my reasonably priced corner apartment only to have Keane come back to Seattle a couple months later asking for his old room back, either because he'd fucked things up with his new girlfriend, Maddy, or because, despite my boy's ebullient charm, he'd found out breaking into modeling and acting in La La Land wasn't quite as easy as he'd hoped.

As it turned out, my low-key worries about Keane Morgan making it in LA were unfounded. After only two months in Tinseltown, it was clear my boy wasn't just killing it in LA, he was mass-murdering it. Just that fast, he'd already shot three small speaking roles and landed two national commercials plus a modeling gig for Calvin Klein underwear. *And* he'd moved off his little brother Dax's couch and into his girlfriend Maddy's place across the hall.

So, what did I do then, when I realized Keane wouldn't be returning to Seattle? Did I ditch Daphne, my girlfriend of mere months, to join my lifelong best friend in LA? No, although that's what I *would* have done if I'd known Daphne was gonna drop me like a bad habit a month later to attend art school in New York. No, back when I thought there was no "I" in "love," when I thought Daphne

2

was all-in the same as me, I did what any man caught between a rock and a hard place would do: I asked Daphne if she'd be willing to transfer to an art college in LA at the end of her next school term.

"I'm one step ahead of you, Z!" Daphne chirped. "I submitted an application to Cal Arts a month ago!"

Of course, I called Keane right away to tell him the spectacular news.

"But what if Daphne doesn't get accepted to that art school in LA?" Keane asked.

"Then Daphne and I will move to Los Angeles after she graduates."

"But won't that be in, like, two years?"

"Don't you worry your pretty little head about it, baby doll," I said to Keane. "Daphne could get into any art school in the country. She's just that good."

"Just promise me this," Keane replied. "If Daphne doesn't get into that art school in LA and you guys wind up breaking up, then you'll get your ass down to LA the very next day after the breakup."

"Jesus God, I don't even know where to begin with your flagellation," I replied. "I know you miss me, Peenie—and I miss you, too, sweet meat—but rooting for the end of Zaphne is the same thing as rooting for the non-existence of my eighteen future babies. I've never rooted for the end of *Kaddy* and the non-existence of *your* eighteen future babies."

"Sweet Baby Jesus, I'm dealing with a madman," Keane replied. "First off, like I keep telling you, Maddy and I aren't *Kaddy*. We're *Meane*. That's way cooler because it's *ironic* on account of Maddy being so damned *nice*. And, second off, don't blame Madagascar for my relocation to the land of avocado toast. I would have moved here, regardless, simply because this is the city where a dumbshit like me can get paid to do nothing but stare into a camera lens like he's getting a hand job under a table. And third off, I'm not actively rooting for the end of Zaphne. I'm merely lodging a request *in case* Zaphne *happens* to implode before Daphne graduates—which ain't the craziest notion in the world, considering your track record for falling in and *out* of love at breakneck speed, big guy."

"Forget all the times I said I was in love before Daphne," I replied. "I'm telling you, Peenie. Daphne is my future."

3

They were famous last words, of course. Not to mention clueless and embarrassing words, too. As it turned out, Daphne wasn't my future. In fact, she was barely my present, as evidenced by the fact that I'm now sitting in the lobby of River Records, mere weeks later, after having been dumped.

"Here you go," Reed's assistant says, drawing me from my thoughts. She hands me a glass of water. "Reed says he apologizes for keeping you waiting. Apparently, he and Barry have quite a bit to talk about."

I lean back against the leather sofa and flash her my most charming smile. "No problem. I just moved here Friday, so my dance card is wide open. Quick question, though. Is 'Barry' Reed's head of security? Reed said I'd be meeting his 'head of security' today, but he didn't give me a name."

The woman nods. "Barry Atwater. He was a celebrity bodyguard for years before Reed tapped him to manage security for all his nightclubs. From there, Reed slowly expanded Barry's duties until, a few months ago, Barry officially became head of security for everything in Reed's world—the nightclubs, the label, and Reed's personal life, too."

I thank the woman for the intel and we chat for a bit longer, and when she leaves, I pull out my phone and search "Barry Atwater." Immediately, a slew of photos pops up, all of them featuring the same large black man walking alongside a different celebrity. *Damn, Gina.* At six feet four and two hundred forty pounds, people often describe *me* as a big black man. But this Barry Atwater has me beat.

I read a snippet about Barry in an article about celebrity bodyguards and discover he's an ex-marine who's guarded some of the biggest names in music and entertainment. Well, shit. How quickly is this badass motherfucker gonna show me the door when he finds out I've got no experience whatsoever in the security industry—that I'm a personal trainer from Seattle who's never even worked as a bouncer at a nightclub? When Reed handed me his card four months ago backstage at one of Dax's shows and told me to text him about a job if I happened to move to LA, he made it sound like my lack of experience wouldn't be an issue. But that was *before* Reed put this Barry dude in charge of security.

"Mr. Shaw?"

I look up from my phone to find Reed's assistant staring at me.

She smiles. "Reed and Barry are ready to see you now."

Chapter 2
Aloha

I finish singing the last note of "Pretty Girl" and, on the final, hard-hitting drumbeat, strike a choreographed pose in the middle of my backup dancers. After weeks of grueling rehearsals, we've finally reached the end of our last run-through before moving to our first arena of the tour for two days of dress rehearsals.

"And... lights out," our director says, though there are no actual stage lights to dim in this expansive warehouse. "That was the best run-through yet, guys."

With a collective whoop, my dancers and I break free from our frozen tableau and begin high-fiving and congratulating each other. As I hug one of my longtime dancers, I notice over her shoulder the most beautiful face in the world smiling at me from across the room.

"Barry!" I shriek. I disengage from my dancer and sprint gleefully toward him. "Take fifteen everyone! Big Barry's in da houuuuse!" When I reach Barry, I leap through the air and physically hurl myself into his massive arms. "I knew you wouldn't let me down. *I knew it.*"

"Hey, honey," Barry says in his rumbling baritone. And, just that fast, from those two words alone, I know Barry isn't here to tell me the news I want to hear.

I disengage from Barry's embrace, a scowl on my face, and pound a closed fist into his hard chest. "*No!* You *have* to come on this tour!"

Barry chuckles, kisses my fist, and guides it to my side. "It's nothing personal, honey. I don't have time to guard anyone on a tour these days, not even you."

I adopt the most adorably persuasive expression I can muster. "But I *need* you. You're my human Valium, Barry. My *rock*."

I might be laying it on a tad bit thick, but it's for good reason. Big Barry has accompanied me on every tour of my life, ever since my first at age thirteen when I traveled the world singing horrendously saccharine songs from my hit Disney show *It's Aloha!* By now, ten years and seven tours later, Barry's more than a bodyguard to me. He's family. And that's not a small thing for a girl whose father abandoned her at age three and whose mother has treated her more like an ATM machine than a cherished daughter.

"You don't *need* me on tour, Aloha," Barry says, patting my cheek. "You *want* me. There's a big difference. Speaking of which, I'm here to tell you how I'm going to staff the security for your tour, whether you *want* it or not. Remember last year when I had to be in Thailand with Reed and 2Real during the Kids' Choice Awards and I assigned—"

"The ex-Navy SEAL?"

"Yes. Brett. I've assigned him to—"

"You can't assign that cyborg tight-ass to guard me for an entire *tour*! I'll have a meltdown within a week and wind up canceling a month's worth of shows."

Barry rolls his eyes. "You'd die before canceling a single show and we both know it. You'd never let down your Aloha-nators. But it doesn't matter because I haven't assigned Brett to be your personal bodyguard. I've assigned him to be your 'head of security' while another guy—Zander—is your actual bodyguard."

I look at Barry quizzically. "You're assigning *two* guys to do the job you've always done for me?"

Barry nods. "Brett will handle the high-level security functions: interfacing with venue security and law enforcement, planning transportation and ingress-egress routes, assuming the anchor spot during your performances. And while he's doing all that, your friendly, easygoing personal bodyguard, Zander, will shadow and escort you, the way I've always done, as well as acting as your human Valium and/or rock, as needed."

I cross my arms over my chest, unmoved. I realize Barry is doing this with the best of intentions, but how could he possibly think this will work? I've grown up with Barry. He's the only person in the world I completely trust. How could he think anyone—whether two guys or one—could possibly replace him?

Barry touches my arm. "Just give this Zander guy a chance. I've got a gut feeling about him. Can he fully replace me *today*? No. But given some time and experience, I believe he will. Experience a man can acquire. The right personality? That's something he's got to have naturally."

I look at Barry sideways. "Just how inexperienced is this guy?"

"This will be his first tour."

I scoff.

"Trust me, though, newbie or not, he's fully capable of doing what I've hired him to do, especially with Brett watching over him. Just give him a chance. He's got a soothing, calming demeanor and a great sense of humor. I'm positive he'll be a perfect fit with you."

"A 'soothing, calming demeanor'?" I say, snorting. "Is this guy gonna be my bodyguard or my service doggie?"

Barry grins. "A bit of both, I'd say."

I roll my eyes. "How old is he?"

"Twenty-four."

My eyebrows shoot up. I assumed my service doggie would be in his mid- to late-forties, the same as Barry, not merely a year older than me. Well, well, well. I can't say I'm *upset* at the idea of some young, big, muscular alpha dude with a "soothing, calming demeanor" escorting me everywhere I go.

"He's younger than I'd have liked," Barry admits, apparently misreading the expression on my face. "But I met him and quickly realized he's a needle in a haystack in terms of personality." Barry crosses his muscular arms over his broad chest and shoots me a snarky look. "So, what's it gonna be, hula girl? You want Brett on his own or Brett *with* the service doggie? Those are your only options because I'm not working this tour."

I exhale and throw up my hands. "*Fine.* I'll give your dog and pony show a try. Or, rather, your *service* dog and *cyborg* show a try. But I'm warning you: Brett's gonna get an earful from me if he so much as scowls at me. And the newbie? God help him, I'm gonna have to test his mettle a bit to make sure he's got the right stuff."

Barry chuckles. "Break the newbie in however you want. Just keep in mind you're going to be stuck with the guy for three months, day after day—and maybe even longer than that if the North American leg works out with him—so I'd strongly suggest you make every effort to get off on the right foot with him."

7

I pull out my phone. "What's his number? I'll text him tonight to 'welcome' him to my team."

Barry gives me Zander's number and adds, "Just so you know, I've encouraged him to be completely himself around you, including *not* tamping down his personality or his penchant for giving as good as he gets."

"Sounds like a challenge to me." I cock an eyebrow. "Let's make a deal, Uncle Barry. If I can somehow get this service doggie to lay down and play dead tonight, will you agree to take his place on tour?"

"I can't do it, Aloha. I'm up to my eyeballs these days."

"Just the North American leg, then. The first three months. After that, I'll suffer silently with Brett across Europe and Australia until you can find me another service doggie to 'soothe' and 'calm' me."

"I can't do it, honey."

I flap my lips together. "Fine. What about this: if I can somehow get my new service doggie to roll over tonight, you'll come on the first *month* of my tour, just for old time's sake."

To my surprise, Barry pauses at this latest suggestion. "I tell you what I'll wager. If you can get Zander to quit tonight, then I'll come on tour for *two weeks* while I look for his replacement. And I'll do it gladly. Because if you can make Zander fold that easily, then he's not the man I thought he was and I don't want him guarding you any more than you do. On the other hand, though, if Zander handles your bullshit the way I think he will, then you've got to promise to stick it out with him for the entire North American leg, no whining or complaining. Obviously, if he majorly fucks up, then Brett will let me know and I'll promptly fire his ass for cause. But, otherwise, if you're merely annoyed or bored with the guy, then you'll stick it out for the entire three months and I won't hear a peep out of you."

I pull a snarky face. *Bastard.* Despite my big talk, I know full well the chances are slim to none I'll get this Zander guy to quit tonight. If Barry thinks the guy is badass enough to handle me, he must be a pretty solid citizen, newbie or not. But, still, having the slightest shot at getting Barry to come on tour with me for any length of time, even if it's only for two weeks, is more than I had a moment ago. "Deal," I say. I put out my hand, but Barry pulls me into a bear hug, instead.

"I'm leaving you in the best possible hands, girlie," Barry whispers into my ear. "Trust me." When he pulls back from our embrace, his dark eyes are dancing with his affection for me. "Just do me a favor, will you? I know you're itching to have some sort of delayed teenage rebellion—I can *feel* it." He cups my face in his large palms and my heart squeezes. "Just make it through this tour as you're contractually required to do without sabotaging yourself. And when the tour is over, you can take a long break, if that's what you want to do, and figure out who you really want to be."

Chapter 3
Zander

Dax takes a long swig of his beer and sighs. "Shit, Z. I thought for sure you were gonna come back from your meeting with Reed and tell us you were coming on tour with *us*."

"I thought the same thing, my brother." I take the last dregs of the joint from Keane, who's sitting next to me on Dax's couch—the couch that's been doubling as my bed for the past three nights—and suck in a long, deep inhale that finishes the thing off. "Oh, *life*."

"Oh, life," Keane echoes. But he's only being a supportive best friend. These days, Keane Elijah Morgan is the last guy on earth who'd bemoan life's ups and downs. Ever since he met Maddy and moved to LA just over three months ago, his life has been hurtling in only one direction: up, up, and up.

"Traveling the world with you would have been sick," Colin, the drummer of 22 Goats, says from a nearby armchair.

"I guess it just wasn't meant to be."

"Well, look on the bright side," Fish, the lanky, bearded, bassist of 22 Goats says from his prone position on the floor. "Even if you can't tour with us, at least you'll get to stare at *her* for the next three months." He motions to the TV. "Yee-gads, son. Now that's a good-lookin' woman."

The five of us simultaneously turn our bloodshot attention to the Aloha Carmichael music video playing on the flat-screen TV—the sixth or seventh such video to grace our eyeballs since I came back from Reed's office and told everyone the shocking news about my new job.

"She's supernatural," Fish says, his stoned eyes fixed on the TV screen. "She's the most perfect female specimen ever created. Those *eyes*."

"Meh, she's all right," I say, and Fish immediately berates me for it. But I'm being sincere. Yes, Aloha Carmichael is objectively beautiful. Light brown skin, lush lips, long, dark, wavy hair streaked with subtle golden highlights. And, yes, as Fish pointed out, she's got incredible emerald-green eyes. But, despite all that, the girl just doesn't do it for me. Mr. Happy typically doesn't stand at attention for painted sirens like the one I'm seeing on that screen—girls who look like they primp for hours before leaving the house. Mr. Happy is typically far more attracted to low-maintenance, fresh-faced, bohemian types—women like Daphne.

Daphne.

With her cute little messy blonde bun and freckles and long limbs for days. Why didn't she tell me she'd applied to that art school in New York?

Keane nudges my left thigh. "Hey, sweet cheeks."

I turn to look at him with stoned eyes.

"You're thinking about Daphne again, aren't you?"

I nod pitifully. "*Help me.*"

Chuckling, Peenie lights a new joint and hands it to me. "Suck on this, baby doll. The guy at the dispensary said it's stronger than that pen light from *Men in Black.*"

"Thanks, honey nuggets. That's why I love you the most."

"So, when do you report for babysitting duties with Aloha?" Dax asks.

I blow out a long stream of smoke into the air and lean back miserably. "Thursday afternoon before her first concert." I hand the newly lit joint to Dax next to me on the couch. "But I'm meeting Barry tomorrow for two solid days of training before that."

Dax blows out a long plume of smoke. "Training on what? How to put a tweener into a headlock without snapping her neck?"

"Hey, tweeners aren't Aloha's only 'Aloha-nators,'" I say. "The tweeners' mommies love her, too."

Everyone chuckles, but I'm not joking. Every day at the gym, I hear Aloha Carmichael songs blasting out of the spin room, particularly during daytime classes filled with nothing but MILFs.

"Should we be worried about your physical safety?" Keane asks. "Like, seriously, is someone sending Aloha threatening notes with glued-on letters cut out of magazines?"

11

"No, this isn't *The Bodyguard*," I say. "I mean, yeah, it's a dangerous world out there for any celebrity these days. But there's been no known threat to Aloha. And if something comes up, that ex-Navy SEAL dude will be there to handle it like the Kevin Costner he is."

"Well, that's good," Keane says, looking genuinely relieved.

"Here's what I don't get," Fish says from the floor. "If that Kevin Costner dude's gonna be there throughout the whole tour, then what the hell is *your* job?"

I shrug. "Just following her around, I guess. I don't know the specifics yet, to be honest. Hence, the two days of training with Barry. I didn't ask Barry a whole lot of questions after he gave me the job today. I was just too stunned. He said he never assigns newbies to tours—he always makes newbies work as bouncers at one of Reed's nightclubs for a while, just to gain experience. Barry's taking a huge chance on me."

"And why is he doing that, again?" Dax asks. "He can't possibly give a shit Reed's best friend married your honorary sister."

"No, Barry doesn't give a shit about that. That only got me in the door for the interview. And just barely, at that." I shove my hand into a bag of white cheddar popcorn on Keane's lap. "To be honest, I'm not sure why Barry hired me. At the beginning of the interview, he acted like he was doing Reed a huge favor, just by talking to me." I look at Keane. "But then, suddenly, his attitude visibly changed when Reed started telling him about *you*."

"About *me*?"

I nod. "Reed started telling Barry about how you and I were 'Frick and Frack' during Josh and Kat's wedding week in Maui, and, suddenly, Barry was like, 'Wow, Zander, sounds like you're skilled at handling people with huge personalities.'"

"He said you're '*skilled*' at '*handling*' me?" Keane booms. "What am I—a boa constrictor?"

Everyone chuckles.

I continue, "And then Reed was like, 'Hey, Z, tell Barry the story of how Keane dyed his hair blue that time to help you get laid.' So I told Barry that whole story and... *boom*. Game over. The job with Aloha was mine."

"How the hell did *that* story land you the job?" Keane says, chomping on some popcorn. "*I'm* the hero of the blue-hair story, not you."

"Not according to Barry. He was like, 'Damn, Z, for a guy to turn himself into a Smurf for you, you're either an amazing best friend or diabolically gifted at manipulation. Either way, I think I've got the perfect job for you.'"

Keane rolls his eyes. "Well, now I've heard everything."

"Am I the only person here who gets what all this means?" Colin says from the armchair, and we all stare at him expectantly. "Reed and Barry obviously think Aloha Carmichael is the female Keane Morgan."

We all look at each other for a long beat... and then burst out laughing.

"Aloha is Peenie with a pussy!" Fish shouts from the floor, his skinny arm raised into a fist-pump, and we all lose our shit.

"So, I guess that makes Aloha your dream girl, Z," Dax says. "I mean, come on: we all know if Keane had a pussy, you two would be married with eighteen babies by now."

"True," Keane and I say at the same time, and then we both burst out laughing again.

"Oh, man, if this girl is Peenie with a pussy, then Z isn't gonna be able to resist her," Fish says. "I'd bet good money on him fucking her within the first week."

"Not gonna happen," I say. "Barry said she's off-limits. Not that I would have touched her, anyway."

"Barry actually said that?" Dax asks. "Or he *implied* it?"

"Oh, no, he said it, son. In no uncertain terms."

"Say it ain't so!" Fish shouts passionately from the floor, clutching his chest like he's been shot.

"He didn't need to say it, though," I say. "I'm gonna be her bodyguard. It's common sense."

"It's not common sense," Keane says. "Kevin Costner fucked Whitney in *The Bodyguard*, and that didn't stop him from taking a bullet for her. Not that any of us wants you to take a bullet for Aloha, mind you. Just sayin' one thing doesn't necessarily lead to the other."

"Well, thanks for looking for a pussy-loophole for me, brother," I say to Keane. "But I honestly don't need one. Like I said before: Aloha's not even my type. And even if she were, I wouldn't be in the right frame of mind to make a move on her or anyone else because, unfortunately, my heart still belongs to Daphne."

Everyone groans and yells at me for being an idiot.

"Who said anything about your *heart* here, Z?" Colin says. "Pretty sure we've been talking about nothing but your dick."

"Aw, come on, Colinoscopy," Keane says. "You know ZZ Top doesn't separate fucking and feelings like most scumbags. My Wifey is a tenderhearted lad. He's not a dapper dabbler by nature, God bless him."

"But he's *capable* of dapper dabbling, right?" Colin says.

"Well, of course," Keane says, rolling his eyes. "One or two times outta ten, I'd say. But the other eight or nine times, Z thinks he's in *lurve* with whoever he's fucking, especially if the sex is really good. God help him if the sex is supernatural, he starts thinking the girl's his future wife."

"Yeah, but what about when falling in love with the girl isn't an option, like here?" Colin says. "Even without Barry's off-limits des, Z's gotta know Aloha's a nonstarter. She's a world-famous pop star and Z's just some nobody fitness trainer from Seattle. No offense, Z."

"None taken."

Colin continues, "You're not even a fitness trainer to the stars. You've got zero chance with her."

"True," I say.

Colin addresses Keane. "If Z were stupid enough to actually fall for Aloha, he'd do it knowing he was for sure gonna end up just like Kevin and Whitney—with Z standing on the tarmac at the airport with his arm in a sling, watching Aloha fly away on her private jet, her head wrapped in a dope scarf and his heart smashed into a million pieces."

Everyone laughs.

I don't need to ask Colin why he's so well versed in *The Bodyguard,* by the way. I'm well aware that Colin, like myself and Fish, spent his formative years hanging out at the Morgans' house. Which means he's probably seen *The Bodyguard* at least four times, the same as me, thanks to Keane and Dax's older sister, Kat, aka Jizz and Kum Shot and The Blabbermouth, who always had it on.

"Colin is right as rain," I say. "Even if, in some fantastical alternate universe, a big star like Aloha were inclined to give a nobody like me the green light, I wouldn't make a move on her. Because I'd know I wouldn't have a shot in hell at anything but a fling. And as fun as that sounds in theory, a little fun ain't worth my balls being ripped off my body."

"Barry said he'd rip off your balls if you touch her?" Dax asks.

"In those exact words."

"Yeesh."

"Meh, fuck Barry," Fish says. "He can suck your big, black cock."

We all laugh. Under normal circumstances, Matthew "Fish" Fishberger talking tough is funny, simply because he's the skinniest, most pacifist dude among us. But it's especially hilarious imagining skinny Fish talking tough regarding someone as brawny and badass as Barry Atwater.

"I'm serious," Fish says. "Barry has no right to tell two grown-ass adults they can't fuck behind closed doors."

"I'd pay to see you say that to Barry's face, Fish Taco," I say, laughing.

"No, I think I'll stick to saying it behind his back in a soft and well-modulated voice. But you know what I *will* shout from any rooftop? *Fuck Daphne.* That woman dumped you, man. There's no reason you should still be pining for her. Even if you're not gonna make a move on Aloha, then at least, for the love of God, make a move on *someone.*"

Everyone agrees.

"That's easier said than done," I mumble.

"It's easy as pie," Colin says. "Just turn the page."

Everyone in the room says some variation of "amen."

I sigh. "Daphne walloped me pretty good, guys. I need a minute."

"Bah," Fish says. "All you have to do to get *over* one girl is get another one *under* you."

Dax chuckles. "Is that what you do when you get dumped, Fish Head? Do you immediately fuck your blues away?"

Everyone laughs. We don't mean to be dicks to Fish. It's just highly amusing to imagine that a dude who looks exactly like Shaggy from *Scooby Doo* would even get the *chance* to hop from woman to woman in the manner he's prescribed.

"Well, no," Fish concedes. "I've never *personally* been given the opportunity to fuck my blues away after getting dumped. But that's what I'd do if I could—if I looked like Zander and had women falling all over me like he does."

15

I scoff. "Aloha Carmichael won't be falling all over me. She can get any guy she wants, literally."

Dax chuckles. "And that guy will be you, Z. At least for a fling. Mark my words."

"Agreed," Keane says. "The pop star is gonna take one look at Zanzibar and slip him her room key the first night."

"Not gonna happen."

"I genuinely think it will," Dax says. "In fact, a hundred bucks says you and Aloha will be flinging from the rafters before the end of month one."

"We won't." I grab a whiskey bottle off the coffee table and take a huge gulp. "Even in this ridiculous fantasy world where a celebrity like Aloha wants to dabble with her nobody bodyguard, I'd politely decline her offer for the three reasons I've already mentioned: Barry said she's off-limits, she's not my type, and I'm still licking my wounds from Daphne. So, drop it."

"You know what?" Keane says, munching some popcorn. "On second thought, I think I'm gonna have to side with Z on this one. I wouldn't bet on him flinging with Aloha, after all."

"Thank you, Peenie. Nice to know you've always got my back."

"Now, what I *would* bet on, though, is Z falling desperately *in love* with Little Miss Disney during the first month of the tour—after which time I predict he'll break down and start 'making sweet love' to Aloha, Lionel Richie style, every night of the tour during month *two.*"

Everyone around me agrees and then begins enthusiastically debating the finer points of Keane's theory. Essentially, they think he's spot-on in concept, but they disagree on the *timeline* for all this fuckery I'm supposedly going to be having.

"Fuck all y'all," I say, bringing the whiskey bottle to my lips again. "I'm not gonna fuck Aloha. I'm not gonna fling with Aloha. And I'm certainly not gonna fall desperately in love with her. I'm gonna be her platonic babysitter-bodyguard, exactly as I've been hired to be. And when my three months are up and I've got some solid experience under my belt, I'm gonna get myself assigned to the 22 Goats tour. And then, and only then, when I'm feeling sufficiently detoxed from my breakup with Daphne, I'll unleash Mr. Happy into the world again to spread his unique brand of happiness."

"Holy shitake mushrooms!" Keane shouts. "Do you mean to tell me you're not planning to have sex with *anyone* during the *entire* tour?"

"I gotta figure out what the hell I did wrong with Daphne so I won't do it again. Because this 'getting dumped' shit is painful, man."

"Then numb the pain with meaningless fuckery, for fuck's sake," Colin says, swigging the whiskey.

"Nope. I'm gonna use the next three months as a detox from the foxes and figure my shit out. It'll be a three-month *de-foxification*."

"I call bullshit," Colin says. "There's no way you'll last three months as a monk, Z. Put Aloha aside. Won't there be hot backup dancers on this tour?"

"Dude, how the hell could I possibly make a move on a hot dancer, even if I wanted to? I'm gonna be stuck like glue to Aloha twenty-four seven."

"Oh, yeah, that's right," Colin says. "Okay, then, we're back to square one: you're definitely gonna fuck Aloha. I'd bet any amount of money on it."

"I'm in for a hundred," Dax says.

"Me, too," Fish says from the floor.

"Same," Colin says.

"Uh-oh, Z," Daxy says. "Looks like you're the only one who's saying 'nay' here." He thwacks my shoulder. "Come on. Throw a Benjamin into the pot that says you *won't* fuck her so we can get an actual bet going."

"Fuck off. I'm not gonna bet on that."

"Why not? If you don't fuck her like you keep insisting you won't, you'll win the entire pot at the end of the tour."

"He won't bet because he knows he'll lose," Fish says.

"No, I won't bet because it's a disrespectful, douchey-ass bet."

"Disrespectful to *who*?" Fish says.

"To Aloha. To womankind."

"Z's actually right about that," Keane says. "Momma Lou would smack the shit out of us if she found out we bet on something this douchey. And if the momatron didn't smack us, then Mad Dog most certainly would."

Dax grimaces. "Well, damn, you know you've unwittingly

17

teetered into douchebag territory if Keane 'the Peen' Morgan feels the need to be the voice of feminism in a conversation with you." Dax rustles his big brother's already tousled hair. "Nice work, Peenie Baby. Tell Maddy she's doing God's work with ya." He addresses the room. "Okay, how's this for a less douchey bet? A hundred bucks says Z will fall deeply and madly *in love* with Aloha before the end of the tour. That's not douchey because, technically, Z could fall for Aloha without so much as a kiss."

I bring the whiskey bottle to my lips again, too annoyed to speak, but Keane declares the newly proposed bet sufficiently G-rated and feminist-approved. Of course, Colin and Fish chime in to say they want in on the new wager, with both of them predicting I'll wind up hurling my "tender heart" at Aloha "with both hands" at some point during the tour.

"*All* of you think I'll fall madly in love with Aloha?" I ask incredulously. "*Nobody* wants to put money on my heart standing firm?"

Everyone looks around for a beat and then bursts out laughing.

"Not even *you*, Peenie? *Et tu, Brute?*"

"Sorry, Zanzibar. I've known you since eighth grade, man. I've got zero doubts you're gonna fall for Peenie with a pussy."

I scoff. "Fuck all of you, Peenie included. I'll bet my Benjamin and take the entire pot three months from now. Count on it."

Chuckling, Keane leans back and spreads his muscular thighs, assuming his classic "I'm so fucking stoned" pose. "Hey, dudes. Since we all know Z's totally full of shit and will most definitely fall for the pop star before the tour is done, I vote we narrow the wagering to whether he'll fall during month one, two, or three."

Chapter 4
Zander

Dax looks down at his phone after tallying the final bets. "Okay, here's where things stand, fellas: Keane, Fish, Colin, Ryan, and Kat say Z will fall for Aloha during month one. Colby, Lydia, Tessa, and me say he'll be a goner during month two. And Josh, the lone wolf, says Z will hang tough until month three."

I shake my head. "You're a sick fuck to solicit bets from your entire family, Dax Morgan."

"It was no big deal," he says. "I just mentioned the bet in our family group chat. You should be happy I got everyone in on this, Z. If you miraculously pull this off like you keep insisting you will, you'll win an even bigger pot this way." Dax's phone buzzes and he looks down. "Ho! Momma Lou just put a Benjamin on month three."

"You told your *mother* about the bet?" I blurt.

"She's in the group chat. And it's a G-rated bet, right? As far as she knows, it's a bet about rainbows and unicorns, not pussies."

I grumble.

"Aw, quit your bitchin', Z. Momma Lou's C-note is as good as anyone's. You're just pissed even Louise Morgan knows you don't stand a chance at not falling for Aloha."

Keane pats my arm. "Don't be fooled by our mother's sweet smile, Z. She's a savage underneath that blonde bob. Where do you think Kat got her blonde savagery? Although I must confess I thought the momatron would be a whole lot smarter than betting on month *three*."

"Right?" Dax says, laughing. "Rookie mistake."

Keane's phone buzzes and he looks down. "Ho! Add another three hundy to the pot, Rock Star. Maddy and Hannah each bet a C-note on month two. Henn's in for month three."

19

"Oh, for the love of fuck," I mutter, palming my forehead.

"Hey, bee tee dubs, bro," Keane says, addressing Dax. "Can we talk about the fucked-up fact that I had to text Maddy about the bet *separately* because she's not part of the family group chat? It should be clear to everyone by now I'm in it to win it with this girl. I say we start giving Maddy a behind the scenes peek at how the family sausage gets made, just so she doesn't get a wicked case of the bends when she's officially brought into the fold."

"Fine by me," Dax says. He taps something onto his phone and smiles at his stoned-as-fuck big brother. "Careful what you wish for, Peen Star. Hopefully, seeing how the family sausage gets made doesn't make Maddy run for the hills."

Keane's dopey face lights up. "You seriously added her?"

"Yup. She's in. Godspeed, Maddy Milliken." Laughing, he looks down at his phone. "Okay. Now that all bets are in, Z is chasing fourteen hundred bucks if he can somehow go completely against character and *not* fall head over heels in love with a gorgeous, talented pop star with a hot body and the personality of his beloved best friend since age thirteen." Dax snorts. "Sounds easy enough, Z. What could go wrong?"

I flip him off.

"Actually, you know what?" Keane says. "You should yank my C-note outta the pot. I should probably judge the contest instead of betting on it. Even if Z *says* he's not in love with the pop star—even if he swears it and honestly believes it himself—I'm the only one who'll be able to look into Z's eyes and know if he's speaking the objective truth."

"Excellent idea." Dax looks at me. "You hear that, Z? Peenie's word is law when it comes to whether you've fallen for Aloha. If you make it to the end of the three months without Keane declaring your undying love for her, then you'll win the whole pot. But if, at any time, Peenie determines you've fallen for her, then the winnings will be divided accordingly." He turns to his big brother. "Raise your right hand, Peen Star. I'm gonna swear you into the bench."

"Oh, this is exciting." Keane raises his palm, his dimples popping. "I wish the motherboard were here to see this. She'd be so proud."

Everyone laughs.

"Keane Elijah 'Ball Peen Hammer Peenie Weenie Fucking Peen' Morgan," Dax says. "Do you solemnly swear to administer your judicial duties diligently, honestly, and without fucking it up at all times?"

Keane nods solemnly. "I will certainly do my best, little brother."

"That's all anyone can ask." Holding the neck of his beer bottle, Dax air-blesses Keane. "You're hereby sworn in, Judge Peen. Make our momma proud."

Keane bursts into singing the chorus of "The Judge" by Twenty One Pilots—specifically, the part of the song that requires him to sing the word "free" in a full, balls-out falsetto, and everyone laughs.

Keane bats my thigh. "Hey, sweet meat. Do you think you could get me two tix for Aloha's show on Thursday night? Maddy sings Aloha Carmichael songs in the shower all the time and I happen to know she never missed an episode of *It's Aloha!* growing up."

"No problem," I say. "Reed said I can get tix for friends and family for any show, including passes to the VIP meet and greet."

"Oooh, count me in," Fish says from the floor. "After watching so many Aloha Carmichael music videos tonight, I think I might be a wee bit obsessed with her now."

"If you want a ticket, just ask Reed," Dax says to Fish. "We're signed to the same label as Aloha, remember?"

"I'm not asking Reed for shit," Fish says. "That guy hates me. You ask him for me. Reed *loves* you, golden boy."

Dax rolls his eyes but doesn't deny the truth of Fish's statement. "I'll ask Reed for tickets for all of us. It might be fun to watch Z do his bodyguard thing for the first time."

A female shriek of joy wafts out of Keane's phone, drawing everyone's attention.

Keane laughs. "Yes, I know. That's why I asked Z for the tix." He grins and his dimples pop. "I love you, too. The absolute most."

My heart melts. Of course, I've known for months Keane loves Maddy. He's told me so himself. But with me living in Seattle these past three months, I've never actually witnessed Keane saying the magic words to Maddy. And I must say, hearing him say them to her—and to witness him looking so *happy* and *certain* when he says them... man, it's pretty dope.

Keane ends his call with Maddy and smiles broadly at me. "Maddy said to tell you thank you and that we'll name our first born Zander or Zanderina to repay you."

I chuckle. "You two are already planning kids, are you?"

"Apparently," Keane says, his face aglow.

"Where is Maddy tonight, by the way?" I ask.

"Oh, she's with her sister, shooting a promo video for one of Hannah's clients... I think. Actually, I don't remember what the Milliken sisters are up to tonight. Dude, I'm a jellyfish right now. I can't be expected to remember my own name, let alone the whereabouts of my smarter half."

"Is Maddy gonna be pissed when she comes home and finds out you've turned yourself into a jellyfish for the first time since moving to LA?" Dax asks.

"Naw," Keane says. "She'll understand tonight is a last hurrah. Plus, it's not like Maddy gave me an ultimatum about smoking out. She just gently *suggested* it might be a good idea for me to lay off the green stuff a bit while I'm trying to get my so-called 'acting career' off the ground. And my smart-girl was right as rain, by the way. Turns out I get shit done when I'm bright-eyed and bushy-tailed."

My phone buzzes with an incoming text and I look down. "Breaking news, fellas. The pop star—or, as she's just referred to herself, my new '*boss*'—sent me a text to welcome me to her team." I read the short text to everyone and we all snicker.

"Kind of low key aggressive for a twenty-three-year-old to refer to herself as your 'boss,' doncha think?" Keane says.

"Barry warned me she'd probably screw with me a bit outta the gate. You know, just because I'm a newbie."

I send a brief reply to Aloha and receive a lengthy, eye-roll-inducing text in reply, which, of course, I read aloud to the guys.

"Sounds like she's trying to get you to quit," Dax says.

"She probably thinks, if she can get rid of me, Barry will take my place. The good news is I've got Barry's unfettered permission to take exactly zero shit from her." A huge smile splits my face as I begin tapping out another text. "Oh, Aloha Carmichael. Let the games begin."

Chapter 5
Aloha

M y tour manager, Crystal, and my longtime backup dancer, Kiera, are screaming with laughter as I stand before them in my hotel suite doing a spot-on imitation of our choreographer. The three of us—Crystal, Kiera, and, I—are having a "girls night *in*" martini party following a long-ass day of rehearsals.

"So, what did Big Barry say to you when he came by today?" Kiera asks as I flop back onto the couch and pick up my martini glass.

"He said he's not coming on the tour, but, never fear, he's hired *two* guys to take his place—a service doggie and a cyborg."

I tell the girls about today's conversation with Barry, including the stupid wager I made with him that I'm surely not going to win—the one about me getting Zander to quit—and my friends laugh and make funny comments until all three of our glasses are drained and Crystal is getting up to refill them.

"Have you texted your new service doggie yet to say 'sit, stay, *quit*?" Crystal asks as she pours the booze.

"No, but there's no time like the present." I grab my phone off the coffee table, tap out a quick text, and read it aloud to my friends. "'Hi, Zander. This is AC, your new *boss*. I just wanted to say welcome to my tour.'" I look up. "I gotta figure a big, strong, muscular alpha dude like Zander will bristle at a twenty-three-year-old woman calling herself his 'boss' out of the gate."

"You know for a fact your new service doggie is a big, strong, muscular alpha?" Crystal asks. She's back in the sitting area now, handing Kiera and me our refilled glasses. "You've seen a photo of him?"

"No, but aren't all bodyguards big, strong, muscular alphas?"

"Kevin Costner wasn't," Kiera notes. "He had an alpha

23

personality, I guess, but he looked more like an accountant than a bodyguard. And remember that documentary you made us watch that time? The one about those secret service guys? Most of them looked far more like Kevin Costner than Dwayne Johnson."

"Hmm," I say, just as my phone pings with an incoming text. I look down and smile. "My service doggie says, 'Hi, AC. I'm looking forward to working with you.' I look up at my friends. "*With* you, I notice—not *for* you. Could that be his subtle push-back on the boss thing, perhaps?" I snicker. "Looks like it's time to get the service doggie to roll over and play dead." I tap out another text, press send, and then read my masterpiece to my friends. "'Hey, Z, I should probably warn you: I'm a huge click-bait target, especially when it comes to gossip about my love life. Given that I've never had a personal bodyguard besides Barry, and you're only a year older than me, I'm guessing the gossip sites are going to be all over us like white on rice. We'll probably get stalked by paparazzi hoping to catch me doing something highly un-Disney-like with you. Being stalked by paps would be a normal Tuesday for me, but it might be highly stressful for a newbie like you, especially if they post crazy stuff like, 'Aloha makes her new bodyguard her sex slave!' So, I'd totally understand if you want to bow out of this shit show before it starts. God help you if you have a girlfriend back home who might believe everything she reads. Or if you were hoping to hook up with someone during the long, lonely months on the road—a backup dancer, perhaps?—and now the gossip sites are going to make that almost impossible for you, just because everyone on my tour, dancers included, will stay the hell away from you, just in case the gossip sites have guessed right about us. (Which won't be the case, of course.) Don't worry, I'm sure Barry will happily reassign you to another tour, like maybe one with a male artist where the paps would leave you alone and the groupies would be plentiful? I truly think it'd be for the best. Take care, AC.'" I look up from my phone, my eyebrows raised. "Well? Do you think he'll take the bait?"

Crystal snorts. "Not a chance."

Kiera agrees.

Two seconds later, my phone buzzes and I look down. "You guys are right. He's not going anywhere. He wrote, 'I have no problem with anyone thinking I'm sleeping with you, AC. I'm single, straight, and you're a beautiful woman. Also, if you're regularly stalked by paparazzi, then that's all the more reason for me to stay on the job and protect you to the best of my ability. See you Thursday, Miss Carmichael. Or I suppose I should say... boss. PS I have zero interest in hooking up with anyone on this tour. I'm here to serve and protect you and nothing else. You're now officially my mission from God.'" I look up from my phone, my cheeks flushed. "*Whoa.* That was kinda hot."

"Smokin' hot," Crystal says. "Simple, straightforward, and take-charge. Dude, this boy's a stone-cold alpha."

"I gotta see him," Kiera says. "What's his last name so we can look him up?"

"Shoot, I don't know. And I can't ask Barry or he'll know I'm up to no good."

"Then cut out the middle man and ask Zander for a recent photo," Crystal says.

"Wouldn't that come off like I'm flirting? If the goal is to make Zander quit, then flirting with him would be the opposite thing I should do."

"Just ask him for a photo in a really bitchy way. Tell him you want to be sure he's 'hot enough' to be seen walking alongside a 'huge star' like you."

"Oh!" Kiera says. "And when he sends the photo, no matter how gorgeous he is, tell him he's simply not hot enough to be seen with a big star like you. With any luck, he'll think you're a narcissistic bitch-nightmare and quit. The chances are low, but it's worth a try."

"Actually," I say, tapping out a text, "I think I've got an even better idea."

Chapter 6
Aloha

Hey, Z, would you mind sending me a selfie? I'd like to know what I'm in for with the paparazzi and gossip sites. If they think you look like "my type," whatever that means, God only knows how relentlessly they'll hound us for that elusive "scandalous" shot. You SURE you want to be a part of my Godforsaken life? Save yourself, Zander!*

After pressing send, I read my message to my girlfriends and they roll their eyes with disdain.

"That wasn't diva-like at all," Crystal complains. "That was self-deprecating and sweet."

"What the hell, dude?" Kiera says. "That's not gonna make the guy quit. It's gonna make him want to stay even more."

Crystal squints at me. "Is *somebody* already too intrigued by her possibly scorching-hot bodyguard to risk making him think she's a narcissistic bitch?"

I bite my lip, trying to hide my smile. "But, guys, he said I'm a 'beautiful woman.'"

We all laugh uproariously.

"You're so damned predictable," Crystal says. "One sexy alpha text from a *possible* hottie and you're already shifting into full-on capture-the-flag mode."

"It can't be helped," I say, waving at the air. "I've got Satan's DNA inside me, after all. And, PS, I don't think Zander is *possibly* hot. My hot-guy radar tells me this man is *definitely* hot as fuck."

"Oh my God," Kiera says, chuckling. "*Sight unseen* you're already considering a tour-fling with your new bodyguard."

"Not a tour-*fling*," I say coyly. "I'd never have actual *sex* with my bodyguard, hot or not. But a tour-*flirtation*? Hell yeah."

"Why wouldn't you have sex with him, if he's hot?" Kiera asks.

"Because he's my bodyguard."

My friends shoot me blank stares.

"Have you both forgotten what happened when I fooled around with that keyboardist two tours ago? After that fiasco, I swore off messing around with anyone on one of my tours. And the keyboardist was just a musician. I shudder to think how badly a tour-fling with my *bodyguard* would blow up in my face if and when the thrill was gone. A guy from the band I can avoid for the most part. A bodyguard? Not so much."

"Bah, that keyboardist was just a fluke," Kiera says. "I've had lots of tour-flings over the years on lots of different tours and they've never once gone sideways on me the way that one did on you."

"Same," Crystal says. "If both people agree up front the fun will end when the tour does, then tour-flings can be fabulous."

"It's different for you guys," I say. "Paparazzi isn't watching your every move, trying to catch you doing something scandalous. You don't have to worry about photos leaking that will traumatize hordes of little Aloha-nators and their mothers. If the paparazzi got wind of me banging my hot bodyguard every night of the tour, photos of us would break the internet."

My phone buzzes and I look down and gasp loudly. "My service doggie sent me a photo, as requested. A *shirtless* photo."

"Lemme see," Kiera blurts. She rips my phone out of my hand... and then gasps exactly the way I did a few seconds ago.

Crystal peeks over Kiera's shoulder at my phone and gasps, too. "What the...? This guy makes Kevin Costner look like Dwayne Johnson!"

It's an understatement. For the love of all things holy, the shirtless man on my phone is a shaggy, pasty-white, lanky hipster with a beard who couldn't weigh more than a buck thirty soaking wet. To say he's skinny is like saying leg amputations are mildly inconvenient. If this skinny man stuck out his tongue, he'd look like a zipper! And to top it all off, he looks stoned as hell—like he just finished scarfing down an entire pan of pot-brownies.

"No wonder Barry hired the cyborg as your actual bodyguard and this guy as your service doggie," Kiera says.

My eyes narrow. She's right. Clearly, Barry hired the cyborg to protect me while this guy was hired solely to, what... *befriend* me? *Amuse* me? *Babysit* me?

Crystal snorts. "So much for that tour-fling with your hot bodyguard, huh? Unless, of course, you've got some kind of fucked-up Shaggy-from-*Scooby-Doo* fetish."

I toss my phone onto the coffee table, pick up my martini, and take a deep breath. "You know what? I'm glad Zander looks like a bearded pogo stick. Forget everything I said earlier about my bodyguard being off-limits. I was lying like a rug when I said I'd never bang my bodyguard. With no Barry to keep me in check for the first time ever, I'm positive I would have jumped Zander's bones within the first week if he'd been even half as hot as I was expecting."

"I've gotta hand it to Barry," Crystal says. "Obviously, he senses you're a horny little thing who's itching to throw a Molotov cocktail at your squeaky-clean image. He must have searched the world over to find the only twenty-four-year-old bodyguard in the world you'd never want to screw."

"You're absolutely right," I say, shaking my head. "Fucking Barry."

"Aw, man, I'm so disappointed," Kiera says. "From the service doggie's texts, I thought he was gonna be a sexy motherfucker. I was so looking forward to grabbing a bag of popcorn and watching from the sidelines as you seduced him."

"I'm pretty disappointed, too," I admit. "I was looking forward to playing a game of cat and mouse with my hot bodyguard for three delicious months. Well, actually, for a week, after which point I was looking forward to the mouse getting screwed to within an inch of her furry little life until the end of the tour—or for however long she remained interested."

"So, what now?" Crystal asks. "Are you gonna tell Barry you've seen Zander's photo and there's no way in hell you're gonna let Shaggy from *Scooby Doo* guard you?"

"I can't do that. I promised Barry if I couldn't make Zander quit on his own tonight, I'd accept his choice without a peep. Plus, if I'm being honest, I trust Barry's judgment too much to question his choice, as bizarre as it seems. If Barry thinks this broomstick with a beard and the cyborg are the perfect combination to replace him, then I have to believe there's a method to his madness."

"Well, if you want to try a last ditch effort to get Zander to quit, you could tell him there's no way in hell you'd let a skinny guy like him share a photo frame with you. It'd be mean, yes, but it might hurt his feelings enough to make him resign."

"Oh, come on. You know I'd never do that. I might be willing to cast myself as a narcissistic diva bitch to get my way, but I'm not going to shatter some poor, skinny guy's self-esteem." I sigh with resignation. "No, I just have to face it: my stupid bet with Barry is dead in the water."

"Aw, come on, AC, where's your fighting spirit?" Crystal says. "Just take a deep breath and disembowel the skinny bastard. You can do it, girl. Be heartless, just this once."

I shake my head. "If Zander had been a hot alpha, I wouldn't have felt a moment's hesitation about giving him shit. Hot guys always need to be taken down a peg or two, in my experience. But now that I know Zander is the kind of guy who's likely been ignored or flat-out rejected by women his entire life, I just can't bring myself to pile on."

"Aw, Aloha. Always such a tender little soul when you get down to the nitty gritty."

My phone pings and I look down.

Sooooo, do you think we're gonna be hounded by paparazzi or what? I'm thinking YES, for obvious reasons. #AbsOfSteel #PaparazziBait #HandsomeAndHappyLad

Laughing at Zander's hashtags, I type out a reply and he quickly answers. And before I know it, we're engaged in a rapid-fire exchange:

Aloha: Although your abs are indisputably epic, I'm thinking the paparazzi won't be hounding us... but only because you look way too smart to get yourself mixed up with a psycho bitch nightmare like me.

Zander: You never know. Maybe I've got a thing for psycho bitch nightmares.

Aloha: Well, if so, then you've definitely come to the right place, hon.

Zander: Uh-oh. Should I be scared?

29

Aloha: Nah. I've decided to go against my inherently evil nature and be kind to you. Welcome to my team.

Zander: I'm confused. I heard from a reliable source you'd mess with me cuz I'm a newbie. Not true?

Aloha: Not true. Your source, whoever he was (Big Barry) has defamed me. I'm actually gonna be sweet to you precisely BECAUSE you're a newbie. #SaintAloha #MotherTheresaWasAFuckingBitch ComparedToMe #FuckBarry

Zander: Wow. To what do I owe this immaculate display of saintliness from a self-proclaimed psycho bitch nightmare?

Aloha: Maybe I'm turning over a new leaf thanks to your abs of steel and undeniable charm.

Zander: Oh, now I've got undeniable charm to go along with my abs of steel? I just keep getting better and better.

*Aloha: Yep. You're a charmsicle left out in the sun, baby. *whispers* That means you're dripping with charm.*

Zander: Oh, snap, boss! Did you come up with that lil gem on your own or is it something the cool kids are saying these days?

Aloha: I came up with it. And lemme explain how things work in my world, dude. I make crazy shit up and THEN the cool kids start saying it. PS About that boss thing... let's pretend I never said that, okay? I was just messing with you. Barry is your boss, not me. I'm just The Package.

Zander: Ooooh, like in a spy thriller? Kewl. But it begs the question: If you're The Package, does that make me The Deliveryman?

Aloha: Only if The Deliveryman has abs of steel and is dripping with charm.

Zander: Aw, you're making me blush.

"Aloha."

I look up, smack in the middle of looking for a melting-popsicle gif to send to Zander, and discover Crystal staring at me.

"What the hell is that service doggie saying to you that's got you grinning from ear to ear over there?"

I blush, clear my throat, click out of the gif menu I was searching, and put my phone down on the coffee table with a thud. "I was just reading something funny on Twitter." I stand and yawn. "I think I'm gonna crash now, ladies. We've got a big day of rehearsals at the arena tomorrow and I need to sleep off those three martinis."

My friends amble to the door and the minute they're gone, I race back to the coffee table and squeal when I see a new text from Zander awaiting me: the exact melting-popsicle gif I was looking for to send to him! Ha! We share a brain. *Swoon.*

Wait.

Swoon?

What am I thinking? I need to get a grip. Zander is a cutie, yes. But *swoon*? No.

This always happens when I drink. I get dangerously flirty. Horny. Uninhibited. All things I shouldn't be in relation to the man who's going to be my babysitter for the next three months.

Deciding I'd better take a little time-out from texting, I head into my bedroom, brush my teeth, wash my face, drink a huge bottle of water and pop two ibuprofen, and, finally, grab my phone and slide my exhausted body into my fluffy white bed. But when I swipe into my texts and discover there's a new text awaiting me from Zander, a tiny flock of butterflies whooshes into my stomach, just like earlier. Holy hell! What's wrong with me? Those three martinis are really messing with my head. Obviously, when the vodka in my system wears off, I won't feel this weird attraction to Zander the Bearded Pogo Stick any longer. But since I'm feeling it *now,* and it's ridiculously fun to feel it, I pick up my phone and text Zander again.

Chapter 7
Aloha

Zander: Did I put you to sleep, AC? If so, sweet dreams. I'll see you at the arena on Thursday afternoon.

Aloha: Yo! I'm awake. Just had to say goodbye to my friends and get into bed. We've got a big dress/tech rehearsal tomorrow at the arena.

Zander: As your bodyguard, I can't in good conscience tell you to break a leg, so I'll just say good luck tomorrow and goodnight, hula girl. XO

Aloha: HULA GIRL?! Did Barry tell you he calls me that?

Zander: No. That was my own genius idea. Is it some special thing between you two? If so, I'm sorry and it won't happen again.

Aloha: LOL. It's fine. Barry is the only one I don't throat-punch for calling me that. But for some reason, I kinda like you calling me that, too. It feels like Barry passing the torch to you.

Zander: Then hula girl, it is. But feel free to tell me to stop if I start to annoy you with it or any other genius nicknames I might come up with. I've been hanging around my best friend's family since I was thirteen and they nickname EVERYONE. Well, everyone they like. And they've totally rubbed off on me.

Aloha: Ahem. You just impliedly admitted you like me.

Zander: Well, of course. What's not to like? #PsychoBitchNightmare

Aloha: I must admit, it makes me happy you like me. Happppyyyyy! Or, wait, maybe that's just the copious amounts of vodka coursing through my bloodstream.

Zander: Yeah, baby! It's a party! At the moment, I happen to have copious amounts of blood in my whiskeystream tonight. I'm also stoned as fuck, too. #winner #jellyfish

Aloha: It's a partaaaay!

Zander: Hold up. Pretend I didn't mention the stoned as fuck thing. For a second there, I forgot the situation and just thought you were some amazing woman I met in a bar or something. Did I mention I'm stoned? #dumbshit

Aloha: No worries. California is the land of legalized Merry Iguanas. Fair warning, though: you'd better not touch anything stronger than Tylenol during the tour, or Barry will fire your ass. And we wouldn't want that.

Zander: Look at you, tryna keep me from getting fired. That's quite the 180 from the girl who tried to get me to quit earlier. But don't worry about me. I'll stay sober as a judge for the next three months, of course. Gotta stay alert to make sure The Package remains safe and sound at all times.

Aloha: *blushes* Thanks, Deliveryman.

Zander: I can't help noticing you didn't deny trying to get me to quit earlier.

Aloha: Why deny it? I tried. I failed. Moving on.

Zander: But why'd you try? So Barry would join the tour instead of me?

Aloha: Correct. How'd you know?

Zander: I'm drunk and stoned, not stupid, dude. So, am I in the clear now or are you gonna keep trying to get me to quit for the next three months?

Aloha: You're in the clear. How could I try to get rid of you now that I know you're so damned cute?

Zander: *blushes*

Aloha: So, tell the truth, Z: are you drunk and stoned tonight because you're celebrating your awesome new job or drowning your sorrows about your horrible new job?

Zander: I'm celebrating my awesome new job and drowning my sorrows about something else.

Aloha: What?

Zander: I got dumped by the girl of my dreams.

Aloha: Oh nooooo! Who? Why? When?

Zander: Daphne. Dunno. Four nights ago.

Aloha: Oh no! You seriously don't know why?

Zander: Nope. She basically said "It's not you, it's me."

Aloha: Ooph.

Zander: Right?!? She found out she got into a prestigious art school in NYC and off she went across the country without looking back.

Aloha: Why didn't you go with her to NYC? Sometimes, ya gotta sacrifice for love, hon. Or so I hear. I've never personally sacrificed for love, but it seems to be a central theme in the Hallmark movies I've watched.

Zander: I offered to make the move, but she said no thanks and buh-bye.

Aloha: Ooph. That sucks. I've given the "It's not you, it's me" speech a few times and I hear it's brutal on the receiving end of it.

Zander: This was my first time on the receiving end of it and I can, indeed, confirm it's broooootal. Hence, I've been drowning my sorrows tonight along with celebrating my awesome new job.

Aloha: Aw, poor little Zan-Zan. You want me to beat dumbass Daphne's ass for you? I've got a mean right hook and a pair of steel-toed boots.

Zander: Um. Pretty sure if I let a former Disney star commit career-ending criminal assault for me, Barry would fire my ass.

Aloha: Good point. Then how about we humiliate Daphne, instead?

Zander: *puts palm to ear* I'm listening...

Aloha: The last stop of the domestic tour is NYC. We could invite Dumbass Daphne to the show and make out in front of her at the VIP meet and greet.

Zander: OMFG. Pleeease tell me you're serious.

Aloha: As a gunshot wound. This is a bona fide offer from me to you, Zanax. Because I'm not sure if I've mentioned this already, but I'm a fucking saint. (Other than when I offer to beat the crap out of art students with my right hook and steel-toed boots.)

Zander: Dude, I'm in...regarding the humiliation, not the criminal assault, just to be clear.

Aloha: Consider it done.

Zander: Yee-boy! The hilarious thing is that Daphne's a HUGE fan of yours. Both your music and the show. She once told me she had an Aloha Carmichael lunchbox in grade school.

Aloha: Sorry, the lunchbox can't save her. She's going down.

Zander: Thanks. And, hey, if you have an ex you want to make jealous, I'm at your service. Can't imagine dangling me in front of any ex of yours would be helpful to you, but the offer is there.

Aloha: No, thanks, but not due to any lack of appeal on your part. I've seen your abs of steel, remember? #hawt The truth is there's nobody I give enough of a fuck about to want to make jealous. I've been single for well over a year now and have no desire to change my status. The last guy I dated was a nightmare. *shudders*

Zander: How so?

Aloha: Jealous. Possessive. He was even jealous when I had to kiss a male model for a music video. I was like, dude, this is my JOB.

Zander: You need to get yourself a guy with genuine confidence next time, hon. Show me a jealous guy, I'll show you an insecure one.

Aloha: You never get jealous?

Zander: Never. Because I've got self-confidence. If a guy has something I want, then I just work that much harder to get it for myself.

I smile broadly. Damn, that's a whole lot of swagger for a guy who could slide through a keyhole. Not to mention for a guy who's nursing a broken heart after getting dumped. Aw, poor little skinny, shaggy Zander. How many times has this guy's self-confidence taken a hit like the one he just suffered mere days ago? How many times has he had to smile through pain and rejection and pretend to have endless swagger? Suddenly, I want nothing more than to raise this sweet boy's confidence. *Yes.* I'm going to make it my mission to boost Zander's ego to the moon and back during the next three months.

Aloha: I love your swagger, Zander! Keep it up. Screw Daphne! You're the bomb diggity. The little engine that could!

Zander: Wow, thanks for the pep talk, Mom. Very sweet of you. But, trust me, I ain't no little engine that could. I don't "think" I can. I KNOW I can. Also, my engine ain't little by any standard of measurement. #BigEngine #NothingLittleAboutIt #NoPepTalkNeeded

I laugh out loud again. Oh my God. Zander is freaking hilarious. Barry said he had a great sense of humor, and, man, was he right. I begin tapping out a flirty little reply, but before I've sent it, a text from Zander lands on my screen:

Zander: Ignore that last text, please. Did I mention I'm drunk and stoned? We've been getting along so well, I forgot you're not actually Keane in a female body or some awesome girl I met online or in a bar. I'm reeeeally sorry if I crossed a line with that last text and made you feel uncomfortable in any way. #BadZander #DrunkAndStonedZander #ToForgiveIsDivine #SorryBoss #Oops #FlirtyWhenDrunk #ForgiveMe

Aloha: No worries! I thought your text was hilarious! Just be yourself with me, Z. No offense taken.

Zander: Promise?

Aloha: Promise. Would it offend you if I said Daphne was a damned fool to dump you? You really ARE the most adorable person ever. #charmsicle #swaggy #BigEngine #swoon #FuckDaphne #GimmeMoreBadZander

Zander: Holy shit, AC. In all seriousness, I feel like I won the lottery getting this job. Barry said we'd get along, but I didn't think it would be this easy and comfortable between us so fast.

Aloha: Agreed. What else did Barry say?

Zander: Nothing much.

Aloha: Spill, Zander.

Zander: Nothing too interesting, I swear. He just said you'd screw with me and I had permission to be myself and push back. And he said you're not my job, you're my "fucking mission from God."

I drag my teeth across my lower lip. My clit has been pulsing for a while now, which makes absolutely zero sense. Am I really *that* tipsy? I think it's the mismatch of his confidence and looks that's got me so intrigued. How'd he get *this* confident, looking the way he does? Does he have the world's biggest dick or something? Maybe he wasn't joking when he said his engine isn't little... Shit, this throbbing I'm feeling between my legs... these butterflies in my stomach... None of it is making any sense. The boy looks like he could fall through his ass and hang himself. And yet... there's no denying what I'm feeling. With a big, naughty smile, I tap out a text to Zander that's got to be fueled by three martinis and a year without sex more than Zander himself:

Just for clarification, because the English language can be so dang tricky... When you said I'm your "fucking mission from God," how did you mean the F word in that sentence? As mere emphasis... or to define the endgame of your mission... from God?

Without a sober thought in my head, I press send... and then instantly freak out. Bad Aloha! Bad, Drunk, Flirty, Always-Seeking-Male-Validation Aloha! What have I done? *I'm pretty sure I just gave Zander the green light to sext me!*

Shit.

There are three wiggling dots underneath my stupid text.

I have to cut Zander off at the pass before his drunk and stoned ass replies.

With clumsy, hasty fingers and a racing heart, I tap out a message to Zander and press send before his reply lands on my screen:

Haha! Thank you, three martinis. All drunken kidding aside, I'm going to crash now, Zandy Man. I'll see you on Thursday at the arena! Nighty night, my friend!

The three wiggling dots underneath my text vanish and three seconds later, a brief and highly appropriate text from Zander appears:

Zander: Good night, hula girl. Slay your rehearsal tomorrow. Roger?

Aloha: Good night, Shaggy Swaggy! I will!

Zander: Noooo! When someone says ROGER to you, you MUST reply with RABBIT. This is the law.

Aloha: Oh, crap, I had no idea. #lawbreaker

Zander: Now, let's try it again. Goodnight, Aloha. Slay tomorrow. ROGER?

Aloha: RABBIT!

Zander: Good girl. *pats the pop star on the head like a puppy*

Aloha: LOL. Night, Z. Sleep well.

Zander: You, too, hula girl.

Aloha: XO

Zander: XO

With a happy sigh, I put my phone on the nightstand.

Wow. I've got to hand it to Barry. He sure can pick 'em. He thought Zander and I would click, and he was one thousand percent right.

I close my eyes, a huge smile on my face.

Happy Aloha.

Happy, Drunk Aloha.

Yay.

Ping.

I open my eyes and grab my phone. It's another text from Zander.

Hey, Aloha, before I pass out in a puddle of my own drool, I feel the urge to confess something to you. Deep down, I'm not actually a skinny, pasty, bearded hipster. I'm actually a six-foot-four black man. Just thought you should know.

I burst out laughing, suddenly picturing a Chihuahua looking into a mirror and seeing a Rottweiler in his reflection. Giggling, I tap out a reply:

Well, that would certainly explain the big engine. Sweet dreams. Mwah!

Ha! It's a good thing Zander *isn't* a big ol' twenty-four-year-old black man. If he were—if he actually had a studly, hunky body to go along with his adorable personality—then there's no doubt in my mind I'd wind up jumping his bones the first week of the tour, simply because I've got a particular weakness for that flavor of man candy and I'm already finding him kind of irresistible as it is. Shoot. A six-foot-four black man with the personality of Zander? Now *that* would have been a fun tour.

With that happy, silly, naughty thought swirling around in my tipsy head, I roll onto my side and pass the fuck out.

Chapter 8
Zander

I want to modify AC's route from the dressing room to the meet and greet."

That's Brett talking—the ex-SEAL who's going to be my immediate boss and mentor for the next three months. But he's not talking to me. He's talking to a squat Latino guy named Javier, the head of security for the Staples Center. Brett and Javier, trailed by Barry and me, are in the midst of a walk-through of the empty arena before tonight's kickoff show of the tour.

Brett continues, "Make sure the tunnel is cleared twenty minutes before AC is set to head backstage, and notify Zander when you've got it cleared."

A female voice blares over the speakers in the large arena. It's the same booming voice that's been doling out instructions to the production crew on the other side of the arena throughout our entire walk-through. "Okay, that's it for lighting cues," the woman says. "Let's run the opening montage while we await AC's arrival onstage for soundcheck."

At the woman's command, the large jumbo screens mounted on either side of the expansive stage flicker to life and begin showing rapid-fire video images of Aloha Carmichael working the camera. She's alternately dancing, laughing, blowing kisses, whipping her gorgeous hair...

"You got that, Zander?" Brett says.

I tear myself away from Aloha's face on the screen and stare at Brett. "Sorry, no. Could you repeat that?"

Brett tells me a logistical detail about the venue-supplied security guards who'll line the stage during Aloha's performance, and I assure him I understand.

Barry leans toward me. "Shadow Brett during every walk-through in every city, Zander. This is where you'll learn the nuts and bolts of the job."

"Yes, sir."

"Hey, everyone, let's do this ish!" an upbeat female voice says through the overhead speakers. It's a different female voice than before—a much younger, spunkier one.

I look toward the stage... *and there she is.* The Package. The woman I've seen on countless TV commercials for shampoo and facial cleanser and bottled water. The woman I watched shake her ass in skimpy outfits in at least a dozen music videos the other day. The face I've glimpsed hundreds of times growing up as my sister sat glued to the TV or, nowadays, as I've mindlessly flipped channels.

Aloha Carmichael is standing front and center on the large stage, dressed in a white tank top, black leggings, and flip flops. Her dark, unruly hair is piled into a messy bun on top of her head. She looks smaller than I was expecting. During training with Barry, he told me Aloha is only five-feet-four, so I should have known. She just seems so much taller than she actually is—larger than life—in all her music videos.

"Can we check the live-feed?" the earlier female voice booms. And a second later, a live video feed of Aloha appears on the jumbo screens, gifting everyone with the up-close-and-personal sight of the woman's makeup-free face.

Wow.

After seeing Aloha's painted and airbrushed image on screens and in advertisements so many times, I guess I'd started to think she actually looks like the marketed version of her—like a perfect doll. But standing there now, Aloha looks *real.* Accessible. Slightly tired. Like any normal, albeit strikingly beautiful, twenty-three-year-old woman I might see at the gym after she'd rolled out of bed for an early-morning spin class. In short, the real Aloha Carmichael is far more attractive to me than the marketed version of her.

"You guys wanna do 'Pretty Girl' for soundcheck this time?" Aloha says brightly into her microphone, addressing the band standing behind her. And, seconds later, she's singing the song.

I stand and watch, mesmerized. When I've heard this song at the gym, I haven't given it much thought. I don't love it or hate it. But now that I'm watching Aloha sing it and I'm seeing that big voice come out of that tight little body and beautiful face... *I fucking love this song.* Why doesn't Aloha sing just like *this* on the recording— with no special effects added? This girl can really sing.

I suddenly realize my group of four has almost reached the stairs to the stage while I've been standing frozen in place staring at Aloha, and I sprint to close the gap. Just as I catch up to the group, Aloha stops singing and signals to her band. The blaring music stops on a dime.

"Everything sounds great," she chirps. She waves to the sound booth at the back of the arena. "Great job, guys! The levels in my ears are purrrfect!"

"Let's do intros now," Barry says to Brett, and our group begins ascending the stairs to the stage.

Oh, shit. I'm suddenly nervous. During training with Barry, I told him about the photo of Fish I'd sent to Aloha on Monday night. I told him I thought I should send Aloha a real photo of me before meeting her in person at the arena on Thursday.

But Barry wouldn't hear of it. "If you send Aloha a real photo of you, you're fired," he said, laughing.

And since I wasn't sure if he was joking or serious, I played it safe and obeyed his direct order. But now, as I walk toward her across the stage, I'm getting the distinct feeling that might have been a very bad idea.

Chapter 9
Aloha

A loha."

I turn from chatting with my music director to find Barry standing with three guys—the cyborg plus two dudes I don't know: a stocky Latino guy and a fine-as-fuck black man in a black button-down shirt. Hot diggity damn, that black dude is one sexy hunk of muscle-clad dark chocolate. High cheekbones. Two diamond studs in his ears. And those lips! Good lord. They're full and gorgeous. But, of course, as sexy as this man is, he's not the one I've been excited to meet since Monday night.

I look beyond Mr. Sexy, hoping my shaggy, swaggy babysitter is bringing up the rear. But, no, Zander is nowhere to be found.

Shoot. I can't wait to meet Zander. When I woke up Tuesday morning feeling fine and dandy, I had the urge to send Zander a text asking him if he was feeling hung over from his prior night of partying. But then I remembered I'm not *actually* Zander's bestie, no matter the chemistry we seemed to share during our drunken text conversation. Indeed, I remembered I'm just a job for the guy. And so, I refrained from texting him.

But then, on Tuesday night, it happened again: I felt the urge to text Zander—this time, when I crawled into bed after a long rehearsal at the arena. I wanted to ask him if he likes watching documentaries and/or live comedy specials and/or horror flicks as much as I do... and if so, would he be down to watch each other's favorites during long travel days? But, again, I refrained, for all the same reasons as before.

And then, last night, I had the overwhelming urge to text Zander *again*, this time to invite him to my hotel room to hang out. Not to do anything salacious, of course. I just thought it might be nice for us to meet in person for the first time in private, rather than at the arena today, when hordes of people would be bustling around us. But again, I refrained, deciding to leave the guy alone until his job officially started. And now, dammit, after all that self-restraint, it seems I'll have to wait to meet Zander just a bit longer. And I'm not happy about it.

"Hey, Big Barry," I say, melting into his embrace.

"Hey, hula girl," Barry coos, giving me an extra tight squeeze. "You sounded great during soundcheck."

"Thanks. You look awfully dapper today."

"It's a new suit. You remember Brett?"

I disengage from Barry and dutifully shake Brett's hand. "Nice to see you again, Brett. Welcome to my tour." My eyes drift to the fine-as-fuck man to Barry's right. Who the hell is this sexy man with the world's sexiest lips? *Damn!* Every cell in my body wants to climb that man like a tree and kiss the hell out of those gorgeous lips.

"And this is Javier," Barry says, drawing my attention away from Mr. Sexy to the chubby Latino guy. "Javier is head of security for the Staples Center."

Ah. So Mr. Sexy must be Javier's right-hand man. "Nice to meet you, Javier," I say politely, shaking his hand.

"It's such a thrill!" Javier replies exuberantly, his dark eyes sparkling. "My daughter is a *huge* 'Aloha-nator.' She knows every word to every song and she's seen every episode of your TV show. For a full year when she was eight, she insisted on wearing a flower in her hair, just like you do."

My eyes flicker to the hottie again, ever so briefly, even as I'm shaking Javier's hand. Why the heck is he smirking at me like he's got a naughty secret? Hot diggity damn, the devilish grin on that man's exquisite mouth is making my skin buzz. I peel my attention away from him and smile at the venue guy. "That's so sweet. How old is your daughter?"

"She just turned twelve yesterday. My wife is bringing her and her best friend to the show tonight as her birthday present. It'll be her first concert ever."

"How sweet. What's her name?"

"Amelia. Funny story, though. When Amelia was in kindergarten, she made everyone call her Aloha for the entire school year."

I laugh. "Oh my gosh. Well, in that case, Amelia and her friend—and you and your wife—will have to be my guests at the pre-show meet and greet. Barry, can you arrange that for me, please?"

"Sure thing."

Javier thanks me profusely—and as he speaks, my gaze drifts to the hottie again. His dark eyes are positively blazing at me. *Oh, my.* Does this fine man get off on random acts of kindness? It sure looks that way. Well, all righty then. Let's see if I can make his dark eyes blaze even hotter.

"What's Amelia's favorite song?" I ask, returning to Javier.

"'Pretty Girl.'"

I address Barry. "Can you ask Shannon to cue me in my ears tonight to give Amelia a little birthday shout-out, right before we launch into 'Pretty Girl'?"

"You got it."

Predictably, Javier thanks me again, this time like I've just offered to donate a kidney to his daughter. As Javier showers me with praise, I sneak another peek at Mr. Yummy. Oh, man. He's buying what I'm selling. In fact, he's looking at me like he wants to bend me over the keyboard behind us and fuck me raw. My nipples harden at the mere thought. *Yes, please.* Okay, that's it. I can't wait a second longer to find out who this sexy man is.

I look straight at the object of my desire. "And you are . . ?"

"Oh, I'm sorry, Aloha," Barry butts in, before the guy can speak. "This is Zander Shaw. Your new personal bodyguard."

In rapid-fire succession, my brain does a double-take and then comes to a skidding halt... and then crashes down a flight of stairs until, finally, exploding into a gigantic ball of flames.

Zander extends his hand, grinning like he just gave me a wedgie. "Hi, Aloha." His voice is a low baritone. Sexy. Just like him. "It's a pleasure to meet you."

I glare at Zander's extended hand for a moment before pointedly snubbing him. "Can I have a word with you, Barry?" I grab Barry's forearm and pull him away from the group, every cell in my body vibrating with anger.

"Is there a problem?" Barry asks when we're away from the group.

"I want him gone," I whisper.

"Why?" Barry smiles. "Zander told me you two really hit it off the other night."

"He sent me a photo of himself that wasn't him. He's a liar."

Barry crosses his mammoth arms over his chest. "The man sent you a photo of the bass player for 22 Goats—an indie rock band signed to your label. And you wanna know why I'm not the least bit pissed he did that? One, because nobody in their right mind would think I'd hired *that* skinny guy as your bodyguard. And, two, because you had no legitimate reason to request a photo from him in the first place. You think this is some kind of beauty contest? You think this is Tinder and you get to swipe right or left on the bodyguards I assign to you? Well, it's not. The man has a job to do and I've specifically told you he's qualified to do it. That's all you need to know—not whether he's going to set your girly bits on fire."

I narrow my eyes. God, I hate that Barry knows me so well.

"And, by the way," Barry continues, unfazed by my death stare. "A deal's a deal. You agreed if you couldn't get Zander to quit on Monday night, you'd accept your fate without a peep. If your bodyguard's only crime is that he weighs a hundred pounds more than you thought—a hundred pounds of pure muscle—then you should be thrilled about that, not pissed. Now, come on. I promised Crystal you'd be sitting down for hair and makeup in five." Without waiting for my reply, Barry grabs my arm and physically pulls me back to Zander and Javier. "Zander, Aloha welcomes you to her team with open arms and a happy heart. She'd like you to escort her to her dressing room for hair and makeup now, please."

"Of course," Zander says in his deep, sexy voice. He shakes Barry's hand. "Goodbye, sir. I promise to take immaculate care of our girl."

"This isn't goodbye just yet," Barry says. "I'll see you at Reed's party tonight." With that, Barry kisses my turned cheek, wishes me a great show tonight, and leads Brett and Javier offstage.

And, just like that, I'm alone with Zander Shaw. The gorgeous man I'm dying to climb like a tree. The man whose sheer physicality is making my knees weak. The man whose texts on Monday night made me smile and laugh and feel all gooey inside, even when I thought he looked like a bearded broomstick.

Zander smiles politely and motions toward the wings of the

stage. "After you, hula girl."

"Don't call me that," I snap. "I gave you permission under false pretenses."

He presses his lips together like he's trying not to smile. "All right, then. After you, *Miss Carmichael*."

I stalk past him with my nose in the air. But even as I do, I can't deny the butterflies releasing in a torrent into my stomach. Or the tightening I'm feeling deep in my core. The unmistakable tingling sensation I'm feeling in my nipples and clit and on my skin. Holy crap. I can't remember the last time I felt this kind of immediate, undeniable sexual attraction to someone, if ever. And it's certainly not helping matters that I'm suddenly remembering what Zander said about the size of his "engine" the other night.

"It's really great to meet you, Aloha," Zander says politely behind me. "I think we're gonna have a lot of fun together."

"I wouldn't count on it," I mutter.

But I'm lying. Because, in truth, I also think Zander and I are going to have a lot of fun together... and just to be clear, by "fun" I mean a different variety than I've had with my beloved honorary uncle over the past six tours. *A very different variety of fun, indeed.*

Chapter 10
Zander

S o, let me get this straight," I say, speeding up to walk alongside Aloha down the long cement corridor leading to her dressing room. "You're pissed you've got a bodyguard who can actually bench press more than fifty pounds?"

"No, I'm pissed I've got a bodyguard who *lied* to me."

"About being a skinny dude who can't bench press more than fifty pounds."

"No, because I *thought* I was going on tour with a quirky, hilarious dude with *inexplicable* swagger—the kind of swagger that's semi-delusional yet oddly inspiring in a *Rudy* sort of way."

"Oh, I've always wanted to see *Rudy*. We should watch it together."

"Fuck *Rudy*," Aloha snaps. "And fuck you."

I laugh. "Well, gosh, that wasn't a very Disney-like thing of you to say, Miss Carmichael."

Aloha picks up her pace down the cement corridor, swinging her arms angrily as she walks. "The point I'm trying to make here, *Zander*, is that, based on your fraudulent photo, I thought you were an improbable underdog with inexplicable swagger. A hipster with a superhero complex. Rocky. The Karate Kid. Those bobsled guys from Jamaica."

"Wow, that's an impressive list of underdogs you've got at the ready."

She scowls at me.

"Aw, come on, now. Don't fall into the trap of judging a book by its cover. Maybe I *am* an 'improbable underdog with inexplicable swagger.' Seems to me you're jumping to conclusions based solely on my appearance. And that's wack, Jack."

She scoffs and motions to my bulging arms. "You're not an underdog, Zander."

47

"Underdogs can't have muscles? I'll have you know sports mythology is riddled with stories of underdogs who—"

"Gah. Never mind! Forget your stupid muscles. I didn't even notice them. It's that cocky look on your face that makes it impossible for you to be an underdog, okay? It's like you know you're some kind of god among men."

I laugh. Oh my God, this is fun. "I've got a *cocky* look on my face? No. 'Cocky' connotes a heightened but ultimately insupportable sense of confidence. And I assure you, my confidence is entirely supportable." I wink at her, just to see what she'll do, and she flashes me a look that makes me want to laugh with glee. "Bottom line," I say. "You're jumping to conclusions based solely on my physical appearance, and that's something any kindergarten teacher will tell you not to do."

"Well, joke's on you because I didn't even go to kindergarten. In fact, I didn't go to school at all. I got cast in my first TV series at age five and was tutored on-set forevermore. But guess what my tutors always taught me, Zander? *You should never lie.*"

"Dude, I showed you a photo of a guy who could never be your bodyguard in a million years, thinking you'd call me out on it or laugh your ass off. How was I supposed to know you'd actually believe me and fall in deep lust with the guy? And, by the way, other than sending that ridiculous photo, I was totally myself with you during our entire text conversation. Probably too much myself. Which means that, walking alongside you now, I've got the exact same 'charmsicle left out in the sun' personality I had on Monday night. So, what's changed? I'm now some 'cocky' asshole, just because I don't look like an emaciated lumberjack?"

She grunts in frustration. "When I thought you looked like an emaciated lumberjack, I wasn't physically attracted to you. And that made me feel confident we could become genuine friends with zero complications or misunderstandings."

"You're saying now that you've seen me, you *are* physically attracted to me... and that means we can't be genuine friends?"

"Exactly!" she says, shocking the hell out of me. "I'm physically attracted to you the same way you're physically attracted to me."

"Oh, now *I'm* attracted to *you*?"

"Um, *hello.* You made that pretty damned obvious back there onstage. You looked like you were getting ready to take a bite out of my ass."

My jaw hangs open. I stop walking and so does Aloha.

She says, "You can't honestly tell me you think we can have an uncomplicated, genuine friendship with all this ridiculous sexual tension between us. Light a match in this hallway and we'd explode."

I'm still too stunned to speak.

"You know I'm right. This is going to be one hell of a ride for both of us. And all I'm saying is it sure would have been nice if I'd known in advance how insanely gorgeous you are so I could have prepared myself to act nonchalant upon meeting you—friendly but disinterested—rather than drooling all over you and showing all my damned cards right out of the gate!"

She begins walking again and I follow suit, my head spinning. *What is this creature?* I thought Daphne was a straight-shooting, confident girl. But this one... She takes straight-shooting self-confidence to a whole new level.

We reach the door to Aloha's dressing room and stand outside it.

"Well?" Aloha says. "What do you have to say for yourself?"

I clear my throat. "About . . ?"

She motions between us. "This. Us."

I have no idea what to say, so I go with the safest bet. "I'm sorry?"

"That's a good start. Now, what are you sorry about?"

"For... drunkenly sending that photo of Fish to you and pretending it was me. It was wrong of me to do it and wrong of me not to send a real one to you the next day after I'd sobered up."

"And?"

Seriously? "And... I apologize if I was looking at you back there in any way that made you feel uncomfortable or objectified or disrespected. Believe me, it wasn't intentional."

"Well, of course, it wasn't *intentional.* Nobody ever ogles another person *intentionally.* That's the nature of physical attraction. It's *involuntary.* Animalistic. Do you think I could control looking at you like I wanted to climb you like a tree and kiss the hell out of you? And, by the way, I didn't feel the least bit uncomfortable or objectified or disrespected by your ogling. In fact, I liked it. The same way I liked it when you flirted with me the other night during our text conversation."

Okay, this girl is giving me whiplash. "I didn't *flirt* with you the other night."

49

"You sure as hell did."

"No."

"*Yes*. And I flirted right back. But only because I was drunk."

"Well, then, if I flirted with you, it was also because I was drunk. And stoned."

"No."

"*Yes*. Why can't it work both ways?"

"Because *someone* had to start it."

I sigh. "Look, how about we both admit we started flirting *simultaneously* the other night, but chalk it up to you being drunk and me being wasted and heartbroken. Okay? Let's start over and move past all that and agree we're going to be nothing but friends."

"Oooh, great plan. Except for this one little glitch: when you looked at me back there like you wanted to take a big ol' bite of my ass and I looked at you like I wanted to climb you like a tree, both of us were perfectly sober. How do you explain that away?"

I pause. Take a deep breath. And speak on my exhale. "Okay, we're both physically attracted to each other. So what? Adults don't always have to *act* on their mutual attraction. An adult is someone who's able to say, 'Hey, wow, there's a person I find attractive and would very much like to kiss. But, oh, damn, that's right, circumstances prevent me from making any kind of move on that person, so I'm just going to be that person's friend.'"

Aloha gives me a slow side-eye. A smirk dances on her perfect, pouty lips. "*Oh.* Okay. We're *adults* who'll maturely decide to be nothing but friends. *Phew.* For a second there, I thought this situation might get a bit complicated." She turns toward the door of the dressing room and puts her hand on the doorknob. But then she stops and smirks at me over her shoulder. "It's a bit of a bummer we're both such mature adults, in full control of our impulses. Because if you were to make a move on me, I most certainly wouldn't turn you down."

With that, she flashes me a wicked smile, opens the door, and strides into the dressing room, leaving me standing in the corridor feeling like I was just hit across the face by an extremely sexy—and dangerous—two-by-four.

Chapter 11
Zander

I'm standing about twenty feet away from Aloha at the VIP meet and greet. For the past forty minutes, I've watched her greet fans in small groups, one after another—and each time, I've been blown away at Aloha's charm and warmth and sincerity toward them. For some reason, it's not what I expected from her.

"Aw, I love you, too," Aloha says. She's in the midst of an ardent hug with an elated, shaking, near-hysterical Aloha-nator—a young woman of about Aloha's age wearing a flower in her hair, the same way Aloha does on the cover of her *Pretty Girl* album.

I shift my weight, keeping myself at the ready, just like Barry trained me to do. According to Barry, the hardest part of this job, especially when guarding someone who's not in any known, specific danger, is not letting yourself slip into complacency. "You have to force yourself to constantly stay on high alert," Barry explained. "Because there's always the possibility some lunatic will come at her, out of nowhere—some deranged fan who's convinced Aloha is his girlfriend and she's somehow spurned him. Plus, there's the added layer that even well-meaning fans can harm her, too. People get so excited to meet her, they sometimes squeeze her way too hard or even scratch and claw at her without realizing it. Just so you know, Zander, if anything happens to Aloha—if she gets the slightest scratch on your watch—I'm holding you personally responsible."

Yeah, that wasn't a stressful conversation or anything.

Another small group of squealing fans is led away from Aloha and the next group is ushered in: the local security guy from earlier today, along with a woman and two little girls.

Aloha immediately showers the two girls with effusive kindness, even going so far as to summon an assistant to bring each of them large gift baskets filled with Aloha Carmichael swag. Finally, when

Lauren Rowe

the happy foursome is ushered away with their gifts, I catch Aloha's eye and wink, telling her I'm impressed at the kind way she handled the birthday girl, and Aloha shoots me a hilarious look in return that says, "Dude, this ain't my first time at the rodeo."

A commotion at the door draws my attention and I'm elated to discover Dax, Fish, Colin, Keane, and Maddy bounding into the room, all of them hooting and barking my name like they're a football team and I'm their star quarterback. I lope toward my friends, greet them exuberantly, and then lead the entire motley crew to Aloha.

"*You*," Aloha says, pointing her finger accusingly at Fish. "You've got some explaining to do, *Zander*. And you'd better make it good or I'm gonna tell my big, beefy, gorgeous bodyguard here to kick..." She leans forward and whispers her next words, obviously not wanting any of the young Aloha-nators waiting out in the hallway to overhear them. "Your *motherfucking ass.*"

Fish laughingly begs Aloha for forgiveness and tries to explain why five drunk and stoned dumbshits thought sending his photo instead of mine was an exceedingly brilliant idea. Aloha assures Fish all is forgiven and begins chatting with Fish, Dax, and Colin about 22 Goats and their upcoming debut album and world tour.

As the boys and Aloha "talk shop," Keane and Maddy migrate closer to me.

"She called you 'gorgeous,'" Keane whispers out the side of his mouth.

"And beefy," Maddy adds.

"She was just being playful," I say. "Aloha and I have already expressly agreed we're friends and nothing more."

"*Oh, really?*" Keane and Maddy say in unison.

"Well, that's interesting," Keane says. "You've been on the job for mere hours and, already, you two felt the need to expressly declare your mutual friend status?"

"Interesting," Maddy says. "I'd think two people wouldn't feel the need to immediately friend-zone each other, unless there were something—maybe some sort of instant spark?—calling their mutual friend status into question."

"Well said, Mad Dog," Keane says. He addresses me. "Look deep into my eyes, Sir Zancelot."

Rolling my eyes, I comply with my best friend's command, but

52

only because I don't want him to make an embarrassing scene in front of Aloha if I refuse.

Keane squints at me. "Have you been struck by one of your famous Zander Shaw lightning bolts, baby doll?"

"No."

And it's the truth. I haven't. Yes, Aloha is hot—way hotter in person than I thought she'd be. But I most certainly didn't experience any kind of "love at first sight" jolt when I met her. Not the way I have in the past with more girls than I care to admit—none of whom turned out to be the great love of my life, obviously. Now, did I experience amusement, infuriation, and extreme exasperation at first sight with Aloha? Hell yes. And was all of it peppered with a healthy dose of lust? Most definitely. But none of that is even in the same ballpark with *love* at first sight.

"You *have* to come to Reed's party tonight!" Aloha says, drawing the attention of my threesome.

"Party?" Keane asks, sounding like a dog noticing a darting squirrel.

Aloha laughs. "Reed's throwing an after-party at his house to celebrate the kick-off of my tour. He always throws parties for big tours. I'm sure he'll throw one in London for Red Card Riot and you guys, too."

Of course, the group enthusiastically agrees to come to the party. More conversation ensues. And, soon, Keane is telling Aloha about Maddy's "amazing," award-winning documentary.

"I love documentaries," Aloha says. "What's it called?"

"*Shoot Like a Girl,*" Maddy replies shyly. "It's about—"

"*The basketball one?*" Aloha bellows, her eyes lighting up.

Maddy looks floored. She nods, apparently too overcome to speak.

"I watched that movie last month and absolutely *loved* it!" Aloha shrieks.

Of course, Maddy freaks out and the two women begin fawning all over each other for a long moment. But when Aloha's tour manager comes by to remind Aloha there's still a long line of Aloha-nators waiting to see their idol in the hallway, Aloha says her goodbyes to the group, but not before first making Maddy swear to continue their conversation at Reed's party tonight.

As the group begins shuffling away, Keane hangs back just long enough to hug me goodbye and whisper, "My family is a bunch of dumbshits, man. They placed bets on which *month* of the tour you'd fall for Aloha, but, clearly, they should have bet on which *day* of the first fucking *week.*"

Chapter 12
Zander

W hen I arrived at Reed's house several hours ago, Barry told me I was off the clock. "I'm here. Brett's here," he said. "And we're among friends. Just have fun with your friends and bond with Aloha. But don't have more than a couple beers because our girl notoriously parties her ass off at opening night parties and it's gonna be your job to get her back to the hotel in one piece. Probably as the sun comes up, if history repeats itself."

And so, I've been having sober fun all night. I've hung out with my friends, belly-laughed at them as they've partied like rock stars, and generally engaged in the best people-watching of my life. But, mostly, I've covertly observed The Package as she's partied and danced with her famous friends and backup dancers. And after watching Aloha for hours now, both at this party and earlier during her impressive show, I've arrived at an inescapable conclusion about her: she's sexy as fuck. Way sexier than I gave her credit for when I drunkenly watched her music videos the other day and pined for Daphne.

At this particular moment, I'm not watching Aloha from afar. I'm standing in a corner with Barry and Brett and another guy, listening to Barry tell a story from "back in the day." At a natural ebb in the conversation, I glance at the dance floor, curious to see what The Package is doing now. But she's not out there. Come to think of it, I haven't noticed Aloha grinding with her friends on the dance floor in quite a while.

"Have you seen our girl lately?" I ask Barry.

"Last I saw her, she was on the patio talking to your buddy and his girlfriend."

"I think I'll go check on her."

"Great idea."

And off I go.

On my way to the patio, I see Fish splayed out in an armchair, looking like he's about to pass out. As I walk by, he slowly salutes me and I return the gesture. I turn a corner and discover Colin talking to a woman I recognize as one of Aloha's backup dancers. As the woman talks, Colin's dark eyes are glued to hers with unmistakable fire. *Go, Colin.* I enter the large patio and look around, but I don't see Aloha, Keane, or Maddy anywhere. I do see Dax, however. He's chatting with a striking young woman in a corner. *Go, Dax.*

I make my way back into the party and do a quick tour of the entire downstairs. But, still, no Aloha, Keane, or Maddy anywhere.

Out of nowhere, an idea pings my brain... a highly disturbing idea. Drunk Peenie wouldn't have coaxed Drunk Maddy and Drunk Aloha upstairs to find a quiet bedroom for a little X-rated fantasy fulfillment, would he? No way. I'm being paranoid to even think it. Keane would never in a million years suggest a threesome to his nerdy, adorable new girlfriend, not even if the third wheel in the arrangement were a world-famous and extremely sexy pop star he'd just watch blow the roof off the Staples Center... right? Because Ball Peen Hammer and his unapologetically manwhoring ways are firmly in Keane Morgan's rearview mirror these days, now that he's head over heels in love with Maddy... *right*?

My heart lurching into my throat, I stride to the staircase. Please, God, don't let my best friend mess up the best relationship he's ever had by doing something stupid tonight. And, even more importantly, please don't let Peenie screw up his relationship with *me* by fucking Aloha before I've had the chance to—

I suddenly hear Keane's voice. I'm on the second floor now and I can hear my best friend's muffled voice over the crashing of my pulse in my ears. I turn a corner... and then another... and Keane's distinctive voice crystallizes. It's coming from the other end of a long hallway, and based on what he's saying, I instantly realize my rising panic from a moment ago is completely unfounded. Clearly, Keane isn't a dude grooming two girls for a *ménage a trois*. He's a diehard momma's boy bragging about his mother's home cookin'.

"Swear to God, brah," Keane is saying. "She makes the best lasagna in the world, hands down."

I turn a corner and there they are: Keane, Maddy, and Aloha, all of them fully dressed and sitting Indian-style on the floor of Reed's home gym. Other than the large bottle of Jack Daniels they're passing around and the loopy expressions on their drunken faces, they look like kindergartners at story time, not swingers planning a three-way. How could I have doubted my best friend, even for a second? I lean my shoulder against the doorjamb and covertly watch the threesome as they chat and pass the bottle around.

"You're lucky you've got such a nice mom," Aloha says to Keane. "I've always wanted a nice mom like yours."

"Aw, poor Aloha," Maddy says, taking the bottle from Aloha. "My mom's not going to win any prizes for mother of the year, but at least she's never made me her meal ticket. Plus, she came to every one of my tap dancing recitals growing up. *As mothers do.*"

"Right?" Aloha booms, throwing up her hands. "The woman's only daughter plays a sold-out show at the Staples Center and she couldn't be bothered to fly in from God knows where to see it?" She looks at Keane. "If your mom were mine, she wouldn't give a shit about my money, would she?"

"Hell no." Keane takes a long swig of whiskey and wipes his mouth with the back of his hand. "My older brother Ryan is rolling in duckets these days—I mean, not 'rolling' like you or my sister's husband—but, still, he's doing well by normal-people standards. And Momma Lou doesn't treat Ryan any differently than me or any of us. I mean, my mom fawns all over Ryan, but she fawns all over all of us, whether we're rich or poor, dumbshits or smartshits."

"Ryan is your oldest brother, right?" Aloha asks.

"Dude. *No.* I just told you the whole damned thing."

Aloha giggles. "Tell it to me again. I'll listen this time, I swear."

Keane sighs. "Okay, but this is the last time. My time is valuable."

Aloha laughs again. "I know. I'm sorry, Peenie."

His dimples popping, Keane says, "Okay, pop star. Clean out your earholes and listen up: The Morgan family birth order is as follows: Colby Cheese, Captain Ryan, Kitty Kat Morgan Faraday—"

"Kum Shot!"

"Correct. Kum Shot, Jizz, Splooge. Any cum nickname you can possibly think of because...?"

"Because Kat's initials are KUM!"

"Gold star, Alo-haha. Kat's also called The Blabbermouth, bee tee dubs, so if you've got a secret you don't want getting out, then, for fuck's sake, don't tell my sister." He rolls his eyes. "Okay, after Kat, there's the most charming Morgan sibling—Keane the Peenie Peen with the Gigantic Peen—and, after me, there's our baby brother, Dax, who's been ready to become a rock star since birth. You got all that, Alo-haha? Colby, Ryan, Kat, Keane, and Dax."

"Rabbit!" Aloha shrieks happily.

Keane laughs. "Dude, you only say that when someone says roger."

Aloha scoffs. "So many rules with you motherfucking Morgans."

"Ugh, they're the *worst*," Maddy deadpans, and Keane laughs.

Keane continues, "Now, if you want some bonus material for your Morgan family DVD, then slip Zander in the lineup alongside me, like we're fraternal twins. Because, at this point, Zander's an adopted Morgan brother. He's right up there with Ryan when it comes to brains and Colby when it comes to kindness."

My heart skips a beat. Aw, Peenie.

"How do I get in on that action?" Aloha asks.

"Just be your badass self and Z won't be able to resist you. In fact, by the way Zander was looking at you at the meet and greet, I'd say—"

Aloha snorts. "No, no. I meant how do I get in on the whole 'getting adopted by your family' thing, the same way Zander did?"

"*Oooh.* Ha! That's funny." Keane shrugs. "You just gotta show up whenever the Morgans are in one place and make 'em fall in love with you. Hell, you've already got a sick nickname, right? That's half the battle. All that's left is for you to show up at a family gathering."

Aloha sighs wistfully. "I wish it were that easy. I'd give anything to be part of a family like yours—to have siblings and friends and a mother who acts like a mom instead of a mom-ager."

"Dude, it's not an impossible dream. Just show up for a family dinner one night and everyone will fall in love with you. What's not to love? You're awesome."

Okay, it's official: I'm the worst friend in the world for doubting Peenie earlier. I should have known my boy would sooner die than give me so much as a paper cut. He's made it clear he thinks I'm gonna fall for Aloha—which, of course, he's dead wrong about. But the point is Keane sincerely believes I will, which means he'd never so much as lay a pinky on Aloha, whether he was with Maddy or not, because he'd be thinking Aloha is mine.

Keane says, "Hey, why don't you come to Thanksgiving at my house, Haha? We can adopt you then."

Aloha hoots excitedly but then says, "Oh, wait, no. I serve homeless people at a soup kitchen on Thanksgiving every year. Shoot. Goddamned homeless people."

Everyone laughs, including me.

"But, hey, my tour will roll through Seattle in a few weeks and I'm free the night after my show. Why don't I come to dinner and get adopted by your family then?"

"*Perfecto!*" Keane says, pulling out his phone. "I'll text the momatron right now and tell her to start stocking up on lasagna noodles and motherly love."

"I can't wait!" Aloha says. "Will you be there, too, Mad Dog?"

"Of course!"

The women squeal and hug.

Okay, I've let this ridiculous conversation go on long enough. Time for the only sober person at the party to step in and restore sanity. "Hey, kiddies," I say from the doorway. "What's going on in here?"

Everyone turns and greets me enthusiastically.

Keane says, "Aloha's comin' to a Morgan family dinner!"

"And Peenie gave me a nickname!" Aloha adds. "Alo-*haha*—shortened to Haha—because, he said I'm 'fucking hilarious!'"

"She is," Keane confirms. "Someone cast this girl in a Disney sitcom, *stat!*"

Everyone laughs, including me.

Aloha says, "And Maddy's gonna send me a preview copy of her new documentary about strippers, starring Peenie!"

"And believe me, I don't send preview copies to just anyone," Maddy says.

Aloha returns to me, beaming. "She's sending it to me because we're besties!"

"We are. *Forever.*"

I chuckle. "Wow. Sounds like the three of you and Jack Daniels have become soulmates in here. But as the only sober person in the room, can I make a suggestion? Perhaps you guys shouldn't make adoption plans when you're shitfaced. Just a thought."

All three drunkards hiss and boo me loudly.

I laugh. "I'm not trying to be a buzzkill. I'm just—"

"No more talking, bodyguard!" Aloha shouts. "Only catching!" Without warning, Aloha springs up from her spot on the floor like a cheetah, leaps, and hurls herself at me—which, of course, prompts me, by default, to catch the woman midair so she doesn't crash onto the floor. And suddenly, I'm holding Aloha Carmichael in my arms while she hangs onto the front of me like a koala in a eucalyptus tree. Aloha shoves her gorgeous face in mine. Her green eyes are blazing. "Dirty dance with me, bodyguard."

"Here?"

"No, silly. Downstairs. Where everyone can see us and wish they were me."

I laugh. "You're drunk."

"And you're sexy as hell. So I am drunkenly *commanding* my hot bodyguard to dirty dance with me!"

"Okay, let's get something straight. I don't care who you are, you don't get to 'command' me to do a goddamned thing—least of all to 'dance.' Whatever you desire me to do, you can ask me respectfully and take your chances."

A wicked smile spreads across Aloha's face. She presses herself into me, making my dick tingle. "Will you pretty *please* dirty dance with me... *Mr.* Bodyguard? I would be oh-so very grateful, if you did, sir."

I look over Aloha's shoulder at Peenie to find him shooting me a grin that says, *You're in trouble with this one, Z.* Smirking, I look away from my best friend and return to Aloha. If I say yes to her request and she dances with me downstairs in a manner that even remotely resembles the way she's been grinding with her friends all night, then Peen's right: I'm in trouble with this one. Big trouble. Because dancing like *that* with Aloha will almost certainly light a fuse between us I won't be able to extinguish for the next three months. But on the other hand, Barry *did* tell me at the beginning of the party to "bond" with Aloha. And dancing is undoubtedly an excellent way to bond with someone...

"Thanks for asking me so respectfully that time," I say. "Yes, I'll dance with you. In fact, it would be my *pleasure* to dance with you, *Aloha.*" I shoot a snarky look over Aloha's shoulder at Peenie again, acknowledging the fact that, yes, I'm well aware I just sent an ill-advised subliminal message to the pleasure center in Aloha's brain by using her name and the word "pleasure" in the same sentence. And the look on Keane's face tells me he thinks I'm playing with fire here. Yeah, he's probably right about that. But fuck it. I'm just gonna dance with the girl, not fuck her. There's nothing wrong with that.

"Let's go, Mr. Bodyguard!" Aloha shrieks, banging on my chest like a madwoman. "I wanna *dance!*"

I laugh. "Okay, okay. *Patience.* Good things come to those who wait, Aloha."

"I wouldn't know."

"Why doesn't that surprise me?"

With that, I wrap my arms tightly around my little koala and bound out of the room toward the stairs.

Chapter 13
Zander

The song blaring is "Dancer" by Flo Rida. To my right on the dance floor is a guy on a popular TV show. To my far left, Colin is dancing with that same hot backup dancer from earlier, and they look like they're getting ready to devour each other. In front of me. Behind me. Off at a diagonal. Everywhere I look, there are drunk, stoned, ridiculously beautiful people, most of them dancing like they're fucking with clothes on. But I've only got eyes for Aloha. Because the way she moves her body when she's dancing... Man, this girl puts the baller in ballerina.

Of course, as I'm watching Aloha move like a little vixen, I'm dancing, too. But only to keep from looking like a pervy customer at a strip club. Because, yeah, that's exactly how I feel right now: like a scumbag with a boner and a pocketful of dollar bills.

Midway through the song, Aloha stops gyrating and strides to me, right on the beat. When she reaches me, she turns around, bends completely over, and shoves her tight little ass straight into my hard-on. And then she *grinds*, right in time to the music, shoving the crack of her amazing ass right against my hard dick.

Aloha's maneuver isn't all that salacious, actually, when compared to the barely disguised make-out sessions happening around us on the dance floor. In fact, I've seen Aloha do pretty much this same thing with her friends—gay, straight, and otherwise—all night long. But with all those who came before me, Aloha seemed playful and fun-loving. Like she was nothing but a party girl blowing off steam with good friends. But this thing she's doing to me? Oh, yeah, she's most definitely getting her rocks off every bit as much as I am. And I'm not gonna lie: I'm digging it.

Unfortunately, I can't return Aloha's enthusiasm the way I'd do it if she were some random girl I was dancing with in a club in Seattle. If that were the case, I'd grab her hips and simulate fucking the living shit out of her in response to her grinding movement. Hey, a woman fucks me on the dance floor, it's only polite to fuck her right back. But, see, my usual instincts have no place here, not when she's The Package and I'm the guy hired to do whatever the hell she wants and needs... *except* fuck her.

Without warning, Aloha strides away from me, leaving my dick screaming at her to *pleeease* come back. She turns around to face me, an evil gleam in her eye, and then charges at me like a gymnast, the same way she did upstairs in Reed's home gym.

Yet again, I reflexively catch her. And, just like that, here we are again, with Aloha wrapped around my torso like a koala in a tree.

"So this is our thing now?" I say, shouting over the blaring music. "You're my little koala and I'm your eucalyptus tree?"

Aloha giggles. "If eucalyptus trees get raging hard-ons, then yes."

"You think this is me with a raging hard-on? Sweetheart, this is me with a limp dick."

She bursts out laughing and so do I.

"I don't think so, Zandy Man," she says, grinding herself into me. "They say Shakira's hips don't lie? Well, Zander Shaw's *boner* don't lie." To prove her point, apparently, she presses herself pointedly into me again. "Also, I'd prefer to think of myself as a monkey in a tree, please, not a koala. Koala's aren't mischievous enough to be my spirit animal." She grins. "But, either way, this tree is most definitely sporting *wood*."

I can't help smiling. "It's pure physiology, baby. Like a dog conditioned to salivate at a dinner bell. Just because the dog drools, doesn't mean he's hungry."

Aloha pointedly rubs her center against my raging boner again, this time with extra sauce. "I dunno, dude. That sure feels like a hungry dog to me. A hungry Great Dane."

"You rub Mr. Happy, he gets hard. It means nothing. We're just *friends*, remember?"

"Do you usually get hard with your *friends*, Zander?"

"When they look like you and rub their un-fucking-believable ass against my dick? Then, yeah, apparently, I do."

Aloha drags her teeth over her lower lip. "Admit it: you're a heartbeat away from making your move. And when you do, just to be clear, my answer will be a resounding *yes.*"

I suddenly realize we're standing in the middle of the dance floor having this naughty conversation—and that we're no longer even pretending to dance. I can't imagine anybody, including Barry— if, God forbid, he's somewhere in this room watching us—would mistake our body language for actual dancing at this point.

I glance around, suddenly feeling like a bank robber with a bag of cash, and, thank God, don't see Barry anywhere. Feeling like I've dodged a bullet, I quickly carry Aloha off the dance floor into a secluded corner of the large room.

"Ooh, we're going somewhere to make out now?" Aloha says gleefully. "Yippee!"

"Cool your jets, horn dog," I say. "I just want to continue our conversation off the dance floor, away from prying eyes."

"You mean away from *Barry's* prying eyes?"

"Bingo."

"Aw, don't stress, Shaggy Swaggy. Barry already left the party."

Every cell of my body sighs with relief. "Are you sure?"

"Positive. He texted me. He said the cyborg's still here if needed and you'll take me to my hotel tonight." She flashes me side-eye. "Barry put the fear of God in you if you touch me, huh?"

"In no uncertain terms."

"Bastard!"

"But he didn't need to say it. You're The Package. It's obvious."

"Fucking Barry. Always trying to ruin my fun." She pouts for a split-second before smiling wickedly again. "But let's forget about him, shall we? He's *your* boss, not mine. I can do whatever I like, with whomever I please." Her green eyes darken with heat. "Now tell me a little bit about this Mr. Happy fellow you mentioned—the impressive dude who's standing at full attention at the front your pants."

"Not much to tell. He's a happy fellow."

"Yes, I've gathered that."

"Aloha, I should put you down now. I'm being Bad Zander again, and this time I can't blame alcohol or weed."

"I like Bad Zander."

63

"Aloha, seriously—"

"I command you *not* to put me down, bodyguard! My feet hurt. Ouch."

I flash her a warning look.

"Oh. I mean, '*Please* don't put me down, *Mr.* Bodyguard. My feet hurt.' Now where were we? Oh, yes, you were about to tell me why you call your dick Mr. Happy."

"It's self-explanatory."

"Maybe, maybe not. I want to hear you explain it in your own enthralling words."

"No."

"Is it because of that old joke: 'Is that a pencil in your pocket or are you just happy to see me?'"

"Basically."

"Tell me *specifically.*"

"I'm gonna put you down now, Aloha. This has gone far enough. I'm fucking up."

"Ouch! My feet!" She smiles. "Do you call him Mr. Happy because when he comes out to play he's *happy* to be alive and free?"

My breathing hitches. She's just pressed herself against my dick again, but this time in a way that's sending pleasure shooting into my dick like a bullet. "That's it. Yep."

Aloha repeats her maneuver, apparently enjoying whatever expression it's eliciting from me. "Is it that whenever Mr. Happy comes out to play, he makes whatever lucky lady feel happy, too? *As a clam*?" Her eyes ignite. She snickers. "Happy as a... *bearded* clam?"

I can't help laughing. "How the hell do you know that slang? Girls aren't supposed to know that one."

Aloha giggles. "Oh, I've heard every slang term in existence for the ol' 'cock pocket.' I've been around crews and musicians my whole life—some of whom weren't aware there was a little girl in their midst with very big ears." She chuckles and grinds into me again. "I tell you what, Mr. Bodyguard. If you tell me in your own words why you call your dick Mr. Happy, then I promise I'll get down, despite my aching feet, *if* that's truly what you want me to do."

My dick is yearning. Throbbing. *Wanting.* I shouldn't do it, but I can't resist. I press my lips against Aloha's ear and say, "I call my dick Mr. Happy because when I'm with my lucky lady, he *always* puts the *penis* in her happiness."

Aloha guffaws and so do I. But then she presses her lips against my earlobe, right up against my diamond stud, like she's gonna take it into her mouth, and purrs, "I could really use some happiness in my life, Zander."

I clench my jaw and consciously force myself not to turn my head, not to claim her perfect, pouty mouth with mine. My brain knows I can't kiss her—that it would be a huge, regrettable mistake for me to do it. But my lips, my dick, my skin, my nipples—they're all telling my brain to take a little nap for a while.

I take a deep breath, trying to get a grip, just as a mob of Aloha's friends descends upon us, shouting, "Shots, shots, shots!"

Thank you, Baby Jesus.

I shoot Aloha a smile that says, "Saved by the bell." And she glares at me like it's my fault these friends of hers just showed up. Sighing deeply, she unwraps her legs from my waist and slides down to her feet, rubbing herself against my aching bulge one last, delicious time, as she goes.

"Don't stray too far, Mr. Bodyguard." She pats my chest. "It's gonna be your job to scrape me off the floor at the crack of dawn and get me to bed." With that, she lets one of her dancer-friends lead her toward the kitchen. But just before she disappears around a corner, she turns around and shoots me a scorching look that says, in no uncertain terms, "You dodged a bullet this time, motherfucker. But next time, your ass is mine."

Chapter 14
Zander

As the sun threatens to rise behind us, I scoop up Aloha's slack body from the backseat of our hired car and carry her like a drunk-ass bride toward the sliding glass doors of the ritzy hotel. As I walk, Aloha slides her arms around my neck and rests her cheek against my shoulder. She's alternately singing, whooping, babbling, and... yodeling? All the same stuff she was doing during the car ride. Dude, I gotta say, this Aloha chick is a *very* happy drunk. And that's what I'm in the process of telling her when, out of nowhere, about thirty yards from the hotel entrance, a guy with a huge camera bounds toward us and starts snapping blinding flash photos.

"*Whoa,*" I say, my heart lurching at the sudden intrusion. "Back off, man."

But Aloha is unfazed. "Hey, Yazeed!" she sings out as the guy trots alongside us, snapping his blinding photos. "How's your brother?"

"Recovering nicely, thanks. Congrats on the new tour."

"Thanks. Is this video yet, hon?"

"I'm switching to video now. And... go."

Without missing a beat, Aloha waves at the camera. "Hi, everyone! Come see my 'Pretty Girl' tour in a city near you!" She blows an enthusiastic kiss to the camera. "I love youuuuu!"

The guy chuckles. "Okay, you got yours, now gimme mine. Who's the guy? Is he your new—"

"*Boy toy!*" Aloha shouts.

"*Aloha,*" I chastise.

We're mere yards from the hotel's front entrance now, so I pick up my pace, hoping to launch myself through the automatic glass doors before the atomic bomb in my arms goes off.

"Well, that's a first," the guy says, chuckling. "Are you heading upstairs to have sex with your new 'boy toy,' Aloha?"

"Don't answer him," I say as I bound the last few feet toward the hotel entrance.

"Sex is most definitely the plan!" Aloha shouts over my shoulder, just as we cross the threshold of the hotel. "And it's gonna be soooo *gooood*!"

The doors of the hotel close behind us, leaving the guy laughing outside.

"*Aloha!*" I chastise.

She grimaces. "Bad Aloha?"

"*Very* bad Aloha!"

Aloha bats her eyelashes. "Oops?"

I roll my eyes. "He didn't know you were kidding."

Aloha kicks her legs like she's doing the backstroke in my arms. "Don't worry, Shaggy Swaggy, the world won't think you're using sweet little virginal Aloha for sex. They'll assume you're deeply, madly in love with her. Which you *are*."

"I'm not, actually. Especially not right now."

"Well, give it a few days."

"Keane told you about the bet, I take it?"

"Huh?"

"Keane told you about the..." I clamp my mouth shut. Aloha looks genuinely perplexed. But, then again, she's shitfaced, so I'd imagine "perplexed" is her current default mode. "Never mind." I step inside the elevator and swipe my keycard to gain access to our restricted-access floor.

"Oh, Zander," Aloha sighs as the elevator ascends. She presses her cheek against my shoulder. "I've never been in love. But if I ever *do* fall in love, I hope it's with someone as beautiful as you."

I pat her drunk cheek. "I hope so, too. For your sake."

She giggles.

Two minutes later, as I lay my drunk ward on top of her fluffy white bed, she moans pitifully.

"The room is spinning."

"It's not the room. It's your head."

"Make it stop."

"You just have to ride it out like all those mortals who did way too many shots at a party before you." I take off Aloha's shoes and stand over her for a moment, trying to decide what to do next. If Aloha were my drunk little sister wearing that outfit—skin-tight black jeans and a beaded, sparkly gold top—I wouldn't hesitate to get her into some soft clothes. If a little boobage peeked out while I was changing my drunk sister into pajamas, then I'd just look away. No big deal. But Aloha isn't my drunk little sister. She's the batfaced pop star I've been hired to protect. The woman who hypnotized Mr. Happy all night long at the party—even from afar—like a snake charmer. "How about I get you some pajamas and leave you to change?" I suggest. I turn on my heel and head toward Aloha's suitcase across the room, but I've no sooner taken two steps than I hear Aloha behind me, making the exact sound every mammal makes immediately before vomiting. *Fuck.* I lurch to her, scoop her up, and whisk her into the bathroom, just in time for her to drop to her knees and unleash the entire fluid contents of her stomach into the bowl, filtered first through her dangling hair.

"Oh, God," Aloha says pitifully, right before heaving again.

I pull back her long, sullied hair and rub her back as she empties herself. "Poor baby. That's no fun."

"I'm gonna *die*," she whimpers.

"You're not."

"I *am*."

"No, honey, you'll survive. But maybe this is your body's way of telling you that, next time, you shouldn't slam a truckload of tequila shots right after guzzling Jack outta the bottle like it was Evian."

"There's not gonna be a next time," Aloha chokes out, her face still stuck in the toilet bowl. "I'm never gonna drink again." Finally, when her heaves have turned dry, Aloha stands and looks at me with exhausted eyes. Her hair is stringy and barf-laden. She looks pale. But despite all that, she shoots me a dopey, droopy-ass grin and says, "Are you in love with me *now*?"

I chuckle. "No, I can honestly say in this moment: not even a little bit."

She taps her finger against her wrist. "Tick tock. It's only a matter of time."

"Says the girl with puke in her hair. Let's get you cleaned up and into bed to sleep this off, okay?"

"Kay." Without warning, she yanks up her shirt, thereby flashing me her beautiful tits—two perfect scoops of light mocha gelato nestled into a black push-up bra. But her efforts to disrobe are in vain. Apparently, the neck opening of her beaded shirt is too small to slide over her noggin, which means the full length of her shirt is now plastered inside-out and upside-down over her head like some kind of fucked up feed bag. "Off!" Aloha commands from behind the beaded fabric of her shirt as she continues wrestling with it. "It smells like barf in here, Zander! Aaagh!"

I laugh, even though I probably shouldn't. "Stop pulling on it. There's gotta be buttons or a zipper in the back that's holding things up. Aloha, *stop*. Pull your shirt down so I can figure out what's going on."

But she doesn't listen to me. She continues vigorously tugging her shirt up, trying desperately to get it off.

My gaze involuntarily flickers to her jiggling breasts in her bra. They're a perfect palmful each. Spectacular. Mouthwatering. *And off-limits*. I clear my throat. "Hey, why don't we call Crystal to help you get cleaned up?"

"Crystal left the party with the cyborg! Leave that poor girl to her fuckery!"

I grab Aloha's arm gently. "Aloha. *Please* let go of your shirt so I can pull it down and get it off."

With an exasperated sigh, Aloha drops her arms to her sides, leaving her shirt draped over her head.

"Thank you." I gently pull the blouse down, unfasten two buttons at the back, and pull the whole thing up and off past Aloha's stringy, stinky hair. But when I return to Aloha after hanging her shirt on a towel rack, it suddenly dawns on me, full-force: this is a bit of a sticky situation. On my first day of employment, right after an entire party of people saw me dirty dancing with her, my beautiful, drunk ward is now standing before me shirtless. Is this the kind of "bonding" Barry was talking about? Probably not. "Hey, let's figure out a female friend to help you get cleaned up and into pajamas."

"No. *You*."

"Any female at all. Maybe even a female hotel clerk? A maid? Anyone but me, basically."

"*You*!"

"Hey, what about that backup dancer you danced with so much at the party? She seems like a close friend of yours."

"Kiera?"

"Yeah. Let's call Kiera and—"

"She left the party with Colin. Leave that poor girl to her fuckery!" She puts her hands on her hips like Wonder Woman, juts her rack at me, and smiles. "You're stuck with the job, Z. And when I say 'job' I mean: staring at my bee-yoo-tiful boobs like you want to gobble them up!"

I quickly look away, my cheeks flashing with heat. *Busted.*

"Aw, you're so sweet," she says. "You're stroking out because I'm in my bra? Ha! Z, don't you know a bra is the same thing as a bikini? And the whole world's seen me in one of those. I can't even count the number of times gossip sites have posted photos of me 'showing off' my 'hot bikini bod' on vacation somewhere." She scoffs. "Now help me get these jeans off, Mr. Bodyguard. The smell of barf in my hair is making me want to puke again." She begins haphazardly peeling off her painted-on jeans, and I offer my arm to steady her. But she's hopeless—incapable of getting her tight jeans all the way off without assistance—so I help her tug them down past her knees.

Finally, when Aloha's jeans are at her ankles, she turns around and bends over, clumsily trying to extricate herself from the last entrapments of the tight denim. And that's when I'm assaulted, in the best possible way, by the sight of the two hottest ass cheeks I've ever been so blessed to behold in my young life—two stunningly beautiful, smooth-as-silk, light mocha ass cheeks hugging the tiniest hint of a pink G-string. Holy fuck.

Her jeans finally off, Aloha straightens up and turns to face me... and when she sees whatever expression of unbridled lust is surely plastered across my face, she giggles, winks, and says, "Looks like my ass just put the *ass* in your happin-*ass*."

I can't help laughing.

"Oh, and now it looks like my tits are putting the *tit* in *titillation* for ya."

"Sorry," I mumble, averting my eyes from her two perfect tits. But there's no safe place for my downcast eyes to wander. Every square inch of her is gorgeous. Her tight abs. Her cute little belly button. Her smooth, tight hips. My greedy gaze halts. There's an angry, deep scratch vertically peeking out from the side-string of her tiny pink panties. I gesture to the mark. "What happened to you?"

Aloha flaps her lips together. "My father left when I was three and my mother has never loved me."

"No, not *that*. Although I definitely want to hear that sad story another time." I point to her marred hip. "*That*. How'd you get that scratch?"

Aloha looks down at the angry mark on her hip. "*Oh*." But then she looks up at me blankly and says nothing more.

"What happened, Aloha?"

She opens and closes her mouth. And then shrugs. "I dunno."

"*You don't know?*"

She shrugs again.

Well, that can't possibly be true. That's a nasty-looking scratch and it looks pretty fresh. Surely, she remembers whatever caused it. But that's a question for another day—a day when Aloha isn't shitfaced and standing before me in nothing but her black push-up bra and practically non-existent pink panties.

I guide Aloha in her barely there undergarments into the shower, grab the handheld shower nozzle, and begin spraying her off like a naughty Labrador who's rolled in mud—all the while trying my best not to peek too long at anything I shouldn't.

"Can you wash your own hair?" I ask after I've thoroughly rinsed her smokin' hot body.

"No. I need my shaggy swaggy to do it."

Sighing, I squirt some shampoo into my palm and get to work on Aloha's barf-laden mane—and the second I begin massaging Aloha's scalp with slow, firm caresses, she closes her eyes and moans like I've just slid a lubed finger inside her. "Oh, yeah. Just like that. *Yes*." She moans again, making my dick jolt, and purrs, "You're my shaggy swaggy... *shampooey*."

I chuckle.

Aloha takes a deep, heaving breath that draws my attention to her tits again and purrs, "You're so good with your *hands*, Zandy Man. Ooooh, you're a sexy, talented motherfucker."

I take a deep breath, internally yell at Mr. Happy to pipe the fuck down, and say calmly, "Tilt your head back."

Aloha complies and I begin rinsing the shampoo out of her hair with warm water.

"So *gooood*," she purrs. "I think I'm in love with you, Zander Shaw. Are you in love with me yet?"

"Nope."

She pouts. "That's 'cause nobody but Barry loves me. That's the way it's always been and always will be."

I scoff. "Aloha, *everybody* loves you. Like, literally, the entire world."

"You wanna know a secret? Being loved by 'everybody' feels a whole lot like being loved by no one at all."

My heart pangs. Not knowing how to respond, I press my lips together and wordlessly begin slathering Aloha's long hair with conditioner.

"They don't love *me*," Aloha continues, her eyes closed. She's hanging onto my bicep to steady herself. "They love their *idea* of me. But God forbid I don't live up to what they want me to be. God forbid I'm not actually perfect like they expect me to be. They'd drop me like a bad habit."

My chest tightens. "Nobody expects you to be perfect, Aloha. Nobody's perfect."

"Aloha Carmichael is."

My heart in my throat, I rinse the conditioner out of Aloha's thick hair, return the nozzle to its holder, and turn off the water. I've somehow managed to keep my pants almost completely dry through this process, but, crap, my shirt sleeves are soaking wet, probably thanks to the way Aloha's been clinging to me. If Aloha were my little sister, Zahara, I'd think nothing of taking off my shirt and hanging it on a towel rack to dry. But there's no way in hell I'm gonna do that with Aloha. One nearly naked person in this situation is bad enough.

I guide Aloha out of the shower and wrap her in two large towels and then help her zombie-like frame brush her teeth—because, clearly, the girl can't handle even the most basic of tasks on her own by now. And then I physically carry her, wrapped in white towels, toward the bedroom as she enthusiastically hums the 'duh duh dum dum!' bride-marching-down-the-aisle song at full volume.

"I'm Mrs. Shaggy Swaggy!" she shouts gleefully.

Chuckling, I place her in a sitting position on the side of the bed. "Now, stay put for a minute while I get some dry clothes from your suitcase." I let go of her shoulders... and then watch helplessly as she flops over onto her side into a deranged, crumpled pile. I prop her up again. "Stay awake for two minutes, Mrs. Shaggy Swaggy. It'll be your wedding gift to me."

"Because we're husband and wife."

"That's right. As your wedding gift to me, I need you to stay awake just long enough for me to get some ibuprofen and water into your system and some pajamas onto your body." *Your hot little body.* "Can you do that for me, baby?"

Her green eyes ignite. "*Baby.* I'm your *baby* because we're husband and wife. Yes, I'll do that for you, *baby.* My beautiful shaggy swaggy *baby.* Because I'd do anything for you, *husband.* My hubby bubby boo-boo-bae. Anything at all."

I can't help chuckling again. "Just stay conscious for one more minute, okay, *baby?*"

"Okay, *baby.* Your wish is my command because it's our wedding night, *baby.*"

"Thank you. Do you have any ibuprofen in your luggage?"

"In that bag." She points straight to the ceiling.

I let go of her shoulders and wait for a beat, making sure she's not going to tip over—and when she miraculously stays upright, sort of, I turn and beeline to her luggage. I find a small bag filled with toiletries and rummage around inside it. But when I pull out the first bottle-sized thing I feel, it turns out to be a prescription bottle made out to Aloha for something called Lexapro. I have no idea what that is, but since it's not ibuprofen, I stuff it back into the bag and rummage around again.

This time, I pull out a bottle of Advil. *Bingo.* I head to a large suitcase and riffle around and quickly find some soft clothes. But when I turn around with the ibuprofen and pajamas in hand, I find Aloha splayed out on the bed crosswise on her belly, her legs dangling off the side of the mattress, her panties and bra flung onto the floor, and her bare, tight, *naked* ass mooning me.

My cock jolts at the surprising—but not unwelcome—sight. "Jesus," I mutter. I force myself to look away from what has to be the Eighth Wonder of the World and grab a towel off the floor. After quickly covering Aloha's nakedness, I somehow manage to rouse her enough to stuff some ibuprofen and water down her throat and help her get dressed. Finally, I move her wet-noodle body lengthwise on the bed, lay her damp head onto a pillow, cover her with the white duvet, and whisper, "Goodnight, hula girl. Sweet drunken dreams."

"*Husband*," she whispers, just before her head lolls to the side and she's out like a light.

I stand over her and stare at her lovely features for a long moment. What demons are lurking behind that beautiful, perfect face? And what the fuck was I thinking tonight, letting her hypnotize me the way she did? Never again. I almost blew it tonight. Fucked up royally. Good God, I can't even imagine the hell my mother would have given me if I had to call her and explain I lost my brand-new job within the first twenty-four hours of my employment because I couldn't keep my dick in my pants. I shake my head at the thought. Yep. That's it. From now on, I'm gonna be a total pro and that's final.

I grab my phone off the nightstand and tiptoe out of the room, feeling like the walls are closing in around me. Actually, I think it's entirely possible I'm not out of the woods yet. I just saw Aloha's naked ass, after all... after putting myself in the *position* to see her naked ass. Would Barry consider that grounds to shitcan me, if he found out? *Fuck, fuck, fuck.* Hopefully, Aloha won't remember any of this when she wakes up and Barry will never be the wiser. But what if Aloha *does* remember and tells Barry everything? Will Barry say I breached some basic tenet of the bodyguard code by showering Aloha in nothing but her bra and undies? Did I fuck up tonight or do precisely what Barry told me to do during my training—take care of Aloha, no matter what? Shit. I don't know if I deserve high-fives right now or a tongue-lashing or worse.

My phone in hand, I bound out of Aloha's bedroom, just as she moans pathetically behind me. I whip around and lope back into the room, poised and ready to whisk her back to the toilet. But, no, she doesn't look like she's on the verge of hurling again... at least not for now. But what if she does need to barf again and I'm not right there to help her? Would Barry consider *that* grounds to fire me? Should I take a seat in that armchair in the corner and watch over her... or crash on the couch in the other room? Shit! As much as I don't want to ask Barry what to do, my gut tells me I should. The man told me he'd hold me responsible for the slightest scratch on "his girl," after all—so I can't imagine what he'd do to me if Aloha were to choke on her own vomit while I slept soundly on a couch in the other room.

Fuck! I hate this job! Why did I say yes to this stupid fucking job?

I take a deep, steadying breath. Damn. There's no way around it: I gotta text Barry. He told me to shoot him a text if I had any questions, day or night, and I promised him I would. As much as I don't wanna do it, I gotta keep my word. And not only that, deep down, I know I've got no choice but to tell Barry the full truth about what went down here tonight and let the chips fall where they may. *Fuck.*

Chapter 15
Zander

ey, Barry. AC is safe and sound in bed. It wasn't a straight shot to get her there, though. She barfed all over her hair when we first got to her room, so I put her in the shower in her bra and undies, plied her with water and ibuprofen, and put her to bed in some soft clothes. I suggested we call a female to help her get showered and dressed for bed, but she refused. Full disclosure: at one point, I turned around after getting her pajamas from her suitcase and discovered she'd pulled off her wet bra and undies and was passed out naked on her belly. I quickly covered her with a towel, helped her dress, and tucked her into bed. I think she's down for the count now, but just to be on the safe side, I'm planning to crash in an armchair in the corner of the bedroom, just in case she needs to barf again. But if doing that would be weird or deprive her of privacy, just let me know and I'll hang out on the couch in the other room. Z*

My index finger hovers over the send button. Man, I don't want to send this text. And I don't want to sit here like a creeper watching Aloha, either. If she were my sister, I'd crash on the couch. But she's not my sister. She's a world-famous celebrity whose care is entirely in my hands.

Fuck.

I press send on my text and drag my exhausted ass to an armchair in the corner of the bedroom. It's now been twenty-four hours since I've slept and I'm dying to close my eyes and pass out. But since that's out of the question until I hear back from Barry, I pull out my phone to keep myself awake.

First off, out of curiosity, I google the name of that prescription I found in Aloha's bag—Lexapro—and quickly discover it's an antidepressant used to combat "panic attacks and episodes of acute anxiety." Interesting. From what I've seen of Aloha so far, she seems like the last person in the world who'd suffer from either malady. But then again, Keane has struggled with anxiety his whole life, and people never guess that about him.

My father left when I was three and my mother never loved me.

That's what Aloha said when I asked about that scratch on her hip. And at the party earlier, she told Keane and Maddy she wishes she grew up with a mother like Keane's...

I google Aloha's name with the search words "childhood" and "parents" and immediately dive into the links that pop up. Unfortunately, there's no singular source that gives me a full overview of the topic—no one article or interview that lays it all out for me. But after reading several articles and watching some clips of interviews, I'm able to stitch together a pretty solid narrative of how the world-famous child star and music artist known as "Aloha Carmichael" came to be:

Aloha's mother, Healani "Lani" Kealoha—who, by all measures, is and always was a stunningly beautiful woman—was born and raised on the big island of Hawaii. After high school, Lani moved to the "big city" of Honolulu and began working as a greeter and cocktail waitress at high-end resorts. In an interview a few years ago, Aloha's mother said two particularly attention-grabbing things about those early jobs. One, she claimed she always earned the most tips of anyone at any hotel where she worked because, according to her, she was "always the prettiest girl on any hotel staff." And, two, Lani said she swore to herself during those early days to one day become one of the "filthy rich guests being served piña coladas by the pool," as opposed to one of the "servants" having to serve guests "with a fake fucking smile."

At age twenty-two, Lani met her future baby daddy, James Carmichael—a twenty-one-year-old marine with a strong jawline, broad shoulders, and emerald-green eyes. Eleven months after her fateful meeting with James in a karaoke bar, Lani gave birth to a little girl she named "Destiny Leilani Kealoha"—a beautiful baby with Lani's coloring and James's striking green eyes.

In a TV interview Aloha gave at age thirteen, she revealed it was her young father, not her mother, who first started calling her

"Aloha." Apparently, Aloha's father chose the name because: one, he hadn't agreed to the name "Destiny" in the first place and never warmed to it, and, two, throughout Aloha's first year, locals kept remarking on the happy baby girl's obvious "Aloha spirit." Surprisingly, Lani adopted the nickname, too, despite the fact that it had been coined by the man who was rapidly becoming her estranged lover, and, soon, baby Destiny was known as "Aloha" by pretty much everyone in her orbit.

A few months after Aloha's third birthday, James Carmichael was transferred from Marine Corps Base Hawaii to a marine base in Okinawa, Japan. By all accounts, Aloha never saw or heard from her father again.

After James left Hawaii, Lani relocated to Los Angeles with her then-three-year-old in tow, determined to fulfill her lifelong dream of becoming a professional model, actress, and/or singer. But when Lani's dreams didn't pan out on a bullet train as she'd hoped and money rapidly became scarce, she began submitting her toddler for modeling and commercial jobs under the name "Aloha Carmichael." In an interview years later, Lani talked about the stage name she chose for her daughter, explaining, "My last name was too big a mouthful and too ethnic. I felt 'Aloha Carmichael' was the perfect shorthand to tell casting directors what to expect: an exotic beauty, but not *too* exotic—a Hawaiian girl with Scottish-green eyes. It turned out to be genius branding on my part, actually. Best decision I ever made."

Although Lani had initially been motivated to hire Aloha out for modeling and acting jobs solely to finance her own dreams of stardom, it soon became clear Aloha had the brighter future of the pair. So much so, in fact, by the time Aloha turned four, Lani legally changed her daughter's name to "Aloha Carmichael," gave up on her personal dreams of stardom, and officially became her young daughter's full-time manager. As Lani put it later in an interview: "I knew then that 'Aloha Carmichael' could conquer the world, if only I managed her exactly right. *Which I did.*"

Man, did she ever. At age five, Aloha was cast in a plumb recurring role on a hugely popular TV sitcom. And at age seven, Aloha landed the titular role in the now-iconic Disney show, *It's Aloha!*—a show about a precocious Hawaiian girl who becomes an unwitting global sensation after a tourist secretly films her singing and strumming her ukulele under the shade of a palm tree.

And the rest, as they say, is history. *It's Aloha!* aired for a full ten seasons, but it only took three for Aloha Carmichael to become a household name. By the time Aloha was ten, she wasn't just America's sweetheart, but the entire world's.

Even today, a full six years after *It's Aloha!* went off the air in first-run episodes, it's still one of the most watched television shows in the world in syndication. Not to mention one of Disney's biggest cash cows. Which is all to say twenty-three-year-old Aloha is a very wealthy young woman. To this day, and probably for many years to come, Aloha earns a fuckton of royalties and residuals from *It's Aloha!*-related enterprises: products bearing her likeness, music recordings associated with the show, and, of course, the constant re-airing of the show in worldwide syndication.

A search for details about Aloha's finances, just out of curiosity, yielded only vague information—nothing that nailed down her annual income or what percentage of it is derived from her adult music career, product endorsements, and cosmetics line versus her *It's Aloha!* past. I found one article estimating Aloha's current net worth at a whopping two hundred fifty million and a second one estimating it at a measly two hundred mill. Either way, give or take fifty million, I was blown away. Of course, I realize information on the internet isn't always reliable, especially when it comes to stuff like a person's net worth. But, either way, Aloha is obviously worth tens of millions of dollars, if not hundreds of millions—a fact I could have guessed for myself from the fact that she bought a nine-million-dollar Malibu beach house for her mother last year and, the year before that, a six-million-dollar Spanish-style home in the Hollywood Hills for herself.

I look up from my phone, suddenly not wanting to read further. I don't know why, but this stuff about Aloha's finances is making me feel sick to my stomach. I knew before reading all this shit I didn't have a shot in hell with Aloha. I understood she was flirting with me and leaping into my arms and grinding against my dick on the dance floor and calling me her shaggy swaggy for sport. To amuse herself. To pass the time. I knew, in my heart, that when she drunkenly referred to me as her "boy toy" to that paparazzi guy, she was actually blurting the truth.

But seeing Aloha's net worth in black and white—even if the numbers might not be precisely right—hammered the point home for me in a whole new way: a big star like Aloha, a girl with all the money and fame in the world, would never be interested in a personal trainer nobody like me. Not for anything long term or real, anyway. I could never be anything but a fling for Aloha. A fun memory, even while I'm still in the room.

My eyelids heavy, I return to my phone. This time, I search "Aloha Carmichael boyfriends." And, immediately, a purportedly "definitive list" of Aloha Carmichael's ex-boyfriends pops up.

I click and read the surprisingly short list. Why the hell does Aloha have so few exes? Is she diabolically good at keeping her relationships under wraps or has she truly dated this few guys? And, shit, have *all* her exes been celebrities—or are celebrities the only guys anybody bothers to write about? According to the list, Aloha's only dated actors, music artists, and a couple famous athletes. And, notably, none of them looks edgy in the slightest. Every single guy looks like he was forged in the same underground Disney factory. Even the purported "rapper" Aloha dated looks like he was dressed by a bunch of middle-aged white women. Shit. That dude makes the Fresh Prince of Bel Air look gangsta.

I'm also noticing Aloha's "relationships," such as they are, don't last long. Not that I'm judging her for that, by the way. Neither do mine. But, still, it's interesting. The only guy that appears to have lasted more than a couple months with Aloha is the first guy on the list: her teenage boyfriend, Jacob Ludeker, a young Channing Tatum type who, like Aloha, starred on a Disney show. Apparently, Aloha dated the guy off and on for four years until finally breaking it off for good with him at age nineteen. The article declares, "Jacob was Aloha's first love and she's never stopped carrying a torch for him." Is that true? Is this Jacob dude Aloha's gold standard—the one that got away? Is she hoping to get back together with him at some point? And if so, what's so fucking great about him?

I search Jacob's name and quickly surmise that, no, Aloha is most definitely not hoping to get back together with Jacob Ludeker. Three months ago, after completing his third stint in rehab for an opioid addiction, the dude came out as gay. Currently, he's living openly with his boyfriend of a year and is a leading voice for gay activism.

My muscles soften. Good. Gay activism is good. Very, very good. My eyelids close. My head bobs to my chest. Darkness descends.

Gah.

I force my eyes open and slap my cheeks to keep myself awake... just as, praise Jesus, my phone pings with an incoming text from Barry:

Hey, Z. I'm coming. Stay put in the bedroom with AC till I get there. Good instinct to sit with her. Confidentially, she once told me that when she was little, she frequently used to wake up screaming in bed with a fever or after having had a horrible nightmare and her mother would never come to her. So, she'd get up and wander the house, crying and screaming for her mother, only to find her passed out cold on the couch with a bottle of wine. Ever since AC told me about that stuff, I've always erred on the side of being there for her when she's sick or sad. As far as you seeing AC's bare ass, I'm sure she'll laugh it off. But be sure to tell her so she can chew you out or complain to me if she wants. Good job tonight, Z. Your instincts are spot-on, just like I knew they'd be. Welcome to the tour. B

Chapter 16
Aloha

I open my eyes to find Big Barry sitting in an armchair in the corner of the bedroom, his chin lowered to his chest and his eyes closed. This isn't the first time I've awakened after being sick as a dog to find Barry unexpectedly sleeping in a chair a few feet away. But I must admit I'm surprised to find him here *today*. The last thing I remember with clarity, Zander was stuffing me into a car in front of Reed's house. When the heck did Barry get here? And where is Zander? Did I scare him off after only one day on the job? As crazy as it sounds, if that's the case—if my purported "wish" came true and my shaggy swaggy bodyguard quit on me—then I'll be deeply disappointed, even if that would mean Barry would take Zander's place while looking for his replacement.

I rub my temple. Gah. I feel like there's a jackhammer pounding inside my head. Holy fuck buckets. I'm never going to do shots again. On my next tour—*if* I have a next tour—I won't give a damn how many people say, "Come on, AC! Aloha Carmichael *not* getting shitfaced on opening night will curse the entire tour!"

I stumble out of bed and into the other room, desperately searching for a bottle of water. And, much to my relief, I find Zander fast asleep on the couch. The man is shirtless and covered in a white blanket just below his nipples. His bulging arms are absolutely *insane* and covered in sexy tattoos. His dark shoulders are muscular and broad and drool-inducing. I swear, every time I see this man, I want to *climb* him like a tree. It's not normal how much I want to hurl myself at Zander Shaw. Cleave my body to his hulking frame. Press my flesh against his and grind into him and then *kiss, kiss, kiss* his sexy, full lips... until, finally, riding his cock like he's a rodeo bull.

Zander's pants are slung over a nearby chair. Which means he's either completely naked underneath that white blanket or he's wearing nothing but his skivvies. Oh, how I wish I were the kind of pervert who'd shamelessly peek underneath a sleeping man's blanket to find out if he's a boxers, briefs, or commando kind of guy. But, alas, I'm not.

I grab a bottle of water and guzzle it down and then stand over Zander and gaze at his striking features in repose. Soon, my mind wanders to last night, to that electric moment when I was clinging to Zander like a monkey, and my lips were mere inches from his, and I truly thought he was on the verge of leaning forward and giving me the kiss of a lifetime. If my friends hadn't pulled me away to do shots just then, would Zander have thrown caution to the wind and claimed my lips with his?

Zander's phone on the coffee table silently lights up with an incoming text, drawing my attention. It's a text from someone identified as "Captain"... a name I find vaguely familiar, though I can't quite place it... and, much to my shock, *my* name appears in the preview pane of the message.

Well, fuck, Z. Apparently, Aloha doesn't mean hello and *goodbye to the Great Zander Shaw. It means nuttin but "helloooooo, baby!" Ha! I figured you'd dive head first into that particular honeypot like Winnie the Pooh on a starvation diet, but I never thought you'd do it on...*

Holy crap. My heart racing, I grab Zander's hand, gently press the pad of his thumb against the thumb-reader on his phone, and head straight to Captain's full message.

Well, fuck, Z. Apparently, Aloha doesn't mean hello and goodbye to the Great Zander Shaw. It means nuttin but "helloooooo, baby!" Ha! I figured you'd dive head first into that particular honeypot like Winnie the Pooh on a starvation diet, but I never thought you'd do it on your first day on the job! Dax said your boss declared the pop star off-limits. Are you playing with fire here, son? If so—and if you wind up getting axed for being her boy toy—I'm guessing it was well worth it. Surely, you blew her mind with The Sure Thing and all the other assorted nifty tricks only we five sex

83

gods know. If not, shame on you. But either way, given the well-known connection between your dick and heart, I'm assuming I'll be taking my beautiful wife out to dinner at her favorite restaurant tonight with my share of the winnings. All I need is for Judge Peen to issue his official ruling on the bet and I'll be up to my eyeballs in Argentinian BBQ. Thanks for being predictable, Z! That's why we all love you the most, sucka!

I look up from Zander's phone, my mind and heart racing in equal measure. Okay, first things first: this Captain guy is clearly one of Keane's brothers. Yes, now that I think about it, I'm positive "Captain" was one of the nicknames Keane mentioned. So, okay... Zander and this Captain Morgan guy bet Dax and Keane that Zander would fuck me. And now Zander has them all convinced he accomplished the task. But what did Captain mean he needs Keane to issue an "official ruling" on the bet? An official ruling about *what*?

I scroll through Zander's inbox, searching for anything more about this douchey bet, and stop on a dime when I stumble upon an exchange between Zander and Barry from earlier this morning.

I read both men's texts, gasping the whole time. Well, now I know why Barry is sleeping in an armchair in the bedroom. And I also know why I've awakened to find my beloved Big Barry sleeping in a chair countless times after I've been a hot mess the night before. My God, Barry is the sweetest man, ever. And so is Zander, too, for the way he so diligently took care of me after the party. No, wait. What am I thinking? Zander's not a sweet man! He's a *douche* who bet his friends he'd fuck me and then lied to them and said he did it!

Just as I'm about to dive back into Zander's texts to search for more clues regarding the bet, a new message lands on Zander's screen—this one from someone named Cheese. And, yet again, I glimpse *my* name in the preview pane of the guy's message! My heart medically palpitating, I swipe into the full message and read:

Day ONE, Z? Come on, man! I know Aloha is beautiful and a superstar, but you couldn't have held off for a month and a day? I had month TWO, you fuckwad! Which, BTW, I only picked because Dax told us your boss designated her OL. Was Dax wrong about that or are you making mincemeat of the rules, Z? Also, I cry foul! Dax only told us Aloha is the female Peen AFTER all bets were placed! If I'd known that little nugget before pledging my Benjamin, I'd have bet month one like Captain. Maybe even HOUR one. As it stands now, I'm gonna have to listen to my brother go on and on until the end of time about how he won and I lost and he's a winner and I'm a loser. Thanks for nuttin, Z. My only solace is knowing you lost, too. I hope you're still employed, boy toy, but if not, I'm guessing it was hella worth it! #stud

I look up from my screen, utterly confused. Another Morgan brother who thinks Zander had sex with me... but this one assumes that means Zander *lost* the bet? How would that make any sense? Don't douchebags who bet their friends they'll bang a girl *win* the bet when they supposedly bang said girl?

I scroll again, looking for answers to this bizarre riddle, and come upon a series of rapid-fire texts from "Peenie" to Zander:

Well, that was quick! Less than a full day and the pop star is already publicly declaring, with video proof, that you're her boy toy? Ha! I knew fuckery would soon be afoot when I saw the way you and the pop star were eyeball-fucking each other at Reed's. Talk about two people with little boners in their eyes! But, even so, I thought you'd at least hold off a couple weeks, just to fight the good fight. FYI, the one-monthers are already demanding I call the bet. Don't worry, I told them I have to look into your eyes on FaceTime before issuing my official ruling, just in case this is a rare time where you're able to separate fucking and feelings. But I gotta admit, given the hard video evidence (pun intended), it's gonna be a tall order for me not to call the bet today, Z. Call me as soon as the world's most famous boy toy comes up for air, so I can look into your baby browns and make my official determination. #MyWifeIsABoyToy #JudgePeenieRules #ZHasZeroImpulseControl

BTW, if you're in lurve, as I'm guessing you are, then this girl is for sure gonna take the top spot on my list of Z's Coolest Girlfriends. No offense, but D was boring as shit. Gorgeous but boring. #FuckYourBluesAway #AdiosD #ZIsMovingOn #AlohaIsTheKewlest

85

Lauren Rowe

Bwahaha! I just realized Daphne is gonna see the video! Damn, I wish I could be a fly on that wall! #RevengeIsSweet #LookAtZNowBitch

OMFG! I just looked up the tour sched and saw it ends in NYC! Was that vid all part of an elaborate ruse cooked up by you and Haha to make D jealous and beg you to take her back in NYC? #MadGeniuses

Okay, there's no way in hell that video was a ruse to make D jealous. I saw the way you and Haha looked at each other at the party and there was no rusing the lust in both your eyes. As we both know, when it comes to Zander Shaw, where there's lust, there's a 50-50 chance love will follow, so just do your best to keep your shit tight so you don't get burned to a crisp by this fire, mmmkay? Of course, if you do get burned, I'll be there to patch you up with bandages and aloe vera. You know why? Because I love you the most! #HappyWifeHappyLife
#MyWifeCannotSeparateFuckingFromFeelings #ButThatIsWhyILoveHimTheMost #TenderHeart #NotAManwhore #PenisConnectedToHeart #MassivePenisAndEvenBiggerHeart #ThatIsWhyILoveYouTheMost

Just to clarify, I love you the most because of your massive HEART, not your massive PENIS. (Though, of course, your penis inspires awe and admiration.)

Call meeeeeeeeeee! (But only when you're done making Aloha see God multiple times in one sesh.) #CannotRushPerfection #DoNotCallMeWhileFuckingAloha #UnlessYouFeelYouMust #OkYeahCallMeWhileFuckingAloha

Okay, my future wife is making me stop drunk texting you now. She said I'm being a dick while you're trying to get your dick on. Actually, no, that's a lie. Maddy didn't say anything even close to that. What she said was I need to stop being a dick and take off my clothes and bone the fuck outta her now. So I'm gonna listen to my woman and make like Zander Shaw now. #IWannaBeLikeZ

86

*#GonnaBoneMaddyNow   #InspiredByZ   #ZsDickIsMyInspiration
#ZsDickShouldWriteInspirationalLiterature*

Surely, Keane's hilarious and oddly endearing texts would be making me smile right now if I weren't losing my mind about whatever video he keeps referring to. There's video "proof" that I had sex with Zander? Did he record me drunkenly babbling at the party about how much I wanted to bone him? And did he then text the video to his best friends with a note that said "Mission accomplished!"? But then why would Daphne presumably see it? Did this fucker text the video to Daphne? Or, holy fuck, post it to social media? Hardly breathing, I scroll through Zander's inbox again, looking for more references to the video, and stop dead in my tracks when I see two unread texts from none other than... Daphne.

Wow, Z. For a guy who said he was in love with me mere days ago, you've sure moved on in record speed. And with Aloha Carmichael?! I am shooketh. Did you fall in love with her at first sight, the same way you supposedly fell for me, or are you really her boy toy, like she said? Either way, I never would have believed you could move on quite this fast. Congrats, I guess.

Oh, for the love of fuck! Daphne's seen this supposed "video proof" that Zander and I had sex? A video in which, apparently, I called Zander my boy toy? Did Zander personally send Daphne this video to make her jealous? My mind racing, I read Daphne's second text to Zander, this one time-stamped about four minutes after the first:

It's not that I didn't love you, Z. I did and still do. Everything I said to you the night we broke up was the truth. You're amazing. Sweet. Funny. And sex with you was mind-blowing, as you well know. Like I told you when we broke up, you were the perfect boyfriend. But that was the problem. I knew if I kept going with you, my future would be written in ink. And I'm not ready for ink yet. Not even close. Would you call me, please? I can't express everything over text. I'm just so... shocked. I always thought we'd end up together one day when the timing was right for me. And now you're with Aloha Carmichael? I can't believe it. Call me.

87

Oh my God, that bitch! When the timing is right for *her*? So she's just gonna keep her hooks firmly lodged in poor, sweet Zander's heart until she's ready to claim him for good... whenever it suits her? I hate her. I want to reach through Zander's phone and throat-punch her! Zander is the sweetest, sexiest, cutest guy ever, and she—

Wait.

No.

The video.

The bet.

Clearly, Zander isn't as sweet as he seems.

I open Zander's Instagram app. No video there. So I open Zander's browser and search my name and... *bingo*. There it is. Everywhere. A video uploaded by *TMZ* this morning for which the frozen screen shot is Zander carrying me into this very hotel.

I sit on the edge of the couch next to Zander's legs and watch the clip, which begins with me calling Zander my "boy toy" and ends with me replying, when asked if I'm heading upstairs to have sex with Zander: "Sex is most definitely the plan! And it's gonna be soooo gooood!"

Oh, boy.

I nudge Zander's legs. "Hey, Mr. Bodyguard. Wake up."

A couple more nudges, and Zander opens his eyes. "What time is it?" He rubs his face. "How are you feeling?"

"Just after noon and shitty. But my headache and sour stomach will pass. You know what won't pass, though? At least not for a solid fifteen minutes, according to Andy Warhol? Your fame, boy toy."

"Huh?"

"You're famous, Z." I hand Zander his phone with the video cued up. "It seems I ran my mouth off a bit as you carried me into the hotel this morning. Whoops. Sorry."

Chapter 17
Aloha

Z ander looks up from the *TMZ* video, looking utterly annoyed. "I told you not to talk to that paparazzi guy."

"Yeah, I probably should have mentioned: I'm kind of a loose cannon when I drink. Also, a fame-whoring dipshit. Oh, and, quite frequently, a big ol' flirt."

Zander plops his phone onto the coffee table, sits up onto his elbow, and rubs his eyes again—and the blanket covering his wide chest slips down to reveal an eye-popping upper torso and the top of what promises to be a truly ridiculous set of abs. "Nothing happened between us, if that's what you're wondering."

I roll my eyes. "No, I wasn't wondering. I don't think for a second you're the kind of guy who'd take advantage of a shitfaced, unconscious woman. Also, I'm pretty sure I'd know it if a penis had recently penetrated me, particularly a 'massive' one attached to an extremely muscular six-foot-whatever black man."

"Six-foot-four. And why the air quotes on the word 'massive'? Was that sarcasm?"

"Uh, no. I have full faith in the sincere massiveness of your penis, Zander. The air quotes were because I was quoting your 'wifey.'"

"Oh, Jesus." Zander shifts his position and the blanket falls even farther down his torso, revealing the most spectacular set of abs I've ever seen... plus, a little something-something extra: a jaw-dropping rod poking straight up from behind the white blanket. When Zander notices the trajectory of my gaze, he glances down, sees his tent pole, and quickly covers his hard-on with his forearm. "Keane told you I have a 'massive' dick?"

"No, Keane didn't say it to *me*. He said it to *you*. In a text.

Lauren Rowe

Specifically, in one of the many texts I secretly peeked at on your phone while you were impersonating Sleeping Beauty."

"*Aloha.*"

"Sorry. But not really."

"How'd you get into my phone?"

"I brilliantly pressed your thumb against the thumb-reader while you were sleeping."

He shakes his head.

"You should thank me for being so considerate. You were sleeping peacefully and I didn't want to wake you to ask permission to hack into your phone."

"Okay, let's set this as a boundary right now: hacking into my phone is emphatically *not* allowed."

"Oh, cool your jets, Zandy Man. You're in no position to chastise me after you committed a far more egregious crime." I lean forward over Zander's legs on the couch and narrow my eyes. "I know about the bet. I know you bet your friends you'd fuck me by the end of the tour—and that they're all convinced you've done it, thanks to that stupid video."

To my surprise, Zander doesn't look the least bit like a guilty man. Just an exasperated one. "I didn't bet my friends I'd fuck you."

"You might want to read the million or so texts on your phone before serving me a steaming pile of cow dung and swearing it's chocolate mousse in a crystal parfait cup."

Rolling his eyes, Zander grabs his phone from the coffee table, lies back—keeping his forearm firmly covering his bulge, I notice—and begins reading his recent texts. But, quickly, he looks up, mortified. "You're totally misinterpreting these texts. I can explain everything."

"Read first, 'explain everything' second."

Zander returns to his phone and reads for quite a while, muttering things like "Oh, Jesus," and "Fucking Morgans" as he does. Finally, he lowers his phone and exhales. "I know this looks bad, but—"

"Just tell me this: Did you, or did you not, bet the Morgan brothers you'd fuck me?"

"I did *not*. Swear to God, the bet isn't about sex."

"I've read the texts, Zander. There's no point in lying to me."

"I'm not lying."

90

"What's the bet about, then?"

He sighs. "I need to tell you how the whole thing unfolded or else you won't believe me."

I lean back against his legs and cross my arms. "I'm listening."

Zander rubs his forehead. "The whole thing came about Monday night—right before you texted me. I was hanging out, drinking whiskey and smoking weed and talking shit with my boys—Keane, Dax, Fish, and Colin—right after getting back from getting this job. So Fish started playing your music videos on a big-screen TV and going on and on about how hot you are. And that led to someone saying there's no way I was gonna be able to resist making a move on you at some point during the tour. So I said 'No, no, it's never gonna happen, guys.' And then someone goes—"

"Stop. Wait. Why'd you say that?"

"Huh?"

"That you'd 'never' make a move on me? If I'm so hot and you knew we were going to be stuck together like glue for a solid three months, why'd you feel so damned sure you wouldn't be tempted, at least *possibly*, to make a move on me at some point? For that matter, how'd you know *I* wouldn't make a move on *you*?"

Zander shifts his hulking body underneath his blanket, momentarily baring his deliciously tented hard-on to me. "I... Because I knew I was gonna be your bodyguard."

"And?"

"And that made you off-limits, as I've already explained to you more than once."

"According to *Barry*."

"According to Barry, but also according to me. According to common sense."

I vaguely indicate Zander's forearm, which at this moment is, presumably, still covering a straining boner. "So I guess Mr. Happy has no common sense, then?"

Zander rolls his eyes. "Mr. Happy always comes out to do morning yoga, dude. Don't take it personally. He's extremely fitness conscious."

I smirk. *Sure, Zander.*

"My eyes are up here, babe," he says, and I let my eyes scorch a path from his forearm, past his impressive pecs, all the way up to his gorgeous dark eyes. He continues, "I told the guys I'd 'never' get physical with you because I knew I wouldn't be able to do this job if I'm chasing you around a tour bus. Plus, let's not forget my state of mind on Monday night: I'd just gotten the shit kicked out of me by Daphne a few days before and I was pretty much obsessed with the idea of winning her back."

Was obsessed. Zander just used past tense in that sentence. Does that mean he's not *presently* feeling that way? Oh, God, I'm dying to know—but too scared of the answer to ask.

Zander continues, "And Dax was like 'A hundred bucks says you'll have sex with her.'"

"Ha!"

"*Listen.* Dax said that, but then Keane goes, 'Hey, guys, that's a douchey bet. Not feminist-approved.' So they all agreed the bet should be whether I'd fall *in love* with you by the end of the tour. So, you see? At the end of the day, the bet wasn't about sex. Not directly, anyway."

"Indirectly?"

He shrugs. "Nobody said it out loud, but let's get real. Even if my friends think it's *possible* for me to fall for you without sleeping with you, I'm sure they assume it'd be a slam dunk if we *did* get it on. Because, see, that's the rap on me in that crowd: 'Z can't separate fucking and feelings.' 'There's a high-speed elevator between Z's dick and heart.' 'Lust almost always turns into love for Z.' And, honestly, they're right to think that way about me, generally speaking. I mean, is it possible for me to separate my dick and heart? Yes. But, truthfully, if I'm having sex with someone I really like, someone with whom I've got great chemistry in every way—which, for me is the preferred kind of person to be having sex with because I'm not a huge fan of sleeping with someone who *doesn't* light my fuse in every way—then why the hell *wouldn't* I develop feelings for the woman?" He shrugs. "But, I swear, sex wasn't an official part of the bet. Just the opposite. At the end of the day, the bet was one hundred percent about nothing but good old fashioned, Disney-approved *love.*" He flashes me side-eye. "But I've got a hunch Keane or Dax already told you all this and you're just fuckin' with me for sport."

"What? No. Nobody said a word about any of this. At least, not that I remember."

"You sure? Because all last night, you kept asking me if I'd fallen in love with you yet."

"I did? Ha! That's funny. No. As far as I know, they said nothing to me."

"Then why would you keep asking me if I'd fallen in love with you?"

I shrug. "Because I'm me."

Zander laughs. "Oh my God, you really *are* the female Peen, aren't you?"

I cross my arms over my chest. "Do you honestly expect me to believe a bunch of straight guys sat around smoking weed and drinking whiskey and watching me shake my ass in a bunch of highly titillating music videos... and then decided to place bets on whether you'd 'fall in love' with me? I find that excruciatingly hard to believe."

"It's the truth and I can prove it. Louise Morgan—Momma Lou—is in on the bet."

My jaw drops.

"Yep. She threw down a hundred bucks on month three. In fact, Dax got his entire family to place bets, just to pad the pot as much as possible."

"That's crazy."

"That's the Morgans."

"What did Captain mean when he said 'Judge Peen' had to issue an 'official ruling?'"

"Keane decided he should judge the competition, rather than bet, because—get this—according him, I might fall madly in love with you without even realizing it myself. He thinks he'll be able to look me in the eyes and tell everyone the truth about whatever's going on with my purportedly tender heart."

"Well, damn, now I'm even more offended. You didn't find me attractive enough to at least leave open the *possibility* that you *might* fall in love with me? How insulting."

Zander palms his forehead. "Oh my God, I can't win with you. Aloha, you know full well I find you attractive. I believe you were *tipped* off—pun intended—about my rather intense attraction to you last night on the dance floor."

I snicker. "Yes, your attraction to me has been a *hard* thing to figure out, but, somehow, I've managed it."

He rolls his eyes. "But being intensely attracted to someone isn't the same thing as *acting* on that attraction. And it certainly isn't the same thing as falling in love."

Okay, now I'm highly annoyed. Doesn't this man realize I'm *irresistible*—at least, when I want to be? That if I were to turn on my charm to full wattage with him, I could bring him, or any man, to his knees? Because, *hello*, guess what's been my job since I was three years old? *Making every creature who comes in contact with me—man, woman, or child—fall in love with me!* The fact that Zander doesn't—

Wait.

Hold on.

It's just occurring to me Zander said he's "intensely" attracted to me a moment ago. Not just attracted. That's new. *The plot thickens.*

"Look," I say, trying not to smile. "I know Barry put the fear of God into you, but forget about him. *If* something physical were to happen between us at some point on the tour, *hypothetically*, thanks to our 'intense' mutual attraction, then you wouldn't have to worry or think twice about Barry finding out. I'd never tell him or anyone about us. And they'd never guess, either, because I'd be discreet. Case in point, I had a tour-fling with a keyboardist a couple tours ago and nobody ever found out. Even when the guy broke the most important rule of tour-flinging and wound up telling me he'd fallen hard for me, I still didn't say a word to anyone about him. Even when everything turned awkward and weird between us after he confessed his feelings, I was a locked vault. In the end, thanks to my steel trap and the guy's NDA, he wound up finishing out my tour and then going on to another, even bigger, one with my full endorsement and recommendation and nobody was ever the wiser about what went down between us."

Zander rolls his eyes. "Aloha, all that just confirms why you're off-limits to me. Don't you see? Forget Barry for a minute. Regardless, I'd be a damned fool to get involved with you. I'm not one of your musicians. *I'm your bodyguard.* I'm gonna be stuck to you like glue every day for the next three months. If we were to mess around and you were to get bored with me a few weeks later—which sure seems like your MO, sweetheart—or if, God help me, one-sided feelings were to develop on my end like they did for that keyboardist—then I'd feel compelled to show myself the door the minute things got 'weird' and 'awkward.' And as far as nobody guessing, that possibility is blown now, thanks to that stupid video. The whole world, *including Barry*, is gonna be watching you and your supposed 'boy toy' like hawks now, waiting for any indication we're actually boning." He shakes his head and exhales. "My buddies were exaggerating when they said lust *always* turns into love for me. But not by a whole lot. I'm not a 'friends with benefits' kind of dude. Can I do it? Yes. I've indeed had flings and casual sex in my lifetime. But never with anyone I really like."

My heart skips a beat. *He really likes me?*

"So, whatever incredible chemistry we're both feeling," he says, "I need to ignore it and do my job."

I can't stop smiling. I realize Zander intended everything he just said to shut the door on a possible fling for us, but I can't help feeling like he just kicked that door wide open. But since no means no, I've got no choice but to respect his stated boundaries and treat him as my friend without benefits... that is, until he finally comes to his senses and makes the first move.

"Thank you for making all of that crystal clear to me," I say. "Now that I understand your boundaries, I, too, will ignore the intense chemistry I'm feeling with you."

Zander looks pained. Ha! For a guy who just won this argument, he sure looks like a guy who *lost* it.

I extend my palm. "May I have your phone, please? I'd like to send a text to Dax."

"Oh, God, Aloha, please don't chew Dax's ass for the bet. We were all stoned out of our minds and drunk off our asses and—"

"I'm not upset about the bet. I want to tell Dax I want in on it."

"Huh?"

I smirk. "I want in on the bet. There's money at stake and I want to win it."

We engage in some back and forth. And then a staring contest. Until, finally, reluctantly, Zander places his phone in my open palm.

"Thank you." I place Zander's thumb against the thumb reader on his phone and head straight into his contacts list. When I find Dax's name, I quickly tap out the following text:

Hey, Dax. This is Aloha on Z's phone. I just found out about the bet. Count me in! Z and I haven't had sex, despite what I said in that TMZ video. In fact, Z just informed me he'll never, ever have sex with me and he certainly won't fall in love with me because he's just going to do his job like a good soldier. Of course, I have full faith in him. If he thinks he can ignore our insane, intense attraction and chemistry, then I'm sure he's right. But just for kicks, just because I like throwing money away, I guess, will you please mark me down for a hundred bucks on month two? I figure when I lose, it'll be another hundred in Z's pocket, right? And I can certainly live with that. Thanks bunches! AC

Chapter 18
Aloha

Zander puts his phone down after reading the text I just sent to Dax.

"Please don't be mad," I say.

"I'm not. He's a Morgan. He'll think you're hilarious."

"No, no. I mean please don't be mad I made everyone on planet Earth think you're my boy toy."

"Oh, *that*." He sighs. "I couldn't care less what 'everyone' thinks. I do, however, care very much what my mother and Barry think. My mom because she was thrilled for me to get this job and I don't want her thinking I couldn't go a full twenty-four hours without bonin' the fuck outta the woman I was hired to protect."

My clit pulses. *Yes, please.*

"And Barry because I'd very much like to keep this job. Not to mention my good name."

"Your *good name*?"

"Barry, unlike my mother and 'everyone,' knows exactly how drunk you were when I brought you to this hotel room. I don't want him or anyone else thinking, even for a minute, that I took advantage of an unconscious or incapacitated woman. That's a crime, you know."

I grimace. "Oh, jeez. That angle didn't even occur to me."

"I don't think Barry would believe your drunk ass babbling in that video over me telling him nothing happened, but what if I'm wrong about that? Or what if a little piece of him isn't completely sure about me going forward? I don't need him or anyone wondering if I'd do something like that, Aloha."

"Shit." I sigh. "Well, unfortunately, I can't do anything to clear things up with your mom. But I can certainly clear things up with Big Barry, which I promise I'll do the minute he wakes up."

"*Wrong.* You most certainly can and *will* clear things up with my momma. She'll be at our dinner with the Morgans. You can tell her then what a fine, upstanding bodyguard I've been since jump street."

I'm utterly confused and I'm sure my face shows it. "Our dinner with the Morgans?"

"On your free night in Seattle."

I stare at him blankly.

"In three weeks...?"

Still nothing.

"*Aloha!* You agreed to have dinner at the Morgans' on your free night in Seattle in three weeks!"

"Have you gone *mad*?"

"Please tell me you're joking."

"Tell me *you* are!"

"*Aloha!*" Zander tilts back his head and rubs his face with his large hands—thereby taking his forearm off his crotch for the first time in a very long time. And, dang it, much to my disappointment, Zander's tent is gone. "Jesus, take the wheel," he mutters behind his hands before dropping them and turning his dark gaze on me. "You don't remember the conversation you had with Keane and Maddy while sitting on the floor of Reed's home gym?"

"Well, yeah, I remember talking to Keane and Maddy in Reed's gym. *Of course.* But we didn't talk about some stupid *dinner.* Maddy told me about her new documentary and promised to send me a preview copy before it releases at some film festival next month. And Keane told me about all the crazy nicknames in his family and I was like, 'Oh, I *love* nicknames!' And he was like, 'Well, then, I hereby christen you Alo-haha because—'"

"*Aloha, think,*" Zander says sharply. "During that same conversation, you told Keane and Maddy your mother doesn't love you and you wish you had a mother like Keane's. A real mom, not a mom-ager. And he said his mother loves all her kids, rich or poor, dumbshit or 'smartshit,' and that she makes amazing—"

I gasp. "*Lasagna!* Oh, shit! And I agreed to come to dinner so his entire family can adopt me!"

"Bingo. And then Keane texted his mom about it right then and there, sealing the deal."

I snort. "Well, obviously, that's not gonna happen. You're gonna have to *unseal* the deal for me."

"No."

"Yes. Text Keane and tell him the dinner is off."

"No way. You made your bed and now you're gonna lie in it. You're going to that dinner in three weeks and you're eating lasagna and getting adopted by Mrs. Morgan and the entire Morgan clan, exactly like you said you would."

"I can't go to dinner at some random family's house in Seattle! That would be a crazy thing for me to do."

"Keane already texted his mother. She was probably beside herself with excitement at her Zumba class this morning, telling all her friends she's gonna be playing honorary mommy to everybody's favorite spitfire, Aloha Carmichael."

I clutch my chest. "Listen to me, Z. I'm not being a diva about this. I *can't* go." I swallow hard, my heart racing. "Zander, I get... *anxiety*."

To my surprise, Zander doesn't look the least bit surprised by my admission. "You'll be fine." He grabs my hand. "The girl I saw onstage in front of tens of thousands of people last night can do anything she puts her mind to, least of all sit at a dinner table with a nice, friendly family and eat a delicious homemade meal."

"You don't understand," I choke out, my heart beating like a steel drum. "I can sing and dance in front of tens of thousands. I can say my lines in front of cameras. I can sign autographs with a painted-on smile. I can do anything that requires me to be the ever-charming 'Aloha Carmichael.' The thing that's hard for me—the one thing I absolutely *cannot* do—is sit in a room filled with a small number of complete strangers—*non-celebrity* strangers—*non-Aloha-nators*—and try to have an actual conversation about normal-people things and still live up to their expectations that I'm gonna be this perfect, dazzling beam of *radiant* light they've 'known and loved' for the past ten years!"

Zander's features are awash in sympathy. He touches my shoulder gently. "Honey, the Morgans don't expect you to entertain or dazzle them. They just want to eat lasagna with you. You don't have to perform. Just *be*." He smiles. "Trust me, when you're with the Morgans, you won't even be the funniest, coolest person in the room. And I'll be with you the whole time. So will Keane and Maddy. So it won't feel like you're eating dinner in a room filled *entirely* with strangers."

"I can't, Z."

"You can, honey. And you will. I promise, the minute you meet the Morgans, you'll feel like you've known them your whole life. Before you know it, you'll feel comfortable enough to turn off the 'Aloha Carmichael' charm and just be yourself."

I don't know what that means, I think. But, of course, I don't say it. Because Zander wouldn't understand. Nobody could possibly understand because nobody has lived my crazy, abnormal life.

Zander strokes my arm, sending goosebumps flashing across my flesh. "I'll be right there with you the whole time, sweetheart," he whispers soothingly. "And I think you're beautiful and amazing and perfect, just the way you are, absolutely no 'Aloha Carmichael' dazzle required." He strokes my forearm. "And this coming from the guy who, mere hours ago, watched you barf into your hair."

I smile. Just this fast, Zander has managed to guide me back from the brink of panic in a way only Barry has ever done before him. I take a deep breath and speak on my exhale. "Okay."

He pats my arm. "Good girl. And while you're eating lasagna at the Morgans' and being your boring, imperfectly perfect self, you'll explain to everyone that you were just acting a fool last night with that *TMZ* guy."

I twist my mouth. "Yeah. About that... Yes, of course, I'll tell the Morgans and Barry and your mom the truth. But, um, do I have to tell the entire *world* you're not my boy toy... or can we just let that ride a little bit longer out there in the general population?"

"I don't follow."

"I've been looking for a chance to show the world I'm no longer the squeaky clean virgin-princess they watched on TV for a decade—that I've become a grown woman of twenty-three. A sexually liberated *woman.* But finding the right way to let them in on that little fact has proved challenging for me. I've got young fans. I'm their role model. Disney princesses aren't supposed to have sex unless it's with Prince Charming in a committed relationship, if ever." I snort. "So, I'm thinking... now that this supposed fling with my smokin' hot bodyguard is out of the bag, I kind of don't want to stuff it back in again. I mean, come on, that video's not all bad for you, is it? You can't possibly be bummed Daphne thinks you're banging the hell out of me."

Zander's wicked grin tells me I've got him pegged right.

I return his smile. "We were already planning to make Daphne jealous in New York. So, why not make her jealous every day for the next three months? Go big or go home, right?"

"I'm in."

I hoot and high-five him. "Now, don't worry. We won't have to actually *do* anything. No faking or play-acting required. I simply won't address or retract the 'boy toy' video. That alone will be enough to keep endless speculation going. As people see us together in photos throughout the tour, even if we're just standing near each other doing nothing, they'll drive themselves crazy analyzing our body language and seeing secret looks and signals that aren't even there. I guarantee you, by the end of the first month, people will be convinced we're ravenous fuck buddies or secretly engaged. Either way, they'll be picturing you banging me every night of the tour, and that will go a long way toward helping me blemish my squeaky clean image without necessarily blasting it to high heaven in a way that would be a bit much for the poor little Aloha-nators to process."

Zander chuckles. "Fine with me, as long as I can tell anyone who actually knows me what's really up."

"Of course."

Zander bites his beautiful lower lip. "Not gonna lie, I'm definitely digging the idea of Daphne thinking I'm fucking you to within an inch of your life every night in cities across North America."

My clit pulses. *Yes, please.*

"Aloha Leilani Carmichael!" a deep, rumbling voice bellows behind me.

I turn around calmly. "Why, hello there, Big Barry. What a lovely surprise."

"Don't 'Hello there, Big Barry' me. And wipe that smile off your face. I just saw the video, Aloha. I hope for Zander's sake you were merely attempting a little drunken revamp of your image, because if your new bodyguard thought it was okay to make a move on the drunk-ass woman he was hired to—"

"No, Barry," Zander blurts. "I swear, I didn't—"

"Back the fuck off, Big Barry," I say. I crawl on top of Zander and splay my body over his like we're in the trenches of a war zone and I'm protecting him from an incoming grenade. "My shaggy swaggy bodyguard has been a perfect gentleman, top to bottom. A perfect bodyguard and babysitter and *friend*. I was just messing with that *TMZ* pap. You know how I get when I drink—what a loose-lipped little hussy-famewhore I can be." I gesture to a nearby armchair. "Now push that bulging vein back into your neck and sit down. We'll have ourselves a little room service and chat like civilized adults before Zander and I need to board my bus for San Diego."

Chapter 19
Zander

I'm watching Aloha from a loveseat on her luxury tour bus as we make the three-hour drive from LA to San Diego. Crystal, Aloha's tour manager, explained to me that, depending on the distance from one city to the next, Aloha will sometimes travel by private jet and other times by this bus—an unmarked luxury behemoth that's configured more like a condo than a bus. For the past hour or so, I've sat and watched Aloha chatting on the far end of the "condo" with her team. Among other items, they're finalizing details for Aloha's performance at the Billboard Music Awards in Las Vegas in a couple months.

Aloha finishes her meeting with a robust "Good work, everyone!" and when her team disperses to open laptops and check phones, she bounds over to me on the loveseat. With a wide smile, she plops herself down and swings her legs over my lap like it's her birthright to do it.

"Hey there, Shaggy Swaggy," she says. "What's shakin', bacon?"

"Nothing much, lettuce and tomato. I've just been chillin' like a villain. Have you been drinking plenty of water like I told you, drunkard?"

"Yes, sir." She holds up an almost-empty water bottle.

"Good girl. Keep hydrating. And when we get to the hotel, I'll lead you through some stretches, just to get the toxins out of your system as quickly as possible."

"Wow, I got me a bodyguard and personal trainer, all in one? Score!" She slides her hand in mine. "So, did your mom reply about the dinner in Seattle?"

"Yep. She'll be there. My little sister, too."

103

"Oh, I didn't realize you have a sister."

"Yeah, she's in her last year at U of Oregon."

"What's her name?"

"Zahara Theodora Shaw."

"Zander and Zahara. Your mom likes Z names."

"My mother's name is Zelda."

"Well, that explains it. Does Zelda Shaw live in Seattle?"

"She does."

"And that's where you grew up?"

"It is."

"Why the short answers, dude? You got something to hide?"

I chuckle. "No. I'm an open book."

"Good. Then tell me *everything* there is to know about you."

"That's a bit broad."

"Okay. Then give me the highlights, starting with your birth."

She snuggles against me and I proceed to do as I'm told—I tell her the basics about my childhood in Seattle. When she asks how I met Keane, I tell her the story of how I met him in eighth grade and instantly knew he was my soulmate. "Everyone thought Keane was nothing but the class clown with a pretty face," I say. "But I could tell there was much more to him than that." I tell her about high school, including plenty of stories involving Keane, and then describe how I became like family to the entire Morgan clan over the years. "Aren't you bored by now?" I say after talking for an outrageous amount of time. "I haven't stopped talking in fifteen minutes."

"You've only been talking for, like, twenty minutes, dude. And I'm hanging on every word. Let's move on to your post-high-school years now. Did you attend college?"

"Yes. I went to Arizona State University on a football scholarship—the same place where Peenie Weenie went that same year on a baseball scholarship."

"Oh my gosh. How amazing to get to go to college with your best friend."

"It was a dream come true. I actually got accepted to U Dub in my hometown, which almost anyone would say is a better school on paper. But I chose ASU to get out of Seattle, even though I love it, and, of course, to get to be with Peenie. As it turned out, it was a great decision. Peenie and I were roommates in the dorms the first year and, after that, we lived together in an off-campus apartment until Keane was drafted at the end of his junior year."

"Keane was drafted?"

"By the Cubs."

"The *Cubs*? Holy crap! I had no idea."

I chuckle. "Yeah, Keane was an all-star star pitcher. All-American. He was the shit."

"All I knew about Keane is he's a former stripper trying to become an actor-model in LA."

"That's Peenie's most recent résumé. But before that, he was a superstar pitcher. Everyone thought he'd get to the majors and lead his team to the World Series one day. Unfortunately, his baseball career crashed and burned in the minors after he injured his elbow, but if it weren't for that, he'd have done great things with that amazing arm of his."

"Poor Keane. Was he really bummed about his injury?"

"He was devastated. I can't even begin to tell you how hard Peenie took it. But he's good now. Chasing a new dream. Plus, he's got the sweetest girl in the world cheering him on."

Aloha rests her cheek on my shoulder. "I love Keane and Maddy."

"They're perfect together."

"I can't even imagine how much fun you and Keane must have had in college."

"Oh, baby girl, you have no idea. Peenie and I were Salt and Pepper—not to be confused with Salt 'N' Pepa, by the way, who were far cooler than us two clowns ever were. But, yeah, we were the party, no matter where we were. The eye of the storm. Double Trouble. The Hype Man and the Headliner. Bonnie and Clyde."

"Which of you was the Hype Man?"

"Peenie, of course. Most days."

"And which of you was Bonnie?"

"Me. But only because Bonnie was way more badass than Clyde. I didn't even wanna be Clyde. We were also Wesley and Woody. Dressed up like them every year for Halloween. And Wesley was unquestionably *way* cooler than Woody."

"*Wesley* and Woody? Don't you mean *Buzz Lightyear* and Woody?"

I chuckle. "Dude, keep up. *White Men Can't Jump*. Wesley Snipes and Woody Harrelson."

"Oh, I've never seen it."

"Then put it on the list of movies we're gonna watch together, right after *Rudy*. You gotta be able to appreciate how perfectly Peenie and I pulled this off." I pull out my phone and show her a throwback Halloween photo of Peenie and me dressed as Wesley and Woody, and then find a photo on the internet of the movie poster for comparison, which we recreated for our photo, and Aloha absolutely loses her shit. Which, of course, spurs me on to show her even more photos of Peenie and me from back in the day, all of which prompt Aloha to laugh and me to tell her story after story. After a while, I find myself talking about the year I stayed in school after Peenie had already gone off to seek his fortunes with the Cubs. "I wanted to make my momma proud and get that college degree. So I stayed in school a fourth year, unlike Peenie, and didn't enter the NFL draft my junior year. I figured I'd enter it my senior year, after I got that precious piece of paper. Unfortunately, things didn't work out as planned. I wound up getting one too many concussions during my senior year and decided the risk wasn't worth it. No sense playing a few seasons in the NFL only to lose my mental faculties for the rest of my life."

"Why so many concussions? What position did you play?"

"Linebacker. And I was good, too. I probably wouldn't have gone first round in the draft, but I was a shoo-in for the second. But, oh well. Wasn't meant to be. After that, I graduated, moved back to my hometown with my degree in exercise physiology in hand, and started my career as a personal trainer while Peenie tore it up in the minor leagues. When Keane's baseball career ended, he moved back to Seattle, we got an apartment, and it was Wesley and Woody, together again."

"And that's when Keane started stripping?"

"Yep. Eventually, he became the top male stripper in Seattle. *Ball Peen Hammer*."

Aloha giggles.

"And now he's in love with the girl of his dreams and working on his dream of becoming the next Brad Pitt or Channing Tatum."

"And what about your dream? What is it?"

"At the moment, to become the best bodyguard I can be for a pop star who won't stop asking me questions."

Aloha twists her mouth sympathetically. "I'm sorry if this job isn't what you've ever envisioned for yourself."

My heart melts at the earnest expression on her face. "Aloha, honest to God, there's no place I'd rather be."

Aloha visibly swoons and we share a smile that sends butterflies releasing into my stomach.

She grabs my arm and snuggles into my shoulder again. "So what's the story with your father? You haven't mentioned him yet."

"Aw, come on, dude. My life is normal and boring. Let's talk about your exciting life now."

"I want to hear more about you. I love hearing about how you grew up in a normal family with a normal mother—a mother who wasn't hell-bent on making you famous. And with friends. Oh my God. So many *friends*."

"Did you have *any* friends growing up?"

"I had one. The girl who played my best friend on *It's Aloha!* was also my best friend in real life. I also sometimes hung out with kids working on nearby sound stages, but I wouldn't call any of them close friends like her."

"You had a boyfriend for years as a teenager, right? Jacob somebody?"

"Ah, you looked me up."

"Did you know he was gay? Did he?"

"Not at the very beginning. But then, when we kissed this one time, I opened my eyes and I could see he was going like this." She scrunches up her nose like she's smelling something unpleasant. "And that's when I knew my gut instinct was right. *He liked boys.* We talked about it and he was so relieved to be honest with me—and with *himself.* But he was also deathly afraid for anyone to find out his secret—afraid his fans would reject him and the studio would cancel his show. So I agreed to be his 'girlfriend' until he was ready to come out. And that was fine because I really did love him. I was never 'in love' with him. He was always like a brother to me. A really messed up brother with a serious drug addiction." She sighs. "Our relationship was one long, continuous intervention, if you wanna know the truth. Not what I'd call fun." She lifts her cheek from my shoulder and flashes me a lovely smile. "So you

107

see, talking about your supposedly 'normal and boring' life is like talking about a lovely fairytale to me. A beautiful dream."

My heart skips a beat at the sincerity on her face. But I'm done talking about me. I'm aching to peel off Aloha's mask and find out who she is behind that pretty smile and all that glitter. "Tell me about your mom."

"Not much to tell. She's Satan."

"Will I meet her during the tour?"

Aloha snorts. "No. My dear mother is presently on a yacht with her new, billionaire boyfriend, traveling the world, and simply can't be bothered."

I grimace.

"Yeah. My mom's a real peach. But let's not talk about her. Back to you. You still haven't told me about your father. Is he in the picture at all? Does he have a Z name, too?"

"No Z name. He's Fred. And, yes, he's in the picture, but three-quarters of his face is cut out of the frame."

"Ah."

"My dad was never fully absent from my life. Just not fully there, either. Sort of in and out. Noncommittal. More like an uncle than a father. My mom has always held down the fort by herself, basically, without any meaningful help, economic or otherwise, from the ever-unreliable Frederick Shaw."

Aloha assesses me for a long beat. "Well, that explains it. You were raised by a strong woman and you've always looked out for your little sister."

"That explains *what*?"

She beams a huge smile at me. "You."

My heart skips a beat, yet again, at the way she's looking at me. "Thank you."

"You're welcome." Again, Aloha nestles against me. "So tell me, Zander Shaw, what did your strict, God-fearing mom think of the amaaaaazing Daphne?"

"I never introduced my mother to Daphne. My mom doesn't even know Daphne existed."

Aloha bolts upright. "But you were 'in love' with Daphne!"

I shrug. "Introducing a girlfriend to my momma is a big-ass deal. Not done lightly."

"*But you were 'in love' with Daphne.*"

I make a noncommittal sound.

"The plot thickens," Aloha says, cocking one of her perfect eyebrows and drumming her fingertips together. "Why wouldn't you tell your mother about a girl you *loved*?"

"Don't read into it too much. I never introduce my mother to girlfriends before six months, no matter how 'in love' I think I am."

Aloha's eyes bug out. "*You and Daphne weren't even together for six months?*"

"Four months."

"Jesus Christ, Zander Shaw! You made Dumbass Daphne sound like the great love of your life!"

I chuckle. "Love doesn't follow a strict timeline. People sometimes get engaged after a month and stay married for fifty years."

"But you dated the girl for four measly months and then went on and on about how badly she broke your heart!"

"She did break my heart. I'm a leaper by nature. If I'm feeling it, I cannonball into the pool without hesitation. It's who I am. When I go in, I go all-in."

Aloha rolls her entire head, not just her eyes. "So, have you called Dumbass Daphne, the great love of your life after four months, as she requested in her 'I am shooketh' text from this morning?"

"I haven't responded to Daphne yet, no."

"You're ghosting her?"

"No, I just haven't responded yet. I don't know what to say."

"Don't you think you owe poor Daphne a reply after those *four* loooong and amaaaazing, earth-shattering, life-changing *months* together? Don't you think a text is the least you can do after she gave you the best four *months* of her life?"

"Enough."

"Hey, let's send the great love of your life a photo!"

"Of what?"

"Of us. Maybe one of me sitting on your face?"

I burst out laughing. "Well, that would definitely get her attention. Not to mention mine."

"Wouldn't that be hilarious? Ha! Let's do it!" Aloha thwacks my shoulder. "Hand me your phone, Mr. Bodyguard."

109

"Oh, my God, Aloha. *No.*" I peek toward the other end of the bus. "Nobody is paying a lick of attention to us at the moment, but I think that would change if you suddenly straddled my head and sat on my face."

"I wasn't serious about that. Duh." She flashes me a snarky look, her hand still extended. "Phone. Now. I'm gonna reply to Daphne's text for you. Ghosting is for pussies."

I look at her sideways. "What are you gonna say to her?"

"You'll see." She bats my shoulder again. "Come on. Not sure if anyone's told you this yet, but I always get my way. At least on tour, I do. It's an unwritten rule: 'Nobody says no to Aloha on tour.' Now do as I say and hand it over."

"No."

"Yes. Trust me."

"See, the thing is: I actually don't trust you as far as I can throw you."

"I'm just gonna take a selfie of us—of our *faces*, not of my twat pressed against your lips. And I won't send anything unless you've approved it first."

I'm too stunned by the image of Aloha pressing her "twat" against my lips to move a muscle for a moment.

"Zander Shaw! Keep up, sexy man! For the love of fuck, give me your phone."

"I... no."

"Yes! I'm the pampered pop star on this bus and you'll do as I say."

"Try again."

She sighs. "Fine. Pretty please, *Mr. Bodyguard*? This is a trust exercise."

"Yet again, it bears mentioning I don't trust you at all."

"Hence, the trust exercise."

Aloha waits with her palm out, until, finally, I slowly place my phone in it.

"Just don't go scorched earth on her," I say. "I'm never an asshole to my exes. *Ever.*"

"*Trust.*" Without the slightest hesitation, she places my thumb on the thumb reader of my phone—like we've both come to some implicit agreement it's her unfettered right to hack into my phone at her whim. She swipes into the camera, and then, much to my surprise, climbs on top of my lap, drapes her body over mine, and bites my ear, taking my diamond stud into her mouth and swirling it with her warm tongue... all of which results in my dick springing to life directly beneath her glorious ass... the amazing ass I saw naked, in all its glory, mere hours ago... which I'm now suddenly remembering in acute detail. Oh, God. That ass! It's a work of ass-art that should be on display in an ass-museum in Massachusetts.

"Oh, hello, Mr. Happy," Aloha says as my dick hardens to steel beneath her. She grinds into me playfully and giggles. "Wow, Z, I'm constantly amazed at how much Mr. Happy likes doing yoga with his platonic *friend*."

"It's pure physiology."

"Mmm hmm. So you keep telling me. Now smile for Daphne, Zandy Man. Smile like you just fucked the living hell out of me and then I sucked you off 'til you passed out."

"Jesus Christ, Aloha."

"Dude. Stop looking like that. You have to look like we just rocked each other's worlds, not like I just punched you in the face."

Without warning, Aloha bites my earlobe, *hard*, making my cock jolt underneath her.

And then I sucked you off 'til you passed out.

Jesus God, I'll never forget Aloha saying those amazing words as long as I fucking live.

Aloha shows me the selfie. "You like?" she asks. "Wait. Don't answer that." She pointedly presses herself into my hard-on underneath her. "Yes, I can surmise that you do, indeed, like it. *You like it a lot.*" She snorts and slides off me, leaving Mr. Happy gasping for air and silently screaming, "Don't gooooo!" And then she hunkers down and begins tapping out a text on my phone like she didn't just send rockets of pleasure shooting into my cock.

I rearrange Mr. Happy in my pants and peek over her shoulder. "What are you writing?"

"A text to go along with the photo. Don't worry. I won't send anything without your approval."

"But what are you gonna say?"

"*Trust.*"

"But, see, I one hundred percent do *not* trust you," I whisper.

111

Lauren Rowe

But then I remain quiet and patiently wait to read whatever masterpiece she's concocting.

A minute later, Aloha hands me the phone and says, "Okay to send?"

Hi Daphne. This is Aloha Carmichael on Z's phone. I just want to thank you for being honest with Zander about your feelings for him (or lack thereof). I'm sure it wasn't easy to break his heart, considering how great he is, but I think it takes a big woman to be honest about her feelings and let someone as amazing as Zander go. If he's not a fit for you, better to cut him loose and let him try to find love (or at least some smokin' hot lust) with someone else. One woman's trash is another woman's treasure, amirite? Thanks again for your honesty and authenticity and for paving the way for me to have such a horny good time with someone who fits me like a glove in more ways than one. Snicker. Love and light, sister! Aloha

Chapter 20
Zander

I can't stop laughing as I read Aloha's text to Daphne. "How'd you get so damned diabolical?"

"The apple doesn't fall far from the tree, I guess. Did I mention my mother is Satan?" She giggles. "Do you want to do the honors and press send?"

"Hell yes." I press the button. "Thank you, Satan's Daughter."

"You're welcome, Shaggy Swaggy. I'm not diabolical thanks only to my demonic DNA, by the way. For years as a kid, I used to have to sit through coaching sessions before going on TV talk shows and press junkets. After all that training, sending a 'fuck you' disguised as a 'thank you' to Daphne is child's play."

"You're amazing, Aloha."

She flashes me a truly adorable smile. "Does that mean you've fallen deeply and madly in love with me?"

"No, but I'm *this* close to falling in heavy like with you." I show her my index finger and thumb, barely a centimeter apart. "But don't tell Keane. He won't believe I'm still on this side of the line and he'll call the bet in favor of the one-monthers."

"Dude, I wouldn't dream of ratting you out to Judge Peen. At least, not during month one. I'm a two-monther, remember? *I want that pot of cash.*" She squeezes my arm. "So riddle me this, Zan-Zan. What was so damned amazing about Daphne that you felt compelled to swear to your friends you'd never, ever, not in a million years, fall for me?"

"Daphne wasn't the only reason I said that, remember. Barry had a lot to do with it, too."

"Fuck Barry. He's not the boss of me."

"Well, he's the boss of me—and not a guy I want to piss off."

113

"Aw, Barry's a softie."

"He's a badass motherfucker."

"With a softie center. But whatever. Back to Daphne. She was at least *part* of the reason you said you'd never, ever touch me."

"Correct."

"Then my initial question stands: what's so amazing about this goddamned girl? Because, last I checked, I'm pretty damned amazing, too."

I chuckle. "You really are the female Keane, you know that? Well, the *pre-Maddy* Keane. Before Maddy came along, Peenie couldn't stand the idea of a single pickle in the world not throwing herself at him, even if he didn't actually want the pickle."

"The pickle?"

"Peenie used to say getting women was like 'picking pickles from a jar.'"

Aloha laughs. "Stop trying to distract me and answer the question: what was so amazing about Daphne you couldn't even *imagine* falling in love with a sexy and irresistible woman like me?"

"I don't know how to explain Daphne's appeal. She was just really attractive to me. Luminous. Kind of, I dunno, mysterious. We had amazing chemistry."

"But was your amazing chemistry with *her* better than your amazing chemistry with *me*?"

"Jesus, you're relentless."

"I am. Which means you might as well tell me what I want to know, because I'll pry it out of you, eventually."

I exhale. "Comparing my chemistry with you versus Daphne is impossible. It's like comparing apples to oranges—pickles to pomegranates—because you and I haven't had sex. " *Yet.* That's the word that just popped into my head. I shut my mouth, making sure I don't say it.

"Okay, then, take sex out of the equation," Aloha says. "Think back to your *pre-sex* chemistry with Daphne. Was it better or worse than ours?"

"That's a hard thing to remember. Daphne and I slept together Lionel Richie style the first night."

Aloha cocks her head. "Lionel Richie style?"

I grin. "All night long."

Aloha hoots.

"That's a Keane-ism," I say, laughing with her. "I wish I could take credit for that one, but I can't."

"Is that typical for you?" Aloha asks.

"Oh, God, yes. I absolutely love going all night long."

Aloha visibly blushes. "No, Mr. Sex Machine. I meant is it typical for you to have sex with someone that fast—the same night you meet them?"

"*Oh.*" My face floods with heat. "Um. It's not *a*typical, I guess. If I meet someone, and we're really vibing, and both of us are sending green-light signals to each other, then why wait? Now, just to be clear, one-night stands typically aren't my jam. But if a woman bowls me over and she's making it obvious she's down to fuck, then I'll roll with it and see where things might lead."

Aloha looks genuinely surprised.

"You've never leaped straight to sex on night one?" I ask.

Aloha shakes her head. "How could I? If the guy is a celebrity—which is almost always the case when it comes to me—then I'm thinking, at least at first, he might be using me for publicity. And if a guy I'm attracted to *isn't* a celebrity—if he's a guy I'm just meeting out in the world at large—I'd never jump into sex with him because I'd be thinking he's probably a star-fucker. Or I'd be worried he might sell his story to the rags or try to jumpstart his 'acting and modeling' career by 'leaking' a private sex-tape. That's why my team is so strict about NDAs—not just with people who work for me, but with anyone who interacts with me in my personal life. You never know what someone might wind up saying or doing."

I grimace. "No wonder you've never fallen in love. You don't trust anyone as far as you can throw them."

Aloha shrugs like that's an obvious statement.

"You don't trust *anyone*?"

"I trust people. But not completely. The only person I trust *completely*, without a shadow of a doubt, is Big Barry. I used to completely trust my best friend, Cassie—the one who played my bestie on *It's Aloha!* She was my sister, the same way Keane is your brother. But after I released my first album and the debut single went to number one, she tweeted that I didn't deserve my success and that I was nothing but a 'puppet' for my label."

"Oh my God. And you'd trusted her the same way I trust Keane?"

"Like a sister."

"Holy fuck. Was her Twitter account hacked, maybe?"

Aloha shakes her head. "That's what I thought at first. But, no. She blamed the tweet on cocaine and went to rehab a few days later. But, come on. Coke didn't create those feelings of jealousy inside her. It just brought them out. She'd put out an album six months before me and it tanked. And unlike me, she'd personally written or co-written every song. So, I actually understood the source of her anger. But, still, having her turn on me like that—and so publicly—made me feel like I can't trust anyone. To this day, I feel like anyone besides Barry is one line of cocaine away from eviscerating me on social media."

Oh, my heart. The tortured look on Aloha's face is ruining me. I touch her cheek, every cell in my body yearning to lean in and kiss that pained expression away. "You're not a puppet," I whisper, my face mere inches from hers. "No one is pulling the strings when you're up there dancing and singing and making an entire arena full of people fall madly in love with you. That's all you, Aloha."

Aloha's chest heaves. She twitches forward like she's going to kiss my lips... but then kisses my cheek. "Thank you," she says softly, just before sliding her arms around my neck and clutching me fiercely.

Oh, fuck. All of a sudden, every cell in my body wants to return that cheek-kiss she just laid on me. I wanna kiss her soft cheek and run my lips along her jawline. But, God help me, if I do any of that, it'll open the floodgates and I'll surely kiss her lips. And that's something I simply can't do.

Aloha sighs, shifts her position, and rests her cheek on my shoulder. "I think I'm done talking for a while, Shaggy Swaggy. Let's just watch the sunset for a bit, okay?"

"Okay, hula girl."

We sit together for a long while, watching the sky changing colors. But after a bit, I can't resist asking Aloha something I've been curious about.

"Why is your relationship with your mother so terrible? Did something specific happen or is it just the culmination of years of mixing business and family?"

She pauses for a long moment. "Long story short, my mother cares about nothing and no one but herself and money. She doesn't have a nurturing bone in her body."

"So I take it she's not on the list of people you trust."

"She is not."

"What about Reed Rivers? Do you trust him at all?"

"Reed's a good business partner. A straight shooter. Is he my friend? No. Would I want to date him? Fuck no. But in a business context, I trust him to do what he says he'll do."

"I've actually been wondering how you wound up on Reed's label. He's not known for pop music, is he?"

"No. I actually signed with Reed because of Barry. Reed had expanded Barry's duties and told Barry he couldn't freelance anymore. Which meant Barry was no longer allowed to guard anyone not signed to River Records, not even me. At the time, I was just about to renew my three-record contract with my first label, so I scrapped that deal and negotiated the same deal with River Records. As part of the agreement, Reed promised to leave me and my team alone to do our thing and I promised to make him buckets of cash. And so far, it's worked out. My first two albums for Reed went platinum and this last one, *Pretty Girl*, is on track to go triple platinum."

"Wow."

"Talk about going out with a bang, huh?"

"Going out? Does that mean you're leaving River Records?"

She shrugs. "*Pretty Girl* fulfilled my contract and I haven't signed a new one. Everyone thinks I'm dragging my feet on the new deal because I want to gouge Reed for more money. But that's not it. I'm just not sure I want to sign a new contract with anyone."

"You don't want to make music anymore?"

She sighs. "It's probably just a phase. But, yeah, lately, I keep finding myself fantasizing about becoming an episode of *Whatever Happened To...?*"

"What would you do instead?"

"I have no idea. Honestly, I don't know who I'd be if I didn't do this." She waves generally at the bus and then exhales. "Don't mind me. I'm just being dramatic. I'm sure if I take a nice, long tropical vacation after this tour, I'll be ready to cut a new album and hop right back on tour in no time."

"And if not, that's okay. This is *your* life. Live it for you and nobody else."

Aloha shoots me a look like I've just said the silliest thing in the world.

"You think I'm naïve for saying that?"

"I think you're sweet. And I think you don't realize how many people count on me. Not to mention how stupid it would be for me to throw everything away just because, 'Wah, wah, being famous is so hard!'"

"Maybe you wouldn't have to throw it *all* away. Just change it up. Slow it down. Maybe you could... I don't know. Keep the parts you like and throw away the parts you don't?"

"It doesn't work that way. It's all smooshed together. It's like how a sailboat needs to have a sail *and* a rudder to function properly. You can have a humongous sail and gale-force winds at your back, but without a rudder, you're just blasting off toward some random spot on the horizon line with no control or way of steering."

My chest tightens. The look on Aloha's face tells me she's just divulged something meaningful to her. I take a deep breath. I'm not sure I should ask the next question, but I do it, anyway. "Do you feel like a sailboat without a rudder, Aloha?"

Her face flushes. She presses her lips together and then nods slowly. "I actually wrote a poem about it once."

"You write poetry?"

"All the time."

"Wow. I'd really love to—"

"No. Sorry. I don't let anyone read my poems."

There's an awkward beat.

"Okay, well, if you ever change your mind..."

"I won't. Thank you. You're sweet to be interested. But, no."

There's another moment of silence between us.

"So... you're big on sailing?" I say. "I seem to recall you doing a lot of it on your show."

"You've seen the show?"

"From afar. My little sister used to watch it."

Aloha smiles thinly. "I absolutely loathe sailing. I get seasick just *looking* at a boat. Moana, I'm not. But all of season eight featured that stupid storyline where Aloha goes undercover as a 'regular teenager' to escape the pressures of fame, and she takes a job giving sailing lessons to the guests at a fancy resort. So I had to take sailing lessons to look like I knew what I was doing. It was *torture*." She exhales. "But enough of my whining. Let's talk about something else. Something *fun*." Her green eyes drift to the passing scenery out the bus window for a moment before igniting with mischief. "I know. How about we play a game? I happen to know a super fun one I think you're gonna love."

Chapter 21
Zander

"Ror the love of fuck, Aloha."

We're still barreling down the I-5 toward San Diego. Sitting together on the love seat at the back of the bus. And, much to my aggravation, Aloha just asked me if I'd rather "do" her or Daphne.

"It's a *game*," Aloha says, rolling her eyes. "It's called 'Who Would You Rather'? Ellen DeGeneres, the queen of nice, plays it all the time on her *daytime* talk show. So it can't be *too* salacious."

"I'm familiar with the game. But the two choices aren't supposed to be two people I actually know. They're supposed to be, you know, celebrities."

"I'm a celebrity."

"But you're not a celebrity to *me*. Not anymore, anyway. You were at first, but now you're just, you know, *Aloha*. The annoying girl who keeps asking me annoying questions about Daphne because she has a Keane-Morgan-like addiction to collecting pickles."

Aloha giggles, clearly enthralled by everything I just said.

"And regardless," I continue, "my two choices can't include someone I've already slept with."

"You haven't slept with *me*."

"But I've slept with Daphne!"

"So you keep reminding me."

"I don't 'keep reminding' you of anything, Little Miss Pickle Collector. You're the one who keeps asking me annoying questions about Daphne. I never bring her up."

She pauses, the expression on her face conceding my point. "Side note? I feel like referring to *me* as a pickle collector has a much naughtier connotation than referring to Keane as one. Don't you?"

I chuckle. "Good point."

She grips my forearm. "Would it entice you to play my reindeer game if I go first? Go ahead. Ask me if I'd rather do Zander Shaw or any celebrity in the world. Pick anyone you want, even Dwayne Johnson, my biggest celebrity crush, and I'll answer with complete honesty."

"I'm not gonna ask you jack shit, pickle girl."

"My answer is *youuu!* Okay. Your turn."

I glare at her.

"Fine. You don't have to tell me which one of us—Daphne or me—you'd rather do, if playing the game makes you clutch your freaking pearls. You can just tell me which of the two of us you find *sexier.*"

"Oh, yeah, because that's not the exact same question phrased another way."

"Booooo!" she booms. She swats at my arm. "You're being a stick in the mud, Shaggy Swaggy."

"How about I tell you who's more *annoying*? Gee, let me think. Oh, I know: *you.*"

She flaps her lips together. "Just tell me. I need to collect your pickle, dude. I've got an itchy pickle finger."

We both laugh.

"Aloha, seriously. I can't possibly say which one of you is 'sexier.' The two of you are just too different to compare."

"In what ways are we different?"

"In every way imaginable."

"Elaborate."

I sigh. "Daphne is this blonde, blue-eyed volleyball player art student amazon. She's almost six feet tall."

"She sounds like a nightmare."

"And she's mysterious. Kind of ethereal. She always kept her cards close to her vest. I could never be sure what she was thinking."

"And you liked that? Shit, she sounds like torture. But enough about stupid Daphne. Tell me about *me.*"

"You're the anti-Daphne."

"Thank God."

"You're a five-foot-four, green-eyed force of nature with zero filter. You say whatever is on your mind at all fucking times. You not only *don't* keep your cards close to your vest—you hurl the entire deck at me twenty-four-seven. You endlessly pester me to answer questions I do *not* want to answer. You hack into my phone like it's yours. And you climb me like I'm your own personal jungle gym."

"You don't like it when I climb you?"

"I *love* when you climb me. But that's beside the point."

Her eyes are dancing. "What's the point? I'm having a hard time discerning it because, sorry, from what you've described, I blow doors on Daphne."

I laugh. "I'm just saying you're nothing like Daphne, which means it would be like comparing apples to oranges to compare the two of you. That's all I'm saying and that's the truth."

But it's not the truth. It's a lie. Even as I'm giving my indignant speech, I'm realizing, without a doubt, that Aloha the Apple is way, *way* sexier to me than Daphne the Orange ever was. If presented with both women buck naked on silver platters, both of them beckoning me with open thighs, it's suddenly crystal clear to me I'd head straight for Aloha with drool running down my chin. And I truly don't know when or how that happened, seeing as how mere days ago I sat on a couch in Daxy's living room watching every one of Aloha's music videos and thought to myself, "How the fuck am I gonna win Daphne back?"

"Was Daphne your first love?" Aloha asks.

"No."

"How many times have you been in love, excluding Daphne and me?"

I laugh. "Five or six. Maybe seven, if you count kindergarten."

"All by the tender age of twenty-four? Holy crap, dude. Put a cork in that bottle on occasion. You're out of control."

"Life is short."

"Yeah, but it's not *that* short. You don't have the lifespan of an inchworm."

I laugh again. Because, apparently, even when Aloha Carmichael is being annoying, I find her utterly charming.

"How the hell have you fallen in love that much?" she asks.

"I don't try to fall in love. I just do. I'm a leaper. It's how I roll. Although, not gonna lie, getting dumped for the first time in my life last week has made me wonder if maybe I should try doing things a bit differently going forward. But, still, I regret nothing. I've had a blast falling in love. It's the best feeling in the world."

"I wouldn't know."

"You've truly *never* been in love?"

"I've been in heavy *like*. And I did *love* my gay ex-boyfriend. But loving someone who's gay and letting him use you as a beard isn't what I'd call being 'in love.'"

I tilt my head. "I find it interesting so many of your songs are about love and heartbreak and you've never experienced either."

"Who says? I've been heartbroken, just not about romantic love. And I've felt love. I just haven't been 'in love.' So when I sing about those things, I just tap into the feelings I've actually had and extrapolate. I don't write my own songs, remember? I just sing what my team tells me to sing and make it work for myself as best I can."

"I assumed your songs were at least tailored to you and your life."

"Nope. I'm a puppet, remember? I just give the people what they want. And what they want is love songs, not 'heavy like' songs. Ha! Can you imagine? 'I've never been in love but I've been in heavy like. So, come on, baby, come on over tonight. Come and be my first, the one who figures out the riddle. Teach me how to feel it, how to break this wretched curse.'"

"Did you just come up with that on the fly?"

"Yeah."

"You should write that song. You could make it a cool twist on a love song."

"That? Oh, no. I was just being silly. That was stupid. I'll leave the songwriting to the professionals."

"What's silly about it? Why not put some of your true self into your music?"

She rolls her eyes. "Now look who's being silly."

"Why? I think your fans would love to hear songs from you that are a peek at the real you."

"I can't do that."

"You can't write a song, or you can't write an honest one? Because, if you ask me, you could sit down and write a song today. You came up with those lyrics right off the top of your head."

"Yeah, I came up with lame lyrics. Big whoop."

"Have you ever written a song?"

"I used to write songs all the time. Not anymore."

"When was that?"

"Years ago. Back when I was still on the show. I was obsessed with songwriting, actually. I'd write lyrics nonstop in my journal—sometimes on napkins or scraps of paper if inspiration was really flowing. Melodies would flood me in the shower and I'd jump out with shampoo in my hair to work out the chords on my ukulele or guitar. I didn't tell anyone about my songs for the longest time, just because I was insecure about them. And when I finally did get the courage up to share my songs, it was a horrible experience. So I stick with poetry now. Lyrics, still, I guess. But lyrics nobody will ever hear set to music."

My heart aches at the look on her face. "What happened when you shared your songs? Why was it a horrible experience?"

Aloha sighs. But she doesn't speak.

I touch her hand. "Tell me, Aloha. Please?"

She twists her mouth for a moment before saying, "I'd just signed with my first label and we were gearing up to record my debut album. I told my producer I wanted the album to be ultra-personal—a window into my soul. A coming-out-party for the real Aloha, as opposed to the Aloha *character* everyone saw on TV for a decade. So my label teamed me up with a couple professional songwriters—the best in the business—and I got up the courage to pull out my guitar and play them a few of my songs. They said they liked them and thought we could build on them. But then my mother got wind of my lyrics and lost her damned mind. She said there was no way in hell she'd let me air my 'dirty laundry' to the entire world. She said nobody wanted to hear about anything but girl power and love songs from me. She said my album would tank if we used any of my stuff, just like my best friend Cassie's had tanked six months earlier. So I gave in and let the professionals take over. I figured when my debut album inevitably bombed like Cassie's had, I'd get dropped by my label the same way Cassie had been dropped by hers, and then I'd be free to write and record any songs I wanted, whether they were terrible or not. I figured I'd release my second album as a little indie passion project on my own dime and write every song for it personally, even if people made fun of me. But, of course, as you know, that's not what happened. My debut album went platinum with four top ten singles, including two number ones. And just that fast, the Aloha Carmichael brand became set in stone. With my second album, we stuck with the proven formula and it was an even bigger smash. And now, here we are, six albums later, and I'm still giving my Aloha-nators exactly what they want."

I touch Aloha's arm. "But you're twenty-three now, sweetheart. You're allowed to take some risks and make art, if that's what you want to do."

She looks entirely unconvinced.

"Will you play me some of your songs?"

Aloha shakes her head. "It's been so long since I pulled out my ukulele or guitar, I couldn't even play them if I tried. And, trust me, you don't want to hear them, anyway. They were total shit. In retrospect, those songwriters were just boosting my fragile ego when they said my songs had potential. Honestly, my mother did me a huge favor by squashing my ridiculous dreams. It's literally the only favor she's ever done me, but she was right."

My stomach tightens. "I'd bet anything those songwriters were being honest with you."

"I guess we'll never know."

Oh, my heart. I wrap my arm around her shoulders and pull her closer to me. In reply, she lays her head on my chest, slings her legs over my lap, and snuggles close. And that's how Aloha and I remain for a very long time, with her legs draped over my lap and our bodies cleaved together and her head on my chest... until, finally, her head lolls against my chest, letting me know the beautiful girl with Satan for a mother has fallen fast asleep.

Chapter 22
Zander

It's a few minutes past eight when our bus pulls up in front of our hotel in San Diego. Aloha is still dead asleep against my shoulder. I'm drunk on the scent of her coconut shampoo. And there's a sizeable throng of enthusiastic Aloha-nators, some of them holding signs, lots of them wearing flowers in their hair, awaiting Aloha outside the hotel entrance. There also appears to be a few local TV reporters and possibly a paparazzi or two, though I'm no expert at differentiating the paparazzi just yet.

When the bus comes to a stop, Crystal makes her way to Aloha and gently nudges her shoulder. "Honey, wake up. We're in San Diego."

Aloha stirs, rubs her face, and looks groggily out the bus window at the waiting crowd. "Oh, God. Not *now*, people."

Crystal follows Aloha's gaze out the bus window. "I'm surprised there are paps waiting for the bus." She narrows her eyes at me. "That's because of you, boy toy. They're obviously hoping for a repeat of yesterday's shenanigans."

"I had nothing to do with yesterday's shenanigans. That was all Drunk Aloha's fault."

"No, it was your fault." Crystal motions to my body like, somehow, my sheer physicality offends her. "They want more shots of *this*."

Aloha says, "I've been meaning to tell you nothing happened between Zander and me. I was just being a famewhore when I talked to that *TMZ* guy."

Crystal looks openly disappointed. Her eyes drift across my body for an unmistakable beat. "Pity."

My cheeks hot, I glance out the window and notice Brett

126

standing out there, already scoping out the crowd. "Let's give Brett a minute to get the lay of the land before we get off the bus."

"Good," Aloha says. "That'll give me time to cover this travesty." She indicates her exhausted, hung over face and calls to her makeup artist on the other end of the bus to "work her magic."

The makeup artist flies into action. And as she works, the Aloha-nators outside the bus begin serenading Aloha with an enthusiastic acapella rendition of "Pretty Girl."

"Aw, listen to them singing for me," Aloha says, her eyes closed as her makeup artist applies shadow to her lids. "They're so sweet."

"They love you," the makeup artist replies. "*Everybody* loves you, Aloha."

My stomach somersaults.

Aloha says nothing.

The makeup artist finishes her work and Aloha stands. She pulls her dark hair out of its messy bun and addresses me. "You ready, boy toy?"

"Ready, Miss Carmichael."

"Now don't forget. Those paps out there are hoping to capture our every lascivious look, so make sure you gaze at me like you just finished fucking me to within an inch of my life."

"I'll do no such thing."

"Well, then, at least look at me like you think I'm beautiful and charming."

"Aloha, I couldn't keep myself from looking at you like that if I tried."

A crooked grin spreads across Aloha's face—her *beautiful* face—and I wink at her. But I sense something dark lurking beneath Aloha's uneven smile—something more than her hangover. Anxiety, if I had to name it.

"You okay?" I ask.

She fidgets and looks out the window. "I'm fine. I just..." She takes a deep breath, like she's trying to force air into her lungs. "When fans are gathered spontaneously like this—when there are lots of them and they're not organized and controlled like they are at meet and greets—and I'm not feeling good, like now—I worry they're going to start crowding me too much and I won't have any personal space and I'll..." She glances toward the members of her team on the other side of her bus and whispers, "I don't want the paps or reporters to capture me having a panic attack on camera. It would go viral. I'd be mortified."

Oh, my heart. How is it the girl I thought had the world at her feet actually has the weight of it on her shoulders? I grab Aloha's hand. "If you're feeling the least bit claustrophobic or anxious, just tap your nose like *this* and I'll swoop in to be your human shield. Tap your nose twice and I'll bend down so you can hop aboard my back, and then I'll whisk you far, far away."

Aloha smiles shyly. "Okay. Thank you."

In my peripheral vision, I sense Aloha's makeup artist and tour manager, Crystal, exchanging a swooning look, but I don't pay them any mind. Aloha is my only concern in this moment. I tap on a window to get Brett's attention outside and he gives me a thumbs-up. "Okay, hula girl. We're good to go. You ready to do this shit, dude?"

She nods. "Ready, dude." But she doesn't look ready. At all.

"You look perfect, Aloha," Aloha's makeup artist says brightly.

"Gorgeous," Crystal agrees.

But Aloha's eyes are still trained on me. Like my opinion is the only one that matters to her.

I nod and smile. "You look like a butt-kicker."

She exhales. "Okay. Let's do this shit, dude."

I move in front of her and lead her toward the front exit. But just before we reach the door of the bus, I hear Aloha mutter to herself, "Panic attacks are for pussies, Aloha."

I stop walking and turn around. "You need a minute, honey?"

She shakes her head. "No, I'm fine." She addresses the bus driver. "Open the door, please, Frank."

The bus driver opens the door and, immediately, a tidal wave of shrieks and cheers slams into us. I step off the bus and guide Aloha to the ground... and, just that fast, the trembling, twitching girl from the bus transforms into Aloha fucking Carmichael. She smiles, whips her hair, and then, her hand gripping mine like a vise, sashays with all the swagger in the world toward her adoring fans.

Chapter 23
Zander

Aloha and I are sitting side by side on a private plane headed for Salt Lake City, the fifth stop on Aloha's tour. And for the first time since we worked out in the hotel gym together in Phoenix and then hung out in her room watching a double feature of *Rudy* and *White Men Can't Jump,* Aloha and I are alone again. Although, technically, we're not actually alone on this jet. The same people in Aloha's usual traveling entourage are scattered throughout this private plane. But sitting here with Aloha in the back of the plane, the armrest between us lifted all the way up and her body snuggled firmly against mine, I can't help *feeling* like we're the only two people on this plane. Maybe even in the world.

"That was incredible!" Aloha gushes as the credits roll on Maddy's new documentary. "And Keane was amazing in it! He lit up the screen! I wonder if Maddy would let me send it to the casting director who used to work on *It's Aloha!*. Even if she doesn't have a project that'd be right for Keane, I bet she knows tons of casting directors who might."

My heart explodes in my chest. "That'd be amazing."

"I just wish I had some sort of Keane highlight reel from the movie. Do you think Maddy would edit something like that for me?"

"Absolutely. Or you could just send your friend links to a few Ball Peen Hammer videos on YouTube. Those are all short and sweet and Keane is just as charming in those."

"Ball Peen Hammer videos?"

"Keane and Maddy didn't tell you about that? Yeah, Keane and Maddy have a web series called *Ball Peen Hammer's Guide to a Handsome and Happy Life.*"

"What?"

"It's awesome. 'Maddy Behind the Camera' shoots videos of

129

Keane talking to his 'handsome and happy lads in training' about all kinds of stuff. In the beginning, before Maddy and Keane were an item, Keane talked mostly about how to pick up women and have phenomenal sex. These days, though, now that Keane is no longer a stripper and Maddy owns his heart, Keane talks about whatever's going on in his life. Peenie thought when he stopped talking about picking up chicks in his videos, he'd lose his audience. But he couldn't have been more wrong. Their audience just keeps growing."

"Well, this I gotta see. Cue one of those bad boys up for me."

"I'll show you the very first one."

I play the video on YouTube and Aloha watches in amusement as Keane explains his one-of-a-kind Ten Year Rule.

When the video ends, Aloha gushes about it for a while and then asks, "Why was his hair blue?"

I tell Aloha the story, which, in summary, is that Keane dyed his hair blue to help me impress Daphne the first night I met her in a bar.

"Did Daphne wind up dyeing her hair blue after seeing the color on Keane?"

"No. After she saw the color on Keane, she decided to go with blonde highlights, instead."

"Bitch! And you actually *liked* this girl? *Dude!*" She swats my shoulder. "Stop talking about stupid, blonde, 'mysterious' and 'luminous' Daphne all the time. You're making my ears bleed."

"You're the one who asked me—"

"Just show me another BPH video. I can't get enough."

I cue a second BPH video, and then three more. And all of them make Aloha laugh that sexy belly laugh of hers—the one I live to hear. Finally, we watch the BPH video in which I shaved down his blue hair to a blonde buzz cut—the clip we shot in our bathroom in Seattle just before Keane flew to LA to get his adorable girl.

"Aw, you and Keane are the cutest bromance ever," Aloha says when the latest video ends. "Would it be okay if I tweeted this one to my Aloha-nators?"

"Oh my God. How many followers do you have?"

"Eighty-two million, give or take."

"Aloha, that would be huge for Keane. Thank you so much."

"You said he's trying to break into modeling and acting. Maybe it will give him a little buzz."

She opens Twitter and writes the following message:

Hey, Aloha-nators! Check out actor/model & life coach Keane Morgan aka Ball Peen Hammer! This clip features BPH and his bestie—my beloved Zander. Show BPH some love, guys! He's a star on the rise! Swoon!

"What's your twitter handle, babe?" she asks.

"I'm not on Twitter."

"*What*? Caveman." She quickly inserts the video link, tags Keane and her casting director on the tweet, and posts it. "There. Hopefully, that little tweet will open some doors for our aspiring little Peenie Baby."

"Wow. Thank you so much, Aloha. Keane's gonna shit his pants."

"I'm happy to do it. No shat-upon pants required. Honestly, the tweet was as much for me as Keane." She snickers. "The Twitterverse will pounce on the fact that I called you my 'beloved.' By the time we land, they'll be convinced we're secretly engaged or I'm pregnant with your love child. Triple bonus points if Daphne sees the tweet, right? *Bitch*." Aloha slides her hand in mine, a huge smile on her face. "*Alexa*, play me some more Ball Peen Hammer videos."

"I'm Alexa?"

"Of course."

We watch several more clips and marvel together at Keane's unique Peenie-ness... until, finally, a video entitled "The Sure Thing" pops up on Aloha's laptop screen as the next video in the automatic queue.

"Uh, let's skip this one," I say hastily, reaching for the keyboard.

Aloha slaps the top of my hand. "I wanna see it. Captain mentioned 'The Sure Thing' in his text to you after the 'boy toy' video. He said he assumed you'd performed it on me."

I open and close my mouth. *Shit*.

"Is it a sexual position?" she asks.

"I don't think we should watch this one."

"Why not? Does Keane do something pornographic in it?"

"No, he just talks, same as usual."

"Then lighten up." She scrutinizes my face, smirking. "Oh my

God. What the hell is this Sure Thing? It's something really dirty, isn't it?"

My face is hot. "No. It's just a technique." I clear my throat. "A sexual technique."

"Oh, holy hell, now I've absolutely got to see this video."

She's quick, but I'm quicker.

"Dude!" she blurts when I tilt her computer away from her extended hand. "What the hell is wrong with you?"

"Your future self will thank me."

"And my present self is about to bitch-slap you. Turn on the freaking video, Mr. Bodyguard. That's an order."

"Aloha, listen to me. If ever... *someone* were to perform this technique on you... at some point in the future... then you wouldn't enjoy it nearly as much if you'd watched this video or heard about how the technique is performed in advance. It works best when the woman doesn't know what's coming. When she can get out of her head and let go and *feel*."

Oh, man. If I thought that explanation would dissuade Aloha from wanting to watch the video, I was sorely mistaken. Her green eyes are on fire. "Tell me every little thing about it right now or I'm gonna push you out of the airplane. My future self will be shit outta luck."

I pause.

"Decide, Zander. Would *you* rather be the one to tell me about this sexual technique, or have Keane do it when I'm alone in my bed tonight, watching the video over and over again with my hand inside my panties? The choice is yours."

Holy fucking shit. My cock pulsing, I clear my throat. "It's a, uh, fingering technique. For bringing women to orgasm." I clear my throat again. "And not just any orgasm—an all-body one, which is way more powerful and pleasurable than a simple clitoral orgasm." I take a deep breath. "The technique usually gets women off more than once in a relatively short amount of time. What we boys call a 'sesh.'"

Aloha's eyes are blazing. "This technique gives women *multiple* orgasms?"

"Yes. Each one better than the last. All of them vaginal orgasms, not clitoral."

Aloha looks beyond titillated. "And you know how to do this to women?"

My dick is thickening underneath the opened tray table above my lap. "Yes."

"But, I mean, have you *performed* this technique *personally* or do you simply know *how* to do it, in *theory*?"

"I've done it. Many times. And very, very successfully."

Aloha's chest heaves sharply like I just slid a finger inside her. "And it's called 'the sure thing' because... it works every time?"

My dick has now hardened to full mast. "Yes. It's pretty much a slam dunk."

Aloha leans forward and whispers, "But what if a woman isn't all that, you know, good at getting off with a partner?"

Oh, Jesus. If I keep talking, there's only one place this conversation will end up: with Aloha asking me to do the technique to her. And that's something I simply can't do. I press my lips together.

"Tell me, Z," Aloha purrs, her green eyes aflame. "What if a woman has *never* had an orgasm with a partner?"

I take a deep breath. "From my experience, it works on anyone, as long as certain preconditions are met. I've done it to a woman who'd never had an orgasm before, not even on her own. And she had three orgasms in a row, each one stronger than the last. She said it was the best night of her life. One of the best of mine, too."

Aloha's chest heaves again. "Three orgasms in what span of time?"

"That particular woman took thirty minutes. That's pretty long. The amount of time it takes varies, depending on the woman. And just to be clear, three Os isn't a guarantee. I can *guarantee* one. Two is almost always a slam dunk. Three Os happen like seventy-five percent of the time. Beyond that, it's a crap shoot. With the right woman and under the right circumstances, I can get a woman doing her multiplication tables for me about twenty-five percent of the time, I'd say."

Aloha looks like she's on the verge of coming right now. "How many Os is 'doing her multiplication tables' and what are the 'right circumstances'?"

I don't know when it happened, but I suddenly realize I'm

holding Aloha's hand and gently rubbing the top of hers with my thumb. "There has to be insane chemistry between the woman and me. Not garden variety. She needs to be relaxed and not too hung up about sex in general. I need to get her ridiculously turned on before going for The Sure Thing—usually by eating her out beforehand. If all that's working for me really well, then I can definitely get three. Maybe even four or five. Five is the most I've ever gotten. It's not easy to get. It's a workout for the woman, you know? By two, she's dripping in sweat. Plus, I don't have the willpower to make it past five. But a couple of the Morgan boys have gotten as many as seven in a sesh. I honestly don't know how that's possible, but they'd never lie about it. But, still, five Os is no small thing, either for me or the woman."

"You don't have the willpower...?"

"Not to fuck her. By *three,* most women are so turned on, they start..." I look around, making sure nobody's eavesdropping on us. "Speaking in tongues. That's the only way to describe it. Women come completely undone at three and start begging me like their life depends on it. And that turns me on so much, I usually can't..." I take a gigantic breath. I'd bet anything my cock is dripping with arousal by now. I clear my throat. "I usually can't hold on any longer. I'm going in."

"You mean they start begging for...?"

I look around again, my heart racing. "Yeah. My cock."

Aloha's lips part with arousal.

I'm fully aware I'm being very bad right now. Very, very bad. But, fuck it, I wouldn't have missed the chance to see Aloha's face like this for anything. It's like she's having a little orgasm right here and now. I continue, "Once I get a woman to three Os before fucking her, then I know I've got a great chance of getting her to four once I get inside her. Because when a woman is that turned on, she almost always comes again when I get inside her. And, God, Aloha, that's the brass ring. It's the best feeling in the world, having a woman come around my cock. And I'm told it's the best feeling for her, too—coming while being filled all the way up. As far as I'm concerned, it's the closest thing to seeing God two people can experience."

A little puff of warm air escapes Aloha's pouty, perfect mouth, followed by the faintest of moans. She shifts in her seat. "What would happen if you didn't give her..." She looks around and then whispers, "Your cock, right away? What would happen if you tried for another O with your fingers before fucking her, even after she starts begging you?"

"I don't know." I chuckle. "When a woman is speaking in tongues and begging me for my cock, I'm gonna give her my fucking cock."

Oh my shit. By the look on Aloha's face now, I know for a fact that if I slid my fingers inside her sweet little pussy, she'd be wet and swollen and ready to go off like a rocket in under a minute. I shift in my seat, trying to relieve the pressure on my hard-on, but it's no use.

Aloha whispers, "And all the Morgans know about this technique, the same as you?"

"All of 'em. The two oldest brothers came up with it in the first place. I mean, not *together*." I laugh. "Ryan figured it out first. He told Colby and Colby worked out a better mousetrap, so to speak. The two of them exchanged notes over time. And then, when they had it working like clockwork, they told the three of us younger guys—me, Keane, and Dax. Plus, they told us about a whole lotta other stuff we needed to know, too. Thanks to them, when the three younger guys started having sex, we were all lightyears ahead of the curve. Nowadays, things have evened out as far as teachers and students. We're all pretty much killing it now. If someone figures a new thing out, he'll tell the group, but we don't need to trade info as much as we used to do, since we're all pretty much cooking with gas by now. Our credo is: if you're not getting your woman off hard and multiple times in a sesh, then you're failing at fucking."

"How is this out there and nobody's ever done it to me?"

"Most guys don't know about it. And if they do, they can't master it. It's not some kind of easy on-off button. It's a full-blown technique. A guy needs to have the right touch. A bit of finesse. Plus, like I said before, the woman's got to be super turned on beforehand and most guys have no idea how to accomplish even that."

Aloha visibly shudders like I've just stroked her throbbing clit. And that's all it takes for a little growl to escape my mouth. I fake a cough and put my hand over my mouth. *Shit.* I've got to stop this right now. I've crossed a line and I gotta get my ass back over to the other side of the line right fucking now.

135

"Zander, " Aloha whispers, her voice laced with arousal.

I wait. Here it comes. She's gonna ask me to do it to her. And what will I say? I'd have to say no, right? Although I suppose I *could* show her how it works, just so she can experience an orgasm with a partner for the first time. Just to show her what her body can do... Not to get my own rocks off, but as a sort of community service type thing...

But Aloha doesn't ask me to do it. On the contrary, she sits back in her seat, shoots me a naughty smile, and says, "I'm tempted to ask you to do it to me, to be honest. But since you promised Barry I'm off-limits—*and* you're still hung up on the amazing girl who gave you the best four months of your life—I'll restrain myself and continue to respect your stated boundaries." She cocks her perfect eyebrow, a demonic gleam in her emerald eyes. "Maybe someday I'll find a guy to do it to me. Who knows? And if I do, hopefully, he'll do it half as well as you would have done." She pats her mouth like she's yawning. "I think I'll take a nap now, Shaggy Swaggy. If I start moaning in my sleep like I'm having an orgasm, just leave me be. Obviously, I'll be dreaming about you doing The Sure Thing to me." With that, she shuts her laptop, pats my hand, and closes her eyes.

Chapter 24
Zander

Aloha styled me with that tweet, brah," Keane says on my phone screen. "I picked up over four million followers practically overnight!"

"That's so awesome, Peenie."

"Couldn't be better timing, too. I've got a huge audition tomorrow and my agent said casting directors love to see a 'robust' social media following. Thank her again for me, okay? Tell her if I get the part, I'll name my first born 'Haha' after her."

"*Haha Morgan*," I say. "That's actually the perfect name for a child of yours, Peen."

I'm sitting on my hotel bed in Boise in swim trunks, catching up with Peenie on FaceTime after a long but awesome day with The Package. As usual, Aloha was unstoppable today. Early this morning, she went to a pancake breakfast to raise money for a local animal shelter. After that, she swung by a children's hospital to visit kids with cancer—the same thing she did in San Diego, Phoenix, and Salt Lake City. After that, the force of nature that is Aloha Carmichael did a couple radio interviews, met with her costume designer regarding some beaded corset-thing she'll be wearing for her awards show performance in Las Vegas next month, and then it was off to the arena for what's become the standard show-day routine.

And now that the show is over and we're back at the hotel, Aloha is still going like the Energizer Bunny she is, even after the crazy day she's had. At this very moment, Aloha's in her hotel room getting into her bathing suit so she can head down to the hotel pool for a midnight swim with her dancers and band. So I'm sneaking in a FaceTime chat with Keane while I wait for her to text me to come get her.

"So, let's cut to the chase, baby doll," Keane says. "You in love with her yet or not?"

"Not."

He sighs. "The one-monthers are going ballistic on me, you know. Especially Ryan and Kat. At this point, they think I'm covering for you." He looks into the camera sideways. "Am I unwittingly covering for you, just because I'm blinded by my deep and abiding love for you?"

"Nope. Aloha and I are still just friends and that's how we'll remain throughout the entire tour, just like I said from the start. She's off-limits, remember?"

"Fuck Barry and his OL des. Aloha gets to say who fucks her and nobody else."

"That's exactly what Aloha said."

Keane's eyes widen. "Well, this is a new morsel of intel. Aloha said she's *not* off-limits to you?"

Crap. How did I let that slip out? "I didn't tell you that?"

"No! And it's a glaring omission! Why would Aloha say that to you, unless she's telling you she wants to fuck you?"

"Aloha was just saying Barry doesn't have a say about her sex life in general, not in relation to *me.*"

"So your sworn testimony before this court is that you two haven't talked about the two of you bonin' down?"

"We have not. We've talked about sex in general only."

"Why do I get the feeling you're dancing between raindrops here, Z?"

"I'm not. All that happened is I showed her some Ball Peen Hammer videos the other day—the day she tweeted about you—and then wound up telling her about The Sure Thing."

Keane palms his forehead. "Oh, for the love of fuck. That's the oldest trick in the book, telling a girl about The Sure Thing. I pulled that exact maneuver on Maddy and look where it got me."

"It wasn't like that."

"Lemme guess: she asked you to do it to her."

"Actually, no. She said she *wanted* to ask me to do it, but she 'respected my stated boundaries' too much. And then she closed her eyes and took a nap."

Now Keane hoots with laughter. "Oh, man, she's good. She's playing you like a xylophone, Z. Ha!"

I roll my eyes, even though I know he's spot-on. That

motherfucking girl is playing me like a goddamned xylophone and it's driving me up the wall.

Keane continues, "She's wagging her little mouse ass in front of you, the hungry cat. She's like, 'Hey, kitty-kitty! Make your move already, you big pussy!'"

I can't help laughing. Fucking Peen. "I gotta go, honey nuggets. I'm sure Aloha is wondering where I am. Good luck at your big audition tomorrow."

"Thanks, kitty-kitty. Have fun with your cute little mouse."

I disconnect the call without responding and head down the hall to Aloha's nearby room. Aloha never texted me, but she's gotta be in her swimsuit by now. But when I knock on Aloha's door, she doesn't answer. So, I send her a text saying I'm standing outside her door and then knock again. Still nothing. I press my ear against Aloha's door... and I'm jolted to hear quiet, muffled crying inside her room.

Panic floods me. "Aloha?" I shout, banging on the door.

The crying stops. But Aloha doesn't reply.

"Aloha!" I yell, rapping on the door again. "Are you okay in there?"

"I'm fine," her feeble voice calls out. "Go to the pool without me."

Shit. I reach into my pocket and finger the keycard to her room. I've never used Aloha's room key before. Crystal said it's only for emergencies, and back when she said that, I understood that to mean physical emergencies, like a fire or something. Does a situation like *this* count as an "emergency"? "Open the door," I command. "Or I'm coming in with my key."

"*Don't come in*," she says. "Go swimming. I need to be alone for a bit."

I press my forehead against the door, my heart racing. "Aloha, I need to see your face or I'm coming in."

"I don't want you to see me. I've been crying."

Fuck. Barry warned me there'd be at least a handful of days on this tour when, out of nowhere, the stress and grind would get to Aloha and she'd have a bit of a cry. Maybe even a meltdown. Indeed, during my training with Barry, he said an important part of my job is gaining Aloha's trust early on so she'd let me be her shoulder to cry on whenever she hit a wall. But things have been going so damned well, and Aloha has been such a machine, day after day, I'd forgotten all about Barry's warning. Until now. "Sweetheart, if you're crying, that's all the more reason to let me in," I say into the closed door. "If you let me in, you won't need to explain your tears to me. I'll just hold you while you cry on my shoulder."

There's a long silence. When she finally replies, her voice is coming from mere inches away, like she's leaning against the other side of the door. "Go swimming, Z," she says. "I won't leave my room, I promise. I just need to be alone and write some poetry and cry. I do this sometimes. I'm fine."

Oh, my heart. "Sweetheart, as your bodyguard, I can't hear you crying and walk away. I just can't. At least not without seeing your face to make sure you're in one piece."

For a long, agonizing moment, I remain still, my forehead and palms pressed against the wood of the door. I hear her sniffling, mere inches from me.

Finally, the doorknob turns... and the door opens, just a crack. "See?" she says through the tiny sliver of an opening. "I'm fine. Just feeling sorry for myself. Being a wimp."

Every fiber of my body wants to push open the door and take her into my arms. But I refrain. "You're not a wimp to be sad and exhausted. You're a human being."

She sniffles.

"Why are you sad, honey?"

She pauses. "I just got off the phone with Satan. And it wasn't a pleasant call. I just need to cry for a bit and write poetry and then I'll be fine in the morning. Go to the pool. Have fun."

I roll my eyes. "I'm not going to 'have fun.' Not with you sitting in here boohooing. I'll go to my room and come back to check on you in an hour. Text me if you need me before then and I'll come running. And by that I mean I'll literally sprint to you, Aloha. As fast as my legs will carry me."

She nods. But doesn't return my smile. And then she silently closes the door in my face.

I grit my teeth. Goddammit, this job is such a mind-fuck! Hanging out with Aloha, day in and day out, has been tricking my brain into thinking we're tight as ticks. Two peas in a pod. But, clearly, she doesn't feel as close to me as I feel to her.

I turn around and begin marching to my room, my heart racing. Fuck! And to add insult to injury, I gotta text Barry now. I text him an update every day, of course. But until now, they've all said the same thing, essentially: *Aloha's great. We're really clicking. Couldn't be better.* But today, for the first time, I've got to write a very different kind of update:

Hey, B. AC is crying in her room. Said she had a bad phone call with her mother. I made her open the door a crack so I could see her. I tried sweet-talking her into letting me into the room to be her shoulder to cry on, but no dice. Heading to my room now. Told her I'd come back in an hour and to text if she needs me before then. Not sure what else to do.

Barry's reply comes immediately:

It's a good sign she cracked the door for you. I'll take it from here. Don't check on her later unless you hear from her or me. And if she acts like nothing happened tomorrow, then follow her lead. Thanks.

If she acts like nothing happened tomorrow, then follow her lead? What kind of horseshit is that? My nostrils flaring, I shove my phone into the pocket of my swim trunks. Fuck! It pains me to think Aloha's in her room, crying her eyes out, and she'd rather be comforted by Barry over the phone than by me in person.

For a split second, I feel the thumping urge to disregard everything Aloha said—everything Barry said—and turn around and run back to her and blast into her room using that emergency key, whether Aloha likes it or not. After all, when Barry trained me, he told me to always trust my instincts, didn't he? He told me to be myself and be a true friend to her... Emboldened, I turn around and head toward her room again. But when I reach Aloha's door, I hear chuckling inside the room, like she's laughing through tears. I can't make out what she's saying, but I can hear Barry's rumbling voice mingled with hers, like they're talking on FaceTime or speakerphone. And there's no doubt he's comforting her effectively—the way I'm dying to do. Well, shit. I'm a day late and a dollar short, son. Apparently, Barry's got this under control and I'm not needed. With a heavy sigh, I turn around and drag my exhausted, rejected ass back to my room.

141

Chapter 25
Aloha

I fall off Kiera's shoulders and splash spectacularly into the swimming pool. Kiera and I have just lost a hard-fought battle of chicken against two of my shit-talking band members. We're in Portland now, just over three weeks into the tour, and we're finally getting around to having that post-show pool party I'd originally suggested back in Boise.

I emerge from my graceless dunking into the pool and immediately search the surrounding patio for my trusty bodyguard. When I find him sitting at the far end of the patio, chatting with the cyborg, I wave my arm and call out to him. When Zander's dark eyes train on mine, his eyebrows shoot up like he's asking if I'm okay. I shoot him two thumbs up and motion for him to join me in the pool.

He shakes his head.

I nod *yes*.

He shakes *no*.

I shout, "I need you to be my partner in chicken! Kiera sucks ass!"

"Hey!" Kiera says next to me, splashing me.

The cyborg motions to Zander, clearly telling him to get his ass into the pool, and Zander, God bless him, gets up from his chair, pats his pants like he's explaining he's gonna get changed into his swim trunks, and then glides out of the pool area straight into the hotel.

And I swoon. He's ridiculously sexy, no matter what he's doing.

Kiera nudges me. "You two getting it on yet?"

"Not yet," I say miserably. "*Yet* being the operative word, I hope."

"How is it possible you two haven't even kissed yet? You guys ogle each other every minute of every day."

"It's gonna happen soon. I can feel it. I mean, for God's sake,

142

how many times can a guy cover his boner before he breaks down and makes his move?"

"Why don't you make *your* move? Who cares what Barry says."

"It's not just Barry. I promised Zander early on I'd back off and let him make the first move. Plus, to be honest, I'm a wimpy little fraidy cat. Afraid of rejection. I don't *think* he's still hung up on his stupid ex-girlfriend, but what if he is? Last I heard, he wanted to try to win her back in New York. I don't *think* that's still the plan, but I don't know for sure. He's never said anything about it, either way."

Kiera shakes her head. "He doesn't want her. He wants you."

"Then he'd better let me know that, once and for all."

She sighs. "How crazy is it the entire world—including every single person on this tour—thinks you two are banging each other's brains out at every opportunity and, in reality, you haven't so much as kissed."

"Please, don't remind me. I've never been so freaking horny in my life." I look toward the entrance to the pool area. "Good God, how long does it take for a sexy man to throw on swim trunks?"

"Maybe he had to jack off in his room before coming back down."

"Are you trying to kill me? I dream about having sex with him every night. Don't put the image of him jacking off into my head, too. I'll spontaneously combust in my sleep."

"Dude, forget what you promised him way back when about not making the first move. Go for it. He won't reject you."

"He might."

"Okay, then, turn up the heat and make *him* make the first move. Things can't go on like this, AC. Something's gotta give."

I pause. "You're right." I nod definitively. "Tonight's the night. One way or another, I'm gonna get Zander Shaw to make his move on me tonight if it's the last thing I do."

"Atta girl."

"I'm *irresistible*, after all."

"Damn straight."

Loud laughter on the other side of the pool draws our attention. A bunch of my dancers are performing a splashing rendition of the choreography for "Pretty Girl." I glance toward the patio entrance again for a long moment, willing my sexy bodyguard to appear. But when he doesn't, I grab Kiera's arm and we join our friends at the other end of the pool to join the dance.

Chapter 26
Zander

C ongrats, Peenie!" I say.

    I'm sitting in my swim trunks and a T-shirt in my hotel room, talking to Keane on FaceTime. Keane's call caught me just before leaving to head back down to the pool and I couldn't resist taking a few minutes to catch up with my beloved Wifey.

On Keane's end of the video chat, he's sitting on his parents' couch in Seattle. He and Maddy arrived in their hometown earlier today in anticipation of Aloha's concert tomorrow night and the big Lasagna Dinner the following night. And, much to my elation, but not my surprise, my best friend just told me he's one of three people still in the running for what he says could be a "life-changing" role for him, a recurring role in a big-money, big-production limited TV series coming to HBO—a show that's going to feature a big-name movie actress in the lead role.

"What's the part?" I ask.

"The movie star is a married college professor and I'd be the student with whom she's having a torrid affair. I'd appear in five of the show's eight episodes, two of which will feature 'highly graphic sex scenes' between me and the movie star."

"Wow. You're cool with doing graphic sex scenes?"

"Bah, it's just skin," Keane says breezily. "The part that actually scares me is what I'd have to do in the fifth episode. The professor breaks it off with her student and then he totally wigs out on her. Like, he starts wailing and telling her he loves her and turning into a total cling-on." Keane chuckles. "So she winds up trying to hire a hitman to kill him in episode six but everything turns to shit on her. How sick is that?"

"You'd have to *cry* if you get this part?"

"No, I'd have to *bawl*. Like, *blubber* my eyes out."

I laugh. "You think you could do that, especially on cue in front of a room full of people?"

"I know it because I already did it. I had to do the blubber scene at my last callback in front of, like, eight people. I actually did the scene with Miss Movie Star herself."

"Holy shit, Peenie! And you blubbered?"

"I bawled like a baby, baby doll. The River Jordan gushed out my baby blues and down my little apple cheeks." He laughs. "Seriously, I smashed it, Z. Obliterated it. I didn't commit murder that day, it was genocide. It was the best I've ever done the scene, by far. Maddy practiced it with me a thousand times and that *one* time, when it really counted, I took it next lev."

"How the hell did you make yourself cry in front of all those people?"

"I just did what my acting coach taught me to do. That whole morning, I thought about something really sad from my life—the day Colby had his horrible accident. And then, when the moment came at the audition, when the movie star broke it off with me, I imagined she'd just told me you'd been killed in a car wreck."

"Jesus."

"And that made me burst into soggy tears. And then, as the scene went on, I imagined myself at your funeral, standing over your coffin, crying my eyes out. I imagined having Maddy whisper to me, right then and there, 'I don't love you anymore, Keane. I'm in love with someone else.'"

"Holy hell, Peenie."

He snaps his fingers and a huge smile lights up his face. "And *boom*. I could barely get my lines out, I was wailing so hard. At the end of the audition, I looked at all the people in the room—the director and casting director and whoever else the rest of 'em were—and I knew I'd slayed it. At least two of them had teared up. Plus, the movie star told me I blew her away."

"Holy motherfucking shit, Peenie. You're totally gonna get this part!"

"Gah. No counting chickens, love muffin. It stresses me out."

"Peenie, there's no doubt in my mind you'll get it and become the next big thing. *I feel it in my bones*."

145

"Dude, don't jinx me. There's still two other guys they're considering, and both of them have tons more experience than me. I'm sure the other guys smashed their auditions, too."

"They'll pick you, Keaney."

Keane shows me crossed fingers. "Worst case scenario, if they don't pick me, I'm pretty sure the casting director will keep me in mind for future projects. She pulled me aside after my audition and said I was 'deeply moving' and 'riveting.'"

"The part is as good as yours, son."

He shudders. "Okay, new topic. I'm shitting my pants just talking about it. My agent says we should find out any day now, maybe even as early as today, and I don't wanna think about it too much in the meantime or I'm gonna barf."

My stomach is somersaulting with excitement for my best friend, but I dutifully move onto another topic. "So how are things going with the lovely Madagascar Milliken? Still great?"

Keane looks behind him, clearly checking to see if Maddy is within earshot somewhere in the Morgan house. "Better than great, baby cakes. Fantastic. Perfect. Blissful. In fact, she's the reason I've even got a shot at this amazing role. Why do you think I told my agent to start sending me out for dramatic roles, and not just frat boys and strippers and football players? Because Maddy encouraged me to do it. She said I'm a whole lot more than a pretty face and I shouldn't let anyone tell me otherwise. She said I've got 'depth and talent beyond just making people laugh or drool'—and that even my Ball Peen Hammer videos are proof I've got a gift to make people *feel*. She said I shouldn't be afraid to let people see all sides to me, not just the joking side. She told me to dream bigger and not let anyone define me but *me*." He smiles broadly and his dimples pop. "The girl totally believes in me, Z. The same way you always have. Man, you should hear the pep talks she gives me. She makes me feel like I can do anything, the same way you always have."

Goosebumps erupt on my arms. "Aw, Peenie. This is music to my ears. And I agree with everything she said to you, by the way. But you already know that."

Keane sighs happily. "I swear, if things keep going this well with that smart-girl, I'll be hard-pressed not to lock her down before our one-year anniversary."

I raise my eyebrows. "Lock her down?" I ask, unsure if Keane's definition of that phrase matches mine.

"Put a ring on it," Keane says without hesitation, much to my shock. "Get down on bended knee. Pop *la grande pregunta.* 'Plight my troth.'"

I chuckle. "Plight your troth?"

He snickers. "It sounds super dirty, huh? That's why I like it. It's actually just old-timey speak for proposing."

"Holy shit, Peenie. Who are you?"

"Crazy, right? Wait. You don't think that'd be seriously crazy of me, do you?"

"Not crazy at all. If you've found The One and you're sure of it, then why wait? Don't dip your toe into the pool of love, son. Cannonball into it, all the livelong day."

"Thanks, Z. So catch me up on everything going on with you."

"There's nothing much to tell. I'm working hard. Learning a lot. Having fun with Aloha."

"Are you learning enough to get yourself onto Daxy's tour after this one is over?"

My stomach tightens. I know that was my original goal when I took this job—using the domestic leg of Aloha's tour as a stepping stone to get myself onto Daxy's tour with Red Card Riot, just in time for those guys to begin *their* domestic leg. But, now, I can't imagine not continuing on with Aloha when she heads overseas after New York. But since nobody has mentioned me continuing on with Aloha, I keep telling myself not to count my chickens. "We'll see what happens," I say. "How's Dax? I saw their first single just cracked the Top 100 on the charts. That's huge."

"I know. He's super pumped about it. Thank Aloha for posting that tweet about his album, will ya? Dax said it was perfectly timed. Did Reed put her up to it?"

"Nope, that was all Aloha. We listened to the album together on a bus ride and she went crazy for it. She posted the tweet right then and there, without any prompting by me or anyone else. Has Dax said how the tour is going so far?"

"Way better than expected. He said Red Card Riot has been super cool to them and the audiences at their first two shows were totally lit. He said it was a dream come true to play a huge, sold-out arena like that, even if nobody came to see them."

147

"I'm so pumped for them."

"Me, too. But enough about Daxy. Let's get to the sex, kitty cat. You fucked the mouse yet? Are you in *lurve?*"

"Enough with the bet. I can't take it anymore. It's nobody's goddamned business."

"Ooooh, that's an interesting response. The guy who swore it'd 'never' happen is now saying it's nobody's business, huh? I'll take that as a 'Yes, Peenie, I am most certainly in love with the pop star.'"

"I'm not in love and I haven't so much as kissed her. I'm just saying the bet is bullshit. Intrusive. Douchey and disrespectful."

"Is that so?"

"Yes."

"You had no problem putting your hundred in the pot almost a month ago."

I sigh.

"Dude, listen to me. The one-monthers only have a few more days to win the pot and they're breathing down my neck. Have you fallen for her yet or not?"

"*Not.*"

"Put your eyeballs right up to the camera and say that again."

I put one eyeball right up to the camera. "Aloha and I are friends. I haven't dabbled with her and I'm not going to. And, no, I'm not in love with her. Now, stop with the fucking bet. I'm done with it."

"Ho-lee shit," Keane whispers, his blue eyes wide.

"What?"

"Okay, Z. The cat's officially outta the bag now. In fact, the damn cat's running around, chasing a big ol' ball of yellow yarn. I'm calling the bet."

"What cat? What yarn? I'm telling the truth. I'm not in love with her."

"You're such a liar. I was almost gonna call the bet the last time we talked, but I didn't out of an abundance of respect for you. But now, I'm one thousand percent positive you're totally and completely in love with the pop star. The bet's done."

"You're wrong."

"You do realize all the one-monthers think you're three sheets to the wind drunk on this girl, right? And I've been the only thing holding them back from staging a coup."

"Keep holding them back. You're on the side of truth and justice, my friend."

"Z, it's not just the one-monthers who think you're gone, baby, gone. It's the entire world. Every human on the planet—and that's not a figure of speech—even people living in mud huts in Malawi—are like, 'Oh, that new bodyguard of Aloha Carmichael's? He's most definitely in love with her!'"

I can't help laughing. "Well, the entire world is dead wrong."

"Come on, brah. Those videos Aloha's been posting of the two of you working out together in hotel gyms across America are like hashtag relationship goals. Not to mention soft core porn."

"Aloha thought it would be fun to inspire her fans to get themselves into the gym."

"Mmm hmm. A plausible story except for the fact that the two of you can't keep your hands off each other in those videos. Dude, when you bench press her, her ass is right in your face. When she wraps her legs around your waist and does those hanging sit-ups, you two might as well be fucking."

"It's a partner workout, dude. Look it up."

"Mmm hmm. Did you know you're a meme, Z?"

"No."

"Hold on. I'll find one. They're hilarious." Keane clacks some keys on his laptop and, two seconds later, he's got his phone trained on his screen—on a photo of me looking adoringly at Aloha as she hugs a young fan at a meet and greet. A caption on the photo reads, "Never settle. Find someone who looks at you the way Aloha's bodyguard looks at her... or die alone."

I laugh. "I'm sure I was just thinking about getting a cheeseburger in that shot. I'm always hungry during meet and greets."

"It's not just the memes that seal this deal," Keane says. "It's all the photos of you holding Aloha's hand. Cradling her shoulders. Guiding her with your hand on the small of her back."

"Aloha feels panicky if crowds press in on her too much. She likes to feel physically connected to me. I'm her human safe space."

"Interesting. Then how do you explain I've seen multiple photos of you two holding hands when there's nary a crowd in sight?"

My chest tightens. "The crowds must have been out of frame."

149

"Mmm hmm. What about photos where you're giving Aloha a piggyback ride?"

"When Aloha feels like people are crushing in on her too much, she gives me the sign and I bend down and she hops aboard my back. She calls me her valiant steed and I call her my pretty Hawaiian princess."

"As all purely platonic friends do."

"Believe what you want. I'm done trying to convince you."

Keane narrows his eyes and leans into his camera, making his bright blue eyes fill the entire screen. "So your sworn testimony before this court is that you only give Aloha Carmichael piggyback rides when she's freaked out and panicking in a big crowd?"

"Yes."

He lurches back, his eyebrow cocked. "Then how do you explain *this!*" He turns his computer around to display a photo I've never seen before—a photo in which Aloha is on my back, her sling-back heels dangling from her extended finger and her head thrown back as she laughs with glee.

I can't help smiling at the photo. Aloha's face in it is absolutely breathtaking. She's the living portrait of euphoria. And, man, my face in the shot matches hers. Which is no surprise, since I remember feeling like my heart was going to explode from sheer, unadulterated joy at that particular moment. So much so, I galloped around with Aloha on my back for what had to be a full two miles like a horse with mad cow disease, simply because I didn't want the sound of her squealing laughter to end.

"That was a one-off," I say calmly. "Aloha's new heels were giving her blisters, so I told her to take 'em off and hop aboard."

"Oh, Z. For the love of fuck. Stop already."

"What?"

"You really think you're convincing me you're *not* in love with her? To the contrary, the look on your face as you spew this bullshit makes me even more convinced I've got this right. *You love her.* Totally, completely, truly, madly, deeply." Keane sighs. "Wifey, I'm sorry, but I gotta call the bet."

Panic rises inside me. "No, Peenie. Don't."

"Gotta do it, baby doll. I took a vow of *judiciousness,* remember?"

150

"Keane, listen to me. I can see how it *looks* from the outside. But I'm not in love with her. Not in the way everyone means for the bet, anyway. Yes, when I watch Aloha performing, I fall in love with her, each and every time—but only the way every person in every arena falls in love with her, too. I'm not *in love* with her the way you're in love with Maddy."

"Z."

"Peenie, listen to me." I take a deep breath, feeling like I'm going to hyperventilate. "You can't call the bet. This isn't a game to me anymore. This is life or death. Yes, I admit if Aloha showed me something unique and special—something just for me—if she let me see the parts of her she doesn't show her 'Aloha-nators'—then, yes, I'd probably fall head over heels for her. But all that's happened here is I've fallen in love with her the same way the entire world has. And that's not love." I sigh. "You know how you used to be addicted to making every girl want you, even if you didn't want the girl in return? Well, that's Aloha. But whereas you were all about making women want to *fuck* you—which, let's face it, was never gonna be fatal for anyone involved—Aloha's all about making men, including *me,* fall desperately *in love* with her. And that's... dude, that's a death sentence for any mortal man, but especially one like me. To her, my tender heart is just another one for her collection. Another one to throw onto the pile or stow in a forgotten drawer. She doesn't want *me.* She wants my heart as a trophy. And once she thinks she's gotten it—once she's got the fix of her drug—she'll stuff my heart into her drawer with all the others and move on to her next conquest. Which is why I *can't* fall in love with her, no matter what... and why, I swear to God, I haven't." A little sound of pure torment escapes my lips and I clamp my mouth shut.

"Holy shit," Keane whispers. "You poor little big thing."

"Dude, you have no idea. Every minute of every day, my heart feels like it's getting ready to burst or break, depending on the moment. And, all the while, my balls feel like they're in a vise. I wanna fuck her so bad, I feel like I'm physically *dying*. But if I fuck her, then I'll fall for her. And I can't do that because I'll get eviscerated."

Keane makes a sympathetic face. "Poor Z."

"Forget poor Z. This is triage, son. Poor Z's balls. Gah. At this point, just a look from Aloha can sometimes give me a boner. And God help me if she bends over... Have I mentioned the glory of Aloha's ass? Oh my God. That ass is stone-cold perfection, son. I have to physically look away from it sometimes so I won't sear my corneas or whimper in pain."

Keane laughs.

"It's not funny"

"It's fucking hilarious."

"Glad you're amused."

"Why not just fuck her? From what I saw at the party, she's definitely down to fuck you. Roll the dice. Risk your heart. Or maybe things won't work out as badly as you think."

"I can't. She's off-limits, remember?"

"Cut the bullshit, Z. It's me, remember? We both know you'd risk it if you thought you could get away with it. *And you can.*"

I sigh. "Yeah, okay. I admit it's not Barry holding me back anymore. I think I've been focusing on the Barry thing as a shield. Because I'm too scared of how badly I'm gonna get burned to a crisp here."

"You're positive if you fuck her, you'll be a full-blown goner?"

"I'll be a full-blown goner if I so much as kiss her, Peenie. I'm hanging on by the barest of threads."

"Then I say do it. Kiss her. Fuck her. Get your woman. Cannonball into the pool, son. Life is short."

"No. If I let myself fall for this girl, it'll be Daphne all over again, only way worse because, this time, I'll be the damned fool who cannonballed into an empty pool *knowing* it was empty."

"Maybe there's water in the pool. Maybe Aloha's feeling the same way you are."

"She's not. She's never been in love and she's only ever dated celebrities." I shake my head. "Naw, Peenie. She's made it clear she's up for a tour-fling with her lowly bodyguard and that's it. And you know flinging ain't my strong suit, man. You guys were right to razz me about the high-speed elevator between my dick and my heart. I'm hopeless."

Keane looks pained. "But maybe this *one time* you could separate fucking and feelings, if you concentrated really hard. Or, shit, maybe, despite Aloha's past track record, she'd want more than a tour-fling with you, after all. Maybe one kiss and she'd fall into the abyss, right along with you."

"She won't, Peenie. Put aside the fact that she's a big star and I'm a working stiff. She's the female you. Well, the *pre-Maddy* female you. She's a pickle collector and I'm nothing but a pickle."

"Well, then, there's genuine hope. I did a one-eighty after meeting my dream pickle, didn't I? So maybe you're Aloha's dream pickle, too."

My skin erupts with goosebumps at the mere thought.

"Or, hey," Keane continues, "maybe you wouldn't even want Aloha after you finally got a taste of her. Maybe you'd fuck her and find out she's too big a train wreck under all that pretty and you'd run away screaming."

I shake my head. "I already know for a fact she's a world-class train wreck underneath all that pretty and that's the thing that attracts me the most. Honestly, if Aloha were to take off her mask with me and fling it across the room and show me the truth, no matter how ugly, I'm positive I'd shove my heart at her with both hands."

"Why do you think she's a world-class train wreck?"

I tell Keane all the ways I'm aware of that Aloha's been abandoned, betrayed, and used. And how I'm quite certain she doesn't know who she is when she's not performing for an audience.

Keane shakes his head. "Sounds like the perfect project for you."

I laugh. "Yeah, I know."

"So much for that three-month detox from the foxes, huh?"

"No, my de-foxification is still on, brother. As long Aloha keeps to her promise not to make the first move, I'm positive I can stay strong and keep Mr. Happy in line. And if I can do that, then I'll be able to keep my heart from falling into the abyss. The good news is there's no way she'll make the first move, no matter how horny she is for me, because I've got her firmly convinced I'm scared to death of Barry and/or still hung up on Daphne."

"You're *not* still hung up on Daphne?"

I roll my eyes. "Of course not. I don't give a rat's ass about Daphne."

Keane laughs.

"It's been torture pretending I do, though. Whenever Aloha and I hold hands and a paparazzi jumps out of nowhere to snap our photo,

153

Aloha's like, 'Oh, Daphne's gonna shit when she sees that one!' And I have to be like, 'Oh, yeah. Daphne's gonna shit!' And all the while, my dick is hard and my balls feel like they're in a vise and all I can think about is how much I wanna eat Aloha's pussy 'til I make it rain all over my face."

"Oh, Zan Antonio. Your poor balls. God help you."

"No, *you* help me and don't call the fucking bet. Having that bet hanging out there is the only thing keeping me strong."

He sighs. "Fine. You've convinced me. You're hanging on by a thread."

I sigh with relief. "Thank you."

"But screw hanging on. Hanging back and being careful and scared of rejection isn't you. In fact, it's a travesty to watch you turn into this sniveling mess, if you wanna know the truth. Okay, so you're not the best at flinging. We all know that. So, fuck it, embrace it. Be *you*. Wear your tender heart on your outlandishly large sleeve. No regrets that way, right? Cannonball into the pool, baby doll."

"I'll think about it." I exhale. "I gotta go, honey nuggets. Aloha's waiting for me to play chicken in the pool with her. I'll see you the night after next at your parents' house."

"Oh, no, you'll see me tomorrow night at the concert. Josh arranged a skybox for the entire clan to come see the show. Everyone but Colby and Lydia will be there to cheer on our favorite bodyguard."

"Awesome. Will Colby and Lydia be at dinner the next night?"

"Yep. They said they can't wait. They just didn't wanna leave Baby Mia yet to go to the concert."

"Understandable. I can't wait to see her." I glance at the clock. "Shit, Aloha's gonna be pissed. I gotta go."

"Cannonball, Z. You got this."

Chapter 27
Aloha

Finally, after what seems like forever and a day, Zander saunters into the pool area like he owns the place. He's wearing bright green swim trunks, a blue T-shirt, and a cocky smile.

He high-fives Brett, the cyborg, who salutes me from across the large patio area and then bolts away like he's got somewhere far more important to be. Well, good riddance, cyborg. I don't want Barry's spy hanging around here, anyway, not when I've decided Zander isn't leaving this pool tonight without making a move on me. *Tonight's the night.*

From across the patio, Zander levels me with his chocolate eyes. He looks like he's making his mind up about something. Or maybe he's just teasing me, drawing out my anticipation because he knows I can't wait to see him take off that T-shirt and show me the goods.

I splash the water in front of me, ordering him to get his gorgeous ass into the water right freaking now, but he holds up his index finger, telling me to be patient.

Finally, slowly, ever so slowly, his eyes trained on mine and a cocky smile on his luscious lips, Zander peels off his tight blue T-shirt, revealing his jaw-dropping torso in all its glory. Chiseled abs. Bulging, tattooed arms. Mammoth chest. His eyes still holding mine, he tosses his T-shirt onto a nearby lounger, takes four slow and concerted steps toward the ledge of the pool, and then, much to my surprise, cannonballs into the center of the pool.

Cheers and hoots abound from everyone already in the water. But Zander can't hear any of them because he's swimming underwater in a predatory line straight toward me. When he bursts through the surface of the water next to me with a loud roar, I shriek and throw my arms around his strong neck and then laugh and laugh.

Without missing a beat, Zander twirls me around in the water, soundly splashing everyone within a three-foot radius of us with my whipping legs.

I can't stop giggling. "What took you so long? I started to worry you'd stood me up."

Zander flashes me a smile that makes my clit zing. "I'd never stand you up, my darling hula girl. In any context. Ever. My Wifey FaceTimed me just as I was heading out the door. We had a lot to catch up on."

I wrap my thighs around Zander's gorgeous torso and tighten my grasp around his neck. "Oh, did you now? Well, whatever you and the missus talked about upstairs, it obviously put you in a feisty mood, so I approve."

"A *very* feisty mood," he says, taking my breath away.

Crystal's movement at the far end of the patio behind Zander's shoulder catches my attention. She's speed-walking in her dripping-wet bikini toward the exit of the pool area. . . and then quietly slipping out. "Crystal just left the party," I whisper.

"Gee, I wonder where she's going?" Zander says.

We share a knowing smile. It's the worst kept secret on the tour: Brett and Crystal have been banging since the night of Reed's party and they're showing no signs of slowing down.

I press my pelvis into Zander's underneath the water, hoping to inspire him to decide to fuck me the way Brett's apparently about to fuck Crystal upstairs. "So, did you and Keane talk about the bet, by any chance, Mr. Bodyguard?"

Zander's nostrils flare as my body rubs against his hard-on. "We did."

My clit is throbbing like crazy as Zander's erection grinds against me just right. "*And?*"

"And the bet continues."

"Boo. Collusion."

Zander chuckles. "Nope. I put my eyeballs right up to the screen and answered every one of Keane's questions and he determined I was telling him the truth: I'm *not* in love with you."

"Bullshit. You're madly in love with me and we both know it."

Zander grinds his hard dick into me slowly—like he's fucking me on a lazy Sunday morning after having fucked me raw the prior

156

night. "Nope," he says, his erection pressing right against my bull's-eye. "Apparently, there's one pickle on planet earth who's resistant to your endless charms, Aloha Carmichael. Sorry to disappoint you, Little Miss Pickle Collector."

He's such a liar. A sexy liar whom I want to lick from head to toe. I press myself even tighter around his torso. "I've got news for you, Z: that pickle ain't resisting nothin'."

He laughs. "My pickle? Not so much. My heart? Yes."

I lick my lips. "Offer accepted. I'll gladly take your pickle today and snatch up your heart tomorrow."

The winning duo from my earlier chicken match bounds over to us, splashing and shit-talking and challenging us to a game. Zander shoots me a rueful look before turning to the duo and launching into an enthusiastic round of trash-talking. But I can't join in on the fun. I'm too aroused. Too *desperate*. I don't want to play chicken. I don't want to do anything but get fucked by Zander Shaw.

"Come on, hula girl! Let's beat these damn fools!" Zander bellows, drawing me out of my horny stupor. He guides me off his chest and effortlessly swivels me around to his back. "Climb aboard, baby. It's whoopin' time."

I sigh, wishing I were hearing those words from him—*climb aboard, baby*—in an entirely different, and naked, context. But, of course, I do as I'm told. As he lowers himself into the water, I slide my thighs onto his broad shoulders on either side of his head, thereby pressing my pulsing, aching, *desperate* clit into the back of his strong neck.

Zander grips my thighs and rises to his full, glorious height. "Show no mercy, hula girl!"

I grip his head. "I know of no other way, Shaggy Swaggy."

And away we go. There's splashing, pushing, and wrangling galore with the other duo. Shit-talking and squealing and laughing, too, as well as cheers and boos from onlookers. And, finally, after a fierce battle, Zander and I prevail over our insipid opponents. *Of course.* Because he's a gladiator and I'm a warrior princess and together we're magic. But if I thought winning the match would keep me from being dunked into the pool, I was sorely mistaken. Right after our opponents are toppled, Zander whoops, tilts back like a felled redwood, and gracelessly crashes both of us into the pool.

My sudden entry into the water sends my bikini bottoms yanking down, but before I've got them back into place, Zander is already scooping me into his arms and twirling me around.

The minute Zander stops spinning me, I hastily pull my bikini bottoms up, trying to keep my lady bits from peeking out. But I'm clearly not fast enough because Zander's gaze is squarely on my pelvis.

"Aloha," he whispers, his voice tight.

Thinking my vag must be hanging out, I look down and discover what's got Zander's attention: a dastardly scab—the healing mark from a deep, vertical scratch on my hip that's now plainly visible due to the displacement of my bikini bottoms. Quickly, I snap my suit over the mark... but Zander is a bloodhound on the scent.

"How'd you get that scratch?"

"Huh?"

"The scratch on your hip. It's healing well, but how'd you get it in the first place?"

"Oh, *that*." I roll my eyes. "During a costume change backstage in Phoenix. I was walking past a wardrobe rack and there was this metal thingy sticking out and it got me."

"As you were walking past?"

"Mmm hmm."

"In Phoenix?"

"Yep."

"I saw that scratch on opening night in LA—when I was helping you shower after Reed's party."

"*Oh.* Yeah. I meant LA. Pfft. All the shows begin to blur together after a while."

"So if I asked Yana about this, she'd remember the incident?"

"I don't think Yana was there."

"But you said it was a costume change."

"I don't think Yana was there that one time. I don't remember who was there."

Zander's eyes are like lasers. He knows as well as I do that Yana, my costume mistress backstage, never misses a step.

"And you were walking past a wardrobe rack?"

My stomach clenches. Why is he so fixated on this? "Yep. I was in my teeny-tiny undies doing a rushed costume change. In fact, now

I remember: I was so rushed, I didn't even wait for Yana to get there—and there was this little pokey thing sticking out of the wardrobe rack and it dug really deep into my hip as I walked past. Hurt like a motherfucker at the time, but it doesn't hurt now. I'd honestly forgotten about it until you pointed it out. It seems to be healing pretty well, luckily."

"Did someone put ointment on it? Who helped you after it happened?"

My heart is pounding. "Nobody helped me. There was no time. I had to get back onstage. And then I didn't mention it to anyone because I just forgot about it. It was just a scratch, Zander. No big deal. I know you're my bodyguard and all, but I promise nobody will hold you responsible for *literally* every little scratch I might get, especially the ones I get from being a klutz." I smile but Zander doesn't return the gesture. He just stares into my eyes for a long beat, his jaw frozen, like he's waiting for me to say more. Like he's waiting for me to confess that I'm full of shit. But I say nothing. At least, not about my traitorous scratch. "So, hey, Shaggy Swaggy," I say brightly. "How about you give me a little piggyback ride around the pool? Or, even better, you give me a piggy*front* ride so we can continue what we started before our chicken match."

Still, Zander doesn't speak. His eyes are laser beams, boring holes into my face. His gaze is unsettling. Unrelenting. *Unconvinced.* He's a PET scan in search of cancer cells. An ultraviolet light in search of blood splatters on a murder suspect's T-shirt. But, fuck him, he can glare at me all he likes. I got scratched walking past a wardrobe rack and that's all there is to it.

"Piggy*front* ride, it is*,*" I say. With a big smile, I slide my arms around Zander's neck and arrange myself around him like a baby in a Baby Bjorn, the same as usual. And, instantly, I'm a horny little monkey climbing my favorite tree, once again. I press myself into Zander's wet, slick, muscular body. "Now, where were we, sexy man?"

Zander lets out a shaky breath and I know I've got him—hook, line, and boner. He's not thinking about my stupid scratch anymore. He's thinking about my almost naked body pressing against his. The sensation of our wet flesh rubbing delectably under the water. The nearness of our lips.

159

"Aloha," Zander whispers.

His erection rises between us and presses against my happy spot. He nestles himself firmly at my entrance and exhales a shaky breath.

Oh, God, all of a sudden, I can't stand this game of cat and mouse another minute. I want him to push the crotch of my bikini bottoms to the side, to bare my entrance to him, and burrow himself inside me right here and now. Nobody will see. The pool lights underneath the water have turned everyone in the pool into darkened silhouettes in the night.

Zander begins grinding into me like before, like he's fucking me on a lazy Sunday morning, and, once again, jolts of pleasure shoot straight to my tip. I moan and he begins grinding me with even more enthusiasm.

Oh, God, I can't take it anymore. Yes, I promised to hold back and let him make the first move, but I'm hanging on by a thread here. In fact, I've been hanging on by a thread for weeks.

Still grinding against him under the water, I skim my lips against his cheek and bite his ear, taking his diamond stud into my mouth and sucking on it. "Hey, Mr. Magic Fingers," I whisper into his ear. "Hypothetically, do you think you could make a girl come in a swimming pool by touching nothing but the outside of her bikini bottoms?"

He slides a palm to my lower back, just above my ass. He's trembling. "*Hypothetically*? Yes. I'm sure of it."

"Even a girl who's never had an orgasm with partner?"

"Absolutely."

I grind myself against his bulge harder, until my clit is throbbing almost painfully. "Prove it."

He exhales sharply... and, as he does, I can palpably *feel* the last shreds of his self-restraint leaving him. His body twitching, he wordlessly slides a hand between my legs over the fabric of my bathing suit bottoms—*hallelujah!*—and when his expert fingers find my hard, swollen tip, he doesn't hesitate. He begins rubbing the bud around and around in tiny circles. Instantly, he's ignited me. I groan at the incredible sensation and Zander replies with a long, shuddering, sexy moan.

"Oh, God," I choke out.

"Good?"

I dig my fingernails into his broad shoulders. "So good."

He doesn't let up. He just keeps on going. And, soon, I'm on the cusp. I moan loudly. So loudly, he clamps his free hand over my mouth. And that simple act turns me on. I bite his fingers. Lick them. Gnaw at him. And all the while his fingers are doing magical things to me underneath the water.

"Here it comes," I blurt. I inhale sharply, stiffen in Zander's arms, and blissfully come. It's the first time a man has brought me to orgasm in my life. And it feels amazing.

When the delicious waves of pleasure cease, I open my eyes to find Zander's dark eyes smoldering at me like burning coals. He removes his hand from my crotch and I press my center enthusiastically into his hard-on, every fiber of my body yearning for him to penetrate me.

"Zander," I purr, just as some dancers make a commotion nearby—a splashing commotion—that reminds me we're not alone. I clear my throat and speak at full voice, loud enough for anyone nearby to overhear. "I think I'm done swimming for the night. You wanna come to my room to watch a movie, Zander?"

"That sounds great, Aloha," Zander says, his rock hard dick pressing against me.

"Why don't we head to our respective rooms, take showers and change into pajamas, and then meet at my room in, oh, about twenty?"

Zander pauses, just long enough to make me think he might throw on the brakes. But then he grinds his cock into me with a particularly enthusiastic thrust, squeezes my ass cheek with gusto, and says, "I'll see you then."

Chapter 28
Zander

I reach Aloha's door, knowing full well I shouldn't walk through it if I want to keep my dick in my pants and my heart in my chest. And maybe even if I want to keep my job. But, fuck it, there's no turning back now. After seeing Aloha's O face in the swimming pool and knowing I was the first man to see it... yeah, come what may—even if walking through that door ultimately leads to calamity for me, one way or another—wild horses couldn't keep me from doing it.

I knock on Aloha's door, and when she opens it, my shallow breathing hitches. She's wearing pink boy shorts and a white tank top. No bra. Her face is scrubbed and moisturized. Her light brown skin is luminous. Her hair is a tangle of waves. She's got a wicked gleam in her emerald eyes that tells me I'm toast. In short, she's sexy as fuck.

"Welcome to my lair," she says. She widens her door to me. *"Entrez vous."*

My brain knows I shouldn't do it, but Mr. Happy is running the show now.

I stride into the room.

"Would you like something to drink?" she asks.

I turn around to face her, my jaw tight. "No. I'm good."

"Then let's get into movie-watching position, shall we?" She literally leaps to the bed and then slowly crawls across it, arching her back and shoving her incredible ass into the air in her itty-bitty boy shorts as she goes. When she reaches the pillows at the head of the bed, she flips over onto her back, stretches her dancer's legs out to full length, pats the bed next to her, and coos, "Come heeeere, Shaggy Swaggy. I've found the perfect movie for our viewing pleasure."

Porn? The girl wants to watch a little porn before we get down to business? Not what I was expecting... but she'll get no argument from me. My heart pounding like a jackhammer, I crawl onto the bed and settle myself next to her.

"Guess what movie I've selected for us?" she says seductively. "I'll give you a hint: it's a romantic comedy from the eighties."

My eyebrows shoot up. Not what I was expecting. Did I misread this entire situation? Did Aloha actually invite me here to watch a movie?

With a little giggle, Aloha presses a button on her keyboard and the movie poster of her selection pops on her laptop: *The Sure Thing.*

Well, there it is. Plain as day. No more dancing around it.

Aloha indicates her screen. "I haven't seen this one yet, but I've heard from a reliable source it's a 'can't miss.'" She grins naughtily. "I'm dying to find out if my source is right about that."

I take a deep breath. Shit. Now that this moment has finally arrived in no uncertain terms, now that my toes are hanging over the bitter edge of the cliff and there's no denying it or walking away, it's suddenly clear to me I can't take this leap into the abyss—I can't take this *risk*—until I get an answer to a riddle that's been plaguing me for weeks now. A puzzle I'd pushed away and stuffed down but which reared its head in the pool again just now.

The thing is, if I'm gonna fuck Aloha—if I'm more than likely going to fall head over heels for the woman as my body enters hers— then I need to solve this riddle first. Because, as much as I wish it weren't the case, I need to know the truth about the woman I'll be falling for. *Who the fuck is Aloha Leilani Carmichael?*

I touch Aloha's thigh and she visibly jolts with excitement. "I'll do The Sure Thing to you if you answer one question first."

Aloha bites her lip seductively and nods, apparently thinking I'm going to ask her something naughty. Something flirty and *fun.* But that couldn't be further from the truth.

I place my fingertip under Aloha's chin. "How'd you get that scratch on your hip, Aloha?"

Her naughty smile vanishes. "I already told you how I got it."

"You told me a *lie* about how you got it. This time, I want the truth."

Aloha jerks her chin away from my finger, indignation overtaking her features. "If this is your idea of foreplay, Zander, I'm not impressed."

I take a deep, steadying breath. "Actually, yes, this *is* my idea of foreplay." I grasp her chin and guide her to look at me. "This is me wanting to know the real you—not the one you churn out on Twitter. Because the thing that turns me on the most, even more than the thought of peeling off those shorts of yours and sliding my fingers inside you and making you come, over and over again, is the idea of getting to do it to the *real* you." I grunt with exasperation. "Aloha, if I'm gonna get inside you, whether it's with my fingers, tongue, or dick—or with my very heart and soul—then I want to get inside *you* and not fucking 'Aloha Carmichael.' And that means I need you to drop your bullshit with me right now because I'm not gonna take this big a risk for the Twitter version of you."

Her chest is heaving. Her eyes are blazing. Everything about her body language reminds me of a trapped animal. "You're calling me a liar?"

"Yes. About this, I most certainly am."

Her nostrils flare. "I told you: I walked past a wardrobe rack backstage."

"My God, you're pathological. Lying straight to my face *again*."

"I'm not lying."

"You are. And you want to know how I know that for a fact?" I lean forward, my jaw tight. "Because it's physically impossible to get a *vertical* scratch on your hip while walking *past* a wardrobe rack. If the scratch had happened the way you said it did, then it would have been a *horizontal* scratch."

Panic flickers across her face. She looks down.

And, just like that, my anger dissipates, replaced by the overwhelming urge to protect her—to take her pain away, even if I'm the immediate cause of it. The truth is I'm taking no pleasure in calling out Aloha's bullshit. I'd much rather my instinct about this be dead wrong. But if she got shitfaced and got hurt somehow, or if somebody laid a finger on her or took advantage of her in a vulnerable state, then getting her to trust me enough to tell me what happened is way more important to me than finally getting to plunge my fingers or dick inside her. I grab Aloha's hand. "Did someone hurt you, sweetheart? If so, you don't have to protect whoever—"

"I did it to myself."

I freeze with my jaw hanging open for a long moment.

She exhales. "With a wine opener."

There's a very long beat of thick silence between us before I gather myself enough to say, *"On purpose?"*

Her eyes water. "Yes."

Holy... fuck. I open my mouth and then close it, too overwhelmed to speak.

Tears flood Aloha's eyes. "It was a one-time slip-up that won't happen again." She swallows hard. "I used to scratch and cut myself all the time, but I hadn't done it in years before this. It was just a blip, Zander. A brief moment of weakness that won't happen again. That's why I didn't tell you—because that's not *me*. Not anymore. And I didn't want to have to explain my whole backstory to you and have you think I'm back in that same headspace again. Because I'm *not*."

I suddenly realize Aloha just used the word "cut." *She used to cut herself all the time.* I've heard that term before... *cutting.* In relation to one of Zahara's friends cutting her arms in middle school. But I've never personally known anyone who did it. And from what little I know about it, I thought people did it to their arms, like Zahara's friend, not their *hips*. "You used to scratch your hips all the time?"

"No, never. This was a first. When I was younger, as a teen, I used to cut and scratch my arms. I only did it to my hip this one time because I knew the tour was coming and I'd be wearing skimpy costumes and I didn't want anyone to be able to see the mark. It wasn't a cry for help. I didn't want anyone to know. I just did it because... " But she trails off and rubs her face.

"Because...? Tell me. *Please.*"

Aloha looks up. "To relieve stress. To get back at my mother. It's really hard to explain."

"Try. Please."

She looks down again. She's shaking. Clearly, she's holding back a tidal wave of emotion.

Oh, God, my heart is bleeding. I wanted the real Aloha? Well, clearly, I just got her. And she's a wounded little animal that breaks my heart. I stroke her hair and coo softly at her, luring my wounded little animal out of the shadows toward the treat I'm holding in my palm. And, finally, after several minutes of gentle prodding and reassuring, Aloha looks up and threads her fingers in mine.

She takes a deep breath. "It was three nights before opening night. And I was feeling especially stressed out about the tour. I knew it was gonna be my biggest one, ever. The biggest arenas. The highest production values and cost. The highest expectations. All of it riding on my teeny-tiny little shoulders." She wipes her eyes. "So, like an idiot—a glutton for punishment—I called Satan to ask her to please, please, just this once, drop what she was doing and fly to LA to come to my first show. But she said no. She and her boyfriend were on a yacht in Greece—taking a vacation bank-rolled by all the money she's 'earned' over the years as my 'manager.' A 'manager' who hasn't done a fucking thing for me in three years, by the way, because I hired an actual manager but kept her on the payroll because she made me feel like doing otherwise would make me the worst daughter in the world."

"Didn't you say your mom's boyfriend is a billionaire?"

"I lied. He's just some twenty-five-year-old dude with washboard abs who's trying to 'break into modeling.'" She snorts through her tears. "My mother pays for everything for him, all of it bankrolled by the money I pay her and the millions she stole from me when I was a minor." Her face turns hard. "I've actually never told anybody that part—that my mother stole millions from me. But she did. My lawyers have told me to sue her ass for embezzlement. But I'd never do that. She might be Satan, but she's still my mother. Plus, I don't need the whole world knowing my dirty laundry."

"Oh, Aloha."

"I'm sorry I lied to you about her boyfriend. I was just so embarrassed. I've always lied about my mother's men my whole life. To everyone. Not just you. My mother's always had what I'd call a defective picker." She rolls her eyes. "So, anyway, that night when I scratched myself, I was sitting in my hotel room, crying about Satan not coming to my show. Crying about the fact that she's my mother at all—about the years and years she's made me feel like nothing but the Bank of Aloha. And, like I said, I was feeling stressed about the tour and..." She sighs. "So, I grabbed a wine opener off the bar and scratched my hip. And the minute I did it, I felt terrible about it. Ashamed. I felt no relief at all, only more pain. And that's when I promised myself I was done forever and would never do it again. And I won't, Zander. I really won't."

My chest is heaving. I move my lips, but nothing comes out, so I clamp them shut.

"Remember when you came to my room the other night?" she says. "That night I was crying and didn't want to let you in? I was crying because I'd just had a horrible phone call with my mother. But guess what? Instead of turning the pain on myself like I'd done that prior time with the wine opener, this time, I handled my emotions the right way. The way my therapist taught me in treatment way back when. I poured the pain into my poetry. I talked to Barry. I took a hot bath and relaxed and went to bed. And when I woke up the next morning, I felt different. *Stronger*. I felt like I'd walked through fire and come out the other side. And that's when I knew for a fact I won't do it again, because if ever there was a time when I was going to slip up and do it again, it was after that horrible, disgusting conversation with my mother. *And I didn't do it.*"

"What was the conversation with your mother about that second time?"

Aloha pauses.

My stomach clenches. "Aloha, please."

She exhales. "You."

"*Me?*"

"My mother thought when I called you my boy toy in that *TMZ* video, I was actually taking a coded swipe at her boyfriend—sending her a secret 'fuck you' for not coming to my LA show." She scoffs. "Because she's the center of the universe, apparently. I couldn't possibly have just been drunk and stupid." She shakes her head. "My mother said all kinds of horrible things to me. She said I'd acted like a 'little whore.' She said my fans would be ashamed of me and ditch me." Her face hardens. "She said I'd committed career suicide by linking myself to a 'nobody' like you."

My heart falls into my toes. Well, there it is. *A nobody like me.* The pink elephant that dances through every room I'm in with Aloha, at one point or another, whether she realizes it or not. I'm a nobody fitness trainer from Seattle and she's a huge star. And being linked to me—for *real*—would be positively unthinkable in her world. I clear my throat. "This from the woman traipsing around the world with some 'nobody' male model twenty years her junior?" But I'm bluffing. Fronting. In truth, Aloha's mother's words have leveled me.

167

"Ah, but you see, my mother isn't Aloha Carmichael. She doesn't have a 'brand' to uphold. She isn't a 'role model' to little girls who's expected to 'conduct herself at all times according to a higher standard of morality.'" She scoffs. "I got off that call with my mother and I was wrecked, Zander. I shouldn't give a shit what she thinks of me, not by now, but hearing my own mother call me a little whore... It made me want to cut open my skin and let her DNA seep out of me. It made me want to cut my other hip to relieve the pain. But I resisted the urge to hurt myself because I knew doing it would only make me feel *worse* in the end. That's what I'm telling you: *I didn't do it.* I was able to think clearly and remember that hurting myself doesn't actually hurt her, only me. I realized I'm done hurting myself. I want to be happy. She always wants to drag me down. She wants my very soul, but she can't have it." She flashes me a look of pure defiance... a look of heartbreaking vulnerability mixed with breathtaking badassery that cracks my heart wide open.

And that's it.

Snap.

The last dangling thread breaks.

In a torrent, all the love I've been holding back and stuffing down and denying for weeks floods every nook and cranny and crevice of my body, heart, mind, and soul. I'm officially a goner. Toast. Done. For weeks, I've been telling myself what I was feeling for Aloha wasn't real. That my emotions were situational. Temporary. A projection. A *wish*. But now, in this instant, looking at this beautiful, flawed, vulnerable, and yet tough-as-nails creature, I can't hold back my feelings a second longer. *I love her.* My heart is hers to do with as she pleases—even if that means she's going to put it into a wood chipper.

A tear falls down Aloha's cheek. "I'm sorry you're finding out all this stuff about me. I like you thinking I'm perfect and have it all together. But the truth is I'm fucked-up and not worthy of being a role model for anybody."

I wipe her cheek with my thumb. "Thank you for telling me. If you're seeing horror on my face, it's not that I'm horrified by you. It's that I'm struggling with how to process this. If anyone else had gouged your flesh with a wine opener, I'd hunt the bastard down and rip their fucking head off. But now that I'm finding out *you're* the

168

bastard who hurt my baby, my brain doesn't know how to react to that news. How the hell do I protect you from *you*?"

Aloha bites her lip. "I'm your baby?" She smiles through her tears. "I'm the bastard who hurt 'your baby'?"

How the hell did I let that slip out? Realizing I love this girl with all my heart and soul is one thing. Letting her know how I feel is another thing entirely. I press my lips together, hoping Aloha will fill the awkward silence by saying something like "You're my baby, too!" Or "Hell yeah, I'm your baby, Zander Shaw!"

But Aloha doesn't say a word.

I let out a long exhale of surrender and whisper, "You know you're my baby." But somehow, thank God, I manage to say nothing more.

Aloha nods, ever so subtly, but doesn't speak.

"What did you use to cut your arms as a teenager?" I ask.

"A razor blade."

I grimace.

"But I barely broke the skin. I only made the shallowest little marks, each one an eighth of an inch apart. I didn't really want to hurt myself. I just wanted my mother to *see*."

"You did this a lot?"

She nods. "Watch any episode of *It's Aloha!* from season six and I'm wearing long sleeves to hide the cuts."

I'm absolutely flabbergasted. "People from the show *knew* you were hurting yourself?"

"Everyone knew."

"Your *mother*?"

"Of course. But I was in every scene of the show and we had a tight shooting schedule. Sending the fucked-up star of a show about a perfect girl to a month-long in-patient treatment program was unthinkable until the entire season was in the can. And even then, it had to be a huge secret to protect the image of the show. But no biggie, right? Why stop production on a cash cow TV show and lose all that worldwide revenue when you can simply cover the annoying star's pesky cuts with pretty hippie-shirts with flowing long sleeves?"

I grab her forearms and turn them over, baring the insides of her forearms to me. Now that I know what I'm looking for, I think *maybe* I see the tiniest scars on her smooth flesh. Or am I imagining those nearly invisible lines?

"I actually started a huge fashion trend that season. Little girls all over the world started wearing flower-child blouses with flowing long sleeves. Because who wouldn't want to be just like Aloha Carmichael?"

I release her arms, shaking my head. I feel physically ill.

Aloha says, "I finally went to rehab when season six wrapped. And it was a Godsend for me. I had tons of therapy and got on meds. But, most importantly, I was encouraged to write poetry every day—to pour my pain onto the pages of my journal instead of turning it onto myself."

"Explain the pain to me, Aloha. And tell me why hurting yourself relieved it."

"I'm not sure I *can* explain it."

"Please, try."

She pauses for a long moment to gather herself and then says, "In my early teens, I started to feel this inexplicable pain inside me. I knew I had no right to feel it. I was on a hit TV show. I had money. Fame. 'Everybody' loved me. But, still, I felt it. I felt lonely. Abandoned. And worst of all, I felt like a fraud. It was hard to be an imperfect, pained teenager playing a perfect, happy one on TV. I felt like a liar every day of my life. And I had absolutely no one to talk to about any of it. So I'd sometimes secretly cut my arms at night. And, somehow, that gave me a tangible way to explain the pain to myself. I gave myself an actual reason for the pain—a hook where I could hang it." She sighs. "When I was little, if I cried about going to an audition, or if I cried because I was too tired to learn my lines or because I wanted to play instead of go to work, my mother would grab my shoulders really, really hard and lean into my face and scream, 'I'll give you something to cry about!' So, I guess, in a twisted sort of way, I gave myself something to cry about. Does that make sense?"

"It does, actually."

"When I felt really stressed out or my heart felt particularly achy, hurting myself always helped. Briefly. When I opened my skin, I could imagine the pain bleeding out and leaving me. I could imagine the poison of my mother's DNA seeping out. I could finally *understand* the pain, if only for a moment. But, of course, the relief didn't last long, so I'd wind up doing it again."

"What about when you dragged that wine opener across your hip? Did that give you relief?"

"No. It was the first time I felt worse immediately after doing it. All I felt was disappointment in myself. Shame. A *lack* of control. Like I'd let my mother win. I knew I'd fucked up and done something I could never do again. So I wrote a poem about it and fell asleep. And when I woke up, I felt like I'd made it through a sort of baptism. And I promised myself I'd never do it again—and I won't."

"I'm surprised you cut your arms as a teen—a place on your body that was so visible. You were the star of a hit TV show. The whole world was watching. Obviously, you wanted the world to see."

"Oh, absolutely. It was a plea for *someone* to notice and help me. My mother. The people who worked on my show. The people watching at home. I just wanted someone to *please* notice the marks and *save* me. But all that happened is my mother had the costume designer cover the marks with long sleeves and we went on like business as usual." She wipes her cheeks. "I should probably mention another piece of this: I took great pleasure in messing up my appearance in a visible way. Because I knew it would piss off my mother to no end. Growing up, I always had to look perfect. If I gained a little weight, my mother put me on diet pills and forbade me to have so much as a cookie. If I had a zit, my mother instantly whisked me off to the dermatologist for an injection. So, clearly, part of it was me wanting to fuck up my body to hit my mother where it counted to her the most—in her money-maker. Honestly, I'm surprised I didn't cut my face and pretend I'd been attacked or maybe shave my head like Britney. I had the urge to do both more than a couple times." She sighs. "But, like I said, when I cut my hip, I realized I'd taken things too far and could never do it again. That I didn't even *want* to do it again. I can't let her win anymore. I shouldn't have let her get to me during that horrible 'boy toy' conversation the other day. Her opinion doesn't matter."

My heart is suddenly clanging. "There's more to that conversation than you've told me, isn't there? She said something else about me, specifically, didn't she?"

Aloha smashes her lips together, confirming my suspicion.

"She's a racist?" I choke out.

Aloha scoffs. "Oh, God, no. It's not that. You could be green with three heads and she'd adore you, just as long as you're someone who can advance my career and therefore pad her bank account." She rolls her eyes. "In my mother's world, I can only be linked to someone with more money and power than me. Someone with more platinum records and fans than me. Someone with whom I can merge Instagram and Twitter followers and take over the world."

Aloha chuckles, but I don't join her. Because even if Aloha doesn't realize it, she's just confirmed she's been brainwashed her entire life to believe normal, non-celebrity guys like me can never be relationship material to her. She might think she doesn't give a shit what her mother says, but that deep scratch on her hip made only a month ago tells a different story.

"You want to read the poem I wrote the night I scratched my hip?" she whispers.

My heart lurches into my throat. "Of course."

Her chest visibly heaving, she rolls onto her side toward the nightstand and grabs a pink journal out of a drawer. She flips through the book for a moment, stops at a specific page, and hands it to me. "You said you want the real Aloha. Careful what you wish for. The 'Pretty Girl' ain't so fucking pretty."

I take the journal from her, adrenaline surging inside me. "Thank you for trusting me with this." My heart clanging wildly and my body visibly quaking, I look down at Aloha's handwritten words.

The Money Tree

Oh, glorious pain
Engravings made in fractions of inches
Bleeding crimson and glitter and
Shining a floodlight on what's hiding
Beneath this flesh in plain sight.
This marking made is a quiet rebellion,
A silent confession that the blinding lights
Of this rarified life so often feel more like
A sniper's munitions than evidence
Of the world's collective adoration.
This cut a slicing reminder that this spotlight
Was neither designed nor invited by me
But supposed and imposed upon me
Unilaterally at the tender age of three.

How could a child who desired nothing more
Than to please be acclimatized to self-realize
When the Woman Who Named Her Destiny
Spied the green in her eyes and surmised
Nothing more than the fertile seeds
Of a Hello and Goodbye Money Tree?
I was a three-year-old seedling
Bred to bloom Benjamins,
A sapling adorned with leaves of dollar bills.
My roots were fertilized not by sunshine and love
But by Instagram followers, greed, and diet pills.
And now this tree that is me blooms vigorously,
My branches wild and touching the sky,
Which perhaps is the reason why no one ever seems
To wonder how come the Woman Who Named Her Destiny
Never stopped to ask or ponder, really,
Whether the three-year-old with eyes of green
Actually wished to grow up to become a money tree
Or if, maybe, just maybe, instead,
There was something else she herself
Might have wished she would one day
Grow up
To be.

Chapter 29
Aloha

I'm trembling as I watch Zander read my poem—stuffing down the urge to snatch the book from his hands and shout "Never mind!" What kind of sorcery has Zander performed on me to make me hand him that sacred book? I've never even shown my poetry to Barry!

Zander looks up from my journal. His full lips are parted, his eyes on fire. "This is incredible, Aloha. You're gifted. A true artist."

I clutch my chest, absolutely overwhelmed. "Thank you."

Zander lays down my journal and takes my cheeks into his large palms. "You're never allowed to hurt yourself again. Do you understand me? As your bodyguard, I won't allow it. And as the man who... cares... *deeply* about you... I forbid it. If you're in pain, then write some more kickass poetry, just like this. And if writing isn't doing the trick on any given day, then come to me and talk to me or cry on my shoulder. And if that doesn't work—if you still feel the need to dig into some flesh to get the pain out—then dig into mine. Cut me, Aloha. Scratch me. *Hurt me*. I can take it. Just so long as I know it'll prevent you from ever hurting yourself again."

"I'd never hurt you," I whisper, just before his greedy mouth lands on mine.

He grips my face and slides his tongue into my mouth as his lips devour mine, and, just that fast, a tsunami of passion and yearning like nothing I've felt before crashes down on me, consuming my every nerve ending and heartbeat. As our tongues swirl and tangle, desire envelops me like a pyre. *I want him.*

His breathing ragged and his entire body trembling, Zander guides me onto my back, crawls on top of me, nestling the hard bulge behind his pants firmly against my clit. I wrap my arms around his strong neck and hoist my thighs around his ribcage and dry hump the tented bulge behind his pants as vigorously as he's dry humping me.

"Condom," I choke out into his hungry lips.

He kisses my neck furiously. "In the nightstand?"

"I don't have any," I gasp out. "Get one of yours."

Zander's hulking body stiffens and freezes on top of me. And, instantly, I know what his body language means.

I jerk back from our kiss, incredulous. "*No.*"

He sighs.

"*You're joking.*"

"I'm not, unfortunately."

I wack him on the shoulder. "*You came to my room tonight without a motherfucking condom?*"

"I didn't bring any on the tour! You were off-limits! This was gonna be a three-month de-foxification!"

"Oh my fucking... After what happened in the pool, you knew you were coming here to fuck me! And you didn't think to swing by the little store in the lobby before coming to my room?"

"I didn't want anyone to see me buying them. And I didn't know *for sure* I was coming here to fuck you. I hoped so. But I didn't want to assume it or jinx it. I figured if we got this far, you'd have one and we'd be good to go."

"Well, I *don't* have one and we're *not* good to go, goddammit! We're fucked and not in a good way!"

He laughs. "Well, why the fuck don't *you* have one, little miss seductress? After what happened in the pool, you *knew* I was coming here to fuck you."

"I didn't know for sure. I hoped, but after all your jabbering about me being off-limits, I thought it was fifty-fifty you'd throw on the brakes. I figured if we got this far, you'd have a freaking condom and we'd be good to go!"

Zander chuckles and sighs. "Well, damn." He smooths a stray hair off my forehead. "No worries. There's plenty I can do to you without a condom. Actually fucking you is only one of the tricks up my sleeve."

I return his naughty smile. "The Sure Thing?"

"No, I don't think tonight's the night for that, actually. I think tonight is when I'm gonna eat your sweet little pussy until I make it rain all over my face."

A shiver of desire races up my spine. "Do with me what you will, Mr. Sex God."

"Oh, I intend to."

He peels off my clothes, leaving me naked and writhing on the bed, and quickly proceeds to devour my breasts and nipples. After a while, he kisses his way down my torso to my inner thighs. And then to my folds. He sucks on them. Nibbles and teases. But he never touches my clit—much to my torture.

Still licking around and near my aching bull's-eye, he slides a couple fingers inside me—and, instantly, my nerve endings zap like live wires. I arch my back and moan. *"Please."*

With his free hand, he pushes my thighs wide, opening me all the way—and then, glory be, he leans in and tongues my bared clit with an intensity that makes me cry out with pleasure. Just a few enthusiastic licks later, and I come. *Hard.* And now I know: the wicked orgasm Zander gave me in the pool wasn't a fluke. He's a man who knows exactly what he's doing and can do it at will.

"So good," I grit out. "Oh, God, *yes.*"

To my surprise, despite my obvious orgasm, Zander doesn't let up on me, either with his fingers or tongue. He just keeps right on eating and fingering me, all the while pushing my thighs apart so he can invade and explore every nook and cranny of me with zeal. And my body is responding like never before. The pleasure he's giving me is slithering up and down my every nerve ending and pooling almost painfully in my clit and core. The build-up of pleasure inside me is so intense, in fact, it's turning me into a ravenous animal, a wanton creature whose sole reason for existence is getting penetrated by Zander's cock—that heart-palpitating bulge straining behind his gray sweatpants.

When Zander slides up to my face to kiss me passionately, I slide my hand into his sweatpants and pull his erection out his elastic waistband—and when I see it bared to me, and the way it's straining toward me and glistening at its tip, my mouth literally waters. I grip Zander's shaft and stroke it up and down, eager to give him pleasure the way he's been giving it to me. I swirl the wetness pooled on Zander's tip, and he jerks and moans in reply.

After a moment, Zander places his hand on my wrist, stopping the hand job I'm giving him. "I don't wanna come," he grits out. "I wanna be hard while I eat you out some more. It turns me on the most to be hard and aching while I make you come."

A shiver of arousal flashes across my skin. I release his cock and nod.

"Get on your hands and knees, sexy girl," he growls. "I'm not done eating you yet. I wanna eat you from every possible angle. I wanna taste every inch of you in every possible way."

Without hesitation, I take the position he's instructed.

"I'm gonna make you feel better than you've ever felt before, beautiful girl," Zander coos behind me, stroking my ass cheeks with his fingertips. When he fondles my slit, I shudder and moan. Anticipate. *Yearn.* Finally, he leans forward and I feel his wet, warm tongue begin licking up and down my entrance a few times, like he's licking a lollipop, and then off he goes, devouring another full meal.

Oh, God, it's too much pleasure. I can't bear it. I dip down to my forearms with my ass up, too turned on, too frazzled and frenzied, to hold myself up any longer, and he responds by opening my folds wide with his fingers—wider than I knew I could be spread—and eating me with even more zeal.

Pleasure tightens inside me. Rises up and threatens to boil over. It rises and rises higher and higher, filling every crevice and stretching my nerve endings to near breaking... until, finally, my core cracks wide open like a thunderclap and begins warping with pleasure from my deepest depths.

Ecstasy.

That's what I'm feeling. It's gripping me and not letting go.

Ecstasy.

Pleasure that feels supernatural. Inexplicable. Inhuman.

I collapse onto the mattress into a sweaty heap, gasping for air and moaning wildly. I flop over onto my back and what I see takes my breath away. He looks like a beast. He's breathing hard. Even harder than me. His huge, hard dick straining out of his lowered sweatpants looks ready to physically blast off his body. It's mushroom tip is wet and shiny and drawing my mouth like a dripping popsicle.

"That was The Sure Thing?" I gasp out.

"No. The Sure Thing isn't oral. And it's not about your clit." He smiles like a shark. "Patience. I'm still enjoying eating your pussy way too much to stop."

He lies on the bed next to me on his back. "Now come sit on my face, baby. I wanna fuck you with my tongue, nice and deep."

177

As aroused and excited as I am, I pause. I've never physically sat on a man's face before. Yes, I've received oral sex, but not by literally *sitting* on a man's face. That's just so... naughty. But when I look at Zander's gorgeous face and see the expression of unbridled rapture on it, I lose my inhibitions.

I crawl over his head and he guides me into position. And the moment I feel his tongue penetrating me, I feel like I've found my new favorite thing. The thing I'll no doubt daydream about all day tomorrow. Hell, for the rest of my freaking life. He adds his fingers into the mix, a maneuver that elicits a growling, keening, cooing sound from me—a sound I've never made before.

As I fuck Zander's face, sweat trickles down the canyon between my breasts. My heart is beating a mile a minute. Every inch of my skin is on fire. My eyes devour his muscled body splayed out in front of me. The tight T-shirt covering his torso. His bulging, tattooed biceps peeking out of his sleeves. His dark cock straining out the front of his sweat pants. Why the fuck isn't Zander naked like me? Being naked while he's clothed is making me feel like nothing but his plaything—

A massive orgasm hits me, without notice.

"I'm coming!" I choke out, gripping Zander's biceps for dear life. And Zander growls his excitement underneath me.

When the waves of pleasure stop throttling me, Zander doesn't let up. He keeps right on going. And, soon, I'm in a frenzy—snapping my hips forward and back on top of his face like a madwoman. But it's quickly clear his tongue isn't nearly enough for me anymore. *I want his cock.* But since that's not gonna happen without a condom, I lean over Zander's torso, grip his hard dick poking out of his sweatpants, and begin sucking on him with my ass jutting straight up in the air above Zander's face. He's too big for me to get completely into my mouth without gagging myself, but I consume as much of him as I possibly can. I feel inspired. I want to give this man a blowjob he'll never forget. I swirl my tongue. Suck and lick. I devour him with everything I've got. And, soon, Zander's bucking and gyrating beneath me like I'm electrocuting him.

"I'm gonna blow, baby," he chokes out. "Oh, fuck, Aloha. I'm gonna come into your mouth if you keep going."

"Mmm hmm."

I double down, making it clear his release into my mouth is

precisely my endgame, even though, honestly, swallowing has never been my preferred ending to this particular game. Actually, neither has spitting, to be honest. But right now, with Zander, there's nothing I'd rather be doing than pushing him over the edge until I'm swallowing down every drop of him.

I voraciously shove my hand into the depths of Zander's sweatpants and fondle his balls and taint as I continue to blow him... and that's the last straw for him, apparently. Ten seconds after my hand invades his sweatpants, his balls tighten in my palm, his dick jolts in my mouth, he lets out a sound of pure euphoria—a sound unlike any man has ever made with me before—a sound that tells me I *own* him—and then the beautiful man explodes into my mouth in a salty torrent that, quite frankly, shocks the living hell out of me in terms of volume and velocity.

My job well done, I begin climbing off him, but he grabs my pelvis from behind and stops me.

"Where ya goin', sexy girl?" he coos from behind my ass. "Not so fast. I wanna try something."

He pushes me forward ever so slightly, until my nose is hovering over his crotch and my ass is sticking up into the air. "You ready to come harder than you've ever come before?" he asks softly. Without waiting for my reply, he slides his fingers inside me and begins stroking a spot deep inside me... a spot that instantly makes my womb tighten and pulse. A spot I didn't know existed until just now.

"Oh, fuck," I gasp out.

"Listen to my voice," Zander says softly behind my ass, like a hypnotist dangling a pocket watch in my face... and then he proceeds to talk and talk. He tells me all manner of arousing things. That I'm beautiful, sexy, addicting. That my pussy tastes like honey. That my ass cheeks in his face are driving him wild. "Whenever I've wacked off this past month," he says, "I've fantasized about eating you. Fucking you. And touching you just like this until you're speaking in tongues."

My heart rate spikes. "This is The Sure Thing?"

"This is it, baby. Through the back door. Now take a deep breath and close your eyes and imagine me fucking you so hard from behind, my balls are banging against you with each thrust."

Oh, God. This man can dirty-talk like nothing I've experienced before. *I love it.*

In short order, Zander's slow-moving fingers inside me are positively owning me. His voice is luring me into some sort of alternate universe where I don't have free will. Muscles deep, deep inside me are tightening and coiling ferociously, straining like they're about to snap.

"Oh, God," I gasp out. "*Zander.*"

"That's it, sexy girl," he whispers calmly, his deep voice in complete control. "That's not my fingers you're feeling, that's the head of my cock pounding against you each time I thrust. Banging you right *here*. Again. And again."

My body stiffens.

Time stops.

"Oh, *fuck*," I gasp out. "Zander!"

And that's it.

Indescribable pleasure slams into me and warps my deepest muscles. If I thought the last orgasms were amazing, it was only because I hadn't felt *this* one yet. A flash of searing heat whooshes through me. Every muscle in my deepest core begins rippling. I begin babbling a slew of incoherent sounds. Warm liquid trickles out of me. And my limbs give out.

I crumple on top of Zander's sweaty body beneath me. *Heaven.* That's the word that comes to me through my rapturous haze. *Heaven.* Surely, I've died and gone there, and I've done it via slingshot at the speed of light.

When the waves of outrageous pleasure subside, I roll off Zander onto my back alongside him on the mattress with my head at his feet. I'm breathing like I've just run a sprint. Sweating profusely. Twitching with aftershocks. I wipe my brow. And then, finally, laugh with glee. "Holy fuck buckets, Zander Shaw!"

Zander chuckles. "Welcome to your first vaginal orgasm, baby. The holy grail. Amazing, right?"

I take a deep breath and exhale slowly, trying to control my racing heart. "Amazing. Oh my God." I run my palms down my torso and they come back soaking wet. "Dude, I'm dripping in sweat."

"Yup. Good things come to those who *sweat*."

I giggle. "That was the most amazing, delicious thing I've ever experienced in my entire life. It was supernatural."

Zander repositions himself so we're face to face and then he props himself up onto his forearm. "That was my first time doing The Sure

180

Thing from behind. I wasn't sure it would work from that angle, to be honest. I've only ever done it with the woman lying flat on her back. But I was getting off hard looking at your ass, so I decided to improvise."

"I think I might have peed a little bit in the throes of it. Sorry. I lost complete control for a minute there."

He laughs. "That wasn't pee. You squirted. Just a little bit, but it still counts as your first time."

"No freaking way."

"Yep. Trust me. I licked it off my fingers. Definitely not pee."

I blink several times in rapid succession, utterly shocked. "I'm a porn star."

He drags his fingertips down my belly. "I hate that women think that way. It's perfectly natural and not shameful at all. When a woman comes epically hard, it can happen to anyone. It just means you went to a brand-new place—a place where you let go completely and lost all inhibitions." He sighs. "And that's so hot, I can't even begin to tell you."

I'm dumbfounded. "I didn't even know it was possible for me."

Zander grins. "That's 'cause you've never been with *me*."

I shake my head, utterly blown away. "That was *by far* the best sex of my life. And we didn't even have sex!"

"Just think how much we have to look forward to next time."

Oh, thank God. After what I just experienced, my worst nightmare would have been for Zander to pull a page out of Kevin Costner's book and tell me he made a huge mistake and can't do it again.

Zander pokes my bellybutton. "I'd better let you get some sleep. The bus leaves for Seattle bright and early tomorrow morning." He pulls up his sweatpants and kisses me softly. "Thanks again for sharing your poem with me. It was amazing." He snickers. "And so was the blowjob." He laughs. "Talk about a one-two punch. *Damn, Gina.*" With a wink, he heads swiftly to the door.

"I had fun, Zander!" I blurt as he opens the door.

He looks over his shoulder, beams me a beautiful smile—a gorgeous smile that sends butterflies whooshing into my belly—and says, "Me, too, baby. Now get some sleep."

The minute he's gone, I put my hands over my face and laugh with glee for a solid minute before finally calling Kiera and shrieking, "Mission accomplished! And it was *sooo* fucking good!"

181

Chapter 30
Zander

I'm a tortured man, Peenie Weenie," I say to Keane on FaceTime. His blue eyes are groggy but full of sympathy. "If I'm this messed up without actually fucking her, I can't imagine how messed up I'm gonna be when I finally get inside her. When that happy day finally arrives, that woman is gonna own me lock, stock, and boner."

Keane yawns. "Hate to tell ya, but it sounds like she already does, sugar nuts."

It's ten minutes before seven in the morning. A half hour before I'm supposed to head to Aloha's room to escort her down to the bus for Seattle. I'm sitting in my hotel room, showered and dressed, my small rolling bag neatly packed. Keane is lying in his childhood bed in Seattle under a blue blanket that perfectly matches his eyes, his blonde hair rumpled and his face creased from sleep.

I rub my face and groan. "I'm exhausted, man. I couldn't sleep after I left Aloha's room last night. Finally, I just gave up trying and started my day at two a.m."

"What'd you do?"

"I texted with Dax for a bit, since it was already late morning for him. And then I went to the hotel gym and worked out for a solid three hours. And then I showered, dressed, and hightailed it across the street to a drug store to run the most important errand of my life."

"Buying a jumbo box of rubbers?"

"Bingo. I'll never *not* have a condom in my wallet again."

"Damn straight, you dumbshit. Ha! That should be our band name. Condom in My Wallet."

"Amen."

"So, how was Daxy when you texted with him?" Keane asks. "He's in Amsterdam now, right?"

"No, Berlin. He's doing great. He can't believe how 'People Like Us' is blowing up. Did you see it just cracked Top 20?"

"Yeah. And the music video is going viral, too. Our boys are legit rock stars, son. It's insanity."

"I know. Dax said people are starting to recognize him on the street."

"Not a shocker. Dax is kind of unmissable on his worst day and he looks like a rock god in that video." Keane laughs. "Did you see the YouTube comments? People are, like, 'I want to lick him from head to toe!' 'I want to have his baby!'"

"I know. Dax was laughing about some of the more aggressive comments—but mostly cringing. You know how he hates people focusing on his looks instead of his 'art.'"

"Yeah, well, if he didn't wanna trade on his looks to sell records, maybe he shouldn't have starred in a music video that's basically soft core porn."

"Right?"

We both laugh.

"Yeah, that's pretty much what Dax said," I say. "He was like, 'Um, I think maybe the music video was a little *too* sexy...? My bad.'"

We laugh again.

"Aw, he secretly loves the attention." Keane says. He yawns. "So, back to you and your insomnia, love muffin. Typically, when you can't sleep and decide to work out in the middle of the night, I know it's 'cause you're grappling with some serious pent-up sexual frustration. But since it sounds like the pop star sucked every drop of pent-up sexual frustration out of your body last night, I gotta think you're simply suffering from an acute case of 'over-thinking.'"

"Oh, God, Peenie, that's an understatement. If there was one night in my life when I coulda used a big fat blunt to dull my over-thinkin' brain, it was last night."

"You know what your problem is, baby doll? You're just too smart. If you were stupid as a box of rocks like me, *not* over-thinking things would be your natural state of being. Shit, I can't even remember the last time I came within a hair's breath of *under*-thinking things."

"You know what, Peenie? You gotta stop doing that. I know

183

you're kidding when you call yourself dumb, but if you do it enough, your subconscious is gonna start actually believing it."

"That's exactly what Maddy always says. She told me to quit it, too."

"Well, listen to her, you dumbshit. She's smart. Not dumb as a box of rocks, like you. Where is she, by the way?"

"She slept in Colby's old room last night." He rolls his eyes. "Mad Dog didn't feel 'comfortable' sleeping in the same bed with me under my parents' roof. Because, you know, my parents don't already know we're living in sin together in LA and bonin' the fuck outta each other every night, Lionel Richie Style."

I laugh. "Cut her some slack. She just wants to make a good impression with the people who might become her in-laws one day."

"Well, mission accomplished there. You should have seen Maddy with my mom last night when we were playing Hearts. It took us forever to get through a single round because my mom and Maddy were laughing so much together. If I didn't already know Maddy's The One before last night, I would have figured it out right then. There's nothing like seeing your dream girl being brought into the family fold before your eyes."

"Aw, that's so awesome, Peenie."

"My mom pulled me aside after the card game and was like, 'Don't live up to your penile nickname and mess this up for me, Keane Elijah!' And I was like, 'Mess it up for *you*?' And she goes, 'Yes. You can't do better than this one, Keaney. *I want her*!'" He belly laughs. "Gotta love the Momatron, especially when she's had a few glasses of merlot. But, come on. You didn't wake me up at chicken-thirty because you wanna hear about my mother. You called because you're a tortured man. Tell me what's got your over-thinkin' brain going into overdrive. I'll fix you."

I sigh. "To summarize, I'm terrified I'm hurtling at the speed of light toward another Daphne situation—only this time, much worse."

"So it's a done deal, then? You're in *lurve* with the pop star?"

"Gone, baby, gone. And you wanna know the craziest part? It wasn't finally getting to taste her that pushed me over the line. It wasn't even getting the best BJ of my life. It was the conversation I had with Aloha right *before* I got her clothes off that did me in."

"A conversation about what?"

"Sorry, love muffin. This is one of the rare times in our marriage I gotta keep the vault locked. She told me some really personal stuff."

"Aw, come on. NDAs don't apply between wives."

"It's not the NDA. It's that I can't betray her trust, not even for you."

Keane grins. "That was the right answer, son." He winks. "So did you tell Aloha she's your primordial destiny yet or what?"

"Of course not. I'm not an idiot. Why do you think I beelined outta there right after she and I finished messing around? I knew if I didn't get out of there on a rocket, I'd start babbling shit I couldn't stuff back in. And thank God I did that, too, because, just as I was leaving, Aloha goes, 'I had fun, Zander!'"

"Ooph."

"*Right*? If that's not code for 'This was nothing but a fling!' then I don't know what is."

"Meh. So what if she thinks you two are flinging from the rafters. All that means is you gotta keep flinging with her like it ain't no thang until you win her over. Keep your big mouth shut and your big cock hard and two months from now, her heart will be yours. I guarantee it."

"Mmm hmm. There's just one little problem with that genius wear-her-down-slowly-without-her-realizing-it strategy, son."

"Naw, it's foolproof. Trust me."

"The bet, motherfucker!" I bellow, much louder than I should. "That's what kept me awake last night. The stupid bet! Realizing that, if you call the bet in favor of the one-monthers, my entire strategy of laying low so as not to scare her off will fly right out the window."

"*Oh.*"

"Yeah, *oh*. I don't even wanna think about how badly it's gonna mess things up for me if you officially declare me 'in love with Aloha' before I'm ready to tell her myself—a full *two months* before I should even *think* about telling her!"

"Okay, you gotta calm down, sweet meat. I see your predicament, but—"

"'*My* predicament'? Fuck you, Peenie. It's a predicament you Morgan motherfuckers created! And now I'm screwed!"

Keane grimaces.

I exhale. "Peenie, listen to me. The last guy Aloha had a fling with on tour wound up falling for her, just like I have, and the nano-second he was stupid enough to tell her about his feelings, she ditched his ass like yesterday's fish special. And let's not forget Aloha read everyone's stupid texts after the 'boy toy' video and therefore knows there's an express elevator from my dick to my heart. Now that she and I finally got down to business last night, I'm sure she's gonna be watching me like a hawk for any sign I'm turning into a stage five clinger on her. *Which I am!* Which means that, no matter what, you absolutely *cannot* call the bet or you're gonna ruin my life."

"Okay, okay. Calm the fuck down. Jazeebabeebus. I won't call the bet."

I stop freaking out on a dime, my jaw slack. "You won't?"

"Of course not. Gimme some credit. I'm not stupid."

"You're serious?"

"Dude, do you really think I care more about my oath of judicial integrity than my wife's lifelong happiness?" He snorts. "I choose *you,* boo. Every time."

I let out the biggest sigh of my life. "Oh, thank God."

"No, thank *me.* God has nothing to do with it. Unless I'm God, which is entirely possible."

"Thank you, Peenie. That right there is why I love you the most."

"As you should." He smiles. "I'm a giver, sweet meat. It's a blessing and a curse."

"Oh, God. I'm so relieved." A reminder goes off on my phone and I look down at the time. "Shit, brother. I gotta get my ass to Aloha's room to escort her to the bus."

"Go be your badass bodyguard self, love muffin. I'll see you tonight."

"I can't wait. I'm gonna get Brett to cover me for a bit during the show so I can come say hi to everyone in the skybox."

"Kewl. Now don't forget, baby doll: absolutely no blurting 'I love you!' or 'You're my primordial destiny!' to Aloha at any time for the next two months. Unless, of course, she says the magic words to you first."

I take a deep, steadying breath. "Roger."

"Rabbit."

"Oh, hey. I almost forgot. There's a present I want to get Aloha, but I won't have a chance to get it myself since I'm stuck to her like glue. Can you get it for me when you and Mad Dog are out and about today or tomorrow? I wanna give it to Aloha tomorrow night at dinner."

"*That's* your idea of playing it cool with Aloha—giving her a present?"

I roll my eyes. "Will you get me the thing or not?"

"Yeah, of course. Just text me the info, Mr. Cool."

"Thanks. Bye, baby doll. I'll see you—"

There's a loud knock at my door—a loud knock followed by a deep, commanding voice barking my name.

"Oh, shit," I whisper to Keane, my eyes wide. "Barry's at my door."

"Oh, shit!" Keane whispers. "News about forbidden-fruit pussy-eating travels fast, huh?"

My mind is instantly reeling. Did Aloha tell Barry about last night? Is there a nanny-cam hidden in Aloha's room? Or, shit, did Aloha tell Crystal about last night... and then Crystal told Brett... who went straight to Barry...?

"Zander!" Barry shouts behind my door again.

"Coming!" *Fuck.* "Wish me luck, Peenie Baby. I'm pretty sure I'm about to get shitcanned. Or worse."

Keane blesses me with the sign of the cross. "Godspeed, Sir Zancelot. I hope and pray the only thing Barry is planning to do to you is fire your ass. But if not, may your balls rest in peace."

187

Chapter 31
Zander

"That's fucked up," I mutter.

I'm standing in my hotel room with Barry and Brett. As it turns out, Barry didn't fly to Portland first thing this morning to fire my ass for feasting on Aloha's pussy last night. In fact, it's now obvious Barry has no idea my tongue was firmly lodged inside his favorite hula girl mere hours ago. No, Barry hopped the first flight to Portland out of LAX this morning so he could personally tell Aloha—after first telling Brett and me—that during the wee hours this morning, some wack job broke into Aloha's empty house in the Hollywood Hills. But not to rob her. To throw himself a perverted little masturbation party.

Based on what the guy confessed to the cops, not to mention the trail of jizz he left behind at the scene, the sick fuck jacked off to completion three separate times in Aloha's house—in her bed, bathtub, and inside a pair of her thousand-dollar Christian Louboutin shoes. And in between jizzing, he also did God knows what with Aloha's panties and makeup and the designer clothes in her walk-in closets. And for his grand finale, he apparently danced around the house buck naked—other than wearing headphones blaring Aloha's music—pausing his dance routine only to rub himself against any surface he thought might, at some point, have been in contact with Aloha's ass cheeks.

"The fucker is being held in a psych ward," Barry says. "I'm told he won't be getting out any time soon. But, of course, Aloha's lawyers are already preparing paperwork for a restraining order, just in case."

"How did he get into Aloha's house?" I ask, my stomach churning. "Doesn't she have a security system?"

"He scouted out the house with long-range binoculars and hit pay dirt when he saw a housekeeper punch in the security code."

I rake a hand over my face and mutter, "Jesus Christ."

"Thank God AC wasn't home at the time," Barry says. "I can't even imagine what might have happened to her if..." He takes a deep breath, composing himself. Clears his throat. "The story hasn't leaked yet, but it will. I've told Crystal to keep AC away from her phone this morning, through any means necessary."

I pace the small room, too amped to stand still any longer. "Going forward, we can't settle for merely reacting to shit as it comes up, guys. We need to be able to spot lunatics like this before they come out of the woodwork."

"There was no way to predict this guy. He was a lurker. He never commented on anything online or otherwise brought attention to himself."

"But surely there *are* sick fucks who bring attention to themselves—guys who are openly obsessed with her online. Whoever those guys are, let's identify them and track their asses. At the very least, let's get their photos so we can see 'em coming a mile away if they come out of the woodwork and come at our girl."

"The PR team who handles AC's social media already alerts us when someone is a bit too fixated, and we alert the authorities. And that's really all we can do. Our job is to protect Aloha's physical safety. We've got to let the online experts track down the online kooks."

I scoff. "But the 'online experts' don't love her like we do, Barry."

Shit.

Did I just say that?

Brett is staring at me like I've just said something highly regrettable. Which means... yeah. I said it. I just admitted I love Aloha... out loud... to Barry. *Fuck.*

But Barry doesn't seem fazed. He says, "That's why I'm having Brett's buddy at the FBI look at AC's social media for us to see if anyone raises a red flag for him."

"No, a 'buddy' doing a favor isn't good enough. I want someone officially on this. Someone paid to make Aloha their top priority." An idea pings my brain. "Do you know Reed's hacker buddy from college, Henn?"

"Reed's mentioned him, but I've never met him."

189

My heart is lurching. "Henn tracked down someone for Keane's big brother, Ryan, a while back, and Ryan said the guy is a stone-cold genius."

"Reed always says the same. Coincidentally, I think Henn is coming to Aloha's show tonight. Reed mentioned his two best friends are coming tonight with a big group. I've gotta think Henn would be included in that group. But if not, I'll talk to Reed about flying Henn to Seattle tonight, so we can talk to him about the project in person."

I exhale. "Perfect."

Barry brings his massive hand to my shoulder. "Looks like the newbie's come a long way since training a month ago, huh?" He smiles. "Brett's been telling me you've been doing a great job—and now I can see for myself he's absolutely right."

"Thanks," I say, even though I know his praise is misguided. It's not accurate to say I've been doing a great job, actually, because Aloha isn't a *job* for me any longer. She's exactly what Barry demanded she be from day one: my mission from God.

Barry scrutinizes my face for a long beat. "You love her?"

I press my lips together. *Shit.*

Barry sighs. "Listen to me, Z. Love is a great thing in general. But in this business, it can make a guy do reckless and stupid shit."

"Or it can make a guy do his job even better," I blurt, and instantly regret it. Why did I say that? It's one thing to say some FBI agent isn't gonna love Aloha the way "we" do, but why the hell am I taking it further and confirming my feelings for Aloha in no uncertain terms... and to my boss, no less? Aloha's father figure? The man who said he'd rip off my balls if I touched her? I take a deep breath. Well, shit. No turning back now. I might as well double-down. "Loving Aloha has never made *you* do something 'reckless or stupid,' has it?"

Oh, fuck. That was clearly the wrong thing to say.

Barry leans forward, his dark eyes blazing. "No. But I've loved Aloha like a *daughter* for a decade. That's a very different thing than her newbie bodyguard thinking he's in love with her after a fucking month." His neck vein pops out. "Believe me, I've seen it all in this business, Zander. I've seen guys 'fall in love' with the woman they're supposed to be protecting and then proceed to fuck her all over kingdom come in unsecured, risky locations. Locations where paps could easily snap photos with long-range lenses or where strangers could easily catch them with their fucking iPhones and upload the clip to Instagram or even extort money. Because that's what happens when a guy lets 'love'—or what he later realizes was nothing but simple *lust*—cloud his good judgment on this job."

I bite my tongue to keep myself from telling Barry to go fuck himself. "Well, no worries there. I'm not in 'lust' with Aloha. And I haven't, and wouldn't, do anything stupid or reckless with her. Not that it's any of your business, Barry, but I haven't had sex with Aloha, if that's what you're indirectly asking me to confirm."

It's a true statement... *technically*. Because my dick has never been inside Aloha and the common understanding of the word sex is fucking... right? So what if, God willing, my statement won't be true before tonight is over; it's still true *now*. Sort of. But either way, whether the statement was technically true or not, I suddenly realize I shouldn't have said it. Because even if I *had* fucked Aloha last night with my big ol' cock, even if I had pounded her to within an inch of her life Lionel Richie style, then I sure as fuck wouldn't be apologizing to Barry for it this morning. Because whether I fuck Aloha or not is none of Barry's business, as long as I do it in a safe, secured location. Indeed, the only person allowed to have an opinion about where my dick goes in relation to Aloha's sweet pussy is *Aloha*.

Barry's hard gaze is unreadable to me. "I didn't mean to imply you've been doing stupid and reckless shit with Aloha. The tabloids have been saying you have, but Brett and Crystal have both confirmed all the crazy stories are false and that you've been nothing but professional throughout the tour. I was just talking generalities—telling you what I've observed as a cautionary tale."

I shoot Brett a look of gratitude, thanking him for whatever he said to Barry when asked about my job performance, and Brett nods in reply. But Brett ain't no fool. He might have told Barry I've been professional on this tour, but he's gotta believe I've been secretly banging Aloha like a drum every night behind closed doors. Brett's seen the way Aloha and I interact on a daily basis. He, along with the entire world, has seen those workout videos of Aloha and me. And he knows I've raced up to Aloha's hotel room to "watch movies" in every city of the tour. Yeah, *I* know Aloha and I have actually been watching movies all those times—other than last night—and that I

191

hadn't so much as kissed Aloha until about eight hours ago, but Brett can't possibly believe that to be the case.

But, see, unlike Barry, Brett doesn't give a fuck what Aloha does in private, as long as she's physically safe. Because Brett, unlike Barry, doesn't have some fucked-up, bizarre notion that Aloha—a twenty-three-year-old *woman*—shouldn't have a normal sex life. I mean, shit, Brett's been sleeping with Aloha's tour manager, Crystal, since night one and nobody's batted an eyelash, least of all me! Why shouldn't Aloha and I be able to do the same thing behind closed doors?

Barry rubs his face and sighs. "I'm sorry, Z. I'm sleep-deprived and worried about Aloha. You've got strong feelings for her, but you're strong enough not to act on them. I respect that."

I swallow down the urge to confess my sins. "No offense taken," I choke out. Oh, shit. I suddenly wanna purge my soul. Because, fuck it, I've done absolutely nothing wrong and neither has Aloha. I clear my throat. "Actually, in the interest of keeping it one hundred with you, Barry..." I clear my throat again. "Rest assured, I take my job very seriously. When I'm on the job, her safety is my only concern. But I firmly believe my job as Aloha's bodyguard has nothing to do with what I might do with her in private... as a man. *If* something were to happen between Aloha and me behind closed doors, it'd be between two consenting adults, and only when I'm sure she's safe and secure and away from iPhones and long-range lenses. And *if* that were to happen, it'd be something private and special and *sacred* between my woman and me—and nobody else's business. Not even yours."

Brett's eyebrows shoot up.

But Barry's face remains impassive. Scarily so.

I wait, watching the vein in Barry's neck throb in and out and his jaw muscles pulse.

The corner of Barry's mouth twitches.

His nostrils flare.

Finally, he says, "So it's like that, huh?"

My heart is clanging. I can barely breathe. I clear my throat. "It's like that."

Barry looks at Brett for a long beat, his dark eyes blazing... and when he returns to me, I think I see the slightest glimmer of a smirk on his lips. Or, shit, maybe that's just wishful thinking. Maybe it's the smile of an executioner unsheathing his sword. "You done spilling your guts now, Zander?"

"I'm done."

"Good. Get your head in the game, man. It's time for us to tell Aloha the bad news about the sicko who broke into her house."

Chapter 32
Aloha

I'm on edge.

Jittery.

Anxious.

Fighting tooth and nail not to have a full-blown panic attack. It's the same way I've felt throughout this entire meet and greet, which, God willing, is almost over. For the past forty minutes—even as I've signed autographs and smiled for selfies and hugged and been hugged by fans—I haven't been able to stop imagining some faceless, deranged wacko breaking into my house and coming all over my sheets. If ever there was a day when I don't want to interact with fans, or anyone, for that matter, today is that day. Except for Zander. I most definitely want to interact with him. Naked, preferably. And Barry, too, of course. Although not naked, obviously. But other than those two, I currently feel like I'm done with people forever.

"You okay?" Barry asks from a couple feet away.

I force a smile as the next group of fans approaches. "I'm fine."

But I'm not fine. I'm shaken. Covertly freaking out. I don't want to be here. I want to wipe off this makeup and take off this sparkling corset thing and rip the sparkling flowers out of my hair and get into bed. *With Zander.* I want to kiss his incredible lips. Get licked into a frenzy. And, finally, blessedly, let him fuck my cares away.

Why can't I have that? In fact, why can't I *ever* have what I want? Goddammit! Everyone always tells me what to do and where to be and I just go along with the program like the good little automaton I am. Even Barry, God bless him, arrived today, out of the blue, and just kind of took over without any regard for the way things run now. He didn't mean to steamroll me. I'm sure he just thought he was taking care of me, like he always has. But things are different now. *I'm* different now. Barry can't treat me exactly the way he did back when I was thirteen. I'm a twenty-three-year-old *woman*. I've got opinions. Plans and desires. But did he ask me what *I* wanted? *No.* When we arrived at this meet and greet, Barry just *assumed* I'd want him to stand by my side, the same as he always used to do. He took the wingman spot next to me and banished my Shaggy Swaggy to stand near the entrance across the large room.

And I let him.

Because I'm a flaming asshole.

Why did I do that? Why did I let Barry banish Zander to Timbuktu? Why didn't I say "No, Big Barry. The wingman spot at meet and greets is Zander's now. I want him and nobody else, not even you!"? *Why didn't I say that?* Because I'm not only a flaming asshole. I'm a wimp, too. Or maybe, more accurately, I'm a cowardly ostrich who was hoping, in that moment, to bury my head in the sand and pretend this morning's hideousness never happened. Yeah, that's probably it. I wanted to turn back time for a while, to go back to when I didn't know there were sickos out there who'd even think of breaking into my house and masturbating in my sheets and shoes, let alone actually doing it. I wanted to return to a simpler time when my only problems were having no friends and no father and not being loved by my mother and having a secretly gay "boyfriend" who was addicted to opioids. Ah, the good old days! But now that I've been standing here with Barry at my side for the past forty minutes, it's clear to me there's no such thing as turning back time. There's only the present. And in the present, the only thing I want is to be alone with a certain hot bodyguard who's standing across the room with his back to me.

I glance longingly at Zander for the hundredth time during this meet and greet. This time, he's talking to the cyborg. Last time, he was scrutinizing the line of fans waiting outside in the hallway. The time before that, he was chatting with Crystal.

Zander turns his head slightly, revealing his phone pressed against his ear. He shakes his head slightly and my brain instantly supplies the word "No" coming out of his beautiful lips. And just that fast, my twisted imagination hears Zander's entire phone conversation:

No, Daphne, Zander says. *I've only been canoodling with Aloha in city after city to make you jealous.*

Well, it worked, Daphne replies. *I want you back, Z. Move to New York today! Quit that stupid job and come to me now!*

"Aloha!" an excited fan shrieks, jolting me out of my bizarre reverie.

"I love you!" another fan in the group squeals.

"I love you, too!" I say reflexively, forcing a smile.

And away we go.

But even as I interact with my fans, my gaze keeps migrating to Zander. I watch him end his call and motion to Brett. They chat and Zander places another call. Okay, clearly, Zander is handling some sort of official bodyguard business over there, not whispering sweet nothings to Daphne. *Of course.* Why did my brain imagine him talking to Daphne, of all people? Zander hasn't mentioned her in forever. It's always me who brings her up, just to test Zander's reaction. Because I'm a flaming asshole. And, anyway, even if Zander *were* inclined to talk to Daphne these days, he'd never do it at a freaking meet and greet while on duty. *Because the man's a pro.*

"I love you, Aloha!" an exuberant new voice says, and my attention is instantly diverted from Zander to the teenager standing before me. And off I go again—smiling, posing, signing, and hugging... all of it while thinking about that sick fuck, whoever he is, who broke into my house. And Daphne. And how much I want Zander's cock inside me. Oh, God, I'm a hot mess.

When the latest group leaves, I glance at Zander again... and this time, glory be, he's looking straight at me. Leveling me with those sexy, chocolate eyes of his. And, just like that, I'm remembering those chocolate eyes looking up at me from between my thighs last night.

Last night.

No wonder Daphne called sex with Zander "mind-blowing" in her stupid "I am shooketh!" text way back when. I haven't even fucked the man yet and it was the best sex of my life. I'll literally never be the same again.

"I love you so much, Aloha!" a woman shrieks, forcing me to take my eyes off Zander's blazing eyes. And before I can say a word to her, the woman lurches at me and enfolds me in an excited, painful hug.

Barry steps forward and politely reminds the woman I'm made of flesh and blood and she releases her tight grip.

"I'm so sorry!" she says, tears streaking down her cheeks. "I just love you so much."

"No worries," I say, even though my arms are throbbing. I pose for a selfie... and away I go again. Twenty minutes later, as the last group is being ushered out of the room, I turn to Barry and whisper, "Thank God that's over. I don't think I could smile for one more selfie if my life depended on it." My gaze flickers to Zander across the room, yet again, and I'm delighted to find him staring at me. And just like that, I can't wait another minute to be alone with him. "Welp," I say, clapping my hands together. "I think I'm gonna chill in my dressing room for a while before the show. Don't worry, I'll have Zander escort me so you and Brett can—"

"Not so fast, hula girl," Barry says sharply, stopping my movement.

Crap. Does Barry suspect what Zander and I did last night? *Gasp.* Did Kiera tell Crystal what I told her... and Crystal told Brett... and Brett told Barry?

Barry continues, "Reed is on his way over here with a group of friends, including a guy named Henn I'd like you to meet. Henn is going to be doing some security work for us."

My entire body relaxes. Oh, thank God. "Oh. Sure. No problem."

"Reed should be here any minute, so you shouldn't have to wait too long to—"

A commotion at the door draws our attention. Speak of the devil. It's Reed Rivers entering the room with a group of people.

As usual, Reed is carrying himself like he thinks he's got the biggest dick in the room—a particularly laughable thought in *this* room, considering Zander Shaw is standing in it.

Reed and his group—four men and five women—greet Brett and Zander at the door—showering Zander, in particular, with effusive affection. And then, all of them, including Zander and Brett, head over to Barry and me for greetings and introductions.

It takes me a while to get everyone in the group straight. But, finally, I do. There's Josh Faraday, Reed's longtime friend since college—a dark-haired hottie in a designer suit who looks like he leaped off the pages of *GQ*. On Josh's arm is his supermodel-looking wife, a blonde introduced as Kat Faraday whom I quickly realize is Keane and Dax's big sister, Kat *Morgan*—the feisty sister Keane said he and his brothers call Jizz and Kum Shot because of the poor girl's initials.

197

The second eldest Morgan brother is here, too. Ryan Morgan—
the one called Captain. And, wow, Captain Morgan is one sexy,
tattooed pirate. Indeed, Ryan Morgan's every smile and look and
movement scream *sex, sex, sex*! But, clearly, he's only got eyes for
one woman: his smokin' hot wife, Tessa Morgan, a big-chested,
small-waisted, dark-haired Latina who could easily claim the Miss
Universe crown, if that's what she wanted to do. Ryan and Tessa
Morgan are so damned *caliente* together, I can't help thinking, while
politely shaking their hands: *I would pay to watch you two have sex.*

The group also includes a stunningly handsome guy named
Jonas Faraday, Josh's lighter-haired fraternal twin who's here with
his lovely wife, Sarah. Like Tessa, Sarah is a beautiful, dark-haired
Latina. But unlike Tessa, Sarah radiates a deep-seated kindness that
takes my breath away. Tessa seems absolutely wonderful, of course.
She comes across as a genuinely warm and wonderful woman. But
she's clearly got a little edge to her, that one. Like, if you were to
cross Tessa Morgan, you'd better cover your balls. But this Sarah
woman? One look at her and there's no doubt she's gentleness and
kindness incarnate.

And then there's sweet and nerdy Henn, the hacker guy Barry
wanted me to meet, whose sweet smile made my heart go pitter-pat
the minute he said hello. Henn is accompanied by his bespectacled
and equally adorable girlfriend, a woman introduced to me by Kat as
"Hannah Banana Montana Milliken." When I asked Hannah if she's
related to my new girl crush and bestie, Maddy Milliken, Hannah
revealed she's Maddy's big sister. Which, of course, made me squeal
and give Hannah a massive hug.

Finally, when all other introductions have been made, Reed
guides the woman who's clearly his date for the evening to me and
says, "Aloha, this is Genevieve." Not "my girlfriend, Genevieve" or
"my date, Genevieve," I notice, so I'm thinking the woman means a
whole lotta nothing to him. Annoyingly, Reed's date, Genevieve, is
the only person in the group who asks me for a selfie and then
proceeds to fawn all over me in a way that makes me feel like I'm at
an official meet and greet, rather than casually hanging out with
Reed's friends. Needless to say, I'm relieved when Zander comes by,
physically peels Genevieve off me, and guides me to Barry, Brett,
and that hacker guy, Henn, for a quick chat.

198

I talk to the "security foursome" for a bit, and just as that brief conversation begins to wind down, Hannah glides over and joins the group. She thanks me profusely for the tweet I sent out about Maddy's latest documentary and informs me that Maddy's movie just won honorable mention at a big film festival. Soon, the other women drift over, too, and the men drift away, and I find myself in the midst of an animated girl party that sends my heart racing with glee. Just this fast, these women are treating me like one of their own—like I'm a friend of Reed's and Zander's, as opposed to "Aloha Carmichael." I've never been part of a female friend group like this, though I've seen the phenomenon in movies, and it's making me feel giddy.

People come and go from my immediate orbit. And I find myself laughing pretty much continuously, no matter who's standing before me. Soon, no matter the combination of people in my midst, I don't feel like I'm making small talk with strangers—I feel like I'm hanging out with good friends. *My* friends. It's the same instant connection I felt with Keane and Maddy. The same one I felt texting with Zander that very first night, back when I thought he was a bearded broomstick.

Zander.

I peek at him across the room to find him standing with Kat, Josh, Ryan, and Tessa—and my mouth physically waters at the sight of him. Whew! That man ain't no bearded broomstick, baby. As I gaze at Zander's group, Kat playfully punches Zander on his shoulder and pulls an expression I instantly realize I've seen before... *on Dax Morgan's face*. And, all of a sudden, I realize Kat's got precisely the same face as Dax, only in female form. Deciding to use this clever observation as an excuse to stand next to Zander, I excuse myself from my current conversation and stride to his side—so close to him, my forearm brushes his.

"Hey, everyone," I say brightly. "Kat, I hope you don't mind me saying this, but I just realized you're the female version of Dax. It's like God got lazy when he was making your brother, so he pulled out his old Kat Morgan mold and said, 'Bah, no one will notice!'"

Kat giggles. "You're not the first person to say that, Aloha. My family has been calling Dax and me the Wonder Twins since we were little."

Out of nowhere, Zander's palm rests against the small of my

back, out of sight from everyone, and my clit pulses at that simple, intimate... *covert* touch.

Ryan chuckles. "Wait till you meet our mother and Kat's daughter tomorrow night. Those two have the exact same face as the Wonder Twins, too. The four of them together look like Russian nesting dolls."

Zander's hand drifts down to my tailbone and rests immediately above my ass crack. My breathing hitches, but I force myself to smile breezily at Kat and Josh and say, "How old is your daughter?"

"One," Josh says proudly. "Gracie Louise Faraday. Little G. Man, is she hell on wheels, just like her fiery mommy."

Ryan and Tessa express agreement with that sentiment and tell me a funny story about an interaction between their son—seven-month-old Zachary—and little Gracie. But I'm only half listening, to be honest. Because Zander's hand has migrated lower and is now resting on my right ass cheek, out of sight from everyone. And the sensation of him secretly groping me, right in front of all his friends... and Barry across the room... is making my clit pound mercilessly.

I look at Zander, my chest heaving, and the look on his face is so sexy—so *hungry*—I have to bite my tongue not to moan at the delicious sight of him.

Josh shows me a photo of his beautiful daughter.

"Wow. She looks *exactly* like Kat," I say.

"Yeah, I've come to the conclusion Kat's a starfish," Josh says. "I think she grew Gracie out of her side like an extra arm bud. Clearly, I had absolutely nothing to do with her."

Everyone laughs, including me, even though I'm highly distracted by the fact that Zander's hand just left my right ass cheek and is now squeezing my left. I glance at Zander, telepathically telling him, *I want to fuck you.* And he sends the message right back to me.

When I tune back into the conversation, everyone is talking about the fact that the eldest Morgan sibling, Colby, and his wife, Lydia, just had a baby girl a month ago—Mia—their first biological child together but the fourth child in their family.

"Does baby Mia have a Morgan-approved nickname yet?" I ask, just as Zander's hand floats back up to the small of my back.

"Mamma Mia," Kat says. "You'll meet her and all the Morgan kiddos tomorrow night at dinner."

Ryan says, "Yeah, if you don't particularly like kids, Aloha, I'd suggest you get shitfaced drunk or stoned out of your mind before heading over to the house tomorrow night. Because at this particular moment in time, the Morgan family is absolutely overrun with little ones."

I laugh and tell the group I love kids and can't wait for dinner tomorrow night. And I'm shocked to realize both statements are true, even the second part—even though, for almost a month, I've been dreading going to the "stupid" lasagna dinner I agreed to while drunk off my ass. Now that I've met these amazing people, the idea of getting to spend more time with them, especially at their childhood home, with their real mom while eating homemade food, doesn't feel like a chore to me anymore. It feels more like an honor.

"Oh, hey, thanks so much for that tweet you posted about Keane," Ryan says. "And for the one you posted about Dax's album, too. My whole family went bananas both times. So cool of you to do that."

"I didn't send either tweet as a favor. Believe me, I was doing my *fans* a favor, both times."

Ryan leans forward conspiratorially. "I hereby officially invite you into our family, Aloha. Please, take Kat's spot. With those two tweets alone, you've already proven yourself a far more valuable family member than our sister ever was."

Kat snorts and swats at her brother's muscular shoulder, not looking the least bit offended. And for the hundredth time since this party with the Morgans and Faradays started, I'm smiling so big, my cheeks hurt.

"I might very well take you up on that offer, Ryan," I say. "Sorry, Kitty Kat, but I've always wanted siblings. A girl's gotta do what a girl's gotta do."

"Hey, I get it, sistah," Kat says, putting up her palms. "I don't blame you. Siblings are the best." She scowls comically at Ryan. "Unless, of course, the sibling in question is Ryan Ulysses Morgan. That guy's a total dick."

Everyone laughs, including Ryan.

"Aw, there's room for everyone, guys," Tessa says. She smiles warmly at me. "Take it from me, Aloha, there are infinite 'spots' in this family. There's no need for anyone to be bumping anyone else off. Right, Zander?"

"True, true," Zander says.

Aw, Zander's words are lovely. But guess what's lovelier? The fact that, as he's saying them, he's squeezing my left ass cheek again, sending electricity zinging straight into my clit.

There's more natural shuffling of conversation partners. I find out that Kat and Sarah—sisters-in-law—were actually besties in college before they met their twin-brother husbands. I also find out the Faraday twins and their wives co-own a bar called Captain's with Ryan and Tessa in Seattle. And that Ryan and Tessa met because Tessa used to be Josh Faraday's personal assistant. Also, that Kat was the one who introduced her friend from work, Hannah, to Josh's college friend, Henn.

"Wow, you're all intertwined like a giant pretzel," I say, laughing.

"Yep, and all roads lead to me," Kat says proudly. "The minute I met Tessa, I knew Ryan would flip out over her. And the minute I met Henn, I knew he'd lose it for Hannah." She leans forward. "That's my gift: matchmaking."

Ryan rolls his eyes. "My sister always says that, but, trust me, she's a broken clock right twice a day."

"Not true," Kat insists. "I *always* know when two people are destined to be together." Her eyes pointedly shift from me to Zander and then back to me again. "*Always*." She winks at me, not subtly, before turning her attention back to the group.

Holy hell. The Bet. How could I forget about that? And the fact that almost all of these people are in on it? Shit. Why did I join in on that stupid bet? Back when I did that, I was just being sassy. Snarky. Silly. *Arrogant*. I was collecting pickles! But now that I've gotten to know my darling pickle... now that I know his heart is mine for the taking, everything feels different—no longer like a lighthearted game of capture the flag. But, come on, how was I to predict back then things could ever begin to feel so... *serious* with Zander? So... real?

I glance at Zander and my heart skips a beat. If I were a betting woman—and let's face it, I am—I'd bet my entire stack of chips Zander's already lost the bet. And that all these people know it. But since the thought terrifies me as much as it excites me—since I can't honestly say I know what I'm feeling or how long it'll last, whatever it is—I force the whole thing down and return to thinking about how much I want Zander to fuck me.

"Maddy and Keane made it to the skybox!" Hannah booms excitedly, holding up her phone. She smiles at me. "It was so wonderful to meet you, Aloha, but I've got to go meet my sister at—"

"Oh, don't go," I say. "Bring Maddy and Keane here."

Hannah's face lights up. "Really? You're sure you don't want to relax for a bit before—"

"No, no. Let's keep the party going."

Out of nowhere, my tour manager, Crystal, appears and places a warning palm on my forearm. "Honey, I think you should see your friends *after* the show to give you plenty of time to relax before—"

"I've got all day off tomorrow to relax. I want to see my friends." I address Kat. "Is the entire Morgan clan in that skybox tonight?"

"No, not the *entire* clan. Dax is still on tour, as you know. And Colby and Lydia are hunkered down with little Mamma Mia tonight. But my parents are there with my aunts, uncles, and my cousin Julie and her husband. And I'm sure Zander's mom and sister have arrived by now. Zander, have you heard from your mom and sister?"

Zander holds up his phone. "Zahara just texted me a minute ago. I was about to slip out for a couple minutes to say hi to them." He looks at Barry. "If that's okay with you, boss."

"Of course," Barry says. "In fact, take the whole night off, Z. Watch the show from the skybox with your friends and family. I'll guard Aloha during the show."

"Wow. Thanks."

"Actually, you know what?" Barry says. "Take tomorrow off, too. Report for duty again first thing Monday. I'm not leaving Seattle until then, so if Aloha wants to leave the hotel at any time tomorrow, I've got her covered."

My heart bounds into my mouth. "That's sweet, Barry. But I won't be leaving the hotel tomorrow. I'm just gonna catch up on sleep and relaxation all day before heading to dinner at the Morgans'. I won't need coverage all day or night."

"All right," Barry says. He claps Zander's back. "Looks like you're officially off-duty until Monday morning, Z. Drink and be merry all you like. Let off steam. You've earned it."

I force myself not to look at Zander. If I do, my face will surely give me away. "I think that's a great idea," I say calmly. "Zander's most definitely earned a little time off."

"Hey, Barry," Kat says. "Why don't you come to dinner tomorrow night at my parents' house? I've been helping my mom cook lasagna for two days, so I know for a fact there's more than enough food. We'd love to have you."

"Thank you," Barry says. "I'd love to."

I look at Crystal to find her nonverbally chastising me for not getting a little rest before the show. But screw her. Life is short. And these people are fucking awesome. "Crystal," I say. "We're gonna have ourselves a little pre-show party. Get some 22 Goats tunes cranking, order a truckload of champagne and snacks to be brought in here, and then bring every human in that skybox to me as soon as humanly possible."

Chapter 33
Zander

Oh, God.
        I'm so fucked.
        As I walk with the entire Morgan-Shaw-Faraday crew back to the skybox to get seated for Aloha's show, that's all I can think on a running loop: *I'm so fucking fucked.*

I thought I'd be fucked when Aloha commanded everyone from the skybox—*including my mother*—to be brought to her in the meet and greet room, but, still, I held out hope I was just being paranoid. But now that I've spent an hour drinking champagne with everyone, and watching Kat eyeball-stalk us and brazenly exchange "secret" glances with Ryan about us, I know for sure: I'm so motherfucking fucked.

The Morgans know. And not only that, my sister knows, too. Only fifteen minutes into Aloha's champagne party—*just fifteen minutes in!*—my sister, Zahara, came over to me and whispered, "Oh, Z, you'd better wipe that look of love off your face every time you look at Aloha or Mom's gonna know what's up and beat your ass for screwing up the best job you've ever had."

"Don't say a word to Mom," I whispered, my eyes reflexively lurching to our mother across the room. As I know all too well, my mother isn't a fan of people risking their jobs by doing or saying anything she'd label "acting a damn fool." Plus, my mom, God love her, doesn't believe a man can fall in love in less than six months under any circumstances and I don't have any desire to hear her strident opinions on that subject yet another time.

"Well, obviously, I won't tell Mom," Zahara said. "But if you really don't want Mom figuring it out, then you'd better get the Morgans in check. I just overheard Kat and Ryan cracking jokes

205

about some bet involving you and Aloha. That's not how I figured it out, by the way. All I had to do was look at you and I already knew. But, still, if I were you, just to be on the safe side, I'd make sure those Morgans aren't gonna start drinking tomorrow night at dinner, or, hell, tonight in the skybox, and start blabbing something you don't want blabbed, right in front of Mom."

And now, here I am, so fucking fucked, walking back to the skybox with the whole, tipsy crew—my mother, sister, Keane, and I walking way up front while the rest of our large, champagne-soaked group ambles behind us. And there's no doubt in my mind I'm heading into near-certain catastrophe in that skybox tonight. And if not in the skybox, then at dinner tomorrow night. Because these people are liquored up and feeling loose and, clearly, they're all convinced I'm in love with Aloha, whether Judge Peen has made his official ruling or not.

But it's not just the thought of my mom figuring things out and reading me the Riot Act that's got me freaking out. Even more so, it's the thought of Aloha herself learning I'm in love with her from a loose-lipped Morgan, rather than from me. God help me if she were to overhear some Morgans whispering about the bet tomorrow night. Or, shit, knowing Aloha, if she were to bring up the bet herself at dinner, thinking she's being snarky, and unwittingly unleash the hounds of hell.

Plus, there's also Barry to consider now, thanks to Kat's spontaneous dinner invitation to him. Fuck! God help me, if Barry catches even a *whiff* of some "bet" about Aloha and me, I'm a dead man. Yes, I know I made my feelings for Aloha known to him earlier today—and I'm thrilled to find myself still alive and my balls intact after doing so. But if, at dinner tomorrow night, Barry were to find out I was involved in some kind of *bet* regarding Aloha...? Baby Jesus, help me. I'm sure Barry would assume the bet was about me *fucking* Aloha, no matter what I might say to the contrary. And a bet like that wouldn't fly with Badass Motherfucker Barry Atwater, no matter what ballsy speech I might have given earlier today about "sacred" shit happening behind closed doors between "my woman" and me.

"And her eyes!" my mother gushes. "So gorgeous!"

"Mmm hmm," I say. "Aloha's mad beautiful."

"And so down to earth, too!" Mom says. "I didn't expect that. Not with all the money and fame she has. But she acted like a regular girl from down the block, didn't she?"

"Mmm hmm. Aloha's always like that with everyone. She's super down to earth."

"Don't you just love her?" Mom says. But thank God, she's talking to Zahara, not me.

"I do," Zahara says. She looks at me, a gleam in her eye. "What about you, Z? *Doncha just love her?*"

I scowl at my sister behind our mother's back and she laughs.

Mom continues, oblivious to the nonverbal conversation happening between her children. "I was relieved to hear Aloha's explanation of that ridiculous 'boy toy' video. Nice to finally put that fiasco to rest." Mom glares at me like I did something to offend her in relation to that stupid video.

"Mom, I told you a month ago Aloha was just drunk and acting a fool in that video. I'm not in any way, shape, or form Aloha's 'boy toy.'" *Oh, God, please, let that be a true statement.*

"Yes, I know what *you* told me," Mom says. "But it was nice to hear *Aloha* tell me herself."

I roll my eyes for my sister's benefit and she laughs.

Mom grabs my arm as we walk. "Just be on your toes with that one, Zander. I know Aloha *seems* accessible and friendly—like she's 'one of the gang.' But never lose sight of the fact that you *work* for her. She's your *boss.* You need to be on your best behavior with her at all times, no matter how casual and comfortable she makes you feel."

Zahara shoots me a look that says, *And here we go.*

"I don't work for Aloha, technically," I say. "I work for the label. Barry is my boss, not Aloha. She's what we call 'The Package.'"

Zahara shoots me a snarky look that says "Oh, yeah, Mom's totally gonna buy that crock of shit," and I glare at her, telling her not to say a motherfucking word.

"Zander, don't play word games with me," Mom says. "I don't care who signs your paychecks. I'm talking about common sense. Common sense is the best sense of all, so how about you use it."

"Yeah, *Zander!*" Keane calls out from behind my mother, out of nowhere. "Don't play word games with yo momma. It's common sense, son, so use it!"

I look over my shoulder at Keane and he flashes me a dopey, stoned look that tells me the huge weed brownie he scarfed down a while ago during Aloha's champagne party has kicked in like a Mack truck.

Aw, poor Keaney. I don't blame him for self-medicating tonight. Apparently, his agent said the final decision will be made today or tomorrow on that huge TV series he's been waiting to hear about. The one with the big movie star that would require Keaney to bawl his eyes out. As Keane well knows, the part will likely change his life if he gets it and devastate him if he doesn't.

"Thanks for your support, Keaney baby," my mother says, chuckling. "Sounds like you helped yourself to some of Miss Aloha's fine champagne, just like me, huh?"

"I sure did, Momma Shaw. Lots and *lots* of it. And you're very welcome for the support, you goddess, you. I love and respect you and always have, because you're a beautiful, wise, and powerful woman."

Mom guffaws. "Oh, Keaney. Always such a charmer."

"Yup, I have *ebullient* charm," Keane says, his dimples popping.

"Yes, you do, sweetie. You most certainly do."

"He's a charmsicle left out in the sun," I say dryly. I look at Keane. "It means you're dripping with charm, son."

Everyone laughs, but nobody more raucously than Stoned Keane. And, of course, my mother simply pats Keane's arm and tells him how much she adores his goofy laugh. Seriously? How is it possible, through all the years of Keane being stoned as shit around my mother, she's never once suspected it? If I were Keane, I'd be offended about that, actually, because it means my mother thinks he's *naturally* that stupid.

"What's funny?" Mom says, looking behind her. "What did you do back there, Keane Elijah?"

"I made a funny face at Zander, ma'am," he says. "But only to lighten the mood because things felt a little bit serious there for a half-second and that felt like a pity considering the celebratory nature of the evening."

Mom laughs and shakes her head. "Well, amen to that. Tonight is a celebration! Ha! I can't remember the last time I drank this much champagne. Woo-wee! That was some good champagne."

"Woo-wee!" Keane agrees.

"I like your girlfriend, by the way, honey," Mom says to Keane. "She's sweet. And sooo smart."

"Woo-wee!" Keane says. "Smartest girl I ever met. That's for sure."

"And I like the way you fawn all over her, even more than she fawns all over you. That's the mark of a healthy relationship: when the man is just a little bit more smitten than the woman. That's how you know it's gonna last."

I look behind me in the corridor, to make sure the adorbsicles and very tipsy Maddy Milliken isn't overhearing this. And it's clear she's not. Maddy's walking quite a ways back with Hannah and Henn, both of whom look as buzzed as Maddy.

"I think you're right about that," Keane says. "Honestly, Maddy couldn't possibly love me as much as I love her because no person in the history of time has ever loved another person as much as I love Madelyn Elizabeth Milliken, so help me God."

My mom exchanges a look with me that tells me Keane just melted her heart.

Keane continues, sounding stoned as fuck to me, but, clearly, not to my clueless mother, "I'm gonna marry that girl one day, Momma Shaw. Maddy's gonna be the mother of my eighteen babies and I'm gonna take care of her and our family till the end of time, just like it's been for my mom and dad."

"Eighteen babies!" Mom says. "Does Maddy know about your big plans?"

"Not yet. We haven't talked about marriage and babies yet. Although, hold up. When Z got tickets to Aloha's show in LA for Maddy and me, Maddy told Z we'd name our firstborn Zander or Zanderina. Does that count as planning for children?"

Mom laughs. "I'd say so."

"Woo-wee!"

Everyone laughs.

"Come here, you sweet little Pooh Bear, you," Mom says to Keane. She links her arm in Keane's, on the opposite side from me, making Zahara step aside to make room for the lovefest. "Now, tell me, honey, how long have you known this girl you're gonna marry one day?"

"Four glorious, life-changing, enlightening months."

Mom can't help but scoff. She isn't doing it in a bitchy way, more like a "Oh, you clueless child!" kind of way. She says, "Four months, and you're already sure you want her to be your wife and the mother of your *eighteen* babies?"

"I'm sure, ma'am."

Zahara flashes me a look like, *You're next in line for the bitch-slapping, dude, so get your cheeks ready.* And I lovingly motion for my sister to fuck off.

"Oh, you think I've forgotten about you over there, Zander?" Mom says suddenly. "I haven't."

Oh, fuck.

Mom links her free arm in mine while continuing to walk arm in arm with Keane. "Now let's have a little talk, honey. I noticed you looking at Aloha like you think she walks on water and I want you to rein that shit in, son."

Zahara and Keane laugh.

Mom continues, "We both know you have an impulsive streak, Zander. A leap-now-and-look-later streak."

"He does. He really does," Keane says. "It's his signature quality, I'd even say. Besides his big, tender heart. The boy wears his tender heart on his sleeve."

"Yes, he does. And while I love that about you in so many ways, I don't want it leading you down the wrong path when it comes to this new career. This is too good an opportunity for you to mess it up by thinking you can let down your guard completely around this woman and say whatever damn fool thing pops into your head. Trust me, you can't say whatever you're thinking with her and you most certainly can't *do* whatever you're thinking."

Boom. Well, there it is. If I'm understanding what my darling mother is telling me, she believes any potential, hypothetical romance with Aloha won't end well for me, either personally or professionally. And, *of course,* it could *never* end with Cinderfella sweeping the pop princess off her feet.

Mom rests her cheek against my bicep as we walk. "Just think with your big head and not your little one, okay? And you'll be fine."

I glance at my sister and she looks sympathetic. I glance at Keane and he looks like a jellyfish. "Thanks, Mom. I'll do my best."

We reach the skybox entrance and stop to wait for the rest of the group straggling behind. As we wait, I lean into my sister's ear. "I gotta talk to the Morgans real quick. Put out this fire. Can you get Mom outta here for ten minutes?"

"You got it." Zahara pinches my arm and then addresses our mother. "Mom, I'm gonna hit the bathroom before the concert. Will you come with me?"

"Oh, yes. I've had *lots* of Miss Aloha's delicious champagne and I don't want to have to get up during the show." She giggles, pats my arm, and winks. "You're such a good boy. You always make me so proud."

"Thanks, Mom. That's always the plan."

I watch my mom and sister walk away and then stride into the skybox with Keane and everyone else, my heart beating like a steel drum. I have no desire to bare my soul to this motley crew right now. But I feel like I have no choice. Almost all the major players on the bet are here, all in one place, while, at the same time, Barry, my mother, and Aloha aren't. The stars are briefly aligned. I've gotta seize the moment.

I work my way to the front railing of the skybox and turn around. "Hey, everyone. Can I have your attention for a sec? Hi. I've got something important to tell you—and I gotta do it fast."

Every eyeball in the skybox trains on me.

I take a deep breath. "With two days still to go in month one, I just want to inform you that I've officially fallen head over heels in love with Aloha."

Ryan and Kat—the two most vocal one-monthers—cheer and high-five each other while everyone else looks some version of surprised, happy, or just plain concerned.

"So congrats to all the one-monthers. Spend your winnings wisely. But here's the thing, guys. I haven't told Aloha how I feel and don't want her knowing yet, if ever. Yeah, I know she's theoretically in on the bet for month two, but she only placed that bet to razz me. She didn't take things seriously back then and neither did I. To both of us, the whole thing was a silly game at first. But it's not a game anymore. At least for me, it's become very, very real."

Kat looks at her mother like "We suck" and Mrs. Morgan clutches her heart and nods in agreement with that nonverbal assessment.

I glance at the door to make sure the coast is clear, and when there's no sign of my mother and sister, I return to the group again. "Unfortunately, I'm positive Aloha's not in love with me. *Yet.* But my plan is to change that—to do everything in my power over the next two months to make her fall for me. And that means I gotta, you know, play it cool for a bit so I can slowly win her over while not scaring her away." I look toward the door again. "Also, I don't want my mother or Barry finding out about the bet or my feelings for Aloha, and both of them are gonna be at dinner tomorrow night. So, please, could you guys keep a lid on this until you've been advised explicitly the cat is outta the bag? No jokes. No funny looks. No innuendos or overt comments. *Please?*"

Everyone simultaneously expresses some variation of "of course" or "we're sorry for being heinous people" or "we didn't mean any harm."

Louise Morgan stands, her hand on her heart. "Oh, our beloved Zander. We're so very sorry if what we thought was harmless fun has caused you a moment of anxiety. *Shame on us.*" She glares at her kids for a long beat. "I'm ashamed of myself for playing along with these hooligans. Of course, none of us will say a word to Aloha or anyone else about your feelings." She looks around at the group. "You got that, you horrible monsters? Let our beloved Zander woo that adorable girl in his own time, without any interference by his so-called 'loved ones.'"

Everyone expresses their promise to stay mum and toe the line.

"Morgan Mafia: activated," Kat says, leaping up and standing by my side. "But just so you know, Zander, if you change your mind and decide you *do* want us to help you—"

"No helping!" I blurt, and everyone laughs. I look at Josh and Henn. "Hey, you two haven't said anything about the bet to Reed or Barry, right?"

Both men say it hadn't even occurred to them to mention it and promise going forward their lips will be sealed.

"Thanks, guys," I say, exhaling from the depths of my soul.

Keane stands. "Okay, new bet, everyone. Who here thinks Aloha will fall for Z before the end of the tour?"

Everyone raises a hand.

"Please, guys," I say. "No more bets, for the love of God."

Everyone laughs.

"For the love of God what?" my mother says, striding into the skybox with Zahara.

Kat slides her arm around my waist. "Oh, Z was just saying he's grateful to God we could all get together tonight because he's missed everyone so much while on tour."

"Amen to that," Mom says. "Praise Jesus." She smiles at me. "I've missed you, too, honey."

The earnest look on my mother's face melts me. She's bossy, my mom, that's for sure—and, man, does she have some strident opinions about a whole slew of topics. But, damn, if that woman doesn't love her kids more than life itself. "Thanks, Mom. I love you."

"I love you, too, baby."

We share a smile, just as the lights in the arena dim.

Instantly, the crowd in the arena—including in our skybox—begins cheering and applauding in anticipation of the show starting any minute. But since I've seen this concert a shitload of times by now—although, granted, never from actual seats, let alone luxury box seats like these—and since I therefore know for a fact there are a solid seven minutes between the lights dimming in the arena and Aloha walking onstage, I settle into my seat, pull out my phone, and begin tapping out a long overdue text:

Hey Daphne. Sorry I haven't responded to any of your texts or voicemails. I didn't mean to ghost you. I just didn't know what to say until now. You were right to break up with me. You did us both a huge favor. I know I told you I loved you, but in retrospect, I didn't know the meaning of the word. My whole life, I've used the magic words far too quickly, too liberally, too casually. I've used them before developing genuine trust with someone. I've confused the promise of love, the hope of love, for love itself. And now I understand, finally, that's what you were trying to explain to me. I now understand that a woman can't feel loved while sitting atop a pedestal. She only feels trapped way up there. Like she's in a gilded cage. I'm sorry I didn't understand. I do now. I truly thought I gave you "everything," but now I see that giving "everything" to someone, when you haven't listened to what they actually want, feels to that person like a whole lot of nothing. D, you're a beautiful, talented, sweet person and I wish you all the happiness and success in the world with whatever and whoever awaits you. I'll always be grateful for what you taught me. And I'll always be your friend, rooting for you from afar. But it will most definitely be from afar. Z

Just as I press send on my message to Daphne, two large screens on either side of the stage begin projecting images of Aloha—visions of her blowing kisses, laughing, dancing, and generally seducing the camera. And everyone in the arena, including me, stands and loses their shit in anticipation of Aloha's big entrance.

The band strikes the opening chords of Aloha's first number, and, of course, everyone freaks out even more.

Thousands of illuminated hibiscus flowers—the flower Aloha so famously wears in her hair on the cover of the *Pretty Girl* album—explode across the pink backdrop of the stage and then burst into a thousand stars. And, again, the arena loses their collective shit. A shock of pink lights and pyrotechnics blast our eyes, leaving every person in the building blinded for a gleeful, heart-stopping half-second before a Plexiglas elevator pops up from beneath the stage and delivers the woman we're all waiting to see. And off we go. As the band whips everyone into a frenzy, Aloha marches out of her Plexiglas cage and begins belting out her monster hit.

Sheer pandemonium overtakes the arena as Aloha struts across the stage in her thigh-high boots and blingy corset and sparkling flowers in her hair, trailed by her armada of insanely talented backup dancers.

"Hellooooo, Seattle!" Aloha bellows between verses of her song, her voice filling every nook and cranny of the huge arena.

And, of course, the crowd responds in kind, welcoming their idol to the Emerald City with open arms and shrieks of euphoria.

"Are you ready to have some fun with me tonight, Seattle?"

The crowd responds enthusiastically.

"Good, 'cause I need to let off some steam tonight! Let's have some fun together and forget the outside world exists! Sound good?"

The crowd roars its agreement.

Right on cue, Aloha falls in line with her dancers and launches into a rigorous choreographed routine that makes the crowd shriek its approval and bop and sing and dance along with her.

And that's it.

I'm gone.

Again.

But not really *again,* actually. No, this time feels different. Because this time, unlike every time before, I've finally got my whole heart to give Aloha. And not only that, tonight, unlike any other night, I can envision Aloha as part of *my* world. Before tonight, I was always Aloha's bodyguard. It was her world and I was just living in it. But tonight, after seeing her with my people—all the people I love the most—after watching Aloha step into *my* world and fit right in, I know in my heart this could work for us. No, that this *will* work for us. Tonight, for the first time, ever, I'm watching *my* woman on that stage... even if she doesn't know it yet.

Chapter 34
Aloha

Best. Night. Ever.

Maybe even literally.

The song blaring is "There's Nothing Holdin' Me Back" by Shawn Mendes. And right now, as I dance at Captain's on a makeshift dance floor with this amazing group of people—this mind-blowing fusion of my peeps and Zander's—the song feels more like the soundtrack of my *life*, rather than a simple tune playing in a bar.

When I headed offstage after my show earlier tonight, I raced to my dressing room, hell-bent on sending a text to Zander that commanded him to meet me in my hotel room with fifty condoms as soon as humanly possible. But there was already a text from Zander awaiting me.

PEENIE GOT THE PART! We "kids" are gonna ditch the parentals and celebrate at Captain's. Ryan called ahead and shut the place down so our favorite pop star can get shitfaced among friends without a care in the world. I'll head backstage to get you right after the show, so shower and wrangle whatever peeps you want to join us at Captain's and tell them to get their asses onto the bus I'm sending to the backstage door. Baby, I'm not your paid bodyguard tonight. I'm your man—the man who's gonna put his penis inside your happiness the minute we get back to the hotel. And, in the meantime, get you nice and wet all night long in anticipation. Z

I replied to Zander's thrilling text with a simple "Yasss!" and then quickly instructed Crystal to herd my peeps onto the bus while I showered. And mere minutes later, I was in street clothes and gleefully racing to the back door to await Zander. When he appeared a couple minutes later, I crushed my lips against his, right then and there, without worrying someone might see me do it—maybe even *wanting* someone to see—and then we boarded the bus together, hand in hand, both of us floating ten inches off the ground.

And now, here we are, dancing the night away at Captain's with this amazing fusion of Zander's peeps and mine: all my backup dancers and musicians, plus, Crystal, and Brett, on my side of the "aisle," and the entire Morgan-Faraday group, minus parentals and plus Zahara, on Zander's side. Reed Rivers is also here, minus his obnoxious date from earlier, thank God, though I'm not sure if he's technically one of my peeps or Zander's. Either way, since he was smart enough to ditch his date and he's clearly having a blast with his best friends, he's more than welcome at this shindig, as far as I'm concerned.

Oh, and last but not least... I almost forgot. An adorable flight attendant also joined the party an hour ago—a short redhead wearing a Delta uniform and rolling a carry-on suitcase who burst into the bar, beelined to Tessa—at which point both women jumped for joy—and then ordered all the tables and chairs in the entire place pushed to the walls and the music cranked up so we could turn our "gathering" into a full-blown dance party. And we've been dancing like fools ever since.

The Shawn Mendes song ends and a new one—"Silvertongue" by Young the Giant—begins. And, of course, I lose my mind. *I love this song!* And by the reaction of everyone around me, they love it, too.

One of my dancers, a guy named Darius, starts doing some acrobatic breakdancing in the middle of the dance floor, and everyone forms a circle around him to cheer him on. And just that fast, we've got ourselves a dance battle, folks. Another dancer takes "center stage" in the circle after Darius, showing everyone what she can do, and the crowd goes bananas. And on it goes, with dancer after dancer coming into the circle to thrill us with their incredible moves.

And then things take a turn to the hilarious when Henn, the hacker, bursts into the middle of the circle to show us *his* stellar moves. Ha! Let's just say Henn should stick to his day job. But even though he's not a talented dancer by any stretch, he's by far the most entertaining dancer of the battle. So much so, he's got every person in the crowd doubled over and crying from laughter.

By the time Henn leaves the circle, we're a voracious mob. Hungry for more. So, Josh and Kat leap into the middle and perform a clothed porno that makes everyone scream and cheer and, I'm guessing, wish they could be a fly on the wall when those two get it on for real. *Damn.*

When Josh and Kat leave the middle of the circle, Ryan and Tessa replace them and dazzle everyone with the sexiest salsa known to mankind. Gah. Again, with the sexiness! What is it with this crowd?

A few more dancers follow until, finally, that redheaded flight attendant pulls an adorable dancer of mine named Kai into the middle and the pair puts on a master class in grinding for our hooting pleasure. Holy hell, if Kai were straight, there's no doubt in my mind he'd get lucky with this one tonight.

When the grinding show ends, the Morgan-Faraday group begins chanting "Ball Peen Hammer! Ball Peen Hammer!" So, of course, Keane answers the call, strutting into the middle like he's the headliner of a *Magic Mike* revue.

After showing us some jaw-dropping moves as a preliminary tease, Keane grabs a nearby chair, pulls his giggling girlfriend into it, and proceeds to give her an enthusiastic lap dance that makes everyone, not just Maddy herself, lose their freaking minds.

Oh, God, I'm lightheaded. I don't think I've ever laughed this hard or had this much fun or been this sexed up in all my life. Is this how normal people live? Without a care in the world? If so, sign me the fuck up.

Out of nowhere, Zander's words from almost a month ago pop into my head: *When you're with the Morgan family, you won't even be the funniest, coolest person in the room.* At the time, I assumed he said those words simply to lure me to show up for the "stupid" dinner I'd drunkenly agreed to attend. It didn't occur to me for a minute he could be speaking the truth... because, come on, I'm Aloha Carmichael. But now, I can see Zander wasn't kidding. If I'm lucky, I'm *maybe* tied for the sixth coolest person in this room. *Maybe.* And, frankly, that's exactly the reason I'm having so much fun tonight. It's thrilling and also a huge relief to *not* be the center of attention at a party. To simply be one of the gang. To just... *be.*

Ball Peen Hammer gets off Maddy's lap, leaving her a blushing, giggling pile of goo. And then, as he stands before Maddy in the chair, Keane grabs at the fabric of his T-shirt like he's about to rip it off. Well, that's Maddy's hard limit, apparently. She leaps out of her chair and skitters into the crowd, laughing and shrieking adorably as she goes.

Belly laughing, Keane starts to follow his shy girlfriend off the stage, shaking his head. But Ryan isn't having it. Nope. He grabs Keane, stuffs a twenty into the waistband of his jeans, and turns his brother right back around. It's a hilarious turn of events that sends the entire crowd into a shrieking frenzy... and visibly ignites our darling former professional stripper.

A hilarious and sexy striptease from Keane follows—a sensual, eye-popping routine that makes it abundantly clear why this boy used to be the top male exotic dancer in Seattle. And the best part? Every time Keane seems like he might be on the cusp of stopping his striptease, one of his family members laughingly stuffs another bill into his waistband, egging him on to take off a little bit more... until finally, Ball Peen Hammer is dancing before us in his Calvin Klein briefs and socks, gyrating his way around the entire circle and getting bills stuffed into his waistband as he goes.

When Keane gets around to me, I motion that I don't have any money. Which I don't. I never carry money or credit cards or my ID while on tour. Crystal carries all that stuff for me. Of course. But I've no sooner gestured to Keane than a twenty magically appears inches from my face.

Giggling like a hyena, I take the bill from Crystal... but then, rather than stuff it into Keane's briefs, as all watchful eyes are plainly expecting me to do, I turn to Zander next to me and slide that sucker into the waistband of *his* pants with a wide and wicked smile.

Well, the crowd goes ballistic at that unexpected maneuver. A chant of "Go, Zander! Go, Zander!" erupts... until Zander answers the call. Without hesitation, he pulls me into the middle of the circle, obviously intending to give me—and the crowd—a show.

But I'm a little bit drunk and a lot bit horny, so I hurl myself at him, the same way I always do, and he catches me on the fly, as usual. But this time—for the first time, ever—I wrap my legs around Zander's waist and my arms around his strong neck, pull myself up to his lips, and kiss him deeply, right in front of everyone.

At the unexpected assault of my lips on his, Zander graces me with the kiss of a lifetime. It's a passionate kiss. An electrifying one that's turning me on like never before—not only because of the brazen sensuality of the kiss itself, but because we're doing it in front of *everyone*. Under the circumstances, this kiss feels more like a coming out party than a simple kiss. A proclamation. We're declaring our mutual, unapologetic desire for each other and daring the world to say a goddamned thing about it.

Zander grabs my ass as he holds me up and kisses the living hell out of me and I clutch his neck fervently and devour his lips with everything I've got. Oh, God, it turns me on to no end to think Zander is kissing me in front of Brett and Reed... both of whom might tell Barry what went down here tonight. Which means Zander is willing to risk his job for this kiss! I mean, in reality, I'd never let Zander get fired for kissing me tonight. At the end of the day, I have to believe it's me who'd have the last word on Zander's employment, not Barry, if I threw my weight around enough... I think? I've never actually thrown my weight around in any context, let alone in the context of keeping a bodyguard employed. But, *still*, I can't imagine Barry could send Zander away against my will. But, regardless, Zander doesn't know that. I'm sure he believes he's taking a huge risk by kissing me... and the realization that Zander is willing to do that is sending me into near-ecstasy.

As Zander and I continue kissing like animals, I sense movement around us. People filling in the circle. General dancing resuming. I break away from Zander's heated kiss, gasping for air, and press my lips into his ear. "*Bathroom.*"

Chapter 35
Aloha

Zander locks the bathroom door behind us, slides me down to my feet and pushes my back against the door, all while kissing me frantically. I reach down and unbutton his pants furiously, reach into his briefs, and grip his hard, silky dick. He moans as I stroke him and I shudder and gasp, on the verge of coming right here and now from sheer anticipation. I'm so aroused, I can barely stand. He hikes up my skirt. Rakes his fingertips up my thigh, pulls the crotch of my underwear aside, and slides a finger inside my wetness, making me gyrate and coo with pleasure. I'm ready for him. Throbbing. Yearning. *Desperate.*

He plunges another finger inside me. Then another. I hump his fingers and claw at his broad shoulders and gulp at the air, on the very cusp of coming undone.

I watch Zander rip into a foil packet and get himself covered like his life depends on it. A moment later, he grabs my ass, slams me against the door, and plunges himself inside me.

I gasp. I've never been filled like this before. He's bigger than I'm used to. Much bigger. But it feels incredible.

Zander thrusts. Once. Twice. Three times. And I come. *Hard.* For the first time ever with a man's cock inside me. It's a delicious sensation.

As my walls constrict and ripple around him, the look on Zander's face is pure rapture. But he continues thrusting into me mercilessly, giving me yet another sensation I've never experienced before—being fucked through an orgasm. It's sublime. Almost too good to bear.

I tilt my hips back and forth to take as much of him as humanly possible. Clutch at Zander's collarbone and tug on him. Until, finally, he picks me up by my ass, crushes his mouth to mine, and impales me against the bathroom door.

The moment comes to me in fits and spurts of sensation. The wooden door against my back. Zander's huge cock inside me. His hands gripping my ass. My heart beating like a jackhammer. The loud music on the other side of the door. The booze in my system. I feel drugged. Here, but not. Like a piece of me—my soul, maybe?—is soaring around the room through it all.

Zander growls and shudders sharply, clearly on the cusp of losing it, and a sound of pure ecstasy erupts from me.

I come.

And so does he, with my name lurching from his beautiful lips.

After he's gathered himself, he slides me down to my feet and leans me against the door with his large frame hulking over me, his forearms and forehead pressed against the wood above my head.

I clutch his torso and press my forehead against his chest, breathing hard.

"Holy fuck," he says.

"In love with me now?" I tease. And instantly regret it. Bad Aloha! Bad, Drunk Aloha!

But just when I'm about to say something to fill the silence, to deflect from my ill-advised joke, Zander shocks me by whispering, "Yes."

I inhale sharply. *Oh, Jesus.*

I'm not shocked by the sentiment itself. I already knew Zander loves me. I wouldn't have given him my poem to read if I hadn't been sure of that fact. I'm just shocked as hell he actually *said* it to me. *Out loud.* Jesus! Doesn't the man know the first rule of a tour-fling?

I remain silent with my forehead pressed against his chest, trying to figure out what to do. What to say. Okay now, logically, there's no need to panic here. Zander's admission doesn't change anything. I fucked him knowing he loves me. So, the only difference now is that he knows I know. And is that such a fatal thing? No. Certainly, if he can handle that slight shift in circumstance, then so can I.

"Shit," Zander mutters after my long silence. "Peenie told me to keep my big mouth shut and my big cock hard for the next two months. He *told* me. But I just..." He sighs. "You felt so good, Aloha. You're better than any drug. It was so good, I felt like I'd been injected with truth serum."

"Zander, look at me."

He sighs, lifts his forehead from the door, and gazes down at me.

"You saying the words out loud didn't let some cat out of a bag. The cat's been poking his head and two front legs out of the bag for quite a while now, like 'meow, meow, me-ow-looove-youuu!'"

I'm thinking he's gonna laugh at my silliness, but he doesn't. He looks anxious. He says, "When the keyboardist told you he loved you, you cut him off. Buh-bye."

I roll my eyes. "Oh, for the love of fuck, I wish I'd never told you about that goober. He's a flea on the ass of an elephant and you're a... what's that huge prehistoric elephant?"

"A mammoth."

"Yeah, he's a flea on the ass of a mammoth and you're the mammoth. He's a moron and you're Einstein. He was as interesting as paint drying and you're the most interesting, entertaining, sweetest, cutest, most thrilling person I've ever met."

A huge smile spreads across his gorgeous face. "Seriously?"

"Yes."

"So... you're not pissed at me?"

"*Pissed* at you? What kind of monster do you think I am?"

He lets out an audible shrug. "I dunno, Aloha. There are still two days left of month one—and you're a two-monther." He winks.

I scowl and pound on his hard chest. "Motherfucker! You couldn't hold on just two more freaking days, Zander Shaw? Jesus fucking Christ, you bastard!"

We both laugh.

"I couldn't help it," he says. "Your magic pussy just squeezed the truth out of me."

I giggle. "If you love me, then prove it. Don't tell the Morgans you've succumbed to my charms, so I still have a shot at winning the money."

"You could live with yourself if you won by cheating?"

"Hell yes. *I want that money!*"

We both laugh again.

Zander sighs. "Yeah, well, it's too late for that. Sorry, but I already told the Morgans how I feel about you earlier tonight."

"You're joking."

"I'm not. I told them in the skybox when my mother went to the restroom. I wanted to be sure none of them would talk about the bet in front of you or my mother or Barry at dinner tomorrow night. Like, I literally got up front and turned around and made an official announcement to make sure nobody breathed a word about my big secret to you." He grins. "Because my big plan was to play it cool with you for the next two months."

"Well, so much for that."

Zander laughs, this time right from his belly, and I can't resist giggling with him. Oh, God, butterflies—no, bald eagles—are flapping around inside my stomach. It's a sensation I've never felt in my life—this electricity surging through my body, especially *after* having sex with someone. When the chase is over. When I've got the pickle collected and firmly stowed in my jar. Oh, wow, this crazy feeling in my heart—this *bursting* feeling—is like nothing I've felt before. *What the hell is it?*

Still giggling with Zander, I tug on his shirt. "Don't you worry about a thing, Shaggy Swaggy. You admitting it out loud doesn't change a thing between us. We'll just pretend you never said it and carry on as usual, okay?"

Zander's wide smile softens. Suddenly, everything about his facial expression screams, *It changes everything, you dumbshit!* But he says nothing. Not with his mouth, anyway. With his eyes, he's quite plainly telling me I've just dragged a razor across his heart.

"I just meant that everything will still be great between us, that's all," I say. "That I'm not panicking. That's a good thing, right?"

His shoulders relax. He sighs. "Yes. Thank God for small mercies."

"So it's agreed, then? We'll still have fun and hang out and nothing will change—except, of course, we'll now be fucking each other every night?"

I smile, but he doesn't smile back. He doesn't look as upset as a moment ago, but he's certainly not jumping for joy at my proposal. But, come on. What does he expect me to say? *I love you, too, Zander?* That's asking the impossible of me. "Look, there's no need to give these feelings we're having any kind of name," I say. "It's not like either of us is going anywhere any time soon. We're gonna be stuck like glue for the next two months, no matter what. So why give it a name when we can just be together for two months, day in and day out, and enjoy ourselves?"

His jaw pulses. "I agree with that."

"Good. Great. Plus, a lot can happen in two months' time. By the time we get to New York, you could be sick of me. You could be the one wanting to end things, not me."

"We both know that's not gonna happen, Aloha. I'm in it to win it."

"You never know. You could sprint away from me in New York like, 'Get me the fuck away from this psycho bitch nightmare, please!'"

His dark eyes are boring holes into my face. "That's not gonna happen. I'm all-in. If you want me, you got me. The ball's in your court. I'm putting it all on the line. *I love you.*"

My chest tightens. The bald eagles in my belly from a moment ago morph into bats. Gargoyles. Velociraptors. The walls in the small bathroom are closing in on me. "I... I can't make any promises to you, Zander," I choke out. "It's just not possible. Please, let's just keep doing this awesome thing, whatever it is, and keep feeling what we feel, and having a blast and plenty of sexy times, but let's not worry about what might happen in the future. It'll be what it'll be when we get to New York. We'll know what to do when the time comes. And if we don't, then we'll talk about it then. *Just not today.*"

Zander moves his mouth like he's going to say something but then thinks the better of it. He takes a deep breath and speaks on his exhale. "All right." He nods decisively. "A tour-fling for the next two months, it is, hula girl. I'll keep my big mouth shut and my big cock hard and play it cool with you all the livelong day. But, just so you know, if the new pickle you're aiming to collect is getting me to declare my undying love to you every time I fuck you, then you're gonna be sorely disappointed. I won't say it again unless you say it first and that's a fact, Jack."

"Thank you, Baby Jesus. I've got no desire to collect that particular pickle. Believe me."

"Good, 'cause it ain't gonna happen."

"Good."

"Good." He pauses. "But just so I don't have any lingering urges to bare my soul to you going forward... there are some things I'd like to get off my chest now, just so I don't unwittingly blurt them at any point over the next two months. Fair enough?"

225

"Sure. Knock yourself out."

Zander takes a deep breath, grabs my hands, and looks deeply into my eyes. "I love you, Aloha Leilani Carmichael. Not only when I'm fucking you against a bathroom door or eating your sweet pussy 'til I make it rain. I love you when we're simply sitting together on an airplane, watching a movie. Or working out together at a hotel gym. I love you when you're onstage and even more when you're off it. I love you when you're all made up to look like a painted fantasy, but even more when you're scrubbed clean and your hair is piled on top of your head. I love you when you're strutting across a stage like you own the place and when you're curled up in a ball, feeling like the weight of the world is crushing you. I love you when you're on top of my back laughing and when you're cradled in my arms sleeping or drunk or crying." He brushes his thumb against my cheek. "I love all the parts of you, Aloha. Not because you were on TV. Not because you've sold millions of records. Not because everybody knows your name. But because you're *you.*" He grins. "Aloha, what I'm trying to tell you is that I love you no matter what. And nothing's gonna change that. Not the passage of two months. Not the passage of twenty years. Not a change of cities. And certainly not the bullshit lie of calling this a fling. I love you and I'm gonna do everything in my power to make you love me back. And when you do—because, mark my words, you will, one day—I'm gonna take care of you and keep you safe, physically and emotionally, in every way. Not because someone's paying me to do it, but because you're my heart beating outside my body. *Because you're my reason to breathe.*"

I stare into Zander's dark eyes, feeling like I'm going to pass out.

"But since you're obviously not ready to accept any of that as The Truth yet," he continues, "then, okay, let's have some bullshit fun together for the next two months. Same as always but with lots of sex added to the menu. I'm giving you my heart with no expectation or guarantees that you'll give me anything in return. It's yours. Do with it what you will."

I wobble slightly, but he holds me up.

"The only thing I ask of you in return, the one thing I require, is the assurance that while we're purportedly flinging from the rafters over the next two months, you won't have any kind of sexual contact with anyone else. Not unless you've first told me you're positive you don't want me. That's all I ask."

I jut my chin at him. "How could you think I'd want anyone but you?"

"I have no idea what you want. Because, clearly, *you* have no idea."

I touch his collarbone and whisper, "I know exactly what I want. You and only you. For the rest of the tour."

He exhales and closes his eyes.

"Side note," I say, filling the silence after a moment. "How the hell would I even be *able* to get with someone else, even if I wanted to? *Which I don't.* I'm glued to your side twenty-four-seven, Zander."

Zander opens his eyes. They're blazing. "No, I'm glued to *your* side, Aloha. There's a difference. You could tell me to go away and that you'll see me in the morning and then you could bring some guy to your room and there's nothing I could do about it. You could send me away for an hour or forever, at your whim. *You've* got that power. *I don't have shit.*"

My heart pangs. Oh, God, I'm evil. Pure evil. The pain in his eyes is making my heart squeeze painfully. "Oh, Zander." I grab a fistful of his shirt. "For the next two months, I belong to you every bit as much as you belong to me. And when we get to New York, we'll know what comes next. Just, please, let's not worry about what the future holds." I pull him down and his mouth crushes mine. He wraps his arms around me and kisses me passionately... wordlessly telling me he's surrendering to my stated terms of engagement.

Chapter 36
Zander

I t's just after three when I lay Aloha down, fast asleep, onto the bed in my hotel room. As we were getting into the back of an Uber in front of Captain's, I asked Aloha, my eyebrow cocked with mock smarminess, "Your place or mine?" I wasn't being serious. The girl's never touched as much as a pinky toe in one of my tiny hotel rooms in any city on the tour. But to my surprise, Aloha replied, "Take me to your lair."

Not gonna lie. I was electrified by that response... that is, until Aloha fell fast asleep in the back of the Uber. I can't blame her for crashing, of course. The girl's had a long and emotionally exhausting day that began in Portland with her finding out a lunatic had broken into her house and ended in Seattle getting fucked against a bathroom door. All things considered, I'm surprised she stayed awake as long as she did.

I sit on the edge of the bed with my back to Aloha's sleeping form and take off my shoes. I'm just about to peel off my shirt when my phone buzzes with an incoming text from Barry.

Aloha's sick?

Wow. Fake news travels fast. When Aloha and I emerged from fucking in the bathroom at Captain's and started making the rounds to say our goodbyes, Aloha surprised me by telling Brett and Crystal, "Hey, guys, I just barfed my lungs out in the bathroom, so Zander's gonna take me to the hotel."

I understood why she said it—that she was trying to protect me in case word got to Barry about our kiss and subsequent disappearance into the bathroom—but I was nonetheless disappointed. In truth, I was hoping Aloha and I would emerge from that bathroom, loud and proud, neither of us telegraphing a lick of apology for what we'd so clearly been doing in there. Indeed, that's exactly how things were going at first, as we said our goodbyes to the Morgans and Faradays: we were loud and proud. Of course, none of my peeps said a word about the fact that Aloha and I had devoured each other in front of them and were now acting like a couple, but everyone was most definitely nonverbally congratulating us.

And I loved it.

And then came our goodbye to Brett and Crystal. And Aloha walked it all back. Suddenly, we weren't loud and proud anymore. We were quiet and ashamed. And I hated it, even though I knew Aloha had my professional interests at heart. Because, fuck it. Barry be damned, this job be damned—this whole new potential *career* be damned—I'd have given my left nut to hear Aloha say to Crystal and Brett, "Hey, guys, Zander just fucked me raw in the bathroom and we can't wait to do it again. So, we're heading to the hotel to fuck like rabbits now. See you on Monday morning!"

Hey, a guy can dream, can't he?

Sighing, I stare at the text from Barry on my screen—the one asking if Aloha is sick—and I realize that, unfortunately, I've got to toe Aloha's line.

Yeah. AC wasn't feeling well at the bar but she's sleeping soundly at the hotel now. Just to be on the safe side, I'm gonna sit here with her. She plans to stay holed up in the hotel today, so she won't need coverage. I'm gonna take it easy today, too, so I'll handle anything she might need or want. We'll see you tonight at Casa Morgan. Z

I press send on the message and put my phone on my nightstand... just as fingertips begin sensuously stroking my tailbone.

"Oh, Shaggy Swaaaaggy," Aloha's voice coos behind me.

Hallelujah. I twist around and smile at her. "Well, hello there, sexy girl. I thought you were down for the count."

"Hell no. I was just recharging my batteries for round two." She flashes me a naughty smile and yanks at my shirt. "Take it off, Zandy Man. I stuffed a twenty into your waistband at Captain's. That means you owe me a striptease." She yanks again. "I've been dying to see you completely naked since the second I laid eyes on you in LA. Gimme."

I rise from the bed, a wicked smile on my face. "Oh, you want a striptease?"

"I do."

"Oh, I'll give you striptease."

As Aloha giggles and hoots, I head to my laptop across the small room and cue up a few songs, the first one being "Dancer" by Flo Rida. It's the song that happened to be playing at Reed's party when Aloha hypnotized Mr. Happy like a snake charmer on the dance floor. I didn't know it then, but I was Flo Rida that night—a guy falling in love with a dancer. Well, God willing, the tables will turn tonight and, as I dance for Aloha, this song will coax *her* into falling in love with *me*.

The song begins playing and Aloha squeals her approval. She puts her hands behind her head on the pillow, readying herself for the show. "Come to momma," she purrs.

I've never done a striptease before. Not even in a mirror. But I've seen Keane do it plenty of times, for audiences big and small. Plus, I've heard Keane recount his "stripping philosophy" more than a couple times, which basically boils down to giving your audience a long tease. *You gotta give 'em plenty of time to fantasize about your cock before you take it all off and show 'em the bulge,* Keane always used to say. *By the time you get down to your itty bitty G-string, you want the mere sight of your bulge to set 'em off.*

Words to live by.

I begin by gyrating my hips to the beat of the music. And when Aloha looks like she's had enough time to simmer at that heat level, I turn up the dial, but only a bit. I pull my shirt above my abs, giving her a peek, and then drop it back down. Rinse and repeat.

Finally when she's screaming for me to take it off, I peel my shirt off sloooowly and throw it at her, hitting her upside the head. And, much to my pleasure, Aloha squeals with glee.

My shirt off, I give Aloha a nice little tour of the gun show and my washboard abs. I flex and pose for a bit like a contestant in a Mister Universe competition—or, I guess, a Mister Bodyguard competition, if there is such a thing. And then I follow that bit of awesomeness by turning around gracing Aloha with some enthusiastic shakes of my rock-hard ass.

"Yassss!" Aloha yells. "Come to mommmmmaaaaa!"

Oh, God. This is fun. No wonder Peenie loved doing this so much.

After some slow thrusts and gyrations of my pelvis, I begin unbuttoning my pants—a maneuver that elicits hoots and mattress-pounding shrieks from Aloha. Laughing, I pull my pants down to the ground, revealing my hard-on straining behind red briefs.

"Red!" Aloha gasps, wacking the mattress with both palms like a seal on a rock. "Perfect! Yes! Red-hot! Oh, baby!"

I throw my pants at her, the same as my shirt, and she catches them and shrieks like she just caught a bouquet at a wedding.

"Don't stop now, Zandy Man!" she yells. "Let's see the *cock*!"

After a few pointed thrusts in my red briefs, I pull down my briefs, freeing one *very* happy Mr. Happy from his bondage. And Aloha loses her shit.

Aloha springs to her knees on the mattress and applauds raucously. She hoots. Grasps at her neck and cheeks like they're on fire, all the while bouncing up and down on her knees. "You're gorgeous! Incredible! *Beautiful*!" she shouts. "Oh my God, you're a god among men, Zander Shaw!"

I'm in heaven. If I didn't already love this adorable, sexy girl, I'd have fallen in love with her just now. I throw my briefs at Aloha and she brings them to her lips and kisses them ravenously—like, seriously, the woman is having a full-on make-out session with my briefs. And I laugh hysterically.

The song ends and the room falls silent.

Our laughter has subsided.

Raw sexual energy is coursing between us. Heat. Desire. *Need*. I'm wearing a wicked smile, a straining boner, and my tender heart on my proverbial sleeve. I'm hers and she knows it, in every conceivable way. I'm free. Unleashed. Nothing to hide now, in any way.

I shouldn't say it, but I can't resist. Apparently, she's not the only one who likes to play with fire. "You in love with me *now*?" I say with a smile.

She giggles. "Not yet. But I'm a whole lot closer than a few minutes ago when you were fully dressed."

Yet. The word sends rockets of excitement shooting straight to my dick. "I'll take it," I say, just as the next song on my playlist—

"Silvertongue" by Young the Giant—begins. I noticed Aloha going ballistic for this song when it played at Captain's earlier, so I figured I'd play it for her again now and see if it got her motor running behind closed doors. And, clearly, I made a wise choice.

I crawl onto the bed and kneel before her, taking the same position on the bed as Aloha. With my dick straining between our bodies, I peel off her shirt and then her bra and guide her back into a lying-down position. I get her out of her pants and undies, my entire body shaking with excitement. She's writhing. Moaning. Ready to go off at the slightest touch. Her thighs are glistening from her arousal. She's beyond wet and ready for me.

I spread her thighs and lap up the wetness on them and then head straight to her hard tip and she comes in under a minute. My entire body on fire, I crawl up to her face, every cell in my body alive with the desire to claim her, press my mouth against her ear, and whisper, "Time to show you what your body can do, sexy girl."

Chapter 37
Aloha

"Oh my God," I breathe. I grab the duvet underneath me with white knuckles. "What are you doing to me? How are you...? Oh, fuck! *Zander.*"

In a torrent of outrageous pleasure, I come harder than ever. Even harder than the last time and the time before that. So hard, I feel like I'm having a seizure. So hard, fluid is gushing out of me. This ain't no trickle this time. I'm a freaking porn star.

It's my fourth orgasm of the "sesh." My third since Zander started doing this crazy thing deep inside me with his fingers. And I swear to God, I think I'm gonna die of pleasure. But, oh, what a way to go.

When I come down from my fourth climax, Zander's already between my legs, lapping up whatever the hell just came out of me. I begin babbling. Thrashing. Gasping. I want to beg him to fuck me. But the syllables coming out of my mouth aren't making sense. I'm a wild animal.

Suddenly, Zander's lips are pressed against my ear, his fingers stroking that same spot deep inside me again, and his voice begins leading me to Nirvana again. Against all odds, his magic fingers are ramping me up to full-throttle, yet again.

"You're gonna come so hard this time, you're gonna crack wide open for me," he says, his voice low and intense. "Do you feel it coming, baby? Do you feel your body getting ready to split apart?"

I whimper and nod, on the verge of shrieking like a madwoman.

"Let go," he coos. "Listen to my voice. Imagine me fucking you hard."

I can't reply. I can only moan. I grab ahold of the bed cover beneath me, instinctively bracing for the looming tsunami...

Zander slides a finger up my ass as he continues stroking that magical spot deep inside me, and it's like he's flipped a switch inside me. A switch I didn't know existed. A next level of pleasure... one that turns me into a raving, rabid, electrocuted animal.

"*Yes!*" I blurt. And it's the last coherent thing I say before the most shockingly pleasurable orgasm of my life—a full-bodied seizure emanating from deep inside my core—rockets through me. Shockwaves of pleasure shoot across my every nerve ending. My walls and womb aren't simply rippling or rhythmically constricting—they're violently slamming up and down. Physically *quaking.* My eyes roll back into my head. I'm seeing flashes of light. Stars. Pinks. Whites. Yellows. *I'm seeing God.*

A stream of gibberish gushes from my mouth—sounds I've never made before, all of them punctuated, over and over again, with pleas for Zander to fuck me.

Without warning, Zander plunges himself inside me and I cry out with pleasure, enraptured.

I'm his. He's mine. He's magic. And I never want anyone else, ever, ever, ever, *ever.*

When Zander comes, he does it like a wild beast, the words *love you* slipping from his lips. He collapses on top of me, sweating profusely, quaking, shuddering, growling, his hard chest crushing my soft breasts.

Our hearts pound together for several minutes. Our breathing is ragged.

After a long moment, Zander rolls off me, breathing like a drowning man just pulled to safety. He pulls off his condom. "*Holy shit, Aloha.*"

"Holy shit."

"*Six*," he says. "Six! A new PR."

"*Damn, Gina,*" I say, and he laughs.

He catches his breath. "You feelin' good, baby?"

"I'm feelin'... dead. But in a good way. As in I'm resting in peace."

He laughs again.

I close my eyes. I wasn't joking actually. I've never felt this "at peace" in all my life. Satisfied. Serene. I feel... maximized. Is that a bizarre thing to think post-coitus? Oh, God, I feel like a freaking superhero. Sleep is coaxing me. Beckoning. The deepest, best sleep of my life. "Toothbrush," I murmur. "Facial cleanser. Moisturizer. Get. For. Me... Please."

He laughs. "I'll get everything you need from your room. You're not leaving my lair until it's time for us to head out to the Morgans' this evening."

"Mmm hmm."

I feel the mattress shift and then rise up sharply... and then...

"Aloha?"

"Mmm."

But whatever Zander says next, I don't hear it.

I'm out like a light.

Like an extremely peaceful and happy and powerful and sexually satisfied... fucking awesome... light.

Chapter 38
Zander

Iknow each and every one of Aloha's forced smiles. Her fake laughs. Her go-to catchphrases. The rote words Aloha falls back on whenever she's feeling anxious or panicky or bored or distracted but nonetheless knows "Aloha Carmichael" needs to do more than interact in any given situation, she needs to be dazzling. And I'm elated to observe that tonight at the Morgans', Aloha hasn't employed a single one of her familiar tricks. To the contrary, from the moment Aloha and I walked through the Morgans' front door three hours ago and immediately got dragged by Keane and Maddy into the garage for a hotly contested round-robin foosball tournament, I haven't observed Aloha switching into what I've come to regard as "Aloha Carmichael mode" even once. And I couldn't be more elated about it.

Watching the *real* Aloha remain "in the building" throughout every conversation and interaction thus far tonight has made my heart variously melt, race, and ache. It melted when Aloha cooed at Colby and Lydia's newborn daughter, Mia. It raced when she asked Ryan, Tessa, and Josh a bunch of questions about their plans to expand Captain's to a location in Los Angeles and then said, "Wow, I can't wait to come to the grand opening!" And it ached to the point of physical pain when Aloha stood in the middle of the Morgans' family room and taught Lydia and Colby's little girls, Isabella and Beatrice, the dance routine from her already-iconic "Pretty Girl" music video... and then, once the girls had gotten the steps, sort of, laughingly performed the dance with them for anyone lucky enough to witness the spectacle. And now, as we eat lasagna with the entire group at two large folding tables set up in the family room, it's plain to see the real Aloha is still very much in the building.

It's the usual suspects seated at the two large tables—all the Morgans and their significant others and kids. Plus, we're joined by the "unusual suspects" of Aloha, of course, my mother and sister, Henn and Hannah, and Barry. And at this point in the party, everyone is loose and relaxed and acting like one big, happy family.

"Hey, Rock Star!" Kat gushes. She's seated at my table, smiling and waving at her phone.

The sound of Dax's laughter wafts from Kat's hand. "Hey, Jizzy Pop!"

"Dax!" Mrs. Morgan chastises from the end of the long table.

Kat laughs. "Oops. I should have warned you, Daxy, I'm sitting here at dinner with the whole fam, including all the kiddos, plus a few guests who probably don't need to know all my lovely nicknames."

"Oh. Well, in that case: hello, sister Katherine!" Dax says, and the pair giggles. "Who all is there?"

"*Everyone!*" Kat says gleefully. She pans her phone around the room and everyone at the two tables waves and says hello to Dax as Kat's camera grazes over them. When the camera lands on Aloha and me, Dax blurts, "Holy crap! What's Aloha Carmichael doing in my house?"

Everyone, including Aloha, bursts out laughing.

"Kitty, bring me to Aloha for a sec."

Kat moves closer to Aloha, as requested.

Dax grins at Aloha. "Thanks so much for that amazing tweet, Aloha. You gave us a *huge* boost at exactly the right time. You're our 'angel investor,' so to speak."

"I was just being honest. I *love* the album. And so does everyone else in the world, apparently. Congrats."

"Thanks so much. Speaking of which... Hey, Kitty, stand at the back of the room so I can see everyone, all at once."

Kat moves to the far end of the room and stands on a chair, capturing both tables of people in her frame.

"I've got some cool news," Dax says. "I just found out 'People Like Us' cracked the Top Ten! It's number *nine*, guys—a worldwide smash!"

Pure pandemonium overtakes the room.

"A toast!" Ryan says, hopping up and raising his glass. "To Daxy and 22 Goats! And to 'People Like Us'—the first of many, *many* Top Ten songs for our boys!"

237

"Hear, hear!" everyone shouts, raising their glasses toward Dax's exuberant face. I glance at Aloha and she's visibly floored at the display of familial affection she's witnessing—staring at the Morgans like she's watching exotic animals humping in a zoo.

"Next stop? Number one!" Keane shouts, fist-pumping the air, and everyone cheers.

"Oh my gosh," Louise Morgan says, fanning herself and slumping against her husband's shoulder. "So much goodness, all at once. Daxy is a rock star. Keaney is an *actor* who's going to *cry* on TV and not just take off his clothes. And, most importantly, Mamma Mia is finally here and healthy and beautiful... " That's it. The poor woman can't go on. She chokes up and clamps her lips together, too moved to continue.

Ryan raises his glass again. "Let's drink to all of it, shall we?"

More cheers erupt.

"Hey, any excuse to drink," Kat says dryly, and everyone laughs.

Ryan turns to Keane. "Congrats, little brother. Slay, Peenie, slay. Chase those dreams and never stop."

Everyone raises their glasses to Keane, who looks moved.

Ryan turns next to Lydia. "Lydi-Bug, great job cooking and pushing Mamma Mia out. She's perfection." He winks at Colby. "Cheese, you did a great job helping Lydia make her, I'm sure, but we all know your job was nothing but the fun part."

Everyone, including Colby, laughs.

Ryan clinks Colby's and Lydia's glasses and resumes his seat.

"Hey, fam," Keane says, standing. "As long as we're going around the table giving props, can we send some love Maddy's way? Her latest documentary got honorable mention at a huge film festival last month."

"Woohoo!" Hannah says enthusiastically, and everyone mimics her and raises their glasses.

Keane smiles down at Maddy, a huge smile on his smitten face. "You crushed it, Mad Dog, because you're brilliant and gifted and the smartest person I've ever met. Cheers to you. This is only the beginning."

The table collectively swoons and exchanges glances like "Who the fuck *is* he now?" and then we all clink our glasses and drink to Maddy's success.

With an excited squeal, Isabella, Colby and Lydia's nine-year-old, leaps to standing with her glass of milk in hand. "Cheers to Theo! Last night, he played me a new song he wrote and it was his best one, ever! When he's a rock star, just like Uncle Daxy, I'm gonna go to his concert!"

Everyone cheers and whoops and laughs, including Dax who's still hanging out on FaceTime.

Theo thanks his little sister and then raises his glass back to her in reply. "To Izzy! She got third place in her school's spelling bee this week."

"To Izzy!" the enthusiastic crowd shouts.

Okay, this is getting ridiculous. I don't know if we're all drunk or what, but the adults at this table are finding this litany of toasts hilarious at this point.

"Yo, fam," Dax cuts in on Kat's phone. "It sounds like this lovefest is gonna go on for a while and I've been up all night. I gotta go. Love you all."

Everyone says their goodbyes to Dax. Tells him to stay safe and check in again soon.

But just before Kat ends the call, Dax says, "Oh, wait, Kitty. Bring me to Theo-Leo real quick."

Kat pans her camera onto Theo.

"I'll call you this week so you can play me that new song of yours, okay, little dude?"

"Awesome. Thanks, Uncle Daxy."

"You bet. Okay, bye, everyone. Be good."

Everyone congratulates Dax, yet again, and, finally, Kat ends the call.

And that's when, out of nowhere, four-year-old Beatrice sitting in my lap—whom I've been assuming has been dead asleep against my chest this whole time—abruptly lifts her head and shouts, "I got to be Miss Yeager's helper at pre-school today!"

Of course, everyone loses their mind at our little Bumble Bea's insane cuteness and we all raise our glasses to her stunning achievement. In the midst of the laughter and love swirling around us, I smile at Aloha next to me and my heart bursts at the glowing smile on her face. The girl is lit up like a Christmas tree and it's a sight to see.

I raise my glass to Aloha. "Can I get a little woot-woot for our beloved Alo-haha? She'd never mention this herself, but she just found out yesterday her *Pretty Girl* album has officially gone triple platinum."

"*Zander*," Aloha says shyly, just as a collective woot-woot rises up from both tables. In a flash, every glass of wine, beer, Scotch, apple juice, milk, and water is raised in Aloha's direction and a tidal wave of love is crashing down on her.

"To Aloha!" I say, and everyone follows suit.

I glance at Barry at the other table and the look of pure love on his face causes a lump to rise in my throat.

"Aloha," my mother says at the far end of my table, and I peel my eyes off Barry to look at her. She says, "I don't know what it means for an album to go 'triple platinum,' but it's obviously a big achievement. And I think that's wonderful, because I've always believed good things should happen to good people, of which you are most definitely one."

Oh, my shit. My normally talkative mother has barely spoken during this entire dinner party, opting instead to dote on the babies and silently watch me like a hawk. To think she broke her noticeable silence to say *that* to Aloha, in front of everyone, is making my heart feel like it's medically palpitating. And one look at Aloha, and it's clear she's feeling the same way.

I glance at my sister at the other table and she's visibly floored. And then I look at Aloha to my left again and my heart explodes to discover she's tearing up. I slide my free hand—the one not cuddling Bea—into Aloha's under the table and try not to well up with tears myself.

Normal conversation around the dinner table resumes. But I'm too mesmerized by Aloha's stunning face—and the palpable energy coursing between us—to focus on anything being said at the table.

". . . for you, Aloha?" Mrs. Morgan asks, drawing me out of my euphoric stupor.

Aloha turns away from me and gazes at Mrs. Morgan, her eyebrows raised in a question.

"I asked, what's next for you?" Mrs. Morgan says. "Where will the tour go next? Are you doing anything glamorous and exciting in the near future?"

Aloha graciously describes her remaining tour schedule. She talks briefly about some promo appearances and late-night TV interviews she's scheduled to do. And then, in wrap-up, she says she's going to perform next month at the Billboard Music Awards in Las Vegas.

"Oh, how exciting!" Mrs. Morgan says. "You must be so excited. We'll have to set our DVR."

My stomach clenches. I know full well, because Aloha's told me so herself, she's not excited about the performance, but, in fact, is dreading it. The same way she dreads all awards show performances and appearances. But will Aloha reveal that to Mrs. Morgan or simply flip into Aloha Carmichael mode?

"Um, actually, to be honest..." Aloha begins tentatively. She clears her throat. "Awards shows really aren't my favorite thing. They're actually extremely anxiety-producing for me."

My skin electrifies. I'm not happy about the sentiments Aloha just expressed, of course. I feel sorry for her. But I'm elated she feels comfortable enough in this crowd to tell the truth.

"Why are awards shows anxiety-producing?" Maddy asks.

"They tend to be particularly chaotic and disorganized. Plus, with so many celebrities, all in one place, all of them with their own personal bodyguards, it always feels like there are too many cooks in the kitchen and security actually feels lacking. Which is counter-intuitive, I know." She shrugs. "Awards shows are just a perfect storm of everything that stresses me out the most. Add to all that, it's a live performance, televised around the world, and I'm always worried I'll have some sort of panic attack in front of millions that will go viral and haunt me forever."

I look around the table at the people I love the most, and not surprisingly, everyone looks sympathetic and not the least bit judgmental. My eyes meet Barry's, and, instantly, I know he's as blown away by Aloha's stark honesty as I am.

"Can I ask what's probably a stupid question?" Kat says. "If you hate performing at awards shows so much, if they cause you severe anxiety, then why do you perform at them? You don't *have* to do them... right?"

Aloha opens her mouth. And then closes it. She cocks her head. "In theory, that's true, but... I don't really have a choice. They're an invaluable promotional opportunity and also a huge way I give back to my fans. Not everyone can afford a ticket to one of my shows. My fans don't know I suffer from anxiety. All they know is they want to see me sing their favorite song. So, mostly, I do it for them."

"You poor little thing," Mrs. Morgan says. "It sounds so stressful for you."

"What triggers your anxiety the most, Aloha?" Keane asks. "If you don't mind me asking."

Aloha twists her mouth. "Crowds, I guess. The feeling that people are pressing in on me and I have no personal space and can't breathe. Even fans who only want to show me love can freak me out sometimes. They get so excited to meet me, they scratch and claw at me. It can be scary. And painful. I've been cut and bruised and tossed around more times than I can count. Felt like I was being smothered. When I was little, I used to think the whole world wanted to hurt me or kidnap me. I'd constantly have terrifying nightmares about people chasing me or suffocating me or stealing me."

You could hear a pin drop in the room, other than the twin snoring sounds coming from little Beatrice in my lap and Colby's dog, Ralph, at his feet. Again, I glance at Barry at the other table and his expression reflects my emotions: heartache, protectiveness, *love*.

"I used to have anxiety when I was a kid," Keane says. "I still get it sometimes now, but not too often."

"I get anxiety," Theo pipes in. "Not as much as I used to, though, because my family and band have helped me so much."

"Your *band*?" Aloha says. "You're in a band?"

Theo grins proudly. "The Bedwetters."

Aloha chuckles. "Wow."

"We call ourselves that because I used to wet my bed—like, right up until last year. I got bullied pretty badly for it. So I decided to do what Uncle Daxy and Uncle Keaney both told me to do: make my most embarrassing thing a badge of honor. Uncle Keane told me, 'When they're running you outta town, get in front and make it look like a parade.'"

"Yee-boy, baby!" Keane shouts.

"So that's what I do."

For some reason, I feel compelled to glance at my mother at the other end of the table, and I'm surprised to find her staring at me, not at Theo as he speaks. And, suddenly, by the look in her eyes, I know my mother will be loving when I finally tell her about my feelings for Aloha. I don't know when that'll happen, of course. I've got no thumping desire to do it any time soon. But when I do, my gut tells me she'll be happy for me... right after she whoops my ass for screwing up the best job I've ever had.

"I'd love to hear that new song of yours," Aloha says to Theo.

"Really?" Theo says excitedly. "I didn't bring my guitar with me tonight, but I'm sure one of Uncle Dax's old guitars is here somewhere."

"There's probably one in Daxy's room," Colby says, popping up.

I have the urge to say, "Hold on, Cheese. Why don't you grab the guitar in Keane's room—the one I asked Keane to buy as a surprise gift for Aloha?" And, indeed, by the look Keane is shooting me, he's obviously thinking the same thing. But, no. I shake my head at Keane and bite my tongue. Now isn't the time to give Aloha that ribbon-tied guitar. My gut tells me I should give it to her in private, when it's just Aloha and me.

"Well, then," Mrs. Morgan says, drawing everyone's attention. Her blue eyes are glistening. She tucks her blonde bob behind her ear, takes a deep breath, and says, "Let's clear these tables and have our cake and ice cream on the couches while we listen to a concert by our very talented singer-songwriter, Theo-Leo. That sounds like a lovely plan to me."

Chapter 39
Zander

There were plenty of wackos and weirdos to choose from," Henn says, shaking his head. "People on the interwebs are scary, guys."

I'm standing in the Morgans' kitchen with Henn and Barry, swiping through photos of men and women, but mostly men, whom Henn, with an assist from Brett's buddy at the FBI, determined are a tad bit too obsessed with Aloha.

The rest of the party is in the family room, listening to Theo perform an original song. The pleasant sounds of Theo's singing and guitar strumming in the other room provide a stark contrast to the thunderous crashing of my heart. The mere thought that any of these "über-fans" might one day creep out from behind their keyboards and come at my baby, even if it's just to hug her way too hard and tell her they "love" her, is making my pulse skyrocket and my skin crawl.

Henn continues, "To be honest, I'm just chasing wild geese here, guys. The odds are high we'll never see hide nor hair of any of these wackos. I just did my best to narrow it down to my best hunches, like you asked."

"No, this is great," Barry says. "Will you send these to me?"

"I just did. Lemme know if you want me to do anything else."

Henn describes the further services he could provide, if desired—hacking and tracking, he calls it—and after a bit of discussion, Barry says that, at this stage of the game, the further assistance Henn could provide isn't justifiable from a cost/benefit standpoint.

"But if Aloha receives any kind of specific threat, whether anonymously or from anyone on our 'watch list,' we'll go balls to the walls with all of it," Barry says. And, begrudgingly, I have to agree it's the right call.

Suddenly, the sound of Aloha's voice mingling with Theo's drifts into the kitchen, and I'm instantly drawn like a moth to flame.

"Thanks, Henn," I say. "Great work. I think I'm gonna head into the other room and see what's shakin'." With that, I fist-bump Henn and Barry and hightail it straight out the door.

Chapter 40
Zander

The entire room erupts in applause when Aloha and Theo finish their song. Apparently, Aloha quickly caught on to the simple chorus of Theo's original song and joined in as his backup singer when the chorus came around the second and third times.

"That was amazing!" Theo says, strumming his last chord. "Can we do it again and get a video of it this time? Just for me. I won't post it."

"Of course. And post away."

Theo looks at his mother, his eyes wide. "Can I, Mom?"

Lydia gives her permission and, just like that, several Morgans pull out their phones as the duo launches into the song again. Only this time around, Aloha's picked up on even more of Theo's lyrics and melodies and she's now adding even more harmonies and vocal flourishes, all of which make the song shine almost like a professional masterpiece. *Wow.* I'd never tell Aloha this, but I'm enjoying what she's doing here with Theo even more than half the over-produced songs she performs on her tour. Those songs are catchy as hell and she's a powerhouse performing them with all the bells and whistles, but I prefer hearing her singing like this, with such purity and raw simplicity and backed by nothing but the warmth of Theo's acoustic guitar.

When the duo finishes singing Theo's song for the second time, the room erupts with even louder applause than before. For my part, I'm overcome with the urge to bound across the room and scoop Aloha into my arms and kiss the hell out of her in front of everyone in this room, the same way I brazenly devoured Aloha at Captain's last night. But I refrain, since Aloha is flanked by Theo and Izzy on that couch. Plus, surely, my every move is being scrutinized by the one-two punch of Barry and my mother.

When the applause dies down, Theo launches into another song. And then another. And with each song he plays, Aloha listens for the first quarter and then joins in when she gets it—each time visibly thrilling Theo and the entire room.

Finally, Theo puts down his guitar and everyone applauds and compliments him and Aloha before dispersing into little pockets of conversation and cake-eating around the room. I watch Aloha chatting with Theo and Izzy for a while, feeling pulled to her like a magnet to steel. And when Izzy bolts off the couch to join Colby in taking his boxer, Ralph, for a walk around the block, I seize the chance to assume Izzy's seat next to Aloha.

"What inspired that last song?" Aloha is asking Theo as I settle onto the couch.

"My dad dying when I was seven."

Aloha blanches. "Oh, Theo. I didn't know. I'm so sorry."

Theo tells Aloha about his late father and Aloha hugs him and whispers something into his ear.

"Thanks," Theo says as he pulls out of their embrace. "I think about him all the time. And when I do, I just do what Uncle Dax taught me to do: I put my feelings into a song."

"That song is so... *honest*. How did you get the courage to write like that—without holding anything back?"

Theo shrugs. "When I got my first guitar, Uncle Dax told me I should think about what kind of songwriter I wanted to be. He said there's music designed to make you tap your toe or shake your booty and music designed to touch people's souls. He said some songs do all three. Some do only one. That there's no right or wrong. But he said for him, personally, songwriting is always about touching people's souls. So, when I said I wanted to be just like him—that I wanted to write songs that touch people's souls, too, Uncle Daxy said, 'Okay, then, you've got to take a vow to be fearless. Not just with your songwriting, but in life. Because there might be someone out there who's going through a hard time and they'll hear your song and you'll help them, but only if you're one hundred percent honest.'"

Aloha is clearly bowled over. "But... how? How did you even get started?"

"I learned a bunch of songs on my guitar first, just to figure out

247

what stuff I liked to play and sing. Uncle Dax told me to learn songs that inspire me, so that's what I did."

Aloha swallows hard. "What songs inspire you?"

"Lots and lots. A biggie for me is 'Brave' by Sarah Bareilles. I play it all the time to remind myself to always say what needs to be said."

"I love that song," Aloha says, but her voice is small. Overwhelmed.

Theo reaches for his guitar excitedly. "You wanna sing it together?"

"No, you sing it to me, Theo-Leo. You're obviously a lot braver than I am. Hopefully, while I listen, some of your bravery will rub off on me."

Chapter 41
Zander

I stride down the hallway of our Seattle hotel, a ribbon-tied guitar in my hand. A while back, Aloha revealed she sometimes feels like a rudderless sailboat: she's got gale-force winds at her back and no way to steer. Well, after watching Aloha sing with Theo tonight, I've got a hunch this guitar might be her rudder.

As a favor to me, Barry accompanied Aloha back to the hotel from the Morgans earlier so I could secretly transport the guitar and give it to her later in private. And now, here I am, the guitar in my hand and excited butterflies in my stomach.

I reach Aloha's room and raise my fist to knock... and freeze when I hear crying on the other side of the door. *Shit.* I lean the guitar against the wall and pound on the door. "Aloha!"

No answer.

My chest tight, I grab the "emergency" keycard to Aloha's room and swipe it, but before I've turned the knob, the door opens and there she is, her pink journal in hand and tears streaming down her cheeks. As I lurch into the room, Aloha drops the journal to the floor and hurls herself at me. I pick her up and, quickly, we've assumed our usual monkey-in-a-tree position.

"Sweetheart," I say as I cross the room with my baby in my arms. "Tell me."

She shakes her head into my collarbone.

I reach the bed, lay her down onto her back, and survey her arms. But, thank God, there's nothing. Just to be thorough, though, I pull down the waistband on her shorts, one side at a time. Still nothing.

"I told you I'm not gonna do that again," she says, wiping her eyes.

249

"Yeah, and I'm gonna make damn sure of it." I sit on the edge of the bed and grab her hands. "Why are you crying? Give your pain to me."

She straddles my lap, slides her arms around my neck, and smashes her nose against mine. "Crying isn't always how I fall apart. Sometimes, it's how I put myself back together. I was writing poetry and it made me cry. But I'm okay."

My shoulders soften. "What were you writing about that made you cry?"

"Tonight. The joy of it. The heartbreak of it. Thinking about the fact that a twelve-year-old is a million times braver than me. I was remembering the look of pure joy on Mrs. Morgan's face when she heard Dax's song cracked the Top Ten. When a song cracked Top Ten for me for the first time, my mother's immediate reaction was to ask about my royalty rate for the song."

I nuzzle her nose. "Family doesn't have to be the people who share your DNA, you know. It can be the people you *choose*."

Choose me, Aloha.

Please, choose me.

I continue, "I know you feel like a canary in a gilded cage. But guess what? *There's no lock on the cage door*."

She crushes her mouth against mine.

In short order, our clothes are off, a condom is covering my hard dick, and I'm pulling her on top of me to ride me like a pony.

"You're so beautiful," I whisper as Aloha's body fucks mine enthusiastically. "Perfect. God, I love you." *Shit.*

But Aloha doesn't even flinch in the face of my latest slip-up. She just keeps right on fucking me, her pleasure ramping up without the slightest hitch.

A jolt of electricity flashes through my entire body like a thunderclap. I cup Aloha's breasts in my palms and lose myself as she fucks the living hell out of me. "*Aloha*," I grit out.

She opens her mouth like she's going to say something in reply. But, instead, her green eyes roll back into her head and she comes like fireworks around my cock.

The pleasure of her muscles constricting around me is too much for a mere mortal like me to withstand. I come so hard, I see flashes of blinding white light.

When we both come down, Aloha hurls herself off my cock and splays herself onto the mattress on her back. After removing my condom, I crash down onto the mattress next to her on my back, sweating and barely able to breathe.

"You're supernatural," I say between ragged breaths.

"Look, I can understand why you're madly in love with me. I'd be madly in love with me, too. But you gotta stop saying the magic words. You're cramping my style."

I laugh. "I'm cramping your style? Baby girl, I *am* your style. I've upped your street cred by a long mile."

"True."

"Don't even talk to me about cramping your style. I've seen the Disney robots you used to date—the *Fresh Prince of Bel Air* reject."

She laughs. "God, he was such a dork."

"Cramping your style," I mutter. "Please."

"But, seriously, dude. Whatever happened to 'playing it cool' for the rest of the tour? Whatever happened to keeping your big mouth shut and your big cock hard?"

"Yeah, that's not gonna happen, apparently. Sorry, not sorry."

She snuggles up to me, pressing her cheek against my chest. "Fine. Whatever. Just keep fucking me like that and you can say whatever the hell you want to me while we're *in flagrante delicto*."

I breathe a sigh of relief. It wasn't an "I love you, too, Zander." But it's progress. "I'll take it," I say. I roll onto my side and kiss her. And I'm relieved and thrilled when she kisses me back with equal passion, not a hint of skittishness about her. Out of nowhere, I bolt upright. "Shit! I just remembered something."

"Huh?"

I bound toward the door, buck naked. "Don't move, hula girl."

"Where the hell are you going?"

"I just remembered I left a little something for you in the hallway. Hopefully, it's still out there."

"You mean a *present*?"

"A present."

"For *meeeeee*?"

"For *youuuuu*."

Aloha sits up. "At least cover yourself with a towel, babe. You don't wanna scare a passing maid with your giant Alabama black snake."

Laughing, I grab a towel, put it around my waist, and fling open the door. And, hallelujah, the guitar is still there. I call to Aloha over my shoulder as I poke my upper torso out the door to grab it. "It's here! Close your eyes!"

"Oooh, this is so *exciting!*"

"Are your eyes closed?"

"Yes, sir."

I tiptoe back into the room with the guitar and stand before Aloha at the foot of the bed, butterflies ravaging my stomach. "Okay, *open.*"

Aloha opens her eyes. Her lips part in surprise, but she doesn't look elated. She looks... *terrified.* Like someone with an acute fear of heights who's just been brought to the bitter edge of a tall diving cliff and been told, "*Jump!*"

"Wow," Aloha chokes out, her chest heaving. "You got me a guitar."

"Dax told me exactly what kind to get."

She presses her lips together for a moment and then says politely, "Thank you. That was very sweet of you."

I chuckle. "And, *boom,* she flips into Aloha Carmichael mode on me." I wrap Aloha's hand around the neck of the guitar and push the base of it onto her lap. And then I grab the pink journal off the floor and put it in front of her on the bed. "You've got the beginnings of a hundred songs in this journal, my love," I say. "Beautiful, amazing, *honest* songs. Don't wait for permission to be brave like Theo, Aloha. Just do it. *Be brave.* Push open the door to your cage. Kick 'Aloha Carmichael' to the curb and decide to be nothing and nobody but... *you.*"

Chapter 42
Zander

I wake up to the sound of Aloha in the next room strumming her new guitar and singing "Brave"—that Sarah Bareilles song Theo sang for her last night. And my heart bursts.

Not long after I gave Aloha her new guitar last night, she started tentatively fiddling with it, much to my relief. She looked up the chords to a few simple songs. Songs with easy chord progressions she could muddle through singing and playing. When she flubbed a couple chords in rapid succession on "Here Comes the Sun," she laughed and said, "I was never an amazing guitarist, even back when I used to play every day. I was good enough to accompany myself in a basic way and write my little songs. So, don't expect musical genius here."

"Babe, you weren't put on this earth to be an amazing guitarist," I replied. "Don't let the guitar hold you back. Let it set you free."

So, she kept at it. And, soon, it was clear her fingers were remembering and her confidence was building. She was still playing and singing when I fell asleep in the wee hours of the morning.

And now, mere hours later, she's in there singing "Brave" like a boss—filling the suite with the most beautiful sound I've ever heard in my life.

I pull on a pair of briefs and beeline into the other room, and my heart explodes at the sight of her. She's in a tank top and undies, playing and singing her little heart out. Her dark hair is wild, splayed around her shoulders. Her face is on fire. If I were tasked with creating an artwork entitled "Woman Doing Exactly What She Was Born to Do," I'd pick Aloha in this very moment as my artistic inspiration.

Aloha's eyes lock with mine. She smiles as she continues playing and singing.

I take a seat across from her, my eyes trained on hers, my skin electrified. She's beauty incarnate in this moment. Breathtaking. Perfection.

When Aloha finishes her song, I applaud softly and rise, my chest heaving. I step forward until I'm standing immediately in front of her, looking down at her glowing face.

She grabs my bare torso and lays her cheek against my abs. "Thank you," she whispers. "I *love* it."

Oh, Jesus. For a split second, I thought Aloha was going to say "I love *you*." I take a deep, steadying breath. "You're very welcome. You sound great."

She smiles up at me. She looks exhausted but radiant. "I just couldn't stop playing and playing. Once I got going, I felt drugged."

"Did you sleep at all?"

"For about three hours. Crystal's gonna kill me for getting so little sleep the night before a show. Not to mention for using my voice all night."

"You'll sleep on the plane. Did you try playing any of your old songs?"

"Not yet."

Yet.

Damn. I'm beginning to love that little word.

"I'm sorry I woke you," she says.

I stroke the top of her hair. "Wake me every day for the rest of my life, singing like that." *Shit.* I add quickly, "I had to get up anyway. In exactly twenty-eight minutes, I'm scheduled to 'pick you up from your room' to escort you down to the car headed for the airport."

"Yeah, I need to get moving. Crystal just texted she'll be here in fifteen and Barry's coming to say a quick goodbye in twenty."

"Well, in that case, I'll shower in my room and report back here in twenty-*five*."

She laughs and runs her fingertip across the waistband of my briefs. "I wish we had a bit more time this morning. I'd give you the blowjob of your life to thank you for your amazing gift."

Arousal floods my cock. "Hold that thought until tonight. *Please.*"

She smiles. "I will."

I grasp her cheeks. "You're lit up, Aloha. Shining like a thousand suns."

"So are you."

"That's what happens when a man witnesses the most beautiful sight in the world." *Fuck, Zander. Stop.* I release her face. "Okay, hula girl. Enough pillow talk. I gotta put on my bodyguard cape now."

She reaches around me and squeezes my ass cheek. "Back on duty you go, Mr. Bodyguard."

I peel myself away from her and head toward the bedroom to grab my clothes off the floor.

"Hey, Mr. Bodyguard?"

I turn around just outside the bedroom door, my eyebrows raised.

"When you're on duty out there and you've got your game face on... if I touch my chin like *this*, just know it means I'm giving you a big ol' telepathic kiss."

I touch my chin and wink. "Right back at ya."

We share a brief smile before I head into the bedroom and start throwing my clothes on.

Aloha appears in the doorway, leaning against the jamb. "Would you do me a big favor on the plane today? Will you read my journal while I sleep?"

I stare at her, my heart in my mouth.

"I've got so much stuff in there, it's kind of overwhelming. Will you read the whole thing and see what leaps out at you? Tell me what you'd focus on, if you were me?"

My heart has resumed beating again, and now it's racing. "I'd be honored. I'm not a songwriter, but I can certainly tell you which poems or lines grab me the most."

"That's perfect. You know me better than anyone and I trust you completely, so I just want to know what stuff strikes you as the most *me*."

My heart is seriously not going to survive this conversation. "I'd be happy to give you my two cents. Of course."

"Thank you so much." She smiles shyly. "Do you have a journal?"

"No."

"If you did, I'd want to read it. Every word."

I bite my lip. "If you want to know something about me—anything at all—then just ask me. I'll always tell you the whole truth. I promise."

"I already know that. But thank you for saying it."

I take a huge breath and exhale before saying, "I gotta dip. God help me if I'm standing here in nothing but my underwear and a goofy smile when Barry arrives."

"God help you," she says, but her smile is every bit as beaming as mine.

I finish throwing on my clothes and bound to her. I kiss her gently. "See you in a bit, hula girl."

"Bye, Shaggy Swaggy."

She touches her chin.

I touch mine.

And then, as my heart explodes and splatters all over the walls of the swanky suite around me, I drag myself out the front door.

Chapter 43
Zander

oly fuck.

My eyes lurch from the opened journal in my hand to the top of Aloha's sleeping head. Aloha and I are sitting together on her private plane. Her head is resting on my shoulder. *And I need the fucking crash cart.*

I've been reading Aloha's pink journal during the flight from Seattle as she asked me to do. And while many of Aloha's poems have elicited strong reactions from me, nothing has come close to obliterating my heart the way this particular one just did. I'm not sure precisely when Aloha wrote it, but based on its content and physical placement in the journal, it's obviously a recent entry. And it's undoubtedly, explicitly about *me.* Or, rather, about *us.*

I inhale the scent of Aloha's coconut shampoo—the scent that's become an addiction to me by now—exhale slowly, look down, and read the entire poem again.

The Bodyguard and the Hula Girl

He's my boy toy
And I'm his hula girl.
He's Mister Bodyguard
And I'm a kitten's breath away
From falling hard.
Or maybe just falling
Into the abyss
And selfishly using his bright smile and kiss
As a breathing apparatus.
Am I toying with this boy's heart?

I don't mean to do it, if I am,
Honestly.
But, yeah, probably, I am.
Because it comes so naturally to me
To tease and please, so damned easily
That I might not even know it
If indeed I'm performing
Or otherwise committing a sin or misdeed.
Is this a yarn I'm spinning
Or a true story with a perfect beginning?
If this is a dream, then don't wake me from it,
Please.
And if it's more than that,
If it's genuine reality,
Then teach me how to believe it,
To know for certain when a romance goes
From ephemeral to irrevocable,
Fictional to factual,
When a fairytale becomes dependable and actual,
Rather than merely hormonal and situational.
Yes, I've been playing with my boy toy,
I'm sure of it now,
All the while praying I don't break him
Or make him hate me
Or leave me,
Or, God forbid, go back to Daphne.
That bitch.
But is she really more of a bitch than me?
Because I've been playing with my boy toy
Shamelessly,
All the while closing my eyes and praying
That when he finds out The Package
Ain't what she's cracked up to be
He'll still somehow, miraculously,
Inexplicably...
For reasons that will surely escape me...
Reject the fate of poor Kevin and Whitney
And decide to stay with me,

His fucked-up hula girl,
His koala in a eucalyptus tree,
His clingy baby monkey.
And by "stay," by the way,
I mean to say not just for a tour,
But until a far-away day...
As far away as...
Maybe...
Dare I say it...
At the risk of sounding silly or naïve
Or even flat-out crazy...
An eternity?

Chapter 44
Aloha

T he production manager presses her headset into her ear and listens for a moment. "Okay, they're telling me four minutes, Aloha."

I'm sitting next to Zander in the green room backstage at the Billboard Music Awards in Las Vegas, awaiting my cue to head to the stage for my performance. So far tonight, I've won two awards and also had the supreme pleasure of introducing a performance via satellite by a hot new indie rock band from Seattle who was added to the show's lineup at the last minute—a little trio with the number one song in the world right now who, unfortunately, couldn't be here in person tonight due to their touring schedule. A little band called 22 Goats.

I look at Zander sitting next to me on the couch. He's got his game face on now, but an hour ago, while watching Dax and the boys perform their monster hit on a jumbo screen, he looked like a little kid on Christmas morning. When I came offstage after introducing 22 Goats and stood next to Zander to watch the boys' performance, it was hard for me to decide where to look: at Dax and the boys slaying it up on the jumbo screen or at Zander's euphoric face. In the end, I wound up missing most of the boys' performance.

But that was then and this is now. All traces of euphoria are gone from my bodyguard's gorgeous face at the moment as he sits next to me in this green room staring stoically straight ahead, his expression telling the world he'll throttle anyone who so much as looks at me funny. Which is wildly unnecessary in this secured green room filled with nobody but production staff and fellow music artists and their entourages. But, whatever. I'm not complaining. Whenever Zander adopts his "badass bodyguard demeanor," it always helps calm me down in stressful situations.

Speaking of which... *ooph*... another wave of anxiety is crashing into me. *God, I hate performing at awards shows.* I close my eyes and focus on my breathing exercises. Surely, once I get onstage and start singing, I'll be fine. It's just the anticipation that gets to me at these things. The chaos that's inherently part of the process.

As I breathe deeply with my eyes closed, I feel Zander's index finger poke against my bare thigh. *Boop.* It's what Zander always does when he's officially on duty but senses I might need a little TLC. *Boop.* Just that little touch to my thigh—or sometimes to my inner forearm—and he always manages to wrangle my spiraling thoughts, at least temporarily. It's like he's giving me a physical spot to stow my anxiety for a minute. *Put it right here, baby. Boop.*

I turn my head toward Zander to find him looking at me, his dark eyes full of concern. I nod, telling him his *boop* helped, and he touches his chin, telling me he's telepathically kissing me—and also, probably, knowing him, thinking a certain three little words. The ones he's been banned from saying out loud until further notice. Zander let those verboten three little words slip out a couple times in Seattle a month ago, but, thankfully, after a conversation we had on the plane out of Seattle, he hasn't uttered them since.

The conversation in question happened after I'd just awakened from a nap on the plane to find him holding my pink journal and looking at me like I was the freaking Virgin Mary appearing in a piece of toast.

"What?" I asked, rubbing my eyes.

"I read the whole thing, cover to cover," Zander replied, holding up the pink journal, a huge smile on his face. "Three times."

"Great," I said, my heart clanging. "As I recall, I was the one who asked you to read it."

He smirked. "You know, Aloha, for a girl who loves coming across like she's got zero filter, you sure think a whole lotta interesting things you don't say out loud."

"Yeah, maybe you should try it some time," I replied. "I know this is a new concept to you, Mr. Spill Your Guts, but it's possible for a person to *not* say every damned thing they're thinking or feeling at any given moment."

Zander laughed heartily at that, grabbed my hand, kissed the top of it, and said, "I'm thinking something right now I'm not saying, actually. Something pretty cool—three little words. You wanna know what they are?"

"No, thank you," I replied. Because, truthfully, as much as a part of me swooned *hard* when Zander declared his supposedly undying love for me those couple of times in Seattle, an even bigger part of me freaked the fuck out. "In fact, here's an idea," I said. "How about you not only *don't* say those three little words out loud now, but you see how long you can go without saying them. Wouldn't that be a fun game—to see how long you can go without blurting those three little words to me?"

Zander winked, patted the cover of my pink journal, and said, "Okay, baby. I'll zip it. For now. Whenever I'm feeling the urge to spill my guts, I'll just open this journal and read some of the words you think and feel but don't say out loud."

"Fabulous."

And that was that. Zander hasn't let it slip he loves me even once this past month.

And, oh, what a month it's been. We've done all the same non-tour-related things we did before we started having sex: watching movies, talking, working out. But on top of all that, we've added a few new items to our itinerary. Sex, of course. Sleeping together in my bed every night. And, last but not least, what I call our "songwriting sessions."

As a point of fact, I'm the only one who writes songs during "our" songwriting sessions. But Zander's contribution isn't insignificant. While I play my guitar and scribble lyrics in my sparkly green journal—a gift from Zander because, he said, it reminded him of my eyes—Zander hangs out across the room and makes me feel like a songwriting genius. Sometimes, Zander plays videogames on his iPad while I'm writing my songs. Other times, he does sit-ups or pushups or stretches on the floor. At times, he exchanges texts with Keane or Dax or his sister. Honestly, I don't always know what the heck Zander is doing on the other side of the room when I'm lost in my writing. All I know is, I can count on him to look up from whatever he's doing every few minutes and say something like, "*Nice!*" or "My baby is brilliant!" or "Now *that's* what I'm talkin' about, Willis!"

And if I want Zander's opinion on something, he's always right there for me. Like, if I look up from my guitar or journal and say, "Do you think this song would sound better if I go like *this*... or like *this*?", then Zander will reply with something like, "Well, I'm no songwriter. You're the genius songwriter here. But if you ask me, then I think I prefer it the second way you did it."

Sometimes, when I'm struggling with where to go with the lyrics on a particular song, Zander will flip open my old pink journal, which he's basically committed to memory by now, and he'll suggest a stand-out line or two. Like, maybe he'll say, "You could patch this line into what you're doing over there, babe. I think that would be tight. But you're the artist, not me, so follow your gut." And you know what? *He's always right.* And yet, even with Zander's amazing track record of always having the perfect idea right when I need it, he never forces me in any particular direction with my writing. Never tries to take over or commandeer my creative process. Because, as Zander always says, he's not my songwriting partner, he's my *hype man*.

"It's time, Aloha."

I look up to find that same production manager with the headset standing before me.

"Will you follow me, please?"

With Zander in front of me, I follow her, winding my way through the sprawling backstage area to the wings of the stage... and then wait again. Typical.

At my new waiting spot, I close my eyes to block out the crush and chaos of people around me. The people wanting to pat me on the back and tell me to break a leg. Thankfully, Zander won't let them get to me, even if they're big artists themselves. He's hunched over me, creating a little Zander-bubble nobody can penetrate.

"Box breaths," Zander whispers across the top of my head, his massive body hulking over mine.

I begin counting the outline of a rectangle—the "box" of the particular breathing exercise he's suggested—until the production manager gives me the go-ahead to take my designated spot onstage.

After a quick touch of my chin directed at Zander, which he returns in kind, I walk on rubbery legs to my mark, wave to my musicians behind me, and try to force air into my lungs.

The production manager's voice sounds in my ear monitors. "Isabel, you're on in five, four, three..."

On a nearby stage, Isabel Randolph, a movie actress, begins introducing me into a camera, her voice sounding in my ear monitors: "...the world's favorite 'Pretty Girl,' *Aloha Carmichael!*"

The audience packed below me at the foot of the stage begins cheering and screaming. The light on the camera in front of me switches to bright red. The voice in my ear monitors says, "Cue Aloha's band!" and my band kicks into gear.

I open my mouth and let my voice pour out and, instantly, my anxiety is gone. I'm Aloha Carmichael, once again.

As I sing, my dancers rush onto the stage, filling the large space with their gyrating, sparkling bodies. When I reach the first chorus of the song, I leave my dancers behind and begin strutting, as choreographed, down a long, narrow strip of stage jutting into the audience in a "T" shape from the main stage. At the midway point of the runway, I turn around, right on cue, to face my dancers gyrating on the main stage... and freeze. *Oh my god.* Some dude is pulling himself up and over the edge of the runway about twenty yards away from me! *How did he get past the security guards lining the foot of the stage?*

The interloper rises to his full height, looking me dead in the eye as he moves. And, instantly, from the deranged look on the man's face, I know he's not a light-hearted prankster. This is no joy ride for this man. This is something dark.

But the man has no sooner taken two bounding steps toward me than Zander appears out of nowhere, charging at him from behind. In a flash, before I can move or scream, Zander lowers his shoulder like a linebacker and body-slams the guy into next week, sending him hurtling off the stage like a monkey-sock-puppet flung out of a toddler's crib.

At Zander's beastly hit, the guy's slack body flies through the air and lands smack on the ground below the stage, just inside a security barrier—the perfect landing spot for two security guards dressed in yellow to pounce on him like ants on a crumb.

My eyes return to Zander charging at me. He didn't break stride when he bounced that fucker off the stage, and now he's still coming at me at full speed like a man possessed.

Before I've even moved a muscle, Zander reaches me, scoops me into his muscled arms, and keeps on running toward the end of the long runway.

"Commercial break!" the stage manager barks in my ear monitors, just before I melt into Zander's chest. Is it possible to swoon to death? If so, may I rest in peace.

Holding me in his arms like a bride, Zander shoots down a metal staircase at the end of the runway, marches straight past two yellow-clad security guards standing at the base of the stairs, and strides straight through the audience, parting it like Moses in the Red Sea.

"Not on my watch, motherfucker," Zander mutters under his breath, a vein in his neck throbbing. He lowers his head and leans into my face. "You okay, baby?"

"I am now."

He pulls me closer to him. So close, I can feel his heart thumping against me. "I'll never let anybody hurt you, Aloha. *Never.*"

"Oh, Zander." I let out a long, swooning sigh. "My shaggy, swaggy... *bodyguard.*"

Chapter 45
Aloha

Zander blasts through some double-doors and we're suddenly being swarmed by frantic people wearing headsets.

I clamp my eyes shut, trying to block out the urgent voices and movement around me.

I feel Zander clutch me even more tightly and then turn sharply and veer off.

A voice is blaring in my ears and I rip my monitors out.

I sense the general ambience around me changing. There's a sensation of relative calm.

I open my eyes. We're in a small room. There's a table with catered food laid out to one side. A bar with a bartender in a bowtie on the other. Security guards are standing at the door. We're obviously in some sort of VIP room. I exhale.

Those same frantic people from before enter the room. I recognize them. They're producers of the show. They want to know if I'm all right. I tell them I'm fine. That I just want to leave this place. That I need peace and quiet. *I need to leave.*

Zander still hasn't put me down. He's holding onto me like I'm the crown jewels. *And I like it.* I clutch his neck and whisper, "Don't put me down."

"I'm never putting you down as long as I live," he replies.

There's a commotion at the door. And then the members of my team in attendance tonight burst into the room—my publicist, my business manager, and Reed Rivers. The usual "suits" who attend awards shows.

I assure them I'm all right. Brief conversation ensues. They tell Zander he's a badass motherfucker hero. Reed Rivers starts giving one of the producers holy hell. I tune everyone out.

After a moment, I realize it's kind of bizarre Zander is still holding me, so I tell him to put me into a chair.

He asks me if I'm sure. I tell him I am. And he begrudgingly complies with my request.

Someone hands me a bottle of water. I drink the whole thing down and ask for a double shot of tequila. Conversation around me turns animated. Agitated. The double shot of tequila I asked for arrives and I throw it back. And tune back out.

And through it all, my gaze continues to be pulled to my hunky, heroic Zander. To his dark, blazing eyes and clenched jaw. To his strong arms and the way he fills out his dapper suit. To the palpable heat wafting off his body and the vein in his neck that still hasn't stopped throbbing. To the pure goodness and kindness and fierce loyalty radiating off him.

I love you.

The words spring to my mind, unbidden, shocking me.

I love you, Zander.

Holy fuck.

I've never thought the magic words about anyone in my life. Not like this, anyway, regarding someone I'm having sex with and sleeping with every night. Yes, I say the words a hundred times a day to strangers and dancers and sound guys and crew. But I've never said them to a man who's licked me between my legs. And yet, here I am, thinking them on a running loop about Zander.

My publicist touches my arm, drawing me out of my shocking thoughts.

"Whenever you're ready."

"Huh?"

"To head over to the press room."

"Huh?"

"The world will be dying to hear from you." She looks at Zander. "And you, too, Z, if you're up for doing some interviews. The two of you will be king and queen of the prom." She looks down at her phone and fiddles with something until her face lights up like the Fourth of July. "Ha! You're already trending on Twitter! A clip of Zander knocking that guy off the stage and scooping you up is already going viral." She looks up, her face aglow. "Okay, on second thought, let's not go to the press room tonight at all. We'll give the world a few days to whip themselves into a frenzy over the video. And then we'll figure out our game plan—whether we want to do an exclusive with one of our favorites or more of an interview tour."

I look at Zander. He's trying to look impassive, but I can read him like a book. The man wants to throat-punch my publicist right now. And I don't blame him. She's not "reading the room" very well, as they say. But what Zander doesn't understand, and I do, is that she's only doing what she exists in my world to do. What she's paid handsomely to do. Maximize publicity for me. Keep me on the tips of everyone's tongues while always preserving my brand. What Zander doesn't understand, but I do, is that this woman's job isn't ensuring my well-being. She's not my friend. She's not my therapist. She's not my bodyguard. She's the woman paid to *sell* me.

I continue staring at Zander, though I'm speaking to my publicist. "I'm not going to talk about this incident in the media, Claudia. Not now or ever. I want to put it behind me, starting now."

Zander's shoulders relax. He nods his approval.

"But, Aloha, the publicity—"

"I don't care about publicity," I snap. "I don't care about giving the world what they want. I only care about giving *me* what *I* want. And what I want is to not talk about this in a goddamned interview." Of course, since what I *also* want is to fuck my man and then, after that, party like a pop star with my good friends, I turn to Reed next. "I'm gonna take a couple hours to decompress and then Zander and I will hit your after-party in a bit. Sound good?"

"You sure you still want to come to the after-party?" Reed says. "It's not a command performance, you know. If you're not feeling—"

"No, no, I want to come," I say. "Wild horses couldn't keep me away, actually."

It's the truth. But the reason I wouldn't miss Reed's party for anything isn't because Reed Rivers' parties are *the* place to see and be seen. It's because a group of people I genuinely like—my new friends—will be there: Josh and Kat, Jonas and Sarah, Henn and Hannah, Ryan and Tessa, and, of course, my favorite duo in the whole world, Keane and Maddy. Plus, Big Barry will be there, too, overseeing security for the shindig. So, why *wouldn't* I want to go, regardless of what just happened?

"Great," Reed says. "I'll see you in a few hours, then."

I smile at Zander. "Ready, Mr. Bodyguard?"

"I was born ready, Miss Carmichael."

With that, Zander scoops me up like a bride, clutches me to him even more tightly than before, and marches out of the room.

Chapter 46
Aloha

As Zander walks through the chaotic maze of the sprawling MGM Grand with me in his arms, people all around us stop and gawk and pull out their phones. They shout at Zander he's "the man" and a "fucking beast" and tell me they love me. But Zander and I only have eyes for each other.

"Where are you taking me?" I ask.

"To grab a cab at the front of the hotel. We had a limo scheduled to pick us up at the back of the arena, but, obviously, that plan got shot to hell."

"Where will we go in the cab?" I ask flirtatiously.

"To our hotel," he says matter-of-factly. "Where I'm gonna fuck you like you've never been fucked before."

Adrenaline floods me. I feel the uncontrollable urge to kiss him. "Put me down for a sec."

"*Here?*"

"Yes."

"*Now?*"

"Yes. Please."

Zander stops. He looks around and then puts me down, as requested. And, immediately, I pull on his shirt and guide him down to my lips... and, in short order, we're kissing passionately.

Cheers and catcalls rise up around us, egging us on. I've never kissed Zander in public before, and knowing this kiss will wind up all over the internet is exciting to me.

"Woohoo!" someone shouts to my right. "Did Zander just propose, Aloha?"

"Show us the ring!" someone else shouts.

"Congratulations!" another person yells.

I giggle into Zander's lips.

"I'm on duty, baby," he whispers. "We gotta stop now."

We break apart, and as we do, someone shouts, "When's the wedding?" And it's only then that we realize we've been kissing the hell out of each other smack in front of a high-end jewelry store inside the MGM Grand. Specifically, in front of a glass display of diamond engagement rings. How did I not notice this store when I told Zander to put me down?

Zander's eyes ignite. "Give the people what they want, right?"

I look at him quizzically.

"Let's do it," he says, his eyes ablaze. "Let's get married, Aloha."

"*What?*"

"Let's get married in Las Vegas."

I open my mouth to speak, but he cuts me off.

"Don't speak. Only listen." He grabs my hands. He's trembling. "I love you and always will. My heart is yours and will be forever. I know you can't promise me forever in return, and that's okay. Because I know in my heart you love me right now, the same way I love you. Don't speak!"

I clamp my lips together again.

"This past month has been heaven, hasn't it? Well, it could be like that forever. I know it could." He beams a heart-stopping smile at me. "Cannonball into the pool with me, Aloha. Be my wife. We're gonna be glued at the hip the rest of the tour, anyway, right? Neither of us is going anywhere for another month. So, be my wife. If you wake up in New York and decide it was the worst mistake of your life, then, fine, annul it. Divorce me. Whatever. I won't fight you. And I don't want a dime of your money. Just marry me tonight and be my wife for the next month, at the very least. Give me this gift, please. Give me the one thing you've never given to anybody else in the entire world. Be all mine legally and under God and let me be yours."

My mind is reeling. My heart is exploding. "Don't we need a marriage license to do this?"

Zander's eyes burst into flames. "Is that a yes?" Without waiting for my reply, he gets down on one knee, looks up at me, smiling, and says, "Aloha Carmichael, my love, will you marry me? I love you, Aloha. Please leap with me. Cannonball into the pool. Say *yes*."

I take a deep breath and then say the unthinkable: "Yes!"

Zander whoops, springs up, and twirls me around. When he puts me back down, we kiss like crazy, much to the glee of everyone standing around us, all of whom are holding up their phones.

Still laughing, Zander pulls out his phone and taps out a search with shaking hands. "Okay," he says. "We *do* need a marriage license to do it legally, *but* it says we can easily get one from the Marriage License Bureau in a matter of minutes." He looks up from his phone, grinning from ear to ear. "They're open until midnight and there's a quickie wedding place right across the street. Holy fuck, it's like God himself wants us to do this, Aloha!"

Excitement surges inside me. In fact, I don't think I've ever been as excited as I am in this moment. "Well," I say, "we can't very well disappoint *God,* can we? Let's go!"

Chapter 47
Aloha

Zander and I burst into the Marriage License Bureau, still laughing from our giddy cab ride. There are several couples waiting in the small, sterile room, and the moment Zander and I walk in, the place erupts. Phones come out. Catcalls and cheers abound. A security guard who was milling in front when we waltzed into the building positions himself outside the door, apparently deciding nobody else will be coming into the Bureau until Zander and I have completed our business. I blow him a kiss and he winks.

When we reach the counter, Zander lays his large palms down and smiles gleefully at the flabbergasted clerk behind it. "Hello there, ma'am," he booms. "My fiancée and I are here for a marriage license!"

"Because we're getting married," I add. "Like, *legally*."

Zander and I giggle at the shocking statement.

Oh, God, I feel drunk, even though I'm perfectly sober. I feel *alive*.

"Congratulations," the clerk says. "Fill out this form. And I'll need to see a photo ID from each of you."

Without hesitation, Zander pulls out his wallet and slides his ID across the counter, but I'm a deer in headlights.

"I don't have my ID with me," I whisper to the clerk, my throat tightening. "I came straight here from performing at the Billboard Music Awards. Literally, I came offstage, still in costume, and came here." I gesture to my sparkling corset.

The woman looks behind her before leaning forward and whispering, "I'll check the box on the form that says I verified your ID." She winks. "You're just about the only person in the world I'd break the rules for, Aloha. But my daughter grew up watching your show and she's one of your biggest Aloha-nators now."

We thank her profusely, fill out the brief form, and then head to

273

a row of nearby chairs to await our license, which the clerk assures us will be in our hands in under fifteen minutes.

Just as we're taking our seats, a woman approaches, her phone in hand, asking for a selfie.

But Zander politely shuts her down. "Sorry," he says. "I've banned selfies for my fiancée for the rest of the night. Just for tonight, she isn't the world's. She's mine."

The woman visibly swoons and says she understands. "I saw what you did tonight," she says to Zander. "It was amazing." She addresses me. "If my man did that for me, I'd marry him, too."

When the woman walks away, Zander holds up a pen and a blank piece of paper he apparently grabbed off the counter. "Time to write our prenup."

"Our *prenup*?"

But he's already scribbling away.

I, Zander Jarvis Shaw, of sound mind and body, want to marry Aloha Leilani Carmichael because I love her and she loves me. If our marriage ends, which I hope and pray never happens, I will leave the marriage with whatever was mine when it started, plus whatever I've earned or acquired on my own during the marriage. Nothing else. I don't want a penny from her, ever.

Zander looks up. "Good?"

I'm speechless. Vibrating. Surging with adrenaline. *Shit just got real.*

"Anything you want me to add or change?" Zander asks. And I can hear his heart beating from here.

If that man thinks he sneaked in "and she loves me" without me noticing, he's mistaken. But I have no desire to make him delete it. No desire, at all. "Looks good," I say, and Zander's face ignites like a thousand stars. "But add that we're both entitled to keep any gifts, past or future. No matter what, I want to keep my beloved guitar and sparkly green journal." I hold up my hand to display the simple band on my finger, bought for me by Zander mere minutes ago at that jewelry store in the MGM Grand. "And, of course, this beautiful ring."

Zander had wanted to buy me a different ring. Something with diamonds he obviously couldn't afford. But I refused. The man wouldn't let me chip in on the purchase, after all, and I wasn't about to let him go into debt buying a ring for a marriage we both know isn't going to last more than a month.

Zander sighs. "I wish I could have afforded a ring with a big, fat diamond on it."

"Bite your tongue, fiancé. I *love* this pretty ring and if you say one more word about wishing I had a different one, I'm calling the whole marriage off."

Zander comically clamps his lips together and zips his mouth, making me chuckle.

I tap on the paper. "Add the thing about the gifts. And make it a two-way street."

Exhaling with annoyance, Zander dutifully writes:

Both Zander and Aloha agree they'll keep whatever gifts they might give each other, whether before or after the marriage. And, thank God for Aloha, that includes any snazzy macaroni necklace Zander might make for her at some point during the marriage.

"This isn't a joke, Zander," I say. "Add 'No matter how big or small the gift might be.'"

"Aloha, no. All that does it make it so *you* can give *me* something and that defeats the whole purpose of this thing. This isn't for *my* protection. It's for yours. The only thing I want is to make it clear to you and the entire world I don't want a damned thing from you, ever. I only want *you.*"

"But I want to give you gifts."

"I don't want gifts."

"You've given *me* gifts."

"That's different."

"How? You're allowed to shower me with gifts and I'm not allowed to do the same for my Shaggy Swaggy Hubby Bubby?"

"Correct."

"That's not fair. Giving gifts feels good, Zander. It's fun. You'd want to deny me pleasure and fun? *How rude.*" I tap on the paper again and insist. Because just this fast, my mind is already teeming with gift ideas—a sick new car, obviously. A closet full of designer clothes and shoes. Oh, and some big-ass diamond studs for his ears—

rocks twice the size of the ones he's wearing now. No, three times the size! Yes! And then, whenever everything turns to shit for us—whether that happens in a month or two—or, shit, in a week?—I'm sure I'll want to give Zander a big ol' chunk of change as a parting gift. A million bucks is what I'm thinking at the moment. And I don't want my lawyers to say boo about any of it when the time comes.

Zander grumbles. Clearly, he's not enjoying this conversation in the slightest. But come on, Zander's the one who brought up the prenup in the first place. If we're going to do it, let's do it right.

At my insistence, Zander finally adds the thing about gifts, big or small, and we sign and date our nifty prenup. That task completed, Zander takes a photo of it and texts the photo to me, since I don't have my phone with me. And then he puts down his phone, takes my face into his large palms, and says, "I can't wait to call you my *wife*."

I'm vaguely aware people are staring, but I don't care. Let them stare. I smile into Zander's beautiful face and say, "I can't wait to call you my husband." And, to my surprise, I mean it. *I can't wait.*

Elation floods Zander's gorgeous face. He leans in and kisses me and I throw my arms around his neck and kiss him passionately in return, eliciting cheers and catcalls from our small audience.

"Zander and Aloha?" the clerk calls out from behind the counter. "Your license is ready."

We break away from our kiss and bound to the counter, our hands clasped and goofy smiles plastered on our faces.

"Hey, would you mind if I texted Keane and Maddy to meet us across the street at the wedding place?" Zander says. "I need my best man."

"Of course," I say. "Hopefully, Maddy will agree to be my maid of honor."

Our license in hand and the text to Keane sent, we bound toward the front door like we're walking on a cloud.

"My mother is gonna *kill* me," Zander says, chuckling.

"Mine, too," I say, giggling with him. "I wish so badly I could see the look on her face when she hears the news."

Zander indicates the people around us in the waiting room. "I'm guessing it won't take long for either of our moms to hear about this."

We reach the front door and the security guard warns us a bit of a crowd has gathered out there.

"Shit," Zander says. "I'll text Brett to meet us across the street at the wedding place, too. I'll tell him to station himself outside. Something tells me we're gonna need a little help getting into a cab after we say 'I do.'"

Chapter 48
Zander

Swirling lights. The crush of writhing bodies packed onto the dance floor. All around us, people, people, people, including some of the ones I love the most, are partying and dancing and letting loose.

The song blaring is "Cheap Thrill" by Sia, and Aloha and I are singing the lyrics at the tops of our lungs. We're living this song! Because I might have no money, motherfucker, but I got myself a *wife*! I still can't believe it. Aloha Carmichael is my *wife*. She's all mine, mine, mine. Can *anyone* else in the history of the world say that? Nope. Just me. Ka-*bam,* son!

I'm drunk. But the good kind. And so is my hot wife. And, yeah, we're practically fucking on the dance floor at this point. But, hey, we don't give a shit who sees us making out, even though we're at this huge party with all these people, lots of them highly famous, because... have I mentioned this yet? Aloha Carmichael is my *wife*.

Brett is officially on-duty tonight, watching out for Aloha from afar in this nightclub, since I'm clearly three sheets to the wind... and... also... It's my wedding night, motherfuckers! But, come on, Brett's not even needed at this party. It's filled with celebrities and VIPs only—and the front door of the nightclub is being guarded like Fort Knox.

Suddenly, even through my drunken, happy, horny stupor, I feel a sharp squeeze to my shoulder. No, not a squeeze, a Dr. Spock death grip. I whirl around, ready to punch out whoever's touching me, and...

Oh, shit.

It's Barry. Looking at me like he's about to body-slam me into the nearest wall.

Barry motions sharply, nonverbally telling me he wants Aloha and me to follow him off the dance floor *right fucking now*.

I look at Aloha and she bursts out laughing. So I laugh, too. Barry wants to fire me for marrying Aloha? Or maybe for whatever video he saw of me kissing her out in public? Well, fuck him. I'm Aloha's husband now. Pretty sure that trumps father figure, motherfucker. And it certainly trumps *boss.* Yeah, Barry can fire my ass but there's no getting rid of me now.

Before following Barry, I glance at Keane and Maddy dancing next to us, and shoot Keane a look like, "I'm busted!" And he bursts out laughing, the same as Aloha a moment ago. Keane flips the bird to Barry's broad back and I laugh and laugh and high-five Keaney as I take Aloha's hand and begin leading her through the dense crowd.

Quickly, I realize this crowd is probably too packed for Aloha's comfort level, so I turn to her, touch my nose twice, and then crouch down and offer her my back. Immediately, she hops aboard. Because she's my pretty hula wife and I'm her valiant steed husband. And it's us against the world, fuckers! Or, I guess, in this moment, it's us against *Barry.* Ha! Well, fuck him. There's nothing he can do about me now. Aloha said "I do" and so did I and it was legal and real and tomorrow we're going to buy side-by-side plots at a cemetery like other married couples do. Well, maybe not the plots. I don't know. That would probably be weird. But the concept remains: *she's my wife!*

As we make it to the edge of the packed dance floor, the song changes to "Counting Stars" by One Republic. And I whoop. I couldn't have requested a better song for this moment. This night. This *life.* It's like God is my DJ tonight. *Thanks, God.*

People are patting me on the shoulder and giving me and Aloha high-fives as we pass. People I've never met, but I'm more than happy to give them a high-five on my wedding night as I follow Big Barry to God knows where to tell him to fuck off.

We pass by Reed and our crew—Josh, Kat, Ryan, Tessa, Henn and Hannah. They're hanging out with that movie star who introduced Aloha at the awards show tonight. And they all look drunk as shit, just like me. As I walk by with Aloha on my back and Barry at my front, my peeps cheer wildly and high-five me and Aloha. Because they know, as well as I do, that Barry can't do shit to me now.

We're off the dance floor now. Following Barry into a hallway and around a corner. We walk through a door into a small office.

279

Lauren Rowe

Fuck you, Barry, I think as he shuts the door behind us. *You want to fire Aloha's husband? Well, fuck you, motherfucker. You don't like that I married Aloha, you can suck my big black dick.*

Chapter 49
Zander

T he small office is sleek and tidy.

"Counting Stars" is blaring on the other side of the door.

"We have a prenup!" I blurt as Barry locks the door behind the three of us. "I don't want a penny of her money. I just want *her*."

Aloha leaps in front of me, like she's protecting me from an oncoming locomotive. "You can't fire him!" she shouts, her arms splayed out parallel to the ground. "I'm the boss here and I say Zander stays!" She leans her back against me, reaches around behind her and grabs me. "Even if you fire him, I'll just *rehire* him, Barry! And if you say, 'Ha! *I'm* in charge of *bodyguards*, Aloha!' Then I'll hire him as my *personal trainer*! So... *ha*!"

"You're drunk," Barry says calmly. "Did you start drinking before or after you exchanged *legal* wedding vows with this man, Aloha?"

"'This man' is my *husband*, Barry. My legal *spouse*. My old man. Please give him the respect he deserves."

"We started drinking afterwards," I say. "Here at the club. We were both completely sober when we got the marriage license and then when we said 'I do.'"

"Well, you're not sober now. Either of you." He holds up his phone. "Do you have any idea how big a story this is—especially coming on the heels of what happened at the awards show?" He leans into Aloha's drunk face. "Is that what you wanted? To blow up the internet? To make yourself breaking news? Because if so, you succeeded."

"I didn't do it for publicity!" she shouts. "I did it because I..."

My heart stops. Every hair on my body stands on end. Please, God, make her say it right now in front of Barry. *Please.*

Lauren Rowe

"Because I... *wanted* to do it!" Aloha says.

Barry crosses his mammoth arms over his chest and shakes his head.

I step to the side of Aloha and snake my arm around her shoulders. "I love her, Barry. It's as simple as that. I told her if she's gonna wind up putting my heart through a wood chipper, I forgive her in advance. At least, she'll have been all mine in a way she's never been anyone else's. So fire me if you must, but I'm not going anywhere. At least, not today."

Barry rolls his eyes. "I'm not gonna *fire* you, Zander. Now that I know Aloha was sober and in her right mind, relatively speaking, I have no intention of doing anything but *congratulating* you."

My lips part in surprise. I look at Aloha. She looks as floored as I feel.

Aloha furrows her brow in disbelief. "Are you fucking with us?"

"No."

"You're not mad?" Aloha asks.

"Mad? Why would I be mad? I'm the one who picked him for you in the first place."

Again, Aloha and I exchange flabbergasted looks.

Barry chuckles. "Do you honestly think I picked a guy with *zero* experience to be your *bodyguard*?" He scoffs. "To be honest, I didn't have high hopes Zander would do the job all that well when I hired him." He looks at me. "No offense, Z, but I thought you're too damned nice for this job. Although you've certainly proved me wrong about that, especially tonight. Damn, boy, you're one badass motherfucker, Zander Shaw. I apologize for underestimating you."

"What the fuck are you talking about, Big Barry?" Aloha booms.

Barry smirks. "I'm saying I'm Match dot com. Only, you know, *Barry* dot com. I'm saying I hired Zander because I thought he was perfect for you, and not because I thought he'd wind up being your long-term bodyguard." His smile widens. "And as it turns out, I was right."

My mind is racing. "But... you said you'd rip off my balls..."

"And I meant it," Barry says. "Nobody touches my girl without honorable intentions. And you can't do this job if you're messing around with The Package in places you shouldn't be." He grins at Aloha. "I also knew my girl wouldn't give you the time of day if I'd

282

told her, 'Hey, honey, I met a great guy I think you might really hit it off with. Maybe you two should grab some lunch!'" He chuckles. "I know full well my little hula girl always wants what she can't have. I'm no fool."

"Motherfucker," Aloha mutters.

"But most of all, Zander," Barry says. "I told you I'd rip off your balls if you touched my beautiful girl because I knew if and when you defied me, you'd be doing it because you'd come to care far more about Aloha than any job. Or your balls."

I'm shocked. "But, Reed...?"

Barry laughs. "Oh, you think I gave you this job because Reed told me to do it? Fuck, no. Reed can kiss my ass. I *interviewed* you because Reed asked me to do it. I gave you the *job* because I had my own agenda. A hunch. Well, more than a hunch, actually. When he insisted I waste my time interviewing you, I figured I'd do it right. So, I called Josh Faraday to ask about you, knowing he'd spent some with you in Maui. And Josh put his wife on the phone, saying she's known you for over ten years—since you were thirteen—that you're like a brother to her. And guess what she said? You've got a heart of gold. That you're loyal. That you wouldn't hurt a fly, unless that fly happened to be threatening someone you love and then watch out— you're a beast. She said you've got a strong, strict momma who raised you right, taught you right from wrong, and a little sister you've always protected and respected. She said you're honest and hardworking and someone everyone respects and listens to when you speak. And, most of all, she told me story after story about you and your best friend, Keane—stories that made it clear to me you haven't just been a best friend to that boy all these years, you've been his service animal. His Godsend. So, based on all that, before you walked into Reed's office, I already had a pretty good idea of what I was dealing with. But then you started telling me about your best friend and how much he means to you and I knew you were a needle in a haystack. The man who could take care of my girl and then some. And I also knew, just by looking at you in your suit and the way you'd taken so much care with that paltry résumé, that you'd do the job to the best of your abilities and respect whatever rules I laid out for you..." He pauses for a moment, apparently feeling overwhelmed with emotion. He swallows hard. "I knew you'd follow the rules unless and until you fell in love with her." He smiles, his eyes glistening. "And rightly so."

"You scheming bastard," Aloha says, but her tone doesn't match her words. She flings herself at Barry and he scoops her up and wraps her in a warm embrace while I stand drunkenly by, feeling like my brain is short-circuiting. I'm having a thousand thoughts, all at once, not the least of which are the following two: one, holy shit, Kat Morgan rocks, and, two, I can't believe a girl nicknamed The Blabbermouth somehow managed to stay mum about her conversation with Barry all this time.

"I just want you to be happy," Barry says into Aloha's hair. "That's all I've ever wanted."

Aloha nuzzles her nose into Barry's humongous chest and whispers three little words that make my heart explode along with my head: "I truly am."

Chapter 50
Aloha

The minute the door to my hotel suite shuts behind us, Zander and I rip our clothes off and begin attacking each other like maniacs. As we kiss and grope and consume and devour, we tumble onto my bed naked, a blur of lips and fingers and warm breath and skin.

Zander begins kissing my entire body furiously. "Mrs. Shaw," he growls, his breath hot against my inner thigh.

"You're my hero," I gasp out. "The way you bounced that guy right off the stage like a rag doll... Oh, God, Zander."

He stops what he's doing, his chest heaving, and looks me in the eye. "I'll never let anyone hurt you."

My heart leaps. My clit jolts. "Holy fuck, get inside me."

A wide smile splits Zander's handsome face. "Patience, wife." With that, he returns to his work, kissing and devouring my thighs, until, finally, blessedly, working his way to my clit.

I grip the bedsheet underneath me and purr as he licks me. A tidal wave of pleasure rises up inside me... hovers over me... and then crashes down deliciously, making my innermost muscles ripple and clench.

"Husband," I purr during my climax. "*Yes.*"

Zander flashes me a beaming smile that makes my heart bound and leap. "This is the best night of my life, Aloha."

I stroke his muscular forearm. "Mine, too."

We share a huge, elated smile.

"Why not make it your best night in more ways than one?" I say coyly. "Let's go for your personal best—lucky number seven?"

He chuckles. "Well, I can certainly try. But it's gonna be hard to do with all that booze in your system. It numbs the nerve endings after a certain point."

"No harm in trying, right?"

"No harm at all."

And away we go. But four orgasms later, I'm done. Too wasted to come again and too aroused to mess around with foreplay anymore. I beg him for his cock and he gives it to me. Oh, man, does he give it to me. All. The. Way. I hike my thighs up around Zander's ribcage and grip his hard ass as he fucks me, every cell in my body reveling in him.

"Mrs. Shaw," Zander murmurs into my ear, his voice telling me he's on the bitter edge.

I press my lips against his ear and purr, "Husband."

And that does it. Zander comes inside me with a loud roar.

When his body quiets, Zander slides off me and pulls me close and I lay my cheek on his heaving chest.

"Was that five?" he says.

"Five."

"Not a PR, but, still, not too shabby."

"Not too shabby at all." I exhale happily.

Zander rises up onto his elbow. He brushes some hair away from my face. "Can I ask you something?"

"Anything."

"Why is it so hard for you to say the magic words?" He doesn't seem upset. Simply curious. "No pressure. I don't need to hear them. I know what we're both feeling. But I'm curious: have you ever said the words to *anyone*?"

"I say the words a hundred times a day."

"But, I mean, have you ever said the words for real? To someone you actually care about? Not even someone romantically. Just... *someone*."

My heart squeezes. "I used to say the words to my mother when I was little. But, no, I haven't said them to her or anyone else since childhood." I take a deep breath. "I just... It's hard to explain to someone on the outside. My mother always used those words like a weapon. To control me. Like, if I didn't want to go to work when I was little, she'd say, 'Do it for me because I love you so much.' Or if I was crying because I wanted to go to a real school and meet other kids, she'd say, 'You can't. You've got a destiny to fulfill, unlike other kids, and I'm going to make sure you fulfill it because I love you so much.'" I twist my mouth, thinking. "At some point, those words just lost their happy meaning to me. They became painful."

"Oh, Aloha," Zander whispers.

I shrug. "And hearing strangers say it to me every day certainly doesn't help matters. 'Everyone' loves Aloha, right? Fans, managers, agents, directors, producers, record label execs. I can't begin to tell you how many times per day someone says 'I love you' to me. A fan who doesn't know me. Someone who's only reason for being in my life is making money off me. Like, I remember I used to have this one agent as a kid. And he'd always say, 'I love you like a daughter!' And I believed him. I didn't have a dad, so what did I know? So, I'd say to him, 'Hey, maybe sometime you could take me a baseball game or something!' And he'd go, 'Oh, absolutely!' But he never did. He just kept putting it off. And then one day my mother fired him for embezzlement and I never saw him again. So much for him loving me like a daughter, huh? After that, I couldn't help thinking maybe people only loved me when they were earning a big fat commission off me."

Zander looks pained.

"I'm grateful when fans tell me they love me," I continue. "I'm glad I've brightened their lives. I tell them I love them in return, because I *do*. Because I'm grateful for how good they are to me. And for giving me this amazing life. But at the end of the day, person to person, I don't know them and they don't know me. So if that's *love*—and I do believe it is, in its own way—then I can't fathom how those same words could possibly be applied to my feelings for *you*." I take his hand and whisper, "My Shaggy Swaggy Hubby Bubby." I bite my lip. "My beautiful, kindhearted, badass *husband*."

His eyes are glistening. He smiles through his emotion. "Sweetheart—*Mrs. Shaw*. Hearing you call me your 'husband' means more to me than any 'I love you' ever could."

He leans in and kisses me. And my heart surges. And for the first time in my life, I finally know what it feels like to be desperately, totally, and completely in love.

Chapter 51
Aloha

Zander groans deeply as I give him a first-thing-in-the-morning blowjob under the covers. "Oh, Jesus, Aloha," Zander growls, his pleasure obviously on the cusp of boiling over. He rakes his fingers over the top of my head. His pelvis gyrates. "Oh, fuck, baby, that feels so good."

A sudden banging at the door jolts us.

"Aloha!" a female voice hollers. "Open this door right now!"

"Satan," I whisper hoarsely, my eyes bugging out.

Zander pulls on some sweatpants, looking like he's about to have a heart attack.

"Aloha! Open this door!"

"Hold your horses!" I yell. "We're getting dressed!"

"He's in there with you?"

"News flash, Satan, we're *married.*"

A minute later, I open the door fully dressed, and Satan marches into the sitting room like she owns the place, followed by my publicist, agent, and Crystal, all of whom look like they're on the verge of throwing up.

Crystal mouths "sorry" to me, but I can't be bothered. I train my eyes on my mother's painted face and grit my teeth, girding for battle.

"You!" my mother says, pointing an accusing finger at Zander. "You gold-digging, money-grubbing—"

"I don't want her money," Zander says, putting up his palms. "I married Aloha because I *love* her."

"Ha!" my mother says. "Con artist!" She whirls around to face me. "I've already got the lawyers drawing up the necessary paperwork for an annulment. They said it would take—"

"I don't want an annulment," I say. "And there are no grounds for it, even if I did. I wasn't drunk. There were no false pretenses. It was spur of the moment, yes, but I knew exactly what I was doing."

"For the love of God, Aloha! You can't marry your fucking bodyguard!"

"Well, the state of Nevada says I can and there's nothing you can do about it. Ha!"

My mother narrows her eyes. "So that's what this is about, huh? Sticking it to me?"

"This has nothing to do with you." I march across the room and grab Zander's arm. "I'm elated you're furious about it. I admit that. But this is about Zander and me and nobody else."

"He's using you."

"I'm not," Zander says, his voice on the cusp of shouting. "I love Aloha with all my heart and soul—which is something you clearly don't know anything about."

My mother shoots daggers at Zander. "You stay out of this, you parasitic opportunist con artist. This is between Aloha and me. It doesn't concern you."

"Doesn't *concern* me?" Zander bellows. He takes a menacing step forward, rage wafting off his every sculpted muscle. "I'm her *husband*. Not her boyfriend. Not her bodyguard. And certainly not her shitty, neglectful, greedy, narcissistic mother. Which means *everything* about Aloha concerns me, unlike you."

My mother looks absolutely shocked. And so do Crystal, my agent, and my publicist, all of whom are standing slack-jawed on the far side of the room.

My mother glares at Zander like she's telepathically ordering a hit on him, and then addresses me with clenched teeth. "Pack a bag. You're coming with me. We're getting this sham of a 'marriage' annulled and that's final."

"Now you listen to me," Zander begins, but I hold my arm across his torso to silence him.

"Thank you, baby, but I've got this." I return to my mother. "I'm not leaving with you, *Lani*. I'm staying here with Zander. My *husband*. But I'll tell you who *is* leaving: you. You're going to turn around and march through that door and never contact me again. You're going to live in the house I bought for you, and spend all the money you stole from me for years, back when I was a minor and didn't understand what you were doing. And in exchange for you disappearing from my life for good, I'm going to refrain from filing a lawsuit against you to get back the millions and millions you've stolen from me. But I swear to God, if you come near me again or so much as mention my name in the media, I'll sic my lawyers on you to get back every dime you stole. And not only that, I'll use the lawsuit as an excuse to go on a full-out media tour—which I'm thinking is something the entire world would tune in to watch, considering the size of the crowd waiting outside this hotel just to get the tiniest glimpse of my new husband and me this morning. And you know what I'll say on that media tour? *Everything.* I'll tell them about the cutting and how you not only didn't help me but actively tried to *keep* me from getting help, all in the name of the mighty green. I'll tell them I grew up with a drunk mother who was *livid* when I wrote her a poem for Mother's Day rather than showering her with diamonds—so pissed, she slapped my face. Remember that, Drunk Mommy? I'll tell them about all the times I cried and cried as a child, alone in my bed or wandering the house with a fever, and you didn't come to me, either because you were high or having sex with some guy at the other end of the house or passed out drunk on the couch."

I feel untethered. Like I'm kicking the cage door wide open. For so many years, my mother told me the world as I knew it would end if I uttered the truth out loud. She told me nobody would love me if they knew my secrets. She said the money and fame would dry up and I'd be poor and miserable and alone. But now I see she was dead wrong about all of it. Because with each word of honesty I'm daring to speak in front of Zander and those three shell-shocked people on the other side of the room, I feel more and more powerful. More and more *free.* Suddenly, I realize it wasn't the truth holding me hostage for so long, it was the lies. It was my mother, who extorted me with my secrets, all in the name of financing her lavish lifestyle.

I take a deep breath and continue, "I'll tell them it was my *bodyguard,* not my own mother, who found me in that bathtub at age fifteen after I'd swallowed all my mother's pills and almost went out like Whitney in a bathtub. I'll tell them it was my *bodyguard,* not my mother, who rushed me to the hospital and got my stomach pumped and got me into rehab. Because my *bodyguard,* not my own mother, was the one person in the world who truly loved me for *me* and not what I could do for him." I look at Zander. "Until Zander came along and loved me that way, too."

Zander's chest heaves. He blinks and a solitary tear rolls down his beautiful cheek.

I smile at him through my own tears until the sound of someone sniffling on the other side of the room draws my attention. It's Crystal, boohooing like a baby. My agent and publicist look emotional, too—but more stunned than anything.

I'm not surprised that they're all surprised. Surely, they've always known I've got issues. Everyone on my tours or who works with me figures that out at some point. But the bare truth—that I was essentially held prisoner in my own mind by my greedy mother for years and years—that she manipulated and mind-controlled and abused and *extorted* me—is something nobody could have suspected. Frankly, even I didn't fully understand the implications of all of it, not really, until I started saying all this shit out loud, just now.

I glance at Zander again. He looks like he's a hair's breadth away from physically removing my mother from the room. The poor guy's got to be wondering what kind of fucked-up wagon he hitched his plow to for "eternity" last night. Yes, I've hinted at some of the stuff I just babbled, but I've certainly never let on just how bad it really was. How crazy I really am. How damaged. How unloved. How desperate I became at one point. Well, now Zander knows: I'm fucked up beyond anything he could have possibly suspected.

I return to my mother, my heart crashing. "It's your choice, Lani. Go softly into that good night right now or have to deal with a 'woke' and extremely pissed daughter who happens to have the entire world's attention right now."

My mother's entire body stiffens. "You've let those doctors and therapists tell you I'm a monster for so long, you've started believing it. Well, shame on them for brainwashing you. I sacrificed everything for you, Destiny. Everything I did, I did it because I love you so much."

Bile rises in my throat. "You've got five seconds to get out."

She wrings her hands for a long beat. "Twenty million," she blurts.

"What?"

She puffs her chest. "That's my price to walk away."

291

I scoff. "Wow. It's oddly comforting when a snake takes off her prosthetic legs and starts slithering around."

"Twenty million and you'll never hear from me again," Mom says. "I'm calling your bluff. We both know you don't want the entire world to know your secrets. Pay me and they'll never have to know."

I swallow hard. *Bitch.* "I'll give you two."

"No," Zander says sharply. "Don't give her a dime, Aloha. She's already taken enough from you."

"You stay out of this!" my mother hisses at him. "Tell your boy toy to keep his mouth shut."

Zander's face morphs into the exact expression he wore last night right before body-slamming that wack job off the stage.

Again, I put my arm across his torso. "Thank you, but this is my fight." I stare down Satan. "Two million or that media tour starts tomorrow. Frankly, you should be paying me *not* to do the media tour."

Mom's eyes fill with crocodile tears. "How can you do this to me—your own mother? I gave you *life.* You owe *everything* to me."

I stare at her like a sniper, my chest heaving and my nostrils flaring. "My offer will terminate in five, four, three, two—"

"Fine," she spits out. Her tears instantly dry up. She points a manicured finger at me. "You're going to hell, you know that? For shame, you'd do this to your own mother!"

I address my agent. "Have my lawyers draw up the papers for this deal today. Make it airtight." I glare at my mother. "You contact me again or speak my name to the media, I'll go after you, guns blazing."

Mom whispers, "Everything I've done, I've done because I love you, Destiny."

"Keep your 'love,' Lani. And don't call me Destiny. I'm not *your* destiny. I'm my own."

Mom's eyes harden. "You ungrateful little bitch. Without me, you'd be nothing. Singing sad songs on a street corner. Modeling in a Sears catalog." She scoffs. "Turning tricks."

"Okay, that's it," Zander says. He points his muscled arm toward the door. "Get the fuck out or I'll escort you out."

"I'd listen to my husband, if I were you," I say, stepping to his side and grabbing his arm. "I don't know if you saw the footage from last night, but he's extremely protective of me when he feels like I'm being threatened in any way."

Mom glares at me for ten seconds like she wants me dead. And then she shifts her Birkin bag on her shoulder, sneers at Zander, and walks out the door.

I stare at the closed door for a moment, my heart pounding like thunder, and finally whisper, "Ding dong, the witch is dead."

Zander slides his arm around my shoulders and squeezes. "Are you okay?"

"I'm good," I say. "A little light-headed, though."

Zander guides me to a couch and sits next to me. "Crystal? Can you bring Aloha some cold water, please? She looks pale."

Crystal flies into action and a moment later, I've got a glass in my hand.

"Thank you," I say.

"You're sure you're okay?" Zander says.

"Yes." But when I sip the water, my hand is shaking. "I should have done that a long time ago."

"You grew up under her control," Zander says. "You didn't know anything else. I guess there was a reason she never let you have any friends or go to anyone's house, huh? She didn't want you finding out what was 'normal.'"

I nod.

"Why'd you agree to pay her two million bucks?"

"Because all of my money from the show is blood money. She was right about that. I wouldn't have any of it without her."

"Baby, no. Your mother brought you to the audition, but after that, your success was all yours."

Crystal, my agent, and publicist, all of whom have seated themselves around me, agree wholeheartedly with Zander's statement.

"No, I won the lottery with that show. It was pure luck." I chuckle. "It certainly wasn't the writing." I sigh and rub my face. "Honestly, I would have paid twenty million to get that woman out of my life for good. I was bluffing when I said two was my final offer." I shake my head. "God, it felt so good to finally say what I've been fantasizing about saying for ten years."

There's a long silence. Apparently, we've all been rendered speechless.

"Wow," I finally whisper. "I'm officially, an orphan."

Zander takes my hand. "You might be an orphan, but you're not without family. I'm your family now. And so are the Morgans and Shaws. Why do you think that whole group flew out to Vegas to see you last night?"

"To see *me*? No. To party in Vegas at one of Reed Rivers' legendary after-parties and to see *you.*"

Zander chuckles. "Yes and yes. But they also came to see *you.* Their beloved Alo-haha. You'd told them awards shows are hard for you, remember? They wanted to support you."

"Seriously?"

"Absolutely. They love you, baby. You're one of their own now."

"Wow."

"And they were psyched to party at one of Reed Rivers' legendary parties."

We both laugh.

"Speaking of family, have you heard from your mom and sister yet?"

"Uh, yeah. I've texted with them. Told them I'd call later. My sister was thrilled. My mom was... very much looking forward to speaking to me."

"Well, call her, then."

"Not yet. In a bit."

I roll my eyes. "Zander Shaw. Nut up and call your momma."

He pulls a face.

"Oh my God. You wimp. I just toppled Satan and you're too scared to talk to your mother on the telephone?" I swat his broad shoulder. "Put on your big-boy pants and call your mommy, or you can sleep on the couch tonight."

Chapter 52
Aloha

T hat's true," Zander says. "I don't deny that." He's sitting on the edge of the bed in the bedroom, talking to his mom on the phone. We moved in here to give my wimpy husband some privacy from my three team members in the other room. He continues, "All true, Mom. But, hey, great news: this *one* time it seems to have worked out pretty damned well for me, don't you think?" He smiles... and then frowns. "Uh, no, Aloha can't talk right now because—"

I rip the phone out of Zander's hand. "Hey there, Momma Shaw! It's me, your daughter-in-law."

"Hello, Aloha," Mrs. Shaw says. "How are you today?"

"Married."

"So I've heard—*but not from my own son.*"

"Yeah, Zander and I are very, *very* sorry about that. Not about the marriage, but that you had to find out that way."

"Aloha, let's just cut to the chase, shall we? Did you marry my son as a publicity stunt? Because that's what the gossip sites are saying."

I look at Zander next to me as I speak. "No, ma'am. I married Zander because he's by far the best man I've ever met. And because he lights up my life and I wanted him to be my one and only."

Zander's mother pauses for a long beat before saying simply, "Welcome to the family, dear."

We chat a bit longer and end the call on a happy, loving note.

"See?" I say, tossing Zander's phone onto the bed. "Easy as pie." I rise. "Come on, husband. This 'do whatever the fuck I want' thing is addicting." I pull him up from the bed and drag him into other room with me. "Okay, team," I say to my agent, publicist and Crystal, clapping my hands. "Change of plans. Crystal, push our flight to Houston back by three hours, at least, please. I've got a few things to take care of here in Vegas before we head out for the next city."

"That won't work," my publicist, Claudia, says. "If we arrive that late in Houston, we'll miss several promotional events and engagements I've got scheduled."

"Send my apologies to whomever and tell them I'll make it up to them one day, I promise. Also, I wanna cancel all promo engagements through the end of the tour. The only non-show things I want on my calendar for the rest of the tour are visits to kids in hospitals and pre-show meet and greets with fans. Oh, and raising money for animal shelters. But no more interviews or promo of any kind through the rest of the tour." I look at Zander and smile. "I want to leave myself as much time as possible to spend with my hubby bubby boo." I address my agent. "Sean, will you please ask Reed to come here for a meeting today? I'm ready to talk about my new contract now. I'll sign a new deal with him today, as long as he'll agree to a few revisions and modifications to the prior deal."

"Reed's not gonna budge on the numbers, Aloha."

"The money is fine. I want Reed to sign off on a new creative direction. I'm going to explore a different sound with my next album. More of a singer-songwriter-alt-pop vibe. And most importantly, I want him to understand that all songs on my forthcoming albums will be written or co-written or personally handpicked by me. If Reed is down with all that, then I'm ready to sign on the dotted line today."

"For three albums, like last time?" my agent asks.

"Let's make it two with an option for a third. Even if I do end up signing with Reed again, I might want to create my own label at some point in the future. Hula Girl Records."

"Uh," my agent says, apparently too shell-shocked to speak.

"I'll play two or three of my new songs for Reed today to give him an idea of what he's signing up for. If he likes what he hears, or at least feels excited about the new direction, I'll sign. If not, then Reed and I will part ways at the end of this tour and I'll release my new music myself."

"Uh... okay," my agent says. His phone pings and he looks down. "Reed says he'll be here at your suite in an hour and he's very much looking forward to it."

"Great. Tell him I am, too." I address my full team. "Guys, when this tour is over, the Aloha Carmichael machine will be out of service. I'm going to follow my heart and be honest. I'm going to be brave. Speaking of which..." I pick up my phone and start tapping out a text to Maddy. "If she's willing, I'm going to hire Maddy Milliken to shoot a documentary about the making of my next album. It'll cover the songwriting process. Recording. Hopefully, some performances, once we get there. And, most importantly, I'll give brutally honest interviews about all of it, including the inspirations and back stories behind my songs."

"'*Brutally* honest interviews?'" my publicist says. "Aloha, I think we should—"

"I disagree," I say. "I think if I'm honest about my past struggles, I could help a lot of people out there. So, that's what I'm going to do." I shoot Zander a look and it's clear he's in full agreement with me. And that makes me feel all the more like I'm sailing in exactly the right direction. I address my entire team. "Can you guys do me a favor and ask Barry and Brett and whatever team of guys they're planning to bring with them this morning to arrive a bit later than originally planned? Maybe about an hour after my meeting with Reed? And can you three head out for coffee for an hour?" I grab Zander's hand. "My husband and I were in the middle of something important when you guys showed up with Satan, and I'd like to finish what we started."

Chapter 53
Zander

Aloha's mouth on my cock is sending me to heaven on a bullet train. But I don't want to come this way. Not after the badassery I just witnessed from Aloha—first with her mother and then with her team. No, after watching all that, I want to fuck my wife until she sees God.

I pull Aloha's mouth off my cock and guide her to standing. My eyes on hers, I pull off her clothes and get mine off, too, and when we're both naked and twitching with desire, I grab her ass and pull her up onto me and fuck her smack in the middle of the room—right where we were standing when her team left the room. Right where she dropped to the floor and started sucking on my cock.

I married Zander because he's the best man I've ever met. Because he lights up my life and I wanted him to be my one and only.

Those are the words Aloha said to my mother on the phone. And when she said them, it was one of the most electrifying moments of my life.

Aloha is unleashed as she fucks me. Her eyeballs are rolling back into her head. I walk with her still fucking me to a chair and sit myself down and she begins gyrating on top of me like a woman possessed. I reach between us and massage her clit and she explodes like a grenade, coming hard around my cock. So, of course, since I'm only human and this has been the best fourteen hours of my life, I follow suit.

But when I come down from my orgasm, I suddenly realize I wasn't wearing a condom.

"Oh, shit," I say. "No condom, baby."

"I'm on the pill."

I exhale. "Thank God. I want babies with you, but not yet."

"Amen to that," she says. But she looks stressed.

"I'm clean," I say. "I always use condoms and—"

"No, no, it's not that." She chews her lip. "I'm just, honestly, kind of... freaking out."

My chest tighten. "There's nothing to freak out about. We got this, baby. It's me and you against the world."

"But didn't you hear all that stuff about me? Clearly, I'm a ticking time bomb, Zander. There's no way I'm not gonna fuck this up with that woman's DNA inside me."

I sigh with relief. For a minute there, I thought she was gonna say she's freaking out about the marriage itself. That she made a mistake and wants out immediately. "Aloha, you can't possibly fuck this up."

"I *can* and *will*."

"No."

"Yes. I'll do something to push you away. I'll test you. Take things too far. I'll do something thoughtless and selfish to make you prove your love, but it'll backfire and then you'll just plain hate me and I'll live the rest of my life regretting whatever stupid thing I did and die alone with my house full of cats."

I chuckle and stroke her hair. "Aloha, stop. I'm not going anywhere. That wedding ceremony was real to me. Every word. Till death do us part. In sickness and in health. I love you."

Her face is flushed. She still looks panicky.

"Aloha, what is it?" I touch her chin and lift her face to look at me. "Talk to me."

She exhales. "The month thing. It's too much pressure. I don't like there being some kind of countdown between us. I don't want to feel like, each day we get closer to New York, we're getting closer and closer to the day when I'm supposed to decide if I'm genuinely ready to promise you forever or not."

Again, I sigh with relief. "Sweetheart, there's no countdown. I said that thing about you being free to annul the marriage at the end of the month simply to coax you into saying yes in that particular moment. But, baby, I tricked you. I was rusin' ya, knucklehead."

"Huh?"

"The truth is you could end this thing today, tomorrow, a month from now, twenty years from now. That's the nature of any marriage.

There's no stress, okay? If you decide you don't want me anymore, then you'll leave. I don't want that to happen. Believe me, I'll move mountains to keep that from happening. But if one day you come to realize with full certainty you genuinely don't want me, then, honestly, yeah, you *should* leave. Because, as much as it'll ruin me to lose you, I only want you if you want me back."

Aloha swallows hard. She still looks stressed.

Well, damn. I thought that was a ridiculously eloquent speech. Reassuring as fuck. Kind of noble, too. "Aloha, what's bothering you? I can't help you if you don't tell me. I'm running out of guesses here, dude."

She twists her mouth for a long moment, considering. "No matter how happy I am with you, I'm still gonna have bad days. I'm not a straight line kind of person. I zig and I zag. It's not going to be rainbows and unicorns with me all the time."

"I get a little ziggy and zaggy myself sometimes, too."

"But not like me."

I sigh. "Yeah, I know. And that's okay. I love you. All of you."

"But what if you take it as a personal insult when I struggle, like I'm somehow rejecting you and the patience and love you've shown to me if I occasionally fall apart a little bit? What if you feel unloved when I struggle and then I've got to worry about your feelings every time I'm not doing well, as well as my own? That's a lot of pressure."

"There's no pressure. I know your issues aren't about me. Of course."

She sighs with frustration. "But you'll need support sometimes, too, Zander."

"And you'll give it to me."

"Will I? Do you honestly think I'm the right person to give you support when you need it?"

I touch her hair. "I do. In fact, I'm positive you are."

"But how do you know that?"

"Because I love you. And you love me. And I have faith we'll both rise to any challenge." I sigh. "Aloha, we're both lots of things. But, most of all, we're badass motherfuckers."

She can't help chuckling at that.

"Okay?" I say.

She bites her lower lip. "Okay."

I wrap my arms around her. Kiss the top of her hair. Stroke her back. "Don't be scared, my little koala in a tree. I know you're not familiar with the concept, but I'm gonna teach you what it means to be loved unconditionally, for no other reason than you're *you*. Just wait, my love. I'm gonna teach you all about it."

Chapter 54
Zander

The crowd at Madison Square Garden is going ballistic for Aloha. A few minutes ago, she left the stage after giving the best show of the entire tour, and she's just come back out for her usual two-song encore.

I'm watching the show from the wings, like I always do. But this time, I'm feeling particularly moved. Two songs from now, it will be the end of an era. A finish line of sorts, in more ways than one. Now that Aloha's signed a two-album deal with River Records that will take her music in a decidedly different direction, will she ever play a huge arena like Madison Square Garden again? She'll always have an audience, of course, but will her Aloha-nators follow her in droves into the next chapter? Will edgier music fans who've never given Aloha a shot before give her new music a chance? Only time will tell. Either way, tonight was the last vintage "Aloha Carmichael" show my wife will play to an arena full of diehard Aloha-nators on U.S. soil. And that feels big to me.

But this concert also feels like the end of an era for another reason: this concert in New York was the one that was supposed to be the finish line for the stupid bet hatched three months ago in Dax's living room. The one prompting me to vehemently swear up and down I'd *never* fall in love with Aloha Carmichael. Surely, if someone had shown me a crystal ball that night, objectively proving to me I'd not only fall in love with Aloha by her New York show, but that I'd be *married* to her by now, my head would have physically exploded.

To say these past three months with Aloha have been an adventure would be the understatement of the century. It's been the best ride of my life, particularly this last month as Aloha's husband.

Each day has been better than the last. Even Aloha's one little meltdown two weeks ago in Raleigh—when she woke up crying hysterically in the middle of the night after having had a horrible nightmare in which, she said, I'd left her for Daphne—strengthened our bond. Of course, as Aloha's tears kept flowing that night in bed, I came to understand she wasn't crying about the dream itself. And certainly not about any actual fear I'd leave her for Daphne. No, I understood that the dream was a symbol of her greatest fears. Abandonment. Loss. I understood that, after finally feeling truly loved for the first time in her entire life, she was suddenly realizing just how *un*-loved and abandoned and betrayed and used and abused she'd always been up until now. And that was a hard thing to grasp, all at once. So she was having a bit of a catharsis. A cleansing. A purging so she could put the past to rest and move forward in earnest.

Of course, I reassured Aloha that night. I told her I was all hers and not going anywhere. That I loved her and only her, forever, no matter what. And, finally, after about an hour of melting down like I'd never seen her before, she calmed down and crawled into my arms and we both drifted off to sleep again.

The next morning, Aloha's eyes were red and puffy, but other than that, she seemed perfectly fine. Better than fine, actually. More in love with me than ever. And I felt more in love with her than ever, too. Oddly reassured that she trusted me enough to lose her shit that completely with me. Because, man, did she lose her shit. But that's when it hit me: it's not the times when things are picture-perfect in a marriage that are the true measure of the strength of the relationship, it's when they're *not*. Frankly, it was that night that made me feel like Aloha's true husband in a whole new way.

The crowd explodes with applause as Aloha reaches the end of her first song of the encore. Holy shit. We're now *one* song away from this North American tour being in the memory books. After tonight, Aloha and I will take a week off here in New York, just to rest and do a little sightseeing, and then we'll jet off overseas for the four-month international leg, culminating in Australia. And after *that*, we'll come back to LA for about a year, probably, during which Aloha will record her new album while I'll start my new career as a celebrity fitness trainer. Thanks to all the workout videos Aloha's posted of us throughout the tour, not to mention the viral clip of me "rescuing" Aloha in Las Vegas,

303

I've already got a mile-long list of celebrities wanting to hire me to whip them into shape. And some of them are household names. Big, big household names. Man, I can't wait. Aloha and I talk about our future life in LA all the time. How dope it's gonna be when the tour is over and we're living a simple, married life together in her beautiful house in the Hollywood Hills. How awesome it'll be for me to watch her making her dreams come true while I'm starting an exciting new career for myself— all while living in the same city with Peenie again. Wesley and Woody, together again! And, of course, when Aloha's new album is released, I'll travel with her on whatever tour. Not just as her husband, but as her personal bodyguard again. Because, as Aloha and Barry both know, I don't trust anyone but me to guard my wife.

"Zander," a female voice behind me says, and I peel my eyes off Aloha singing her final song onstage.

It's Crystal standing before me... accompanied by... *Oh my fuck.* A woman I never thought I'd see again.

Daphne.

How is this possible? How is she here? My gaze flickers down to a VIP backstage pass dangling from Daphne's neck... and my brain melts again. How did she get that?

I glance at Crystal to find her glaring at me with hard, disapproving eyes. She says, "I've asked Brett to accompany AC to her dressing room when she gets offstage, as you requested."

"As *I* requested?" I say lamely.

But I'm saying the words to Crystal's back. She's already stalking away in an angry huff.

My gaze darts to Daphne. I can't for the life of me fathom how... or *why...* ?

"Hi," Daphne says. "I was so excited to get your text. And to get this." She touches the backstage pass around her neck. "Thank you."

Why is she thanking me? "How are you here?" I blurt. "*Why?*"

Daphne looks around. "The music's way too loud for anyone to overhear us. Can't we talk for real, just for a couple minutes?" She looks around again. "You know, about what you said in your text?"

"My text? The one I sent *two months* ago in which I said I'd always be your friend *from afar?*"

Daphne rolls her eyes. "The text from two weeks ago." She leans forward. "The *secret* one, Z."

My heart is thumping painfully. I exhale. "Daphne, can I see this text, please?"

Daphne's face tightens. "You don't need to delete it off my phone. I swear I haven't shown it to anyone and I won't."

"Daphne, please. Whatever it is, I didn't send you a text two weeks ago. I've sent you nothing since the 'friends from afar' text over two months ago."

Daphne looks utterly confused for a moment... and then crestfallen. But being the sweet, kind-hearted girl she is, she pulls out her phone, fiddles with it for a moment, and hands it to me.

I look down and, sure enough, there's a text exchange between "me" and Daphne that ends with me confirming the logistics for her attendance at this concert tonight. The whole text conversation makes my head spin and my stomach lurch, but none of it more so than "my" opening text:

Hey D. I don't know how to say this so I'm just gonna spit it out. My marriage to AC was just a publicity stunt. She wanted to revamp her image so I agreed to be her "boyfriend" in the media for the first two months of the tour and her husband for the third. We're gonna get the marriage annulled after the NYC show and she's gonna pay me a cool mill for my trouble. When I'm officially a free man again after NYC, I'm hoping you'll be willing to hang out and see if maybe the spark is still there. Will you come to the NYC show as my guest? I know you're a huge fan of AC's, so I'll arrange for you to meet her backstage. Don't worry, AC won't care. Like I said, our thing is just for show. The only thing is you have to promise to play it cool and act like we're just friends in case anyone is watching. Wouldn't want to blow AC's cover or blow my payday. Looking forward to hearing from you, Z

The arena explodes in applause as I look up from Daphne's phone. Apparently, Aloha just finished her song—the very last song of her North American tour. Her last "Aloha Carmichael" performance on U.S. soil. And, thanks to my psychotically insecure wife, rather than soaking up this one-of-a-kind moment as I should be doing, I'm standing here dealing with a shit show.

"I didn't write this to you," I say, handing Daphne her phone.

305

"I'm sorry. I have to go now." I shout to a nearby crew member who happens to be walking past, and when he approaches, I bark at him to escort Daphne to an unrestricted area. But when I return my attention back to the stage, Aloha is long gone. Apparently, Brett has already escorted my lunatic wife to her dressing room, just as "I" requested.

I'm enraged. Livid. Furious. Although, hey, I can't say my wack job wife didn't warn me. On day one, Aloha told me she's a psycho bitch nightmare, didn't she? I guess I should have listened. My heart crashing in my ears and my blood on the cusp of boiling in my veins, I take off sprinting toward the dressing room.

Chapter 55
Zander

When I arrive at Aloha's dressing room, she's not there. "Fuck!" As I'm turning to leave, my phone buzzes with a text from Brett.

Escorting AC to the back door to sign autographs outside. She says she'll meet you on the bus.

I'm so pissed, I can barely breathe. I take off sprinting in the direction of the back door, winding my way through the hectic backstage area—past milling backup dancers and musicians and crew and costume racks—and finally spot Aloha just as she and Brett are reaching the back door.

"Aloha!" I boom.

She turns around. And the minute she sees the look of fury on my face, she balks. And I don't blame her. I've never shouted at her like I just did. Never had anything even resembling anger in my voice when addressing her before now.

"I've got her, Brett," I grit out when I reach the pair. I clutch Aloha's upper arm, keeping her from going any-fucking-where, and force myself not to sound as furious as I feel. "Let's make sure the venue guys have the barriers set up properly out there before she starts signing."

"Yup."

And off Brett goes through the door.

I grip both of Aloha's shoulders, my chest heaving. "You invited *Daphne* here from my phone? How could you do that to me?"

Tears flood Aloha's eyes. "I... I don't know why I did it. It was two weeks ago, right after I had that nightmare. You fell asleep and I couldn't sleep for hours and I couldn't stop thinking about my dream and I guess I just—"

"*You trust me that little?*" I bellow, my eyes bugging out of my head.

I know I should keep my voice down. Keep my anger in check. People are watching. And Aloha looks like a trapped animal. But I can't keep my cool. I've been nothing but loyal to this woman. Reliable. Kind. Loving. Patient. Every breath I've taken for the past three months, I've taken for her. And this is how she treats me? Like a puppet in some sick little puppet show? Like my love is some kind of game to her, to be toyed with on a whim?

To my surprise, she comes out guns blazing. "I knew this would be the last show in the States and then we'd be heading overseas and after that... *what?* You actually think I'm capable of playing happily ever after with you in LA? *Forever?* How the hell am I not gonna fuck that up? I mean, reality check, dude, do you know who you're dealing with here? So I just thought, 'Well, shit, if I'm gonna fuck this up and push him away and then get decimated, I'd rather he leave me now before I get in so deep, I need him to breathe. Before I need him to smile. Before I won't be able to physically survive it when he leaves!'" She bats on my chest. "If you're gonna leave me, then just do it now! Because I can't keep doing this with you, knowing it's only a matter of time before you go!" She turns sharply, yanking herself out of my grasp, hurls the back door open—a surprise move that makes me lurch backward to avoid getting clocked in the forehead by the heavy door—and off she runs.

"Jesus Christ," I mutter. I march through the door after her and watch as she runs straight toward the bus... straight toward Brett, thankfully... and, also, straight toward a cluster of excited fans standing to the side of the bus behind a barrier...

My eyes lock onto a woman in the crowd. She's elbowing her way violently to the front. *I recognize her.* Where have I seen that woman before? *Henn's pile of photos.* Oh, God.

No.

I take off running, just as the woman blasts through the simple barrier and straight into Aloha's path of travel.

"Aloha!" I scream, my legs pumping.

As if in slow motion, I see the woman reach for something in the pocket of her trench coat and every instinct in my body tells me to leap. *To protect my wife.* So that's what I do. I leap through the air toward Aloha and tackle her, just as a loud pop thunders through the night air.

In a flash, a searing pain scorches through me. I thud to the ground. Hysteria unleashes all around me. I look up, ready to defend Aloha against any threat, and immediately see Brett tackling the woman and a pistol skittering across the asphalt.

Oh, fuck, I can't breathe.

I'm suddenly in too much pain to force air into my lungs.

I can't breathe.

But, no, I have to breathe.

For Aloha.

To protect her.

Aloha.

Yes.

She's my reason to breathe.

I suddenly realize Aloha is shrieking underneath me. Has she been shot? *Please, God, no.* I tilt myself as best I can to let Aloha squirm out from underneath me. She scrambles to my side on the asphalt. She's screaming hysterically.

"Are you hurt?" I choke out.

But she doesn't answer me. She's shrieking for an ambulance.

Does she want it for me... or for her?

Her hands are slathered in blood. Is that mine or hers?

"Are you hurt?" I choke out again, but I can barely get the words out.

I can't breathe.

"I'm not hurt," Aloha gasps out. "Oh, God, Zander!"

Relief floods me. Yes, I admit it's less than ideal that the blood all over Aloha's hands came out of me. But better me than her. At the end of the day—and it looks like this might be the end of my very last day—all that matters to me is that Aloha is safe.

Aloha is safe.

I can go now.

My eyes flutter closed.

Darkness descends.

"No!" Aloha shrieks. She grips my hand hard, jolting me back to consciousness, just for a second. Just long enough for me to hear her scream, "*I love you*! Zander, no, don't close your eyes! Don't go! *I love you*! You're my everything!"

Somewhere my brain registers the happy thought that Aloha just now used the magic words—and she was talking to *me*. I must admit that makes me happier than I ever thought it would. I genuinely thought I didn't need to hear those words from her, but now that I have, I realize I did. Just once. And now my life is complete. I got the best going-away gift from my wife possible, and now it's time to go.

There's only darkness now.

I can't hear anything happening around me anymore. Is there anything else anymore, but this serenity? This love I feel for Aloha? Because that's all I can feel. *Love.* Well, that, and the life force seeping out of me. No, flooding out of me, actually. Wow. I think I can actually feel my heartbeat slowing down. *Thump, thump... thump...*

Thump.

I wish I could open my eyes so I could see Aloha's beautiful face one last time. I wish I could speak so I could say, "I love you, too. Now, don't be scared. You got this, baby. Be brave, Aloha. Be *you* and be brave." That's what I'd say to my wife if I could. And if, by some miracle, I could say a little bit more, I'd also tell her I'm at peace. That this is exactly how I'd want to go out. Protecting her. If I could speak, I'd tell her that, if given the chance, I'd do exactly what I just did a hundred times out of a hundred. With no regrets. Because she was my reason for living. In fact, now that I'm here, I'm positive I fell in love with her in the primordial goop eons ago, and only arrived on earth in my present form when it was time for me to get on track to do what I just did... because she's my destiny. My primordial destiny.

But before I can open my eyes to behold my wife's emerald green eyes one last time or get a single word out... not even a simple "*love*"... I feel the last drop of life force trickle out of me... and my heart thump one last whisper of a time... Visions of Aloha, Peenie, Mom, and Zahara flicker weakly across my brain like static on a walkie talkie. And then the world, and my mind, fade to black.

Chapter 56
Aloha

T hanks for the update," Brett says into his phone. He's talking to someone from NYPD. I'm wringing my hands. Doing my breathing exercises.

We're sitting in a hospital waiting room. Crystal is sitting between us.

Brett looks somber. Exhausted. Tormented. He's still got Zander's blood all over his shirt from when he gave him CPR and applied a tourniquet.

Crystal looks like a zombie.

And me? I haven't looked at myself in a mirror, but I'm sure I look every bit as bloodstained as Brett and ten times as zombified as Crystal. Because I've never felt soul-rending despair like this. Heart-wrenching torment. As I sit here with Zander's blood all over me, I feel like I'm a heartbeat away from having a full-blown psychotic break.

Crystal offered to grab me some fresh clothes from the hotel a few minutes ago, but I refused. I don't want to wash Zander's blood off me until I know for sure he's going to live. If my husband dies because of me, because of my recklessness, my craziness, if that saint dies saving my worthless, stupid life, especially after the stunt I pulled, then I've already decided I'm going to lie down next to his body, covered in his blood, and perish along with him. Because it's abundantly clear to me now I can't live without him. And I certainly couldn't live with myself if he died, knowing he traded his beautiful, bright, pure soul for my tainted, damaged, selfish, hideous, worthless one. If I hadn't sent that text to Daphne, none of this would have happened.

"We don't know yet. He's still in surgery," Brett says on his phone call. He listens for a moment and then says, "Will do. And you do the same." He ends his call and looks at me sympathetically. "Do you want to hear the news?"

"Yes."

"She was devastated by your marriage to Z. He was her target, not a mistake. But she was gonna be gunning for you, right after him. If she couldn't have you for herself, then she didn't want anyone to have you."

"Jesus," Crystal mutters.

"I'm sorry, Aloha," Brett says, his voice breaking. "I fucked up so badly."

I look at him, incredulously. "You were a hero tonight."

"No. I didn't spot her when I went out there. If only I'd—"

"You tackled her to the ground, Brett. You got the gun away from her. And, most importantly, you saved Zander's life. You heard the doctor. If it hadn't been for the CPR and aid you administered, Zander would have been dead on arrival at the hospital."

"But I had her photo on my phone. *And I didn't notice her*." His eyes are full of anguish. "But Zander did. He recognized her right away. I could see it on his face the minute he came out the door. That's how I knew to run over there: the look on Zander's face told me you were in danger."

"Brett, stop. Please. It's my fault, not yours. I'm the one who sent my husband's ex-girlfriend a text, pretending to be him and inviting her to my concert. I set everything in motion tonight. It was *me*." I put my hands over my face. "Oh, God. I'm going to hell where I'll have to live for eternity with my mother instead of up in heaven with my beautiful Zander. And I'll deserve it."

"Don't say that," Crystal says fiercely, grabbing my arm. "Aloha, you made a mistake, but one thing has nothing to do with the other. A text didn't get Zander shot tonight. And, more importantly, nobody's going to heaven or hell any time soon because Z's gonna pull through this."

We both look toward the door of the waiting room at the same time, willing the surgeon to walk through it and give us good news, even though we're well aware the surgery won't be finished for hours.

Crystal's phone buzzes and she looks down. "The Seattle group just took off. The LA group should be taking off in about twenty minutes. I booked Zahara Shaw on a commercial flight out of Portland in the morning. Sorry, that's the first flight I could arrange for her from there."

"Zander's mom?"

"She's with the Morgan group that just took off from Seattle."

I wipe my eyes and nod. "I just hope and pray his mother will forgive me."

"Aloha, stop that. A text, even a stupid one, didn't get Zander shot by a deranged lunatic."

"Mrs. Shaw?" a male nurse says. He made the mistake of calling me Miss Carmichael earlier, but I corrected him.

I stand, panic slamming me, and the man's face immediately melts.

"Don't worry, I just came out to reassure you that the surgery is going well so far, but it's still going to be hours yet. So if you want to wash off that blood and change, maybe head to the cafeteria for a bit, you won't miss anything."

"I'll wait here."

The nurse touches my arm. "Aloha, please. Go wash off the blood so Zander doesn't see it when he gets out of surgery and wants to see your beautiful face. We don't want him waking up and thinking, even for a second, that you've been injured."

My chest heaves. "Will he wake up?"

"The doctor said it's looking good. So let's have faith, okay?"

I wipe my eyes and nod. "Thank you." I rise, determination flooding me. "You're right. Zander's going to wake up. And when he does, he'll need me to be the strong one. And that's exactly what I'm going to be."

Chapter 57
Aloha

I tiptoe into Zander's room in the ICU.

He's lying on a metal bed, hooked up to tubes and wires. His breathing is slow and rhythmic. The heart monitor next to the bed is beeping. His right shoulder and upper chest are bandaged. His arm is in a sling. He reminds me of a sleek racehorse felled on the track. How can someone so strong and powerful look so vulnerable and powerless? The sight of him is breaking my heart.

I bend down and kiss Zander's full lips, ever so gently, and his groggy eyes flutter open.

"Hi," I say softly.

"Hi," he whispers, almost inaudibly.

"I love you," I say. "With all my heart and soul. Forever."

He smiles weakly. Mouths the words "I love you," and drifts off again before I can launch into the apology I have on the tip of my tongue.

A nurse appears and tends to him.

I take a step back and give her a wide berth to perform her duties. She takes his vital signs. Checks his IV bag and bandages. She taps something out onto an iPad and then leaves.

Not knowing what else to do, I sit at Zander's bedside, thread my fingers into his, lower my head, and sob.

Chapter 58
Aloha

S unlight is streaming into the hospital room, bathing Zander's beautiful features in ethereal light. I haven't left his bedside for three days, other than to shower in a hospital facility and grab an occasional bite. Zander's mother, sister, Keane, and Maddy, are in the same boat as me. None of them has left Zander's side, either. The rest of the family—the Morgans and Barry—have camped out in the ICU waiting room. I'm not sure about their comings and goings.

Zander woke up minutes ago seeming not nearly as drugged out as he's been before. Particularly alert and talkative. So, of course, every person in the room, except for me, has taken the opportunity to chat with him. To tell him how much they love him. How worried they've been. How they can't live without him. Keane just left. Once he got talking, he started bawling like a baby and had to leave the room. Maddy followed him out. And now there's only Momma Shaw, Zahara, and me standing over his bed. And I'm the only one who hasn't taken advantage of his alertness to say what needs to be said. Because, of course, what I need to say must be said in private.

I ask Zander's mom and sister if they wouldn't mind clearing out for a few minutes so I can talk to Zander alone, and, thankfully, they don't seem the least bit offended.

The second they're gone, an apology hurtles out of me.

"Nothing to apologize for," Zander says softly. "The woman was deranged. You can't blame yourself for attracting—"

"No, I'm sorry for hacking into your phone and making Daphne think you'd invited her to my show. Zander, I don't deserve your forgiveness, I know. But I'm begging you for it, anyway. I'm so, so sorry. I'll never forgive myself for putting you in the path of danger."

"The path of danger? Aloha, you sent a text. A batshit crazy text

315

that made me furious with you. A text that hurt my feelings. But your text didn't get me shot. A deranged woman with a gun did that."

"But I set everything in motion."

"Aloha, no. Listen to me. This isn't up for debate. *You sent a text.* A bullshit, cray-cray text that pissed me off. But all you did was invite my ex—a flower-child art student who wouldn't hurt a fly—to your concert. You didn't think I'd want Daphne. Of course, not. You just wanted to test me—to see if I'd get pissed enough about it to leave you. It was stupid and insulting and batshit. But it wasn't getting me shot, Aloha." He pauses. "Look, I know why you did it, baby. It was just another form of cutting. You didn't do it to hurt me, you did it to hurt *you.*"

My lips part with surprise.

"But you know what? I'm the guy who told you to give me your pain. The one who told you to cut me, instead of you. So, in the end, I can't really be angry with you if that's exactly what you did."

Tears flood my eyes. "I'll never hurt you again. I'll never test your love again. If you'll let me, I'll just love you. And trust you. And be yours. If you'll just, please, forgive me."

He touches my hand and I grasp it like a lifeline.

"Aloha, of course, I forgive you. And, of course, I still love you and want to be loved by you. There's no cut or mark or fuck-up or insecurity or insanity that will make me stop loving you. Don't you get it? There's no need to push me away before I leave first because *I'm not going anywhere, ever.*"

I clutch his hand, relief and love flooding me. "I love you so much."

"I know you do. Because I'm irresistible. If I were you, I'd be madly in love with me, too."

I laugh through my tears. "I'm going to spend the rest of my life trying my damnedest to deserve you."

He beams a smile at me... but his eyelids are starting to look heavy.

I stroke his forehead for a moment. "Time to rest, my love."

He yawns.

"I'm gonna take such good care of you. I told Crystal to cancel the international tour so I can be your nurse."

He looks crestfallen. "Man, I was really looking forward to the international tour. I've never even been out of the States."

"Honey, you don't need a tour to see the world. You're married to me, remember? And I love to travel. When you're all better, we'll go anywhere you want to go."

"Do you think you could keep the last month of the tour on-calendar? Maybe just Australia? It would motivate me to get better. The timing for the Australian dates would be perfect, based on what the doctor said."

"Sure, honey. We can always cancel the dates later, if needed."

"Won't be needed. You heard the doctor. I'm gonna be as good as new, doing partner workouts with my wife again, in no time."

A lump rises in my throat. "You don't regret making me your wife?"

"Are you kidding? I've never regretted anything less in my life. I'd marry you all over again tomorrow."

I clutch my heart. "Let's do it, baby. The minute you're out of the ICU, let's get married again for real, this time in front of everyone we love the most."

"For *real*? Vegas was real."

"No, Vegas was *legal*. Maybe semi-real. But when I said 'I do,' I wasn't fully on-board like I should have been. I loved you and wanted to take a leap with you. I was exhilarated. But was I thinking I was vowing *forever* to you? Hell no. In fact, I might have crossed my fingers during my vows at one point. Maybe. It's all a blur."

"*Aloha*."

"You should be happy about that. All it means is you get to marry your hot little wife again, only this time in front of everyone you love. Really, you should thank me."

He smiles. "Thank you."

"You're very welcome." I clasp his hand. "So you'll marry me again in a couple days?"

"I'll marry you any ol' time you like, as many times as you'd like."

"Wonderful. This time, Z, I promise: when I vow to be yours forever and ever, for eternity and beyond, I'll mean every freaking word."

Chapter 59
Zander

D o you, Aloha, take Zander to be your lawfully wedded husband, forsaking all others as long as you both shall live?"

It's the hospital chaplain asking that question. And just to be clear, he's asking it of the spectacularly beautiful and talented, but slightly unhinged, woman who's already my wife.

Aloha smiles down at me in my hospital bed, and answers the chaplain with words that are music to my heart: "I do."

"Lemme see your free hand, wife," I say, and Aloha holds up the hand that's not clasped with mine, splaying her fingers to prove she's not secretly crossing them.

"Toes?" I say. "Somebody do a toe-check for me, *pronto.*"

"She's good," Keane says, looking down. "Those pedicured toes are most definitely *not* crossed, sweet meat."

"Excellent." I nod to the chaplain. "Proceed."

The chaplain chuckles along with everyone else. "And do you, Zander, take Aloha to be your lawfully wedded wife, forsaking all others, as long as you both shall live?"

"I do," I say. "Longer than that, actually. Because I'ma tell you right now, I'm planning to listen to Aloha sing to me in heaven, the same way she used to sing to me when we were little blobs floating around together in the primordial goop."

Aloha giggles. *"Zander."*

I glance around the large room—the well-appointed "VIP" hospital room Aloha snagged for me when I got out of the ICU two days ago. And, as I look at all the faces of the people I love the most, I'm slammed with yet another tsunami of gratitude that I'm alive and kicking. Holy Baby Jesus, I thought I was a goner as I lay on the asphalt outside Madison Square Garden a week ago. From what I've been told, I actually cheated death that night. Maybe even technically died at one point before the ambulance arrived. If it hadn't been for Brett flying into action at the scene, all these people would probably be sobbing over my casket right now instead of crying happy tears at my second wedding.

Speaking of which...

The chaplain says, "By the authority vested in me by the State of New York, I now pronounce you husband and wife, Zander and Aloha Shaw. *Again.*"

Everyone chuckles.

"Zander, you may kiss your beautiful bride."

"*Again,*" Aloha whispers, just before leaning down and pressing her perfect, pouty lips against mine.

Everyone claps and cheers. Someone pops a champagne bottle. Plastic cups come out. A heartfelt toast is given by Mr. Morgan—which is a surprise, since the man hardly ever talks—and then by Barry. Hugs and kisses abound. Mom sheds some tears and tells me to always treat Aloha right, to which I reply, "Mom, I took a bullet for the woman. Not sure how much more 'right' I can treat her." And, finally, everyone clears out to let me rest and hang out with my wife.

Aloha takes her usual seat by my bedside and slides her hand in mine. "Get some sleep, Hubby Boo. The doctor said sleep is the most important thing for your healing."

"You should go to a hotel and sleep for a bit, baby. I know you love me. Get some sleep in a comfortable bed."

"I'm not leaving you."

"Then at least sleep on that cot over there."

"I want to hold your hand."

I sigh. "Babe, when I sleep, I don't even know you're holding my hand. Sneak over to that cot and catch some Zs while I'm sleeping."

She squeezes my hand. "I'm catching all the Zs I want right here."

"Aloha, I'm serious. I feel too guilty waking up and seeing you sleeping in that weird position all the time. You're gonna permanently wrench your neck. And then how will you do music videos looking like *this*?" I wrench my neck and make a funny face.

"I'm right where I want to be, doing what I want to do. Isn't that what you always tell me to do? 'Be brave.' Well, guess what? This is me, being brave. Doing what I want to do. Now get some rest. The wedding was exciting and the doctor said you have to take it easy and get plenty of rest, especially after something exciting."

"Wow, look at you acting all wifey-like."

"*Sleep.* Like this."

She presses her forehead against the mattress, presumably showing me how it's done. But I'm too amped to close my eyes. I stare at the top of Aloha's head for a moment, my heart melting with love for her. My gaze drifts to our clasped hands. I take in her slender fingers. Her manicure. The simple band on her finger—the ring I bought for her in Vegas because I couldn't afford anything more elaborate.

Aloha lifts her head and glares at me. "If you don't close your eyes, I'm gonna get Zelda Shaw in here to give you a tongue lashing."

"Oh, shit. You're savage."

"Damn straight." With that, my bossy little wife gets up, kisses me on my lips, nose, and forehead... and then lays her palm over my eyes, forcing me to close them... and, soon, what do you know, with her hand over my eyes, I drift off to sleep with a smile on my face.

Chapter 60
Zander

I stand on the tarmac with my arm in a sling, watching Aloha, flanked by Crystal and Brett, disappear into the private jet. Apparently, my wife needed to get onboard to talk to the pilot about some flight paperwork or customs shit. I don't know. She was vague about it. All I know is Aloha asked me to stand out here so Peenie and Maddy's driver can clearly see which plane is ours.

Speak of the devils, I look toward the entrance to the tarmac and see a black stretch limo pulling through the gate. I wave with my good arm and the limo heads straight for me. When it parks, Peen Star and Mad Dog pop out, their faces aglow.

"Australia, here we come!" Keane booms in a terrible Australian accent.

"Best day evah, mate!" Maddy shouts, her accent no better than Keane's.

The three of us hug and high-five as the limo driver unloads their luggage from the car.

"How are you feeling?" Keaney asks.

"Great. Better every day. I'll be back to my old self in no time."

"Yee-boy! Where's Haha?"

"Already on the plane. She had to talk to the pilot about something."

Out the corner of my eye, I see Maddy flash a thumbs-up signal in the direction of the plane, and then hold up her phone, trained on me.

Reflexively, I wave at Maddy's camera, figuring she's probably shooting a little something for *Ball Peen Hammer's Guide to a Handsome and Happy Life*—which, by the way, has become quite the viral cash cow for Kaddy these days. But before I can think too much

321

about what Maddy is shooting, she trains the camera on the jet, just in time to catch Aloha descending the steps, her head meticulously wrapped in a scarf. And just that fast, I know exactly what's going on here. Bodyguard. Arm in sling. Tarmac. Private jet. Pop star in a head scarf descending plane steps and running toward her bodyguard. Holy fuck! I'm unwittingly starring in a remake of the last scene from *The Bodyguard*!

With Maddy's camera trained on her, Aloha lopes across the tarmac to me. When she reaches me, she does exactly what Whitney did in this scene: she barrels into me for a kiss. Of course, I play my part, embracing her with my good arm and kissing the hell out of her, just as Keane bursts into singing the chorus from "I Will Always Love You" at the top of his lungs. It's a vocal performance that ain't gonna win the boy any Grammys, but it's on point for the moment.

I don't know who's responsible for this dope-ass homage to Kevin and Whitney—my wife, Wifey, or Maddy. But whoever's behind it, I suddenly feel the urge to add my own flavor to the scene.

I was planning to give Aloha the ring in my pocket somewhere in Australia. Maybe in front of the opera house in Sydney? But, see, that's the earmark of an intelligent man: he knows when to pivot. Because the truth is that the simple ring I bought for Aloha in Las Vegas has weighed heavily on me. Talk about a mismatch between a woman and her wedding ring. Aloha is a lot of things, but simple and understated, she is not. Which is why, last week, I called Barry in LA and asked him to do me a favor: sell my prized possession for me—the shiny car I scrimped and saved to buy two years ago—and wire me the cash.

I break free from my kiss with my wife, pull the ring box out of my pocket, sink down on bended knee, and open the box to reveal an emerald surrounded by diamonds.

"Zander!" Aloha gasps. "Oh my God. It's beautiful."

"Aloha Shaw, my beautiful wife times two, will you make me the luckiest man in the world for the third time and marry me in Australia?"

Aloha's green eyes light up. "Yes! *Oh!* Let's do it in front of a koala in a tree this time, while I'm clinging to you like a koala in a tree!"

I laugh. "Perfect."

As Maddy and Keane cheer, I slip the ring onto Aloha's finger, get up, and wrap her in a one-armed hug.

"I love you so much," Aloha says into my chest, her emerald eyes blazing even brighter than the rock on her hand.

"I love you, too, my beautiful hula princess."

We begin walking toward the jet, with Keane trailing behind us, still singing horribly—and *very* loudly—and Maddy walking alongside us capturing every smile.

"Whose idea was this re-enactment, anyway?" I ask.

"Kat's," Aloha says. "When she found out we were flying to Australia via private jet, she said she'd never forgive me if we didn't do it." She holds up her hand to display her sparkling ring. "Thank you for improving the scene."

"You're welcome. I always hated the ending to that movie. I wanted them to end up together."

With that, I grip my wife's hand and lead her up the steps of the plane, so we can do the one thing poor Kevin and Whitney never got to do: fly off together to our happily ever after.

Chapter 61
Aloha

Sydney, Australia

I'm standing at center stage, soaking in the tidal wave of applause and love crashing down on me. It's my last show of the "Pretty Girl" tour. My last show I'll ever do quite like *this.* After tonight, I'll be free. The master of my own destiny in a way I've never been before.

Normally, at this point in the show, I wave to the arena and race offstage to take a quick bathroom break and change costumes before coming back out for my two-song encore. But tonight, for the first and only time, I've got a little something special up my sleeve. Something this crowd, and none other, will get to witness.

"Thanks for coming to my last show of the tour!" I bellow. "I'd like to take a moment to thank some people." I thank my band and dancers and crew and the arena applauds raucously. "I also want to thank my husband." I look to the wings to find Zander standing with Keane and Maddy. "Come out here for a minute, Hubby Bubby Boo."

Shaking his head, Zander ambles to the front of the stage next to me and I hand him a microphone off a nearby stand.

"Say hi to all my new Australian friends, honey."

Zander brings the mic to his luscious lips and waves with his free hand. "Hi, everyone."

"Isn't my husband *sexy?*"

The crowd agrees.

"Zander and I have had so much fun traveling with our two best friends through Australia. Have you guys seen them—Keane and Maddy—or as we like to call them *Kaddy?* They've been all over my Instagram and Twitter lately."

324

The audience roars.

"Have you guys watched their 'Ball Peen Hammer' videos, like I told you to do?"

Again, everyone applauds and cheers.

"Let's get them out here, huh?"

The audience goes ballistic.

I look toward the wings just in time to see Keane pulling Maddy toward me while Maddy shoots me an expression that says, *What the fuck are you doing*? "Maddy, you should record this," I say. "It's pretty cool to stand at center stage in a packed arena and have all these nice people cheering for you."

Laughing, Maddy pulls out her phone and dutifully captures the moment as she continues walking across the expansive stage.

When the duo reaches Zander and me, Keane grabs the mic from Zander and bellows, "Hey, Sydney! How's it going, mates?"

Everyone screams.

"Hey, do you Aussies wanna see something super *cool*?" Keane yells.

The crowd indicates that, yes, they do.

"Awesome. Watch this." Keane turns to Maddy and smiles. He takes a deep breath. "Madelyn Elizabeth Milliken..."

And that's my cue. I grab Maddy's camera from her and continue filming as she looks at me like, *Huh*?

"Maddy, yo, back over here," Keane says. "You don't want to miss this." He grins. "Maddy, you're the best thing that's ever happened to me. You put the happy in my every meal and hour and birthday. You're the happy *and* the lucky in my happy-go-lucky. The happy in my handsome." He takes another deep breath. Shifts his weight. He's visibly shaking. "Mad Dog. Madagascar. Mad Genius. Madelyn the Badasselyn. Maddy Behind the Camera. I'll never want anyone but you. I want to grow old with you. I want to take care of you. To be your husband. I want to have eighteen babies with you."

"Huh?"

Keane pulls a ring out of his pocket, kneels, and holds it up to her. "Madelyn Elizabeth Milliken, will you marry me?"

Maddy clamps her hand over her mouth and nods profusely.

Keane leaps up, slides the ring on his woman's finger, and kisses her... and, of course, the entire arena loses their freaking minds.

Keane and Maddy embrace, and Zander and I simultaneously tackle them and the four of us hug and laugh and wipe away tears. I feel euphoric. Like the final piece of some sort of cosmic jigsaw puzzle just snapped into place for me. These people. Right here. *This is my family.*

Suddenly, I remember where I am and that there are more than a few people waiting on me. I turn to the crowd. "Hey, everyone, thanks for coming to our best friends' engagement party!"

Everyone roars their excitement.

"Now let's *celebrate!*"

Epilogue
Zander

Two Years Later

I'm standing in the wings in Seattle, watching my wife sing one of the biggest hits off her new album. *Aloha the Brave* was Aloha's seventh studio album, but the first released by her as "Aloha." No last name required. It was the first of Aloha's albums to be categorized as singer-songwriter-alt-pop. The first comprised solely of songs she personally wrote or co-wrote. And the first to garner *two* Grammy nominations for her, personally. One for writing and one for performance.

The song Aloha is currently singing to the packed crowd in this arena is called "Boy Toy," a quirky little jam with a genius melody that uniquely showcases the texture and warmth of her voice. A "story song," it tells the linear tale of a horny princess imprisoned by an evil witch in a tower. One night, the princess scales down the wall of her prison in search of sexual gratification. When the princess finds a suitable boy toy—a dude with "chocolate skin, muscles on top of muscles, and diamond studs in his ears"—she rides his back through thorny, scratchy bushes to a nearby cave where she proceeds to have her way with him, every which way, "Lionel Richie style," night after night. Finally, one morning, the princess awakens in the cave with the boy by her side and realizes he's no longer her boy toy. He's magically become her knight in shining armor.

Needless to say, I love this song.

And I particularly love watching Aloha perform it live. She always slays this one. But tonight, especially, my wife is slathering it with extra sauce, probably due to the fact that everyone she loves the most is sitting in a skybox watching her, all of them elated to be

327

witnessing the one-two punch of Aloha followed by the headliner of this world tour, the band that took off like a rocket two years ago and hasn't let up since, 22 Goats.

The simple truth is that Aloha took a couple steps back in her career when she rebranded herself and released music in a new market—a market filled with the kinds of music fans who, by and large, would consider attending an Aloha Carmichael concert a fate worse than death. But that's exactly what Aloha has loved most about doing this tour with 22 Goats—getting the chance to earn audiences' respect the good old fashioned way: by pouring out her heart and soul onstage every night. And, man, does she ever. In each and every new city, my brave little wifey walks onstage to face a firing squad. And, every night, she walks offstage with an entire arena's worth of hearts in her pocket.

It's been a joy to witness, which I do from the wings in my capacity as Aloha's husband and personal bodyguard, and also as the co-head of security, along with Brett, for the entire tour.

Handling Aloha's personal security on this tour has been worlds different than the last tour, when she was "Aloha Carmichael." First off, she's not the headliner. And the arenas aren't filled to bursting with Aloha-nators. I'd estimate Aloha-nators make up only about twenty-five percent of every audience. So that right there makes things more relaxed than the old days.

Plus, people don't get nearly as bold and hands-y with her as before, now that she's married to me. I also tend to think people treat Aloha more humanely now as a result of seeing Maddy's amazing documentary. Yes, people still ask Aloha for selfies and autographs all the time. And, yes, people still hug her and cry when they meet her—even more so, nowadays, since people often feel deeply moved by Aloha's revelations in Maddy's movie. And, yes, paparazzi still pops up regularly, sometimes annoyingly so. But, generally speaking, the world is a far gentler place for my beautiful, fragile, strong, iron butterfly of a wife than ever before. And it's allowed her to blossom in a whole new way. It's been a pure joy for me to witness.

Onstage, Aloha finishes her song and everyone in the arena applauds enthusiastically. Aloha thanks the crowd and says, "This last one is extra special to me. It's about someone I love with all my heart. Someone who helped me figure out how to steer my sailboat. I hope you enjoy it."

The band plays the opening riff, and, as they do, Aloha glances at me in the wings. She touches her chin. I do the same. And then Aloha returns to her microphone and begins to sing:

I was a sailboat,
Adrift, afloat
Wind at my back
A noose at my throat
Full steam ahead
But didn't know where,
Out of control,
No rudder to steer

I was rudderless
Rudderless
Hopeless
And loverless
Orphaned and motherless
Waiting for you

Rudderless
Rudderless
Hopeless
And happy-less
Orphaned and fatherless
Not understanding why I was so blue
No way to know I was looking for you

And now I'm...

Rudderful
Rudderful
Happy and
Wonderful
Life is so lover-ful
'Cause, babe, I got you

Rudderful
Rudderful

329

Life is so
Beautiful
Wherever I'm goin'
It's always with you

Rudderful
Rudderful
Life is so
Beautiful
Life is so
Wonderful
Wherever I'm goin'
I'll always love you

By the time Aloha reaches the end of her simple love song, my heart is exploding with unadulterated joy and love, the same way it always does. "Rudderful" isn't a complicated song, but the way Aloha sings it... straight from her heart... with such *honesty*... oh, man, watching her sing this one always gives me goosebumps on top of my goosebumps.

The band strikes the last chord of the song and the audience graces Aloha with their most ardent applause of the night. And, once again, my baby's leaving the stage with every audience member's heart in her pocket—even the ones who came here tonight loathing her.

Aloha takes a bow, thanks her band and the crowd, tells everyone she's honored and thrilled to be opening for 22 Goats, her "favorite band in the world!" And then she waves, blows kisses, and beelines into the wings and straight into my arms.

"Best show yet," I gush as she crashes into me.

"Having all our peeps here tonight got me feeling so *pumped.* Oh, God, I feel *amazing* right now! *Euphoric!*"

I laugh and kiss her. "Hold that thought. After we party with everyone at Captain's later, I'm gonna take you back to our hotel and go for a new PR. And euphoria is always helpful when going for the gold."

She giggles and I nuzzle her nose.

"I sure do love you, Mrs. Shaw."

She skims her lips over mine. "And I love you. *My beautiful rudder.*"

Author Biography

USA Today and internationally bestselling author Lauren Rowe lives in San Diego, California, where, in addition to writing books, she performs with her dance/party band at events all over Southern California, writes songs, takes embarrassing snapshots of her ever-patient Boston terrier, Buster, spends time with her family, and narrates audiobooks. Much to Lauren's thrill, her books have been translated all over the world in multiple languages and hit multiple domestic and international bestseller lists. To find out about Lauren's upcoming releases and giveaways, sign up for Lauren's emails at www.LaurenRoweBooks.com. Lauren loves to hear from readers! Send Lauren an email from her website, say hi on Twitter, Instagram, or Facebook.

Lauren Rowe

Music Playlist

"The Judge"—Twenty One Pilots
"Dancer"—Flo Rida
"There's Nothing Holdin' Me Back"—Shawn Mendes
"Silvertongue"—Young the Giant
"Brave"—Sarah Bareilles
"Here Comes the Sun"—The Beatles
"Cheap Thrills"—Sia
"Counting Stars"—One Republic

Acknowledgments

Thank you to Jarvis Albury, the fitness trainer in San Diego who, while kicking my butt in the gym, became my inspiration for Zander. What a positive, hilarious, kind, force of nature you are! And, as always, thank you to my dear readers. You're the best!

Additional Books by Lauren Rowe

All books by Lauren Rowe are available in ebook, paperback, and audiobook formats.

The Morgan Brothers Books:

Enjoy the standalone Morgan Brothers books in any order, but suggested reading order is as follows:

1. *Hero.* The epic love story of heroic firefighter, **Colby Morgan,** Kat Morgan's oldest brother. After the worst catastrophe of Colby Morgan's life, will physical therapist Lydia save him... or will he save her? This story takes place alongside Josh and Kat's love story from books 5 to 7 of *The Club Series* and also parallel to Ryan Morgan's love story in *Captain.*

2. *Captain.* A steamy, funny, heartfelt, heart-palpitating insta-love-to-enemies-to-lovers romance. This is the love story of tattooed sex god, **Ryan Morgan**, and the woman he'd move heaven and earth to claim. Note this story takes place alongside *Hero* and The Josh and Kat books from *The Club Series* (Books 5-7).

3. *Ball Peen Hammer.* A steamy, hilarious enemies-to-friends-to-lovers romantic comedy. This is the story of cocky as hell male stripper, **Keane Morgan**, and the sassy, smart young woman who brings him to his knees on a road trip. The story begins after *Hero* and *Captain* in time but is intended to be read as a true standalone in *any* order.

333

4. *Mister Bodyguard.* This is the story of honorary Morgan brother, **Zander Shaw**, and the pop star who brings this tender-hearted, hard-bodied man to his knees. This story begins three months after *Ball Peen Hammer* but is intended to be read as a true standalone.

5. *Rock Star.* The love story of the youngest Morgan brother, **Dax Morgan,** and the woman who rocked his world, coming early 2019!

The Club Series (The Faraday Brothers Books)

If you've started Lauren's books with The Morgan Brothers Books and you're intrigued about the Morgan brothers' feisty and fabulous sister, **Kat Morgan** (aka The Party Girl) and the sexy almost-billionaire who falls head over heels for her, then it's time to enter the addicting world of the internationally bestselling series, *The Club Series.* Seven books about two brothers (**Jonas Faraday** and **Josh Faraday**) and the witty, sassy women who bring them to their knees (**Sarah Cruz** and **Kat Morgan**), *The Club Series* has been translated all over the world and hit multiple bestseller lists. Find out why readers call it one of their favorite series of all time, addicting, and unforgettable! The series begins with the four-book story of Jonas and Sarah and ends with the three-book story of Josh and Kat, to be read in order:

-*The Club* #1 (Jonas and Sarah)

-*The Reclamation* #2 (Jonas and Sarah)

-*The Redemption* #3 (Jonas and Sarah)

-*The Culmination* #4 (Jonas and Sarah with Josh and Kat)*

-*The Infatuation* #5 (Josh and Kat, Part I)

-*The Revelation* #6 (Josh and Kat, Part II)

-*The Consummation* #7 (Josh and Kat, Part III)

*Note: Lauren intended *The Club Series* to be read in order, 1-7. However, some readers have preferred skipping over book four and heading straight to Josh and Kat's story, beginning with *The Infatuation* (Book #5), and then looping back to Book 4 at the very end. This is perfectly fine because Book 4, *The Culmination* is set three years after the end of the series.

Does Lauren have standalone books outside the Faraday-Morgan universe? Yes! They are:

1. *Misadventures on the Night Shift* –Find out what happens when a night shift clerk at a hotel encounters her teenage fantasy, Rockstar, Lucas Ford.

2. *Misadventures of a College Girl*—Find out what happens when a theater major meets a cocky football player at a college party—and nothing goes according to plan.

3. *Misadventures on the Rebound*—Find out what happens when a woman on the rebound runs into a hot stranger on her way to Las Vegas.

4. *Countdown to Killing Kurtis* –When a seemingly naive Marilyn-Monroe-wanna-be from Texas discovers her porno-king husband has thwarted her lifelong Hollywood dreams, she hatches a surefire plan to kill him in exactly one year, in order to fulfill what she swears is her sacred destiny. This is a sexy psychological thriller with twists and turns, dark humor, and an unconventional love story (not a traditional romance).

Be sure to sign up for Lauren's newsletter or for text alerts to make sure you don't miss any news about releases and giveaways:

US ONLY: Text the word "ROWE" to 474747
UK ONLY: Text the word "LAURENROWE" to 82228
NEWSLETTER: http://eepurl.com/ba_ODX
www.laurenrowebooks.com

Also, join Lauren on Facebook on her page and in her FB group (search for Lauren Rowe Books)! Look for her on Twitter and Instagram @laurenrowebooks. And if you're an audiobook lover, all of Lauren's books are available in that format, too, narrated or co-narrated by Lauren Rowe and award-winning narrator John Lane!

Lightning Source UK Ltd.
Milton Keynes UK
UKHW010622060319
338571UK00001B/86/P

9 781732 670402